# it's the not knowing
## or Whatever Happened To William Butler Skaife?

a novel by Kenneth T. Phigs

It's The Not Knowing

## *CONTENTS*

# PART ONE. 1977.

## A New Neighbour

If push came to shove, I suppose I'd have to say I'd lived there for maybe five months; six at the most. I was on good terms with the neighbours; I sorted the post on the hall table, put everything into piles arranged by door number and, obviously, by colour of envelope. That goes without saying, I should hope. I made sure the bin bags were put out on the days when they had to be put out. I made no noise (nothing excessive anyway), I didn't throw parties, never slammed the door when I came home late and whoever the cabbage boiler was, the one who stunk out the building, it wasn't me. I don't eat cabbage, anyway, particularly when it's been boiled. Some smells bring back memories. There's nothing you can do about that and, if I ever catch a hint of boiled cabbage now, I am immediately taken back to this period. Live and let live and if you don't like the smell, you know what to do.

I was the most considerate man I know, and I was a good neighbour – the kind of neighbour most neighbours would want to be neighbours with, if they were able to choose. I know what I'm talking about. I'd lived in a few places since I left the family home, and I never gave cause for complaint at any stage – nothing that would stand up in court. Anyone who'd lived where I'd lived would say the same about me if push came to shove.

There was one fellow who lived in the flat upstairs; he didn't seem threatening but wasn't friendly either – the type who keeps himself very much to himself. No doubt he could smile when a smile was called for, I'm sure you can imagine that type of situation but, as a rule he had what might be described as a blank expression. Gave very little away if you know what I mean. I knew his name, this neutral neighbour, and not by snooping either. His name was Joe Boyle. His post, if you must know, consisted mainly of brown envelopes and the odd postcard – he'd recently received one from two losers called Mike and Joyce, wishing he were there because they were having a 'great time with excellent accommodation.' I didn't read it; I'm a good neighbour, not a nosey one.

Anyway, that's how I came to know his name. I thought he might have worked in physical education in some capacity: PE teacher, personal trainer, something along those lines – maybe a professional jogger. In describing his dress sense, if I really had to, I'd be likely to refer to it as casual but not trendy. And that was alright by me because I've never been interested in clothes or fashion or anything like that. The morons I went to school with seemed obsessed with wearing the same things as everybody else and that was great because that's what they liked and if they all looked the same it was easy to spot them and avoid them. I always tried to wear things that nobody else was wearing. I look back now and think, "yellow blazer, beige slacks. Nice look." That's what I liked at the time.

I often saw Joe going out in the morning and returning in the evening, casually dressed, carrying a kit bag (like the sporty types do). I don't mean one of those drawstring things your mum might have made to keep your pumps in at school, not at all. I mean one of those big kit bags with compartments and zips and handles and straps and a logo. I had no problem with that. He had his life and I had mine. Like I said, I was a good neighbour.

If my calculations are right, it would have been around the first week of February when I got to know Joe Boyle better, to a point where I think I could reasonably refer to him as *plain Joe*.

One evening, there was an incident, and it's still fresh in my mind. I hadn't been in long (as if you needed to know that!), and I was starting to settle after a long day. I don't think I was planning on going out, although I would say that in any seven-day period I would be in the pub on at least four of those nights. There's nothing wrong with that. Anyone wanting to get away from those four woodchip walls, pale green and cold, with black spot mould highlights would be showing good judgement. At that time, I was interested in the history of the British Monarchy since the Normans and had devised a way of remembering them in chronological order:

*Why would he still have raspberry jam? He even eats eggs raw* and so on, and so forth.

I was resting my eyes and trying to remember who was on the throne in 1320. I had wrongly convinced myself that it couldn't have been the second Edward, when I heard three distinct thumps, clear as day and quite regularly spaced timewise, one after the other. This preceded a period of silence which lasted a few moments before it repeated: first thump... second thump... third thump. Then again, as before, the same arrangement of silence and thumps. This went on for some time and was becoming a nuisance –

considerably so, in fact. It won't come as a shock, I'm sure, when I tell you I was irked. Not knowing how long this disturbance was likely to go on for had me thoroughly perturbed. What was it? And who was doing it – the cabbage boiler? It was clearly someone with little or no consideration for the neighbours, and obviously not a good neighbour. I was a good neighbour!

Normally, it wouldn't have bothered me; I like to live and let live but I sensed that, as things were, I wouldn't be able to settle, not fully. Left unchecked it could escalate; something had to be done and, as I couldn't imagine anyone else doing it, it looked like it would be left up to me, but I didn't mind that. As I said, we all have to live together: I would do anything for anybody and was always happy to oblige.

It seems strange now to think, but who could have foreseen at that time how this combination of circumstances would have such an outcome? No-one, that's for sure and I know what I'm talking about.

Home was a handsome Victorian house built in the 1850s and positioned on one of the main roads leading into the town. Blackened on the outside by years of traffic pollution, it had a small garden to the front hidden behind a huge laurel hedge, now overgrown and wild. Nothing grew in the garden (as far as I can remember) except grass in the role of unwanted weed. After an impressive start to life the building, like all the others in the road, had fallen on hard times and was now a house of multiple occupancy with the sense of social failure this entails. No house can resist the inevitable decline after the bedsitters move in.

# It's The Not Knowing

This one now had nine individual addresses, spread over three floors, with each abode as damp, dark and gloomy on the inside as the house was on the outside. I lived on the ground floor in Flat 2, the one nearest the main entrance which might be why I felt quite territorial about this shared space. I felt it had been entrusted to me in some way.

Switching on the feeble light, I went and stood by the foot of the stairs, head cocked and listening. This hall would have been quite grand and impressive in its heyday, but was now overrun with junk, building up relentlessly and greedily devouring the space. A rusty bike, a Windsor chair in need of repair and a tallboy – water-damaged and losing its veneer – all took up space for no good reason. Only one piece made a useful contribution: the drop-leaf table. This is where I laid out the post each morning.

It sounded to me like the thumping was taking place upstairs so that's the way I went – up to the first-floor landing and then left along the airless corridor with its scarlet walls buried beneath, perhaps, a dozen coats of emulsion slapped on unsympathetically over the years. Each layer contrived to reduce the available space so that the elbow room was undoubtedly less than a Victorian would have known and enjoyed. This reduction was not inconsiderable and was, perhaps, something in the order of one centimetre on each side so we're talking 2cm in total. That's getting on for the best part of an inch. Of course, if you'd said 'centimetre' to the average Victorian he wouldn't have had a clue what you were talking about, being strictly imperial. He might have taken you for a lunatic and thrashed you. It's possible, it's always possible.

## It's The Not Knowing

I made my way along the corridor, the old floor creaking in pettish indignation as I passed. My sensory organs were becoming gradually accustomed to the gloom, particularly the ears, and I heard the three thumps again, louder than before. Unfortunately, I maybe hadn't depressed the time lag switch downstairs adequately and this might explain why the lights went out sooner than expected. It might just have been faulty anyway, in which case, no blame can be attached to me. In all probability, this would not have been a problem in the grand scheme of things but, by a stroke of ill fortune which deserves to be cursed to this day, at the very moment the hall was plunged into darkness, my foot caught a solid object, something carelessly abandoned in the gloomy passage, with the result that I stumbled and gashed my head on the handlebars of a bicycle which had been chained to the first-floor bannisters (by somebody clearly lacking foresight).

The ridiculously dull light came on almost immediately and as I looked around there was this fellow Joe, the owner of the obstacle but not (so I'm led to believe) the bicycle.

"Oh Jesus, I'm so sorry, are you OK? Oh Christ, *that's* a bit of a mess!" he said, noticing the fresh blood glistening from the gash, "I only left the holdall (*holdall!*) there while I was putting the – you OK? Are you concussed?"

I wasn't sure whether I was in the best position to answer that, and he continued, "how many fingers am I holding up?" It was three and so obviously three that I didn't waste my breath. "OK, it was three, but never mind. Tell you what, I've got a first aid kit inside, some plasters and stuff, let me see if I can patch that up…"

It's The Not Knowing

"You a doctor?" I asked by way of conversation.

"I dabble," he grinned. It was a line I thought I'd heard somewhere before and perfectly appropriate in the circumstances. *So, he does smile, or grin at least, when the occasion demands. I suspected he might; the cool, expressionless exterior will always slip eventually.* He picked up the guilty holdall (as that seems to be what we're calling it now) and pushed open the door to his room.

"Nice place!" I said, but we both knew I didn't mean it. In the tradition of any other 1970s bedsit, its shabby and uncoordinated brown furniture was glued to a sticky brown carpet which had quite possibly started life in some other area of the spectrum. The usual charity shop trimmings had been strategically arranged to create a Bohemian atmosphere or, to the untrained eye, a sense of random tat strewn in arbitrary fashion bordering on haphazard. No doubt some of these artefacts, to the same untrained eye, might once have seemed desirable *must-haves* in the charity shop *milieu*, where some should most certainly have remained. Charity shops are such a bad idea. The room itself was dark, drab and unwelcoming with the heavy old curtains successfully keeping out the streetlight whilst successfully keeping in the stench of damp and decay. The odour of Village Hall seeped from the pores of every surface.

On one of the walls there was a *Sounds* poster of the singer from Aerosmith, I think. It could easily have been Carly Simon, though. Hard to tell since the teeth and jaws are similar. As I pondered this, Joe reached under the bed and brought out an enamelled biscuit tin ingeniously converted

10

to a storage unit for first aid equipment: bandages and gauze dressings, safety pins, thermometers, that kind of thing. As he was searching, I went back to noting the details of the room. It was slightly bigger than my own place, I decided, and a lot less tidy. He'd stacked a number of beer cans in a pyramid on the mantelpiece, as if it were big and clever. Whether he'd drunk the contents or was still to drink them wasn't evident from where I was standing. The mantel had been repeatedly overpainted down the years – most recently in a shade of lime green which, if I'm honest, offended my eye. A minute or so later, despite my protestations that there really was no need and that I was a quick healer – possibly the quickest in the county – he'd cleaned the wound, smeared it with Germolene or some other unguent before applying a wad of cotton wool held fast by a strip of sticking plaster.

Thump... thump... thump...

"That's the best I can do but it should be OK, now. I'm Joe, by the way, Joe Boyle, but my friends call me Joe Boyle," he said, proffering his hand. I didn't know whether he'd just made a joke, so I laughed anyway and shook it.

"Wilfred Mold, call me Wilf Mold or just Wilf," I said, "and I don't *have* any friends," I joked (obviously). He didn't seem to realise this.

"Oh, right," was all he said.

"I live downstairs."

Thump... thump... thump...

It's The Not Knowing

"Yes, I've seen you about, I think. Isn't it you who sorts the mail and looks after the bins? Bloody good work, that, and a thankless task I should imagine. Do you do laundry?"

"Laundry? No, I think you've er…"

"I'm joking!" he said.

Thump… thump… thump…

I could still hear it thumping in my head. What the hell was it?

That was definitely the day of our first meaningful conversation. I don't mean meaningful in a deep spiritual sense, nothing like that. It wasn't the Dalai Lama and Gandhi chewing the fat over a pie and a pint, but he seemed like a reasonable bloke and my first impressions were favourable. I thought he was OK, as neighbours go, and, if nothing else, he wasn't a moron. I hate morons, particularly the stupid ones. I don't suffer fools gladly, either. Fools who are morons have no place in my life. I found out he wasn't a doctor (he was joking after all) and that he didn't have anything to do with physical education which *did* surprise me. No, he worked in a warehouse of all things. He began to tell me about it, but I couldn't concentrate; the three thumps were still making a noise and it was hard to focus fully on anything else (I wasn't really interested in what he did, if I'm being honest). He was a blasphemer, and a boozer (that much was clear) and certainly not a Royalist, if his *'stuff the jubilee'* badge was anything to go by. On first inspection he was friendly, public-spirited (despite the fact that the accident had been entirely of his making), and he hated the Royal Family of Spongers (not the Queen though, she's alright). So, yes; he was fine. And that was a relief because I'm a people person.

"What about you Wilfred? What do you do, what's your line?" he asked, as if he was interested.

"It's Wilf. Oh, dunno really, bit of this, bit of that… bit of the other," I laughed. Truth is, I didn't have what you might call a job. I hadn't worked for a long time and didn't really have the desire. I did, however, have a regular income of sorts and it was enough for me. I'm not going to go into details if you don't mind. Maybe one day.

"Ah! I see, ha ha… anyway, I'll be going out in a few minutes, Wilf. Pub. Darts match, with my mate next door, Bryan. Have you met him? I suppose you can hear him practicing now; that's him making all the noise… Anyway," he said, opening the door with indecent haste and in a tone which suggested he thought he'd done his bit and now wanted me to depart the scene. It made me uncomfortable if you really want to know. Say what you like about me, but I instinctively know when I've outstayed my welcome or when someone's got a monk on and taken against me – call it a sixth sense – and, as I said, I'm a good neighbour.

As I was being ejected I noticed he had a bookcase, which I hadn't spotted when I was browsing earlier.

"Ah! '*The Origin of Species*,'" I said. "You read it?"

"Yeah, had to when I was at Uni. It's interesting, I suppose. Have you?"

"Me? No, not for ages. But yeah, it's interesting. Makes you think: How can there be a God? And yet…nobody's ever proved otherwise, have they?"

"Well, you can borrow it if you like – maybe see if there *is* a God?" So, I did. I didn't know why, really. I thought I'd just take it and never give it back. Compensation for all the grief, possibly.

"And again, I'm really sorry about that, mate," he said, nodding towards the dressing as he manhandled me and the tome out of the door. I told him not to worry about it, as any good neighbour would. As I headed back down the stairs I tore off the sticking plaster and the cheap cotton wool. "Mate," is it?

I heard them later, going out, their heavy inconsiderate footsteps on the stairs, laughing out loud, with no attempt to keep it to themselves. A few hours after that I heard them coming back in although they weren't laughing then. They were noisy, as if they were trying too hard to be quiet. I wasn't at all resentful in any way. Far from it, in fact. It's true: I hardly knew them to talk to and it's no great surprise they didn't call for me but, at the same time, it might have been nice to have been asked to go and play darts with them; it wouldn't have hurt them just to ask. I'd never played it in my life but I'm sure it can't be that difficult. I've seen them on the telly sometimes, the professionals. They make it look easy, of course. If they didn't they wouldn't be on there would they? But Joe and the other one, Bryan, hadn't asked me, for whatever reason so let's not dwell on it. I won't mention it again.

It's The Not Knowing

There was nothing on the telly, so I picked up Darwin's novel. I'd never read it in my life. I'd heard about it, of course. I wasn't exactly sure what he was getting at, but it always seemed to me that he'd missed the point. Correct me if I'm wrong, but the idea that all life started in the trees seemed flawed in so many ways. For instance, what is a tree if not a life form? Where did that come from, then? It couldn't have come from a tree. If you thought about it logically, Darwin was an idiot. I flicked through the pages. There were about seven hundred! Ridiculous! Who has the time to read seven hundred pages?

That's when I saw it. Tucked in the middle somewhere, at the start of a chapter on '*Instinct,*' something I know a lot about.

It was a glossy colour photo, about 8 inches by 5 inches: three young people grinning optimistically in their flares. Pictured from left to right: someone who looked a little bit older – every inch the hippy with a grant, in the middle a really beautiful dark-haired girl then, on the right, a slightly younger *plain Joe*. Snapped by Kodak in a pub beer garden by the look of it. Two pints of mixed and a barley wine by the look of it. Typical know-all-know-nowt students by the look of it.

I saw that Joe, a couple of days later. I was in the hall gathering up all those free newspapers that nobody reads, tidying things and suchlike when he came home. It must have been around six thirty, that's the time he usually got back.

"Hi, mate," he said, grinning. He commented that the wound was healing quite nicely as he passed, hauling his big bulky sports bag.

"Been working?" I said, as I caught him up at the foot of the stairs.

"Yes, another day another dollar, as they say." He climbed the stairs, two steps at a time, like he was in a rush.

He was fumbling for his keys and didn't notice that I'd gone up just behind him. I think he was quite surprised to see me up there; I suppose I could move quite stealthily when I had to. I noticed the old bike was still there.

"You alright?" he said, taking a step back, which seemed almost aggressive.

"I've got your post here," I said, handing him a posh-looking white envelope. It was from Everest Double Glazing. I'd heard of them, and it looked quite important.

He took it, looked at it and dismissed it with an ungrateful, "just crap," which I thought was a bit rude, but I'm not one to point out other people's failings. I offered to take it away, but he didn't seem keen, preferring to turn down my kind offer without giving it much thought, it seemed to me.

I was disappointed by this and couldn't help but wonder about his attitude. He had caused me serious physical damage by his recklessly abandoning an obstacle on the landing in league with an unknown accomplice…and now this: snubbing someone who was only trying to help. Joe Boyle, it seemed, was quite content to have me deliver his post in person with not even so much as a thank you. If you scratch the surface looking for gold, don't be surprised if you find pig iron. If he didn't want to be civil, that was his right, as a sitting tenant. But be careful if you're a sitting tenant; be careful you don't upset other sitting tenants around you or you'll get your come-uppance. You won't have a leg to stand on when the shit hits the fan. And it will!

The next night at around six thirty, once again it just so happened I was in the hall when Joe got back from wherever he'd been. Working in a warehouse, probably. It wasn't a coincidence, obviously. But, if I or any of the other sitting tenants wanted to stand there at that particular time there was nothing he or his brainless mate could do about it.

He barged in, with that stupid holdall again. It was raining outside, and he was wet through; I was half expecting him to twist and shake like a dog, scattering the droplets from his greasy long hair onto the lino. It's quite a trek from the bus stop where, I know, he gets off the number seven, to the house. I imagine him as one of those people who think there's an optimum speed at which to walk through the rain to minimise exposure to the water as it tumbles from the sky. Obviously, there isn't. That would be too good to be true.

"Hey Wilf, how's it going? Bloody pissing it down out there," he said, shaking water off his holdall, stamping his feet and sending little beads of water in all directions.

"Hello, mate," I replied, "it's going OK I think. And I'm a bit dryer than you... actually, I'm wondering if I lost something in your room the other night? The night I fell over your bag if you remember? I've looked everywhere:

on the stairs and on the floor outside yours but it's not there… my inhaler, you haven't seen it on your travels, have you?"

Of course he hadn't, but he did point out, between bouts of stamping and shaking his coat, that his room wasn't the tidiest so it was definitely a possibility that it might be in there. His greasy face and hair would have glistened if there'd been sufficient light to glisten by. As it was, he looked like a drowning bat flapping in the dark. He'd "give me a knock" if he found it. That's all very well, I said, but how was I supposed to breathe in the meantime? No problem, did I want to go up while he had a look later? He said he'd have to get out of his "damned wet clothes" first.

I made some wheezing noises as though I was having trouble breathing. He suggested it might be worth getting another one. "Have you been to the quacks, he'd sort you out, wouldn't he? get you a replacement… if you need it to help you breathe…he'd sort you out straight away, I bet," was what he said. Used those very words, but it was the way he said it – sort of hostile and stand-offish – like it was somehow my fault I'd lost it! What was his problem? I didn't answer his question; instead, I asked him how the darts match had gone. They'd lost, apparently. Oh no! They'd lost, what a shame. Joe and Bryan had lost at darts. This made me happy, but I honestly can't think why. Anyway, if he wanted to make enemies he was going the right way. But he didn't want to make an enemy of me, he really didn't. People who made enemies of me might not even live to regret it. I could mess with him at the drop of a hat, see how he liked it. Have him waste his precious time looking for something which didn't exist. I liked that idea, a brilliant way to teach him a lesson. And maybe he could get his darts mate to help him look while he was at it. I told him I would really appreciate it if he could look now. Did I pretend to wheeze again? What do you think?

He took off his coat and left it on the banister, dripping into the hall below, which he had already soaked with his stamping and shaking. "Come in, then," he said, rattling the key inside the lock. He had a quick look on the floor – cursory, rather than sufficient – while I went through the motions, knowing there was nothing to find; I've never had an inhaler, never needed one, but he didn't know that. He kept saying he was quite sure it wasn't there but promised to "keep an eye out for it." There was something about the way he said it which made me suspect he wouldn't, and I suppose it was that in particular that set me off. I wondered if, despite his efforts to portray himself as the *People's Friend*, he might not be all he made himself out to be. I couldn't put my finger on it, but it was a feeling I couldn't have shaken even if I'd wanted to.

I edged myself across the room, making mental notes for future reference just in case. They say, "keep your friends close but keep your enemies closer." What they should also say is, "make sure you know the lie of the land before you attack."

"Tell you what, while you're looking for that I'll go get something I found in the book, something you might have lost."

"Yes, OK…" he said from behind a cupboard, like he was hardly interested.

I rushed back downstairs to grab the book and was back before he could say, "Are you sure you haven't got another one anywhere?"

"Don't worry about that now," I said, "I found this!"

"Found what?" he said, irritably. Don't worry, it was all being noted.

"This!" I said, as I thrust it under his nose. "Is this you?"

"Is *what* me?" he said, snatching the photo. Then he gasped. "Oh my God! Yes, that's me. In my mad student days... Wow! ... that's Bryan next door on the left and someone... someone who—"

"I know her," I said, cutting him off and tapping the young woman on the head. I took another look for effect. "Yes, definitely. I'd never forget that smile."

He took the picture and looked at it with the makings of a smile of his own, but a wistful one. "I thought I'd lost this..."

## Suze Moon

A few moments earlier I reckon he'd been about to make some excuse about being wet, needing to change and kick me out, having better things to do, apparently. Not now. No, now he wanted me to stay. Wasn't so keen to get rid of me now. Odd how things go, isn't it?

"*You* do?" he said, stressing the 'you,' as if someone like me couldn't possibly know her. "You *know* Suze? Really? I mean, that's weird, isn't it?"

"Oh, I know lots of people; I'm a people person. I still hear from her, as well – every year she sends me a Christmas card (although I never send cards myself). Bet she sends them to everyone; she's a real Christmas person, as you know."

"No, I don't know… I never got a card from her, and I haven't seen her for years. Wow… Suze Moon… wow… we can keep looking for your inhaler thing if you like, mate; do you have to dash off yet? Can you tell me anything else? I mean, like, how do you *know* her? I'm actually lost for words. All this, your knowing her – it's really unbelievable. Bloody small world or what! Did you know her when she took off – did you know about that? Vanished suddenly, a few years ago now, no explanation or anything… Disappeared one day and haven't heard from her in all the years. So, is she still around? Wow, I really am lost for words!"

He did seem genuinely excited. And he wasn't exactly lost for words, he seemed to have too many words, if anything.

"Sorry, but I do have to go," I said, looking at my bare wrist. "I have to be somewhere, and I really can't be late, but I might be around tomorrow evening… if you're not playing darts with *Barney?*" I said, getting the name wrong on purpose. That's how insignificant he was to me. I turned and moved towards the door, knowing I'd deflated him. Yes, I was beginning to dislike Joe Boyle and his creepy friend Bryan.

Maybe it was time to do something about it.

# It's The Not Knowing

The next day, I went out a bit earlier than usual – that would be about five o'clock – thinking I might go to a pub in time for Happy Hour. I always liked that one hour when the drinks were quite a lot cheaper, and you could save a lot of money during that period by drinking to excess. No, not excess, exactly but you know what I mean and, of course, it was helping the pub in financial terms, otherwise they wouldn't do it. So, yes, I was quite willing to drink my share and help out. I was a good patron.

The downside of such an arrangement was that it attracted the worst type of clientele – people who thought they could just come flooding in after work, drink like fish on an empty stomach, get a fish supper on their way home and end up in in the gutter covered in puke, their marriages broken. So many wretched lives, so many miserable Happy Hours for those who didn't know what they were doing. I know what I'm talking about; I've sat there with a treble for the price of a double, watching them cram themselves into the lounge bars in their cheap suits, swilling and shouting and talking too loudly. Those with the least to say always have the loudest voices – people like that make people like us sick – and will always make a show of themselves; sometimes their behaviour might culminate in punches being thrown but that never bothered me; I could hold my own in a brawl – sometimes more than my own. I'm a peace-loving people person and I don't like to see people behaving like animals.

I had gone out early for other reasons, though, not just to take advantage of the generous discounts. I was rather keen to avoid you-know-who. Speaking frankly, which has always been my way, he was definitely getting to be annoying, like a rash. He was the sort, I had decided, who would give anyone a rash, no questions asked. Not only did his attitude towards the missing inhaler stink – it never turned up, incidentally – but his pestering me for information about that girl, Suze would rile me in the end. He hadn't said anything as such – I hadn't given him the chance! – but I knew it would only be a matter of time before it started. I imagined it might begin with him hanging around in the hall, popping up every time I was there, and so frequently that it had to be more than mere coincidence. "Oh, hi *mate*, if you've got a minute…?" or maybe him putting the bins out when he knew full well I'd be doing it, acting surprised and somehow turning the conversation to whether I'd found her address or phone number; he'd be wanting to know personal details next. Stalkers, that's what they're called, people like that. So annoying and so creepy. As it turned out, I outwitted him. I sat in the pub all evening and only went home when I was sure the coast would be clear. I'd decided to let him stew if that's how he wanted to play it. Just like a stew, revenge was a dish best served cold. Or hot – either was good, really.

It wasn't until the next evening that he made his move and showed his hand. He was nothing if not predictable. I was watching *Parkinson* when I heard the knock on the door.

"Oh, Hi Wilf, how's the head? Thought I'd pop by and see how you were doing. Healing nicely, I see. That's good. Listen, I was wondering if you'd remembered any more about our mutual friend Suze or if you'd found her address maybe? I don't want to sound pushy, but it would be great if you knew anything that might, y'know, help me find her?"

*Pop by*? People who 'popped by,' as he called it, were a bloody nuisance, everyone knew that! I noted it for future reference. I briefly considered acting puzzled, pretending I didn't know what he was talking about. That would have been funny. But I didn't. I made all the right noises and invited him in, realising later that he was the first person I'd invited through that door. I told him to 'take a seat, not literally.' It was a joke, but he didn't seem to get it. He perched right on the edge of the sofa, probably quite tense, I thought. That sofa was a shapeless, sunken old thing lurking under a pale green candlewick bedspread. It did a job, though, in the sense that it was something to sit on. I wasn't bothered about trivial things like furniture. The counterpane was different though. I'd brought that from home, and it had sentimental value. I was suddenly irked to think of someone else sitting on it and letting off.

"Hey, do you play darts? Me and Bryan thought you should come and play up the pub, next time you're about. Are you up for that and a few bevvies?" So, he was trying to bribe me now? So pathetically transparent and sordid. And as for so-called Bryan, why didn't he have the decency to ask me himself?

"Yeah, definitely. That would be brilliant, cheers. I haven't played for a while, but I used to be quite handy with the old arrows," I said, making a throwing motion. "Nice one, look forward to it! And thank you to Bryan!" Then, I smiled excitedly because I thought that's probably what he was expecting. As I said earlier, I'm a people person.

It's The Not Knowing

"What can I tell you about her? Well, I haven't seen her lately, but I used to see her around town sometimes. We'd stop and chat and say we'd meet up again, but we never did unless by accident, never prearranged. She seemed to move around a lot; I remember that every time we bumped into each other she'd have a new address and phone number... having said that, I don't recall that I ever called her or that she ever called me although, I don't know if I had a phone at the time, probably not..."

"You didn't? Christ, why not?" he laughed, as he rudely interrupted. I could see he was quite agitated by this.

"Was she with anyone else, y'know, when you saw her?"

She wasn't, no, she was always on her own, and that's what I told him.

"Right, I see... and you said you knew where she is now didn't you?"

Oh, the look of disappointment when I told him I didn't. Poor Joe. Then the look of hope renewed when I said, "but, you never know, there might be something in here somewhere. I'm a bit of a hoarder..."

I shuffled things around in a drawer for a bit, making searching noises. "There's so much junk in here!" I said, just to increase the tension. The drawer was, in fact, immaculately tidy. "Ah, hang on... what's this? No, that's not it. Hmm, ah! *There* you are! I've been looking for that receipt." I knew he was dying to get in there and have a root around, so I closed the drawer. If you've ever closed a drawer dramatically then, you'd have a fair idea of how I closed this one. I still didn't trust him and saw nothing in his manner to suggest I ever could or would. In everything he did and said it became easier for me to dislike him. I can get on with anyone, always have, but with him? I rustled a few pages from a notebook I'd put there earlier and exclaimed, quite theatrically, "Bingo! Got it! Here we are... (papers rustling) Suze open brackets Moon close brackets."

By now he was positively beside himself, I feared he might even have a little accident on the candlewick and that was quite a worry until he settled down a bit.

"You've found it? Brilliant! Where is she, then? Somewhere round here?"

"Where *was* she," I corrected him. "She might still live at this address but there's no guarantee. As I said, she did tend to move around quite a bit, free spirit, and all that."

"But it's a start, even if she's moved there might be a forwarding address, and surely nobody moves forever, do they?"

"Nomads," I said as I handed him a blank page ripped from a little red notebook I'd bought in the Arndale Centre. I'd used it to write the address, which I'd selected at random from the phone directories in the library earlier in the day.

"Got a pen?" I dictated as he scribbled.

I had deliberately avoided a local address, one he could get to with a quick bus ride, because I didn't want to make it easy. And he had a Metro Card I bet, and, if he did, it wouldn't cost him anything. No, it had to be somewhere more distant. I was keen – I could hardly wait! – to witness the look of disappointment on his face when he returned empty handed, none-the-wiser and, hopefully, inconsolable. Equally, I wanted to avoid the easy option and instant gratification; there was something very appealing about keeping him dangling before delivering the fatal blow. And revenge, as my old mentor used to say, was a dish best served with coleslaw.

Having considered a few options, I picked a place at random. It could have been anywhere really; the whole country was my oyster in that regard. I considered Ludlow but the name didn't appeal. Neither did Bristol, or Bath and Manchester was just a shithole anyway… then I thought that should be *exactly* where I ought to be directing him. I quickly dismissed it as too unpleasant. I'd spent time in Manchester, and I didn't want any memories of that place rekindling.

In the end, I settled on New Barnet which turned out to be down near London. Who'd ever heard of that? Not me – and I've been around.

You know what? It was quite nauseating to see how genuinely happy he was, mooning about and clutching that little bit of paper where he'd copied the address and phone number, his stupid heart going nineteen to the dozen. The address was real enough, someone must live there, but I'd invented the number. I felt nothing but contempt as I showed him away from the counterpane and towards the door. Then he seemed to reappear suddenly, as if he'd been away.

"I owe you Wilf. Fancy a pint? Or several? Least I could do."

I declined, told him it was a kind offer, don't be silly, he didn't owe me anything, I was delighted I could help, hoped it would all work out, was he going to phone her tonight, maybe best to leave it, think about what he might say?

What I actually said was, "Don't like to rain on your chips, but she might not want to be found, have you thought of that?"

As I said it, just for a fleeting second, some niggling doubts crept in, like they do. It crossed my mind that I might have misjudged him and that maybe I was seeing demons where there weren't any. Seeing the cess pit half full instead of half empty, as a wise man might have said. All things considered, he'd been quite friendly and decent today, showing concern for the wound he'd caused, the invite to play darts and all that. I did wonder whether I was taking things a bit too far. He had most certainly annoyed me, him, and his creepy sidekick, but was I being just a bit, y'know, spiteful? Was I taking it too far? Had his appalling behaviour really merited all this?

I was quick to dispel those thoughts. Such thoughts weren't warranted. It was all good.

## New Friends

The next day, at my usual time, I was taking my weekly bath in a shared bathroom, which was not ideal. A cold, damp space, benefitting from a high ceiling where cobwebs could live undisturbed, about ten feet by eight of floorspace, with a modern suite in a hideous shade of sick. It was right at the end of the landing. I know for a fact it was never cleaned – whose job it was I do not know – and it fell dangerously short of my own expectations and high standards. Live and let live is my approach but some animal in that house, one who shall remain nameless, needed to go back to potty-training school. Dirty bastard. I am a people person but I'm definitely not a dirty person person.

There was one little window which wouldn't open because some unskilled amateur decorator had glossed over the frame – the first coat probably applied between the wars with the subsequent layers laid down at irregular intervals since the end of hostilities. Sometimes when I went in there it stank, the kind of stink that a bowl of stale and dusty potpourri could never hope to mask. Those shavings had been there so long, in fact, that they'd started to take on the flavour of excreta and spores. The whole set-up was a breeding ground for mould, the kind of place where the World Health Organisation or anyone with a bacteria-obsession or even a basic medical background would have had a field day. And the worst aspect? What was left to grow in the plughole in that bath; it makes me honk even to think about it. It needed pulling out but why the hell should I do it? I didn't leave it there. The tub itself was struggling against a layered build-up of scum and body fats, many years in the making and so bad that you'd never want to recline and have a soak. No chance, you'd end up scummier than when you went in. Dirty bastards. And thieving bastards! I left some shampoo in there once by accident and I went back the next day to find the bottle almost empty. I served them right, though, I taught them all a lesson. I filled the bottle from the toilet bowl before I flushed and left it back in the same place. Head and Shoulders? Head and Floaters, more like!

As I was sitting in there, knees up and shivering I could hear voices on the landing outside the door. It was Boyle and someone else. Not so-called Bryan, I could tell that from the way they were talking. It was all rather stiff, as if they hadn't been formally introduced.

I didn't catch most of it – it was quite muffled – but I definitely heard: "I'm Joe, by the way, Joe Boyle, but my friends call me Joe Boyle." They both laughed as if it was the funniest joke ever. Well, it certainly wasn't, and it wasn't even original. I couldn't hear the other one's name – if he even *said* it – but I did hear him say something about going to the shops for somebody who lived at the end of the hall in number 8. The weird thing about number 8 is the occupant. I suspected he was blind which, I reckoned, was why there was never any personal post for him – just brown bills, never a postcard. I would have been happy to do that kind of thing for a blind man, bit of shopping and what-not… he only had to ask. But he hadn't and because of that somebody else was inconvenienced as a result. Serve him right. From his tone he sounded like a do-gooder, anyway. Don't get me wrong, I'm not one to judge a book by its cover but he did have that air about him, if you know what I mean? Sunday schooler. It sounded like their little tete-a-tete was over as there was a bit of a silence. The water tank was filling and making too much racket, the pipes were clanking too, so I missed some of it. I thought I heard something about darts. Then there was a shout: "We're

going now so, see you in there. I'll get you one in. Lager?"
followed by the sound of feet pounding down the stairs and
the slamming of the front door.

Just when you think you know someone you realise you
don't. Asking me to go with them, and now it was obvious
they weren't being sincere, probably didn't even want me
to go in the first place, The superficial actions of shallow
people. They hadn't asked *me* if I wanted lager – just made
a vague reference to a 'few bevvies.' That could have been
anything: ales, stout, *lagers*... Black Tower... pathetic!
What was their motive? Had to be a motive, nobody does
anything for anybody without a motive. Why would they?
It's always been like that. There are so many self-centred
people about.

The more I thought about it the less I wanted to associate
with that kind of crowd. Very cliquey. The so-called in-
crowd had just counted me out – not that I was ever in.

There was a knock on the door shortly after that.
"Anybody in there? Going to be long?" What did he think?
That the door locked itself? "Five minutes," I said. I didn't
mind; I'd been in there an hour, and it was the neighbourly
thing to do. I hate selfish people. I waited exactly five
minutes before opening the door. "All yours," I said but
there was no-one there. That's their problem. When I got
back to the room someone had slipped a note under the
door.

*Wilf – tried Suze number. Not recognised. Might have
written it down wrong? Gone to pub if you fancy a pint?
Joe*

I got dressed up and went to the pub. I was going to call his bluff. The note hadn't specified which pub, but I knew where they went, those two. I'd seen him in there a couple of times when I'd gone to the front window and pressed my nose up against the glass. The Shipwreck – *The 'Reck* – had a bad reputation and, as bad reputations go, this one was reputedly quite bad – and well-deserved if the gossip was to be believed. I don't listen to gossip myself; I take people as they are. I don't need idle chit-chat telling me who I should hate. The regulars were mainly students and other species and sub-species of loser. Didn't take kindly to outsiders, I supposed. Didn't bother me at all. I preferred the other pub, over the road. I went inside anyway, as I'd been invited.

The landlord looked up from his slops tray and scowled. I'd heard people say he was a misery guts and this confirmed it. He had a huge gut, and he was miserable, if my first impression was anything to go by. Call it a gut instinct if you want. I will, next time I tell anyone about him. I was about to scowl back when, above the strains of *Hotel California* on the jukebox, I heard: "Wilf! Over here." I looked across and saw Joe Boyle heading towards me waving some money. "I'm buying," he crowed, with a huge inane smile on his blotchy red face. I could tell he'd been drinking. I could always tell.

"You saw my note, then? Couldn't get through on that number you gave me, y'know. Sounded like it was out of order or a wrong number maybe. Anyway, I've got another plan. Pint of lager? Skol OK for you? Three pints of Skol please, Jill, when you're ready." he said, waving his cash again and smiling at the barmaid.

I thought Skol was fine for me. We waited for his change
and then headed over to the corner table where the other
one was sitting. Funny, that I'd never met or spoken to him;
I wasn't sure I'd even seen him even though we lived in the
same building. He looked a bit older than me and Joe, in
his early thirties, probably. But they had been at university
together so, what was the story there? Mature student?
He'd maybe failed in the big wide world so thought he'd
'go back to school.' Yes, that was possible. He looked like
someone who might have failed spectacularly at some
stage.

"Have you two met? Bryan. Wilf," he said, handing him
the pint and sitting down. Bryan was inspecting me closely
and nodded, without actually speaking. If you've ever been
scrutinised, you'll know how I felt.

"Yes, I've seen you about," I said, taking a seat. "How's
it going?"

"Yeah, not bad. Yourself? Don't think I've seen you in
here before, have I? Do you go to 'The *Other* Place?'" He
said that last bit in a faux-dramatic voice, then he laughed.
Quite mellifluously, actually.

"Usually, yeah – for my sins!" and I said that last bit in a
proper theatrical voice, making my mouth into the shape of
a rectangle and popping my eyes before chuckling. I could
be mellifluous, too. Then we all chuckled together, like
mates do.

"Anyway, cheers!" said Joe, and we all clinked our Skols.

We sat and chit-chatted for a minute or so: Did Bryan like
boiled cabbage; did anyone? Parkinson, football, and

rubbish like that while the glasses were steadily emptied during a few awkward silences. The sight of three empty vessels sent Bryan scurrying to the bar for refills, while Joe went for a slash. He came back quite quickly, I thought, which made me wonder whether he had a small bladder (and therefore penis) or a highly efficient evacuation system... or maybe a bag? A question for another day maybe, though probably the former.

"Cheers!" *Clink.* I went to the bogs, just for a slash, and when I got back, I had the impression they'd been talking about me. My ears did actually feel hot.

Bryan was the first to raise the subject. That surprised me, as I thought Joe might have been the one, but I was wrong (No Crackerjack pencil for me, thank God).

"Joe tells me you knew Suze? That right?" Joe raised his eyes and rolled them in mock exasperation, then he chuckled.

I didn't deny that our paths may have crossed.

"You weren't an item, were you? Thing is, and this *might* have been before your time, our Joe had a bit of a thing for her all those years ago. And they *were* an item, they were actually 'walking out together,' weren't you Joe, and he's never forgotten her, have you Joe?" and he laughed and he teased and ragged and ribbed and he took a swig of Skol and he punched Joe on the arm in a playful way and he winked at me, conspiratorially. It was exhausting just watching him.

"I don't deny it," said Joe. I thought he was slurring suddenly, and they're not easy words to slur.

34

"I may have carried a torch for the young lady at one time, it's true. Guilty as charged, m'Lud. But she went and left, and I never heard from her again – *actually,* were you and her, y'know… an item, Wil'?" he said, as if it had only just occurred to him that this could ever be a possibility. "Must have been after me, then, 'cos she never mentioned you."

I was quick to clarify the position, told them that even though I'd had women, loads of women, actually, and some good ones amongst them, Suze had never had the pleasure of my individual attention, we were just friends; that was all there was to it. Nothing more.

"There you go!" said, Bryan as he slapped him on the shoulder. "I told you,  said she wouldn't be Wilf's type, I knew it!" and he laughed. They had definitely been talking about me.

"Oh, I wouldn't say she wasn't my type, she very much was, but we never… y'know." Instantly, I wished I'd said I'd 'bonked her brains out, loads of times,' just to see the look on his flabby piss-head's face. Too late, as loudmouth still had the talking cushion, apparently.

"Hey, you've got competition, Joe! How *do* you know her, anyway?" asked Bryan, peering at me and chuckling like the nosey bastard he was. I knew the signs. Bryan, the former mature student was getting drunk.

"Skols all round?" I said, as I stood up and headed for the bar. That was when I resolved to teach them both a lesson for talking about me behind my back. I had tried very hard to give them the benefit of the doubt and it pains me to say I was wrong. They were both evil.

# It's The Not Knowing

After an eternity I finally managed to get served. They were definitely giving preferential treatment to their regulars; that was patently obvious. The fat landlord stayed at the far end of the bar and didn't look over in my direction once. He was probably scared of me, with all the revenge scowling that was going on. I wondered whether I'd suddenly become invisible. I seethed in his direction, until the barmaid, Jill, finally got around to taking my order: "Same again, is it?"

"Hooray! Yes, please"

"Remind me, again?"

Having thus succeeded in getting three pints of Skol and my change, I made my way back to the table where I found the two of them roaring with laughter about something. I have to admit it did seem genuine, not at all like the ostentatious display of the other night.

"What's funny? You're not talking about me, are you?" I asked, putting the three pints on the table, and spilling some in the process. That's what beer mats are for.

"Cheers!" they said in unison. "Bryan was just telling me about a time... no, you tell it Bryan," said Joe, as he reached across for his pint, wiped it on the mat and took a slurp.

"Well, there was this party, see, years ago at some house, and I turned up pissed, all day session, and what have you... well, let's just say it was a crappy party, so I thought I'd go home. Problem was that it was miles away and there was no bus at that time, so..."

"He took one of the kids' bikes!"

"Yes, alright, I'm telling the story, aren't I? Yes, I did; I took one of the kids' bikes, from the front garden. And not a full sized one, either. It was like a really little kid's one. God, I was pissed. Anyway, thought I'd pedal it home and chuck it in the river when I got there. You'd have done the same; anyone would in that state."

"Indeed."

"Needless to say, I'm not proud of this. So, there I am pedalling for miles, sobered up after about an hour of this sheer bloody physical exertion and realised what a stupid idea it had been, that I was a twat and that I should have stayed at the party and kipped on the floor or in the shed or even in a bus shelter. Finally, though, I get somewhere near home and the birds are just about starting to tweet so it must be almost dawn, so I was probably pedalling this stupid little bike for… God knows how long, when I get pulled over by the police."

"No!" I said, as Joe roared: "There's more, listen!"

"I should just mention that this bike had no lights. So, they said: 'What do you think you're doing?' And I panicked and told them the whole story, but I said I'd *borrowed* the bike. Then I added, 'You'd have done the same!' They didn't laugh, coppers don't laugh, but they did say they could understand my reasoning. Then they asked for my name and address."

"What did you tell them?"

"I told them my name and address."

## It's The Not Knowing

"Your REAL name and address?"

"Yes. I couldn't think of a false name. I'd been pedalling a little kids' bike all night. Fifteen miles, you should try it sometime."

Joe roared again; he was finding this all quite hilarious. I thought it was reasonably funny but was more concerned with the poor kid whose bike had been stolen in a drunken moment. Although, if it wasn't chained up, the kid was partly to blame...

"Anyway, the copper says: 'OK. Keep to the footpath for the rest of the way.' So, I did. When I got to the bridge over the river, I knew I couldn't just chuck the bike in as I'd planned. I was now on file; they'd taken my name and if it washed up somewhere, they might trace it back to me. Irrational, I know, but I wasn't thinking straight. So, I pedalled home and went to bed. I woke up early, really early. And then I suddenly remembered what I'd done and all I could think of was: 'Shit, what do I do now?' So, although I was nearly dying, I got up and pedalled to the bus station."

"This is the best bit, wait 'til you hear this!"

"And it was all looking good, there was a single-decker going back to where I'd 'borrowed' it. It was just about to set off, so I sprinted, and I got to it just in time. The smell of the diesel was nearly making me puke and the noise of the engine was banging in my head. I thought I'd be able to have a nap on the way and just take it back and leave it in the garden with a clear conscience."

"And?"

## It's The Not Knowing

"The bastard driver wouldn't let me on with a bike."

Joe snorted and a jet of lager flew from his nostrils and mouth, going in all directions. He howled with laughter and slapped the table. It was infectious, and I found myself chuckling, then seriously chuckling, then shaking, and finally howling and slapping, same as Joe. I don't think I have ever laughed so much. I liked it. I never knew laughing could be such fun.

"I'm glad someone finds it funny!" he said, "anyway, I pedalled it back. Another fifteen miles with the worst hangover ever and the sun burning holes in my eyes. I put it back in the garden, just where I'd found it, and scarpered. Right, I'm thirsty! Who's buying?"

We stayed in until closing time by which time they were both quite drunk. I wasn't, I can hold my ale. I suppose I'd have to admit that it had been a good evening, all things considered. Enjoyable. It was a change from my normal pub experience, where I would spend the session on my own. There I go, making out like I'm some sort of social leper. I'm not, obviously. Don't even imagine I was on the periphery or that I was a loner. Far from it. But, if I were, then it would have been totally my choice; sometimes it's good to be alone and lost in your own thoughts, have time to think and to see things with a clarity you can't get when people are buzzing around. Who can honestly say they have not, at some time, wished everyone would clear off and leave them alone… and stop talking at them? People can be so irritating, and I don't say that lightly; I am a people person, as you know.

# It's The Not Knowing

Occasionally, I might not be on my own. I might have company; I might sit at a table where others were also sitting, strangers and the like. After a time listening to them, I would add my own views and we'd get talking until they had to leave, for whatever reason. These were people I'd probably never met before and who would stay for a while before they remembered they had to go. It was all part of the experience. I regarded it as a social experiment. I was quite interested in people watching and such things, actually. I might write a book about it. Or maybe a poem. They were sorry to have to go, I know that. I could tell that. I hoped that. I know people.

As I said, we left at closing time, when Ronnie, the landlord with the beer gut shouted from the bar: "Time now, Joe. C'mon Bryan, you can come back tomorrow. Let's have your glasses now, please…"

He was messing about with bar towels and drip trays and the bar staff were going around yawning and collecting the empties, tipping out the ashtrays and wiping the hammered copper tabletops with a filthy rag before putting the upturned stools on the table. As if the rag hadn't spread enough germs, the seats would now make their contribution. On top of greasy snack spillage, I'm sure most people who'd sat on them would have farted out gaseous vapours at some stage and maybe worse, each particle seeping into the fabric. It's called capillary action. Or maybe osmosis. I know what I'm talking about, there was something on Schools Programmes about it.

I was quite impressed, is that the right word? Yes, impressed that the fat man knew their names. He clearly didn't know my name, so I scowled at him. Just because he thought he owned the place didn't mean he couldn't be scowled at.

## In The Park with Victoria

The next day I felt rough. I'd obviously had more beer than I thought. I told you I can hold my ale, and I can, but I suspected there might have been something wrong with it. Maybe the fat landlord hadn't kept his pipes clean, or whatever it is that they're supposed to do with them. And those filthy tables, I remembered those. He wanted reporting if that was the case. But what's the use? He wouldn't listen. Live and let live. Eventually, having waited for a load of other pages to display, I saw the weather forecast on Ceefax. It looked like it was going to be a sunny day, so I thought I'd sit in the park, get some fresh air and cheer myself up.

I went out and something very unusual happened: I didn't sort the post in the hall. Just didn't feel like it. Nobody ever said thanks for doing it, anyway. That's not why I did it, for the thanks, but it suddenly seemed quite irrelevant. They'd probably pick up their post eventually, regardless of whether it was sorted by size and colour and all that. Not the ones who didn't live there now, of course, the ones who'd left no forwarding address – and that was all of them! – but the current residents. So, I left it on the mat and just stepped over it. I didn't think I would ever sort it again. And that seemed quite relevant, actually.

There's a bench in the park I like. I like where it is. Right opposite a statue of Queen Victoria, 1837 to nineteen something. I have a mental block about her dates. I know she followed four Georges and a William: *Good Grief! Grahame Greene watching videos, even goats eventually get excited...*

There was someone sitting on my end of the bench when I got there. I know some people are funny about sitting next to a stranger on a municipal bench, scared that they might be taken for a nonce or a loser. It never bothered me. I went and sat down next to this person. Looked like an OAP, wearing OAP clothes, you know the kind of thing, big coat, and trousers from an old suit. Shoes, sometimes. Rheumy eyes. If you don't believe me, next time you see an OAP go up and take a close look at their eyes. They're always rheumy. It doesn't bother me, though, OAPs kitted out in clothes more suited to a charity shop. If that's what they like, I'm not going to say anything, am I?

The OAP got up almost as soon as I set myself down and, as they moved away, I spread myself out to enjoy the unseasonal warmth of the sun. I heard the sound of twittering. Birds, probably. I closed my eyes and breathed in the warming air, the traffic on the bypass offering up its unrelenting, pitch-perfect drone to accompany the sweet birdsong as it swooped and soared, its lilting, playful melody in glorious, majestic, and perfect harmony with the whisper of the breeze and the gentle rustle of the litter as it skipped, pizzicato across the land. The earth, now feeling the heat from a low but persistent sun knew instinctively that the time was almost upon us, that a beautiful change was coming. Oh, what a glorious time to be alive! Was ever one so blessed by the sheer and overwhelming anaesthesia of being? I could feel my mind shrinking, but I was powerless to stop it; my senses became numb and fell deep below the earth into a lifeless, deathless and painless state, where the only sound was from the descending, calming bass tones of the topsoil and the subsoil and the weathered rock before resolving in the bedrock of nature and, as the light began to dwindle and die, I thought I had died. I liked it. It was so warm, so motherly and so restful, being cocooned like that in perfect stillness. I've never been to Nirvana, or anywhere abroad, in fact, but I imagine that's how it must feel. Like a feeling of nothing. And then, against my most profound and deep-rooted longing to be left there in peace and to fade away blissfully, I slowly began to regain the sense of the everyday; the light and the sound increased, imperceptibly at first and then steadily. It felt like I'd been plucked from a special place and returned to a waking hell. No, not hell, but somewhere not very good. I was back, there. On a bench in the sun, just me and Vicky, with me wishing for all the world that I could have more of what I'd just had.

In the distance there was another bench, on the brow of the hill from where the land swoops down to the river. I have enjoyed that bench myself, sometimes, and it's a nice view, it must be said. I liked my Victorian bench better, though. I felt quite at peace there, somehow, just me and The First Empress of India. What I liked about it, I suppose, was it was rather like having a friend on my terms, someone to talk to when the mood took me. And, if I didn't like the way the conversation was going, I could just ignore it or get up and go. Friends don't ask questions.

I was watching that other bench with interest. Not because I felt like going up there but because it was now being used.

I could make out, at that point, three people. Two had turned up to start with. They were sitting together on the right-hand side. Then, a short while later, the third one came along and sat down, but on the left-hand side. Nothing strange about that, I thought. It seemed unlikely they could know each other, particularly with a seating arrangement like that. But then, a fourth one turned up and sat down in the middle. Again, quite unremarkable except that suddenly, and with perfect synchronisation, the first three got up as one... and walked off together, stride for stride. I observed the lone figure for a while, but it made no move, staying quite motionless as the other three headed off towards the town.

The sun disappeared behind a huge black cloud which had formed suddenly in the southern sky and the brilliant greens of the grasslands became a more sombre shade of pale sage. I looked up at the blackness and then at the solitary figure on the bench.

And, as I pondered, I became quite melancholic. It sometimes happens like that.

Then a nonce came and sat down on my bench so I got up and left.

I headed off towards the town as the sky, by then a threatening black canopy, gave up the fight and dropped its guts. I sheltered under a tree for a bit, for all the good it did, cursing the weatherman. They'd guessed wrong again, but who could be surprised by that? I think they provide a disservice. If they hadn't said anything today, if they hadn't promised sunshine with no possibility of rain, if they'd just kept their big mouths shut, then I would most likely have

44

taken a coat that day rather than the lightweight blue velvet jerkin I was wearing, huddled under a leafless silver birch getting wet. After a time, the rain clouds passed over, and the sky cleared. Too late for me, though; I'd left the park before then, having decided I'd take it on the chin and just get wet. It was just typical, though. The minute I decide to leave, it decides to stop raining. You couldn't be blamed for thinking someone somewhere had it in for you, could you? By then, it must have been sometime around mid-afternoon, I think. I remember looking over at the clock on the Church, but it was slow. In fact, now you mention it, I think it was permanently stuck at 11.30. A useless service, same as the weatherman; public disinformation at its most lethal. But I couldn't waste time, whatever it was, worrying about things like this. I thought I'd go and dry out in the pub, see if anyone was in. I decided I'd go to the 'Reck rather than my local. It does you good to have a change of scenery, sometimes. I was thinking of changing anyway. I'd been going in there, my local, for years but I had been getting quite fed up with it of late, if I'm honest. Same old faces, same old banter. Boring!

I pulled the front door open, and the smell of beer and disinfectant hit me immediately. There were subtle vomit notes too. It was the kind of smell you normally get until the place fills up, when it probably gets breathed in and vanishes. The place was almost empty, and I thought that strange for a mid-afternoon. Apart from me, there was just one other customer that I could see, and that was an OAP. An old fool, drip-feeding his meagre pension into a hungry fruit machine. And I don't mean he was buying fruit. Not hard to see why he was wearing old suit trousers, giving his pittance away like that. Not my business though, was it? I like people, even old people, and I like to help all kinds of people, but there are some people beyond help. It wasn't my place to interfere, so I said nothing.

"Now then, what can I get you?"

It was the fat landlord. He'd come out of some hole somewhere and was now standing behind the bar. I hardly recognised him from last night. He wasn't scowling. If anything, the cruel thin lips were arranged in such a way as to suggest a smile. Not a friendly smile. Not the kind of warm and welcoming smile that comes naturally to a people person, but it was a good effort. Certainly better than yesterday's thin cruel lip arrangement.

"Pint please, Ronnie."

He stuck the glass under the Skol tap and pressed go. He knew my drink. I didn't have to tell him. It was like being a regular. Well, I could play that game, too. I asked if he'd been busy. I think I said: "How's it going?"

He then let me in on a few things: It had been quiet, people were probably skint at this time of the week, and he hoped to sell a month's worth of drinks on the day of the Jubilee.

We discussed how the Queen was alright, but the rest of 'em? No thank you, spongers, the lot of 'em. Ronnie was quick to point out that we were better off with them than without them. No, I hadn't considered the tourist trade and the millions of visitors they attracted to this country, and yes, I suppose they were great for the economy. But how did it benefit the likes of him, this far from the tourist trap? Wasn't it just the cockneys who benefited, the hot dog and fizzy drink sellers in Trafalgar Square? Hadn't he heard they charged two quid for a can of coke? Yes, he had. So, that made him think twice and re-examine the facts. He changed the subject.

"Where's your mates today? Bit early for them, I suppose."

So, he thought they were my mates, did he? I would hardly call them mates. What time was it anyway? It was 11.45. I told him I hadn't seen them but thought they might be in later. And I suppose I hoped they would. Anyway, I didn't have time to stand there chatting, even though I had suddenly gained a few hours I thought had already gone, so I took my drink and my change and headed towards the fruit machine as it belched out the OAP's winnings.

"How much did you win?" I asked, by way of conversation. The miserable old goat didn't even look at me. And he didn't answer straight away. Just kept staring at the machine with his rheumy eyes, as he stuck his wrinkly old mitt into the trough and retrieved a single coin. He put it straight back in the slot and slapped the button. Two bars and a... cherry. Slap, no good either. Slap, c'mon... shit a brick! still no good: You Lose! A fanfare of beeps and grunts and flashing lights snaked their way across the display before disappearing into a black hole. No-one likes a braggart.

"Ten pence," he said.

"Excellent!" I said.

"I put two fucking quid in," he said, picking up his half and shuffling from the scene.

47

## It's The Not Knowing

I wasn't going to put money into that robbing bastard. I won thirteen quid once on a machine like this. It cost me twenty pence. So, I haven't played since. The odds of winning big again are nil. So, I'm well up on the deal. I sometimes think that was my lifetime's achievement. Put in those terms, it sounds feeble and insignificant but, at the time, it was big news. I suppose if you compared it to some people's lifetime achievements, high-flyers, and whizz-kids, you'd be right. You'd have a case. It was nothing much. It was alright by me, I don't care. Look at Ronnie, the fat landlord, cleaning his bar and checking the pipes and all that. Is that his lifetime's achievement? Is that what he amounts to? Can he honestly look back with anything but shame and horror on a life lived like that? Early mornings, late nights, always at someone's beck and call, and for what? Two weeks in Spain every year and a souvenir donkey? Yes, I know those slops trays need emptying and pipes need checking and barrels changing, I know all of that but, really – is that all he's got? Next time you're taking the piss out of someone who won a thirteen-pound jackpot, you just remember Ronnie. Everything is relative. I know what I'm talking about.

I went up to the bar and got another Skol. It was going down nicely, in a hair of the dog kind of role. A few more people had come in by this stage, so I went and sat down, next to a couple of types. They were deep in conversation when I arrived. I gathered, from what I could make out, that they were both teachers, taking time off from marking books and setting tomorrow's lessons. I wasn't eavesdropping; they were talking quite loudly. It wasn't a case of me listening in deliberately, like the Stasi or anything.

One of them got up to go to the bar. Spotting a lull in the conversation, I leaned over and mentioned to the remnant that I had great respect for the teaching profession. I told him I used to go to school, myself, and the teachers were very strict back then. And they all seemed so old. Now, I said, the teachers all look so young! We laughed. I went for a slash and when I came back, they'd gone – they were now sitting on another table on the far side of the room.

I wasn't in the mood for talking, anyway. Just as well, they'd gone. I needed space to think about the Joe situation. I know he'd tried to phone the fake number and obviously that had been a dead end, exactly as I'd expected. I wondered what he was intending to do now, only so that I might keep one step ahead. He mentioned he had a plan last night but didn't expand. His next option would be to write to the address, surely? And that could only result in one of two outcomes. Outcome A: No answer, or Outcome B: Not known at this address – Return to Sender – but then he would know something at least. If he had any sense, he might write to the current occupier at that address and explain the reason for his enquiry. That could only result in one of two outcomes. Outcome A: No answer or Outcome B: Sorry Mr Boyle, she's not known here and, as far as we know, she has never lived at this address, and we've been here ten years blah blah, we wish you well etc. And that's where his hope would crumble and die, knowing that he was now clutching at a straw which was about to break the camel's back. What would he do then? Probably blame me for having a wrong address, of course, with little chance of getting the right one. My plan would have worked out nicely. I took another swig of Skol. You might think I'd have been happy with the way things were going to turn out, wouldn't you? And you'd be right. Sort of.

I was still thinking about the bench on the hill earlier. The single figure. Sitting alone up there. I don't know why, but I couldn't get the image out of my head. And that's not like me because – Oh for God's sake, not *Hotel California* again! – because I never worry much about other people; life's too short. No, take that back, that's not strictly true, I think about other people all the time. I like people, I really do. Why had the other three moved away when he (or she, it might have been a *she*, but it walked like a he) sat down? There, that was it. That's what was bothering me. If they'd waited a few minutes before getting up. If they hadn't all stood up at the same time. If they'd gone off in different directions, even, that would have been something... but they hadn't done that.

I had another couple of pints. It was getting busier now, as the late afternoon crowd drifted in. I should have eaten something to soak up the drink, but I didn't. I can take my ale; it wasn't a problem. I watched someone else feed the fruit machine for a long time. It was voracious, and the moron must have lost at least five pounds. He was medically angry by the end, and he gave the '*thieving fucker*' a retaliatory shove. This toppled his untouched pint from the top of the machine, sending it sloshing down the back of a loser who was sitting close by. The loser leapt up in shock, clutching the back of his neck and fingering his collar. This knee-jerk reaction caused him to rock the table where he and his mousy girlfriend were sitting which, in turn, sent a half of Guinness and a brandy and Babycham sliding into the ungrateful lap of the girlfriend. Luckily, she had already eaten the glace cherry, or things could have been much worse.

It was a beautiful and natural thing to see, two apes squaring up, while a mouse tried frantically to minimise the textile soiling. I hadn't seen a fight in a pub, not one that I wasn't directly involved in, at least, in a long time and this had all the makings of a good one. And so, the two parties engaged in a spot of shoving and grunting, with a couple of dirty tables sent sprawling the most notable casualties. The two sluggers were eventually wrestled apart and kicked out by the fat Royalist landlord, who immediately went up in my estimation. The mouse tottered out after them as I leaned forward and folded my arms on the table, rested my forehead on top and laughed like a donkey. I laughed so hard and so violently and so hysterically, that the tears dripped from my cheeks. Maybe if I'd been upright, they would have rolled down them.

Then, it turned weird, and I felt like crying. Not crying with happiness or joy, either – more like the other, original type. It's a thin line. If I'd had sails, I'd have just had the wind taken out of them. If I'd had wind… it doesn't bear thinking about. I felt quite deflated.

I was just wondering whether it might be worth going to the window, maybe see if they were fighting in the street, when something heavy brushed my shoulder. I looked up and there was Joe, his holdall only recently tossed in my direction, now on the floor. "Missed!" he said, "I thought it was you. What are you having, pint?

"Pint."

## The Suze Crisis

I went for a slash and when I came back, he'd been served, and two pints were sitting on the table.

"We don't see you in here normally, what's happened over the road? You been banned?"

I played along, told him I had.

"Crap pub, that one, anyway. Right, here goes, cheers!" He drank it down in one, sniffed, slammed the empty glass down on the table and belched a sustained belch of epic proportions. A magnificent, world-class belch. People actually turned and stared, and some applauded. I was both impressed and taken aback in equal measure. If it were a thing, I think he could have belched for England. Maybe even Ireland, with the right grandparents.

"Needed that. C'mon, get it down your neck, it's your round."

"Blimey, what's the hurry? Where's Bryan; is he coming in?"

"Got a raging thirst, here! Bryan? Who knows?"

"Bad day at the office?"

"Ah, y'know, the usual crap. Hate this job, woe is me, that kind of thing."

I'm not sure now why I did, with him being in what had the makings of a volatile state, but I asked anyway: "How's the search going?"

# It's The Not Knowing

He sat back and looked up at the ceiling. Then leaned forward, folding his arms.

"It's not going. I tried that number, like I said, but it's permanently out of order, no ringtone or anything, it's just dead. Like my beer, by the way… c'mon, more beers!"

"You could try writing to her?"

"Yeah, yeah, I know all that… I could write, I could send a hundred bloody letters but, who knows, there's no guarantee she's still there, is there. I've thought about this a lot, since you found the photo; *she* disappeared, it was *her* decision, right? And whatever reasons she had for not saying anything before she went – wherever it was she went – who's to say those reasons don't still apply, eh? You said it yourself, didn't you: she might not want to be found. Yeah, she might not. I have to leave it where it is. In the past and finished with, I know that. I do. If it was because of something I did, I don't think I really want to know now, not after all this time. I think it would be too much, y'know, I think the sense of regret would be… y'know? Anyway, enough! Enough of this shit! Are you buying me a beer or what?" and he rattled his glass on the table.

That really hadn't gone as I'd thought it might. I went and bought him another pint, I got myself a tomato juice with vodka and Worcester sauce. It counted as food. I got some crisps as well. They didn't count as food.

"Aye aye, here's Bryan! Bryan! Get 'em in, while you're there!" he shouted, waving his half empty glass in the air, spilling some, obviously. It takes great skill to do that without spilling any. I know people who can do it, so I'm speaking from experience.

By this stage Joe was semi-drunk and a quarter maudlin; abstract concepts are hard to quantify; I hope you appreciate the effort. Myself? I was OK and comporting myself with dignity and decorum. I told you already, I can take my ale. It was the vodkas that did for me in the end, I suppose.

Did we want crisps, nuts? I declined but Joe, who pronounced himself "officially starving" accepted the offer and within a minute or two he was feasting and drinking like a fish.

"Y'alright, Wilf?"

"Very well, thanks," I said. He was being particularly friendly, I thought, but I suppose that's what mates are. Friendly.

Before we got to kicking out time, by which time at least two of us were as drunk as a skunk, the topic came up again: The Suze Crisis. Joe was adamant he would not look for her. There was nothing to be gained and it could only end badly, he said. As he continued to drink and slipped further into a stupor, he let down his guard and became ever more vocal and insistent regarding the qualities, as he remembered them, of Suze Moon. The loveliest, kindest, and sexiest woman he had ever, EVER known, know wot I mean? …gorgeous face, the most amazing, amazing smile, beautiful smile she had, Wilf, you know Bryan, you remember it, a smile could light up a room, a beautiful room an' all, beautiful breasts, the loveliest, roomiest breasts and on and on he rambled, slurring ever more. His face was a picture of contentment, with its dopey grin and glazed, unfocussed and unblinking eyes. When you lose the use of your eyelids, you know you're in trouble. She did sound too good to be true, though, and I really wished I'd known her.

It was Bryan who had a better idea. Or an idea, at least. I'm not sure he boasted about a better idea, *per se.* He's not like that, Bryan. I think what he said was:

"I've got an idea."

"Wossat, then, Bry? Is it this: we get some cans and go home and get arseholed?" he said, slipping effortlessly from his stool and banging his chin on the filthy table as he passed.

"You already are. Get up, you tosser! No, I already told you this; I want to go see our kid in London soon. I'm taking the car, so, how about this for a wizard wheeze: You come with me, split the petrol money, we go via Barnet, it's on the way, give or take a couple of miles; we turn up at the address, you knock on the door, rose-covered cottage, I should think, she opens the door, and you say –"

"No, you never told me that… anyway, forget it, told you it's over. It's too much."

"OK, forget the petrol money. I'm going anyway, why don't you come with me? Weekend away in London, drinking crappy southern beer, kip on his hard floor, see the sights… better than moping around here, surely… I'll ask you again, tomorrow; you're pissed now, you've got your pissed face on. Look at you, all pissed and… more pissed.

## It's The Not Knowing

It's just one tiny little knock on a door, you never know. The photo was found for a reason. Maybe, anyway. Maybe it was destiny that Wilf borrowed that particular book, not any other book, but *that* book, and destiny that he found the photo… destiny that he recognised Suze, someone he knows. I mean, what are the chances?"

"If you believe all that destiny bollocks!"

"Yeah… OK, forget the Suze bit, let's just have a piss up. You'll like my brother, he's an arsehole, just like you."

Bryan punched him on the shoulder. Something else mates do. It's not just for muggers and assailants.

"Like you, y'mean! Anyway, but… I'm telling you; she doesn't *want* to be found; she just fucking upped and went, remember?"

"I know, and maybe she *does* want that now, maybe she'd be *happy* to see your fucking stupid miserable face again! Think positive!" and he slammed the filthy table with his paw as he ordered: "More beer, now!"

Was he really going to see his brother? Or was he doing this for Joe? Maybe he was trying to be some sort of hero, the one who rescues the good Samaritan? I wondered.

Two things occurred to me as I was waiting at the bar. The first was that it was obvious that Bryan was increasingly seeing himself in the role of the great mate, the hero taking Joe to the place where he thought his great love was living, Bryan the shameless, matchmaking glory hunter. He was making all these suggestions, organising things and I didn't know how I felt about that, really. In one way, it was good if he did a bit of the work, and it meant I could take a back seat for a while, get on with other projects. Maybe find other old scores to settle. In another, it was bad. It was my idea, not Bryan's; it was me who had the grievance, it was *my* game, not Bryan's! I'd been the victim in all this, let's not forget that. But... if Bryan was going to drive him hundreds of miles, thinking he was going to get a gold star at the end of the rainbow, then he had another think coming, and that would be a bonus, because he'd look like a fool when it became obvious she'd never lived there. Priceless! So, for no extra effort on my part, I would have got one over on him, as well. Two birds in the hand smashed to a pulp with one stone. But then again... he was doing it for good reasons; he would come out of this smelling of whatever. He'd still be the good friend or best friend... "*Ah well, it wasn't to be but thanks, Bryan, you've been a real mate. Have a gold star, anyway.*" Please! Give me a bucket! What would I be? The enemy: the one who'd cocked up and got the address wrong. They'd think I was a loser, and I'd be a cross between a black sheep and a scapegoat.

The second thing that occurred to me was quite surprising, I suppose. It was a sentiment I hadn't come across that often. I'm not sentimental, I'm a realist, but I realised I actually liked Joe and Bryan. I liked them a lot, in fact. I realised they were quite a big part of my life; they were on their way to becoming my best friends; maybe they already were my best friends, and I didn't know how to recognise it. My only friends? No, that's not true. So, I bought probably my two best friends a pint of Skol, some KP nuts and took them back to our table.

## It's The Not Knowing

We were the last ones to leave, once again escorted to the door by Ronnie who wished us all a good night. That was nice of him. As soon as I got out of the fug and into the fresh air, I had a chemical reaction and one day's worth of alcohol rushed to my head. The rest is a bit of a blur. We must have gone for something to eat, somewhere; I wouldn't have remembered what, if I hadn't found some of it in the bed the next morning. Fish and chips, apparently. And mushy peas. At least, I hope that's what they were. I really did feel grim, and that's not like me. I tried to remember if I'd done anything that could be used against me in a court of law? I looked over at the pile of clothes, heaped just as I must have left them when I got in − whenever that was. I was quite sure, I think, that I'd successfully managed to get home with all the clothes I'd gone out in, so, that was something, at least. I could see the velvet jacket, the tangerine corduroys... One boot... where's the other? Is that...? Two boots, phew... no underpants. No underpants? Really? Oh, God! I panicked, briefly, until I realised I was wearing them. Socks, I'm not wearing them, can't see them but, that's not a problem. It's an inconvenience, but not a problem. There's not much you can do without socks that could land you in trouble. I'm sure of that. Shirt? Where's my shirt? Did somebody take my shirt? This brought back bad memories, something that happened, where I lost my shirt. Not on purpose, obviously. Is that it? Yes. How did it get there? And why are my socks stuffed in the pocket? Anyway, it appeared that I had indeed managed to return home with all clothing intact. And that's a good start to any day.

After that, my mind turned to other troublesome matters. Joe and Bryan. How did I get myself out of this? Have you ever had an out-of-body experience? I have. Loads, actually. Most nights. Some people call them dreams, but not me. In one out-of-body experience, I could see a bench and there was one person sitting in the middle of this bench. I sensed that the person was me. It wasn't a loser, anyway. It was nothing out of the ordinary, just a common or garden bench. Then two people came and sat down on the end, but they didn't say anything to me. I didn't mind. I was quite happy for them to be there, as they weren't interfering with me. A few minutes later, without a word being said in all that time, a third person turned up and sat at the other end, making a total of four people to one bench. And then I stood up and walked away. Deep down, though, my mind was telling me to stay.

## Cold Feet and Crosswords

It was around that time that I started to think I should call the whole thing off. I didn't want to play the game anymore. I've never been petty or vindictive, and certainly never petty AND vindictive at the same time but this, I thought, was just that – petty and vindictive. I'd probably overreacted, and now it was time to stop and pull the plug before things went too far. Things were good now, things were looking up and I wanted it to stay that way. It was good to have friends. It was actually better than good and I *liked* them, so it was even better.

I'd heard Joe go out earlier but, paradoxically, much later than his usual time. Probably overslept. I'm sure he must have been suffering and I wondered if he'd found food in his bed too? Maybe he was going to the phone box to tell them he wouldn't be coming in today. What would his excuse be – diarrhoea? migraine? Both? That's what I'd say, if I ever had to. Twenty minutes had passed since I'd put Ceefax on, and he hadn't come back, so, that suggested to me, at least, that he'd made the supreme sacrifice and gone in.

I went up the stairs to the next floor. That bike was still chained there, with microscopic scrapings of my skin on the handlebar. Do you know, in all that time I'd never once even considered letting the tyres down? It would have been quite justified if I had, really. But I hadn't. That must count for something.

I knew Bryan didn't go to work some days. I think he was a freelance something but don't quote me on that. He was a bit vague about what he did, which some people might think suspicious, being secretive and evasive. It was his business and nothing for the likes of you to worry about. I wouldn't say he was exactly 'loaded or even *minted*,' but he always brought enough money for beer when we were in the pub, always bought his round. You can quote me on that if you like.

I knocked on the door and a few seconds later I could hear signs of life, like a corpse, I imagined, stirring from the murk of a supreme hangover. The door opened and there he was. Not the wreck with which I'd been preparing myself for some jokey banter about hangovers and never quaffing again, but a smartly dressed young blade, a paragon and pin-up boy for the Salvation Army Temperance fascists.

"Wilf! Good morning, sir. How's your head today? Spinning and throbbing, one trusts?"

He was far too perky for this time of the day. But it was, at the same time, reassuring. It proved, if nothing else, that the human body and mind is quite capable of the most extraordinary feats of resilience in the face of adversity and strong lager and/or vodka and tomato juice.

"Not too bad, mate," I said.

"Still got all your clothes? Nothing missing this time?" He laughed and chortled. I had this strange sense that he was laughing *with* me and not *at* me. Have you ever had that feeling?

"Totally satisfactory situation on the garment count," I laughed, even if he didn't.

"What's up then? Lost another inhaler?"

"No, still got all those. It's alright, I don't want to come in…"

"Good."

"OK, it's just… I was thinking about what you were saying about going to Suze's place soon. I mean, do you think that's wise?"

"Don't you?"

"Well, he said it himself, she might not want to be found, she might never want to see him again, for whatever reason, and that's her choice, but y'know, is it fair on him? I mean, it could all blow up in his face couldn't it? It could break him. What if she slams the door in his face, spits in his eye or puts turds in his shampoo... y'know?"

"Turds in his shampoo?"

"But it makes no sense does it, to go all that way? On the off chance? And I've been wracking my brains and I remember now: that address... it's... it's an old one. I'm sure she gave me that one years ago. I remember she left there and moved somewhere else. And even... I mean, think about it – if you think you'll just carry on and have a great weekend in that London, you won't – you can't, because Joe will be so down and so deflated if she isn't there. You've seen him get morose, you've seen him, last night even. I mean, has that ever crossed your mind? All that way, building up his hopes even more? They're sky-high now. We both know what he still feels for this girl, this *woman*, it's like he never got over her and stuff..." I'd lost my thread at this point. "She won't be there; I can guarantee it!" I said, in summary.

Bryan looked down at his shoes. A pair of sensible brown brogues. He made a clicking sound with his tongue on his palate. He wasn't showing off, anyone can do it. He did it again, like he was taking it in, the excellent advice I'd just given him.

"I know."

"Good, so you won't—"

"I know, because I know where she is – and I know where she isn't."

He leaned out from where he was blocking my entry and peered through the gloom towards the top of the stairs.

"Come in."

"Nice place," I said. It was, and much nicer than Joe's. He'd done it up a treat, sort of warm and homely. Quality furniture, but old. I wondered which charity shop he used? Books and more books. No posters but a framed portrait of some bloke I thought I recognised; this time I really did. Was it one of those late-Victorian writers? There was a writing desk under the window with a fantastic lamp, one of those with the springs that you can adjust. I always appreciate a good lamp. On the desk, there was a sheet of paper with a crossword and a big old dictionary.

"What are you stuck on?"

"All of them!" he laughed. "I've only just started writing it; it's what I do for a day job. Did I mention that I'm a cruciverbalist?"

"I finished a crossword once," I said, but I could tell he wasn't impressed.

"That's one for the memoirs, then. Take a pew." I was quite amazed that he did, indeed, have a pew. A proper church thing, solid oak. I had no idea he was so religious. Just goes to show, doesn't it?

"Right..." He closed his eyes, and I thought we were going to pray. I closed my eyes too.

"...the thing is, and this is strictly between you and me, I *do* know where Suze is. She wrote to me at the back end of last year. Totally out of the blue, after all this time. She'd written to me once before, a few months after she left, we're talking 1972, but not a peep in between. The first letter... we'd just come back, Joe and me, after a month spent hitch hiking and camping in Ireland. Pissed it down solid. Suze hadn't gone with us; they were an official 'couple' at the time, but it wasn't really her thing, I suppose. It was while we were away that she upped and went. The letter was slipped under the door *in absentia*, probably by the nosey old bloke who lived in your flat at the time. She tried to explain why she'd done what she'd done: she was 'scared of commitment' – her words – and a job offer had come up, had to move quick, that kind of thing... and she asked me not to tell Joe that she'd written, she was very specific about that. Thought a clean break was for the best and didn't want to upset him any more than she had, maybe. She really didn't want anyone to try and find her. The fact she hadn't included an address sort of proved that. So, I didn't say anything about the letter. I didn't know whether I should, really, at the time, but the longer it went on, the easier it got. She'd gone and that was that."

"You didn't want to upset him, I suppose. You were right, absolutely! not to say anything. I'd have done the same."

"Maybe so, but was I being selfish? There's no question! Of course I was. I was just thinking: 'Stay here Joe, let her go, plenty more fish and all that.' I might even have said that, in so many words..."

"It's a good way of putting it..."

"But it was so disloyal... Joe's my mate, my best friend y'know...? I should have said something. Something more than 'look on the bright side, you're a free agent again, a free agent with your own shagging palace!' That was pathetic; not my finest hour."

"No, but maybe it was a good thing you said that. Make him see the positive side. Definitely."

I suddenly found myself unable to do anything other than agree with him. I wondered about it later, was it because I was in his territory and that his territory was just a bit more… impressive, more imposing, and grandiose than mine? I'm not normally overwhelmed by such trifles. I take as I find.

"No, it wasn't."

"Er… no, you're right, it wasn't. Absolutely."

"He was very down, probably clinically depressed, for a long time. I should have said something."

I wasn't sure whether I should agree or disagree. The role of subjugated toady is never easy.

"Then she wrote again, last year, as I said. Unexpected. And this time, she included her address. She was living somewhere in Edgware, close to her work."

This was concerning. Edgware?

"Yes, north of London on the A1. She said she was doing fine, still working for Green Shield Stamps, but now called Argos, business was booming, she'd been promoted, travelled around and all that. She asked about Joe, how he was, was he married, engaged, divorced, did I still keep in touch with him, y'know, the usual stuff…"

"Oh yes of course, the usual stuff. That's not unusual, stuff like that."

"She said she was maybe going to be moving back here; there was an opportunity, apparently, on the career front. They would pay for relocation… I could see where this was going, and I didn't like it. I think she was testing the water, wanting to come back and hoping Joe might still be an option. I'm a selfish bastard, I really am. I didn't tell him about the letter. I didn't say anything at all. And I didn't send her a reply…"

"Probably just as well?"

"Was it? He had a right to know, it would have blown his mind in a good way… but the problem was it might upset things here for me. That's what it boils down to. Selfish bastard Numero Uno. The truth is I didn't write back because I didn't want to lose my mate, my best mate… so, there you are. That's why. You can understand that, can't you? And it had started to fade away, the sense of guilt… until *you* turned up!"

"Me?"

"Yes, you! At first, I didn't believe it, when Joe told me. I wondered what you were up to. No, hang on, before you start… I mean, it wasn't a normal turn of events, was it? You just *happening* to find a photo in a random book you'd just *happened* to borrow, seeing Suze, telling Joe you knew her and all that...

At this stage I might have been shifting uneasily in the pew.

# It's The Not Knowing

"…but you never really explained *how* you knew her or *where* you'd known her; you never said anything much at all, did you? Nothing concrete. That's what Joe told me. So, I told him to get you out for a pint, so I could take a look at you. And I watched you, in the pub, wondering what you were about. It crossed my mind a few times, that you might be some sort of, what's the word…I should know this… begins with p?"

"Paragon?"

"Psychotic. Yes, I thought you were psychotic. No offence. I was considering beating you to a pulp. But then…"

"You realised I wasn't so you wouldn't. Good!"

"Then, I dunno. We were having a laugh and maybe I forgot it... When Joe first showed me the address you'd given him, I didn't recognise it. I thought 'I'm sure that's not the one on the letter,' but he didn't know about that, so I couldn't say anything. I thought, if you *were* up to something, if you'd invented the whole thing – for whatever reason – you'd just shot yourself in the arse. I'd never heard of New Barnet. Plain Barnet yes, Barnet Fair, Battle of Barnet, and all that, but not Barnet *Nouveau*. So, I looked in the atlas, and it wasn't in there. But neither was Barnet! So, next morning I went to the library. I went to the map section and, sure enough, I found it. Right on the doorstep and handily placed for someone working in Edgware, in fact… exactly the right area. And, I suppose, that's when I gave you the benefit of the doubt, 'cos I didn't believe anyone would attempt to make up an address without at least basing it on where she worked. And, if you knew where she worked then, it follows, that you obviously knew her. Maybe she'd lived there some time before she wrote the letter so, Wilf my friend, I'm sorry I doubted you... I really am, I know you're a sound fellow."

I never doubted it, but I was relieved. I know he'd been joking when he said about beating me to a pulp, and I know I can handle myself, but he was a big bloke, looked like he was no stranger to the ways of the navvy or beating people to pulps. But yes, how *had* I come up with such a good address? Pure skill would be my guess.

"And if you're not going to tell us how you know her, fair enough. That's your business. We all have secrets."

"Yeah, you're so right, Bryan. Good things to have, though." Toadying was getting easier again now.

"Anyway, what was I saying?... Yes. He's been like a bloody jitterbug since all this cropped up again. It wasn't right, what I was doing; I know that. It was totally and utterly wrong and selfish, I know, I'm a miserable sinner! Unless you've been there, though, with the weight of the guilt that builds up, then you've no idea how much mental effort it takes to keep a stiff upper lip and all that bollocks..."

"Dead right, who needs stiff lips, anyway... or bollocks?" I offered in support.

"But... I can put it right! And that, my friend, is exactly what I'm going to do. We'll drive down to her place, me and him. I won't push the Suze thing before then; as far as he knows, we're having a lads' weekend on the beer with our kid. Obviously, I'll write to her first and tell her we're coming. She's hardly likely to say no… unless I've misread the situation, which I haven't… I know he will never understand why she went and what-have-you, but he'll forget all that. When we get there, I'll say it's our kid's place, and as soon as she opens the door, or the gate or whatever it is he'll be blown away, I know he will; I can't wait to see the look on his dopey face!"

He laughed. It was almost an expression of relief, as if he'd just worked it through in his own mind.

"It will be your atonement. You will be free of your sins," I said, from the pew. "Amen."

"It certainly will! Anyway, I need to crack on with this grid now, but here's one for you to mull over: 'Perfect example of standard silver working.' Seven letters. Easy! Will you close the door on your way out? Cheers Wilf."

I left and went back down the stairs to mine. The annoying crossword clue would have to wait, I had weightier matters to consider, such as: How do I explain myself when, in a few weeks' time, we are formally re-introduced, and she tells lover boy that she has no idea who I am? Would it end in a fight, maybe in the street, with a crowd baying for blood? Whose side would they be on? I could handle Joe; he was not the fighting type, but Bryan was a different kettle of fish. Big fish, the kind of fish that kills other fish or even big sharks.

I wouldn't say I broke out in a cold sweat exactly, I'm not a cold sweater… it was more like… you know they say: 'There's no such thing as a problem, just a solution waiting to happen?' Well, it was more like that – a sort of a challenge. This was something I hadn't planned for, and I'm normally good with things like that. Eventualities, they're called. Some things often just work themselves out but, more often than not, they don't – they just end badly. I was beginning to nudge this one towards the second category. I'm not one of those people who like things when they end badly, that's not my style. And I've been there, believe me. If it was a case of kill or be killed, then I didn't want to be killed.

I needed to go to the bank, get some cash and order a cheque book. I think I must have lost the other one, but I don't know when or where I lost it. Obviously. That really annoys me, that, when you tell someone you've lost something and they say: "Where did you lose it?" and I say: "If I knew *that* it wouldn't be lost, would it!" Morons. I needed to get out and think anyway, so after transacting my business at Barclay's, I went to the park and headed for the bench, thankfully unoccupied. It seemed to me there were a few possibilities.

- First possibility: Deny all knowledge. That didn't seem like a viable option at this stage.
- Second possibility: Accuse her of lying. Maybe get them on my side and gang up on her. *Fight?*
- Third possibility: Leave town a) until the heat died down or b) forever or c) until I could think of a better idea.
- Fourth possibility: Tell them it was an aptitude test in 'people finding' and they had passed with flying colours. Maybe get some certificates made up at Prontaprint for authenticity?

- Fifth possibility: Be amazed at the striking similarity between Joe's Suze and the other Suze, the one I claim to know as Suzanne – what are the chances! Could be identical twins with nearly the same name. This one might work.

I wondered how Victoria would have wriggled out of a situation like this. She would probably have had a flunkey to do the wriggling, so, that didn't help.

The bench on the hill was unoccupied, by the way.

I walked back, having decided I'd give the pub a miss. Both of them. My one and their one. The door briefly opened as I passed the 'Reck and I could make out the guitar duet in *Hotel California* just getting going. I couldn't face them, not until I'd worked out my next move. On the way I popped into the Superette to buy a tin of pineapple chunks for dinner. Yes, that's right – I'd started *popping* since I'd been hanging around with those two, and I hadn't even realised until now.

You know how some places feel like the atmosphere has been sucked out – a place where, when you enter, you immediately think you've just found a new and previously unknown level on the Tawdry Scale? The Superette was such a place. It was somewhere between a pig's ear and a dog's dinner in terms of layout with, it seemed to me, very little in the way of logical planning. For the life of me I can never understand why the shelves are not arranged alphabetically, so that, for example, pineapple chunks would be located between pineapples and pins (if stocked). Corned beef would be between corkscrews and cornflakes, and so on and so forth. Despite the unhelpful layout, I found what I was looking for eventually but, at the counter I noticed the can was dented. Don't you hate that? I left it there and went back for a proper one. I paid in cash and as I was counting out the pennies I offered the girl a friendly word of advice: I suggested that she might want to ensure stock on the shelves was in a saleable condition next time. I also asked her what time she finished and did she want to go for a drink after work. She definitely didn't; she was most insistent on that point. I thanked her for her time and left. I heard the door being bolted after I'd stepped outside. It seems I'd got there just in time, it being early closing day. I offered up thanks for this slice of good fortune as I headed towards home and a slap-up meal of delicious chunks.

The post was lying scattered on the floor in the hall when I got back. I picked it up instinctively and scanned the pile to see if there was anything for me. There wasn't, so I left it on the table. Someone else could sort and arrange it, I had better things and a lot of thinking to do. I also managed to retrieve one of those excellent free newspapers which, miraculously, nobody had yet walked over in wet and muddy footwear or kicked under the table.

There was a knock on my door later that evening; I held my breath, and I didn't answer. I'm pretty sure it was them. They knocked again and there was a gap of about fifteen seconds before I heard voices mumbling, followed by the sound of footsteps receding and, finally, the slamming of the front door. Then, and only then, did I resume breathing. At least now I had an idea of what they thought of me – I was a two knock, fifteen second friend. Not bad, really. At least I knew where I stood.

## It's The Not Knowing

I opened the free paper and looked for the property section. I'd decided that there was really only one way out of this mess and that was to pack up and move. Drastic, perhaps, but it was preferable to getting pulped when the shit hit the fan. And it would! Another option would have been the 'unbelievable-coincidence-same-name-same-face' ploy but that, I felt, would have called for a degree of stagecraft of which, sadly, I knew myself incapable. I once trod the boards, briefly, in an amateur capacity and it did not end well. You must believe me when I say that being booed off stage and pelted with overly ripe fruit, as I once was (when playing Jesus in *Godspell*), is not something you forget in a hurry!

I flicked through the pages: adverts for this, that and the other. No thank you very much! Not looking for a third hand car with the mileage wound back – and certainly not a Vauxhall Viva for £100, don't need any gutters cleaning or French oral lessons… in fact, there was no property being advertised. What a damned cheek, pushing crap like this through the letterbox every week!

I heard them coming back later but, by then I was well tucked up in bed and wouldn't have opened the door even if they'd knocked. Which they didn't. I had what a medicine man would call a 'fitful night,' mulling things over in my head. The only idea that came to me as I tossed and turned into the early hours was that I should put a notepad and pencil by the bed in case I came up with an idea. Apart from that, there was nothing - but it was a start.

The next morning, I heard Joe going out at his usual time. I knew Bryan didn't leave much before the middle of the day when he would go to Himmler's Patisserie on the parade for a freshly baked sausage roll. This took him about forty minutes, usually. I obviously had matters to attend to outside, the free papers having failed so miserably; it was therefore essential to arrange my own departure accordingly so as to eliminate any possibility of paths crossing. I was keen to avoid unnecessary confrontations wherever possible, as you can imagine.

Local legend had it that the evening papers were the best bet for rented accommodation adverts and, if I could get one hot off the press, it would improve my chances of grabbing a desirable property before a loser saw it and jumped in first.

It was an overcast and gloomy day in many ways and the weather didn't help. I went to the Superette again, where I saw that girl, the one from yesterday. I flashed her my nicest grin. As our eyes made contact, I winked, respectfully, I hope. Her attempted smile in return put me in mind of a rictus as she turned and disappeared through the stylish yet tired orange bead curtain which lived behind the counter. I like that in a girl, a diffident bearing. It's very attractive and makes me feel somehow in control. I wasn't too keen on the rictus, though. I imagined she'd gone to make herself more presentable; that's not a bad thing but she really didn't have to bother on my account. When she came back I'd tell her she looked 'charming, quite charming,' and then follow up with a casual 'Do you, by any chance, know whether the evening papers have arrived?' I'd mention I was looking for a bachelor pad with inside toilet. That would break the ice.

I hung around near the hugely impressive range of chewing gums, keeping an eye on the counter and the beads. Eventually they rattled and parted; she had transformed into her father, turban and all. If I'm being honest, I didn't like the way he looked at me when I eventually bought a paper, a packet of Juicy Fruits and a gobstopper.

I exited the shop and, pausing only to throw the gobstopper at a pigeon, made my way back in contemplative mood. My plan was: check the ads, do the spot-the-ball, find a suitable flat and go round and see it. If all went well I could be moving my gear this time tomorrow.

## Wheels in Motion

Bloody hell, wouldn't you just know it! I was almost at the gate when Bryan rounded the corner, clutching a sausage roll. I knew he'd seen me, so, any attempt to jump into the laurel hedge would have seemed irrational. And that's one thing I'm not. I'm not always rational but I'm never irrational. I don't know what the middle state is called, when you're neither one nor the other, but I bet some brainbox somewhere has given it a name.

"Hey, you! Yes, you! You dosser, where've you been hiding?"

I've noticed this about blokes. When they first meet you, they're all polite but then, when they get to know you better, they call you all sorts of horrible names, and you know they don't mean it. I'm pretty sure that's how it works. The worse the name, the better they know you. Sometimes though, when I meet people for the first time they call me horrid names right from the outset. I don't care; maybe it shows they like me immediately.

"Hello there," I said, "Wasn't expecting to see you out this early." which was true. It had come as 'quite a surprise,' I said.

"Good timing, anyway. Joe's on his way, said I'd see him in the pub in twenty minutes. You coming?"

Shit. "Great!"

This could potentially be a problem with my chance to find alternative accommodation seemingly scuppered for the present.

"Where've you been, then?" he asked. Previously I would have marked him down as a nosey bastard but not this time. It seemed genuine enough. I told him about the Superette and the meddling father, poking his nose in and cramping my style.

"Cramping your what? Your style? Ha ha, that's quality!" I don't know what he found so funny, and I told him so.

I then asked him where *he'd* been, see how *he* liked it. Himmler's Patisserie, on the sausage roll run – like I didn't already know that! He'd posted a letter on the way and then made a few 'phone calls… That didn't sound good, sending a letter.

"You've written to Suze already?" No, not to Suze; he wasn't going to write to her at all, he confided.

"Hallelujah! Common sense prevails!" I shouted or, at least, my inner self shouted. I was relieved to hear that, though.

"Changed your mind, then?"

"Not at all, it's just I don't need to arse about writing a letter, buying a stamp and all that...

He smiled a self-satisfied smile with a hint of smug.

"... since I found out her telling bone number! Easy really, I phoned directory enquiries and, a few minutes later, Bob's your uncle. Thank you very much." Cocky bastard. He punched me on the arm, and I told him that was excellent news.

He seemed horribly happy now, considering he might soon be losing his best mate. Probably make up for it by beating me to a pulp. Who would he go drinking with when that happened? Me, unpulped? But, I was hoping to leg it any day now. You can see my quandary.

'*You can check out any time you like, but you can never leave*' came booming from the speakers as we pulled open the front door. Was this the only flipping song on the jukebox, or what? It was Bryan who bought the beer, said he'd just been paid for doing a crossword or something, I wasn't really listening.

"Are you going to call her, then?" I asked. I had to know; this might really put the cat among the pigeons.

"I did earlier, no point hanging around. Cheers!"

I said "Cheers" back, but my heart wasn't in it. The Skol started to taste like a really weak, watery, and possibly inferior brew. That's what a growing unease can do to the senses.

He told me with great enthusiasm: she was 'gobsmacked' when he rang, she was incredibly surprised – that'll be why she was *gobsmacked* then – any fool could have told him that! – and, did I know, she sounded 'all tearful' by the end. That's why they don't have women in the army, I said. She couldn't wait to see them both, apparently. Of course, they could stay at her place if they wanted, apparently. And yes, she was still at the same address. Apparently.

"And er… you didn't ask her about living in New Barnet, then?"

"No, it didn't matter, did it. I might, though. Anyway, if Joe has managed to get the time off tomorrow… it'll be 'All systems go, chocks away.' He won't have a clue!"

He took a huge celebratory swig as, all of a sudden, my mouth became as dry as the dust on a sunburnt camel's arse.

"And by the way, he doesn't need to know any of what I told you the other day. You remember, the letter and all that, OK? As far as he knows, it's just a lads' weekend away on the booze, right?" He fixed me with a stare I might describe as 'pleading with menaces.' Was this something I could use to my advantage? Maybe shift the blame onto him, have him turn out to be the villain? "It was him, Joe, he kept the letter from you and it's only thanks to me… etcetera," but that wasn't my style. I was an honourable coward. I tried ratting once, at school; I told on someone to Mrs Boyle. I had to. I was being blamed for something I didn't do, and it wasn't even my copy of Razzler in the first place. The real culprit got a serious talking to. And I took a serious beating after school from the culprit and his mates.

"Oh… you know what? I forgot to mention you when I was on the phone. I'm sorry about that. But, if there's any message you'd like to send I'll make sure she gets it, OK?"

Right Wilf, the writing's on the wall and the cat is looking through the brochures, selecting which pigeon to chase first… stay calm, you know there is always a solution. Always.

Joe came in, in the manner of someone who had just booked a few days off work and was looking forward to a period of heavy social drinking in the nation's capital. He was lugging that holdall around again, like it was a real statement piece. I didn't care; he had his life and I had mine. Then his stupid mate asked if he had really managed to book the time off at such short notice? No, he hadn't. As notices go, it was too short by half. What happens about the weekend away? They're still going. They're still going? Yes. He threatened to walk out so the arsehole boss gave in; he won't get paid, but he doesn't care. He owes them nothing. So, they're still going?

"Yes! We're still going! The weekend starts now, with maximum exposure to the amber nectar. Get 'em in!"

The afternoon passed in a haze; I remember hearing *Hotel California* a few times but of the rest… nothing. There must have been an evening, but I don't know if I was there or if I was anywhere. I told you I can take my ale. I was lying. I can't. And that's not the only lie I've told. I'm probably the biggest liar you know.

I woke up in the early hours, fully clothed. At home, though. Not a bus shelter or anything like that. I couldn't get back to sleep, my head was spinning for hours.

I went to look at a flat and it was perfect and being offered at less than my current rent. This is fantastic and the indoor toilet definitely swings it – I'll take it, I said. I was gloriously relieved. 'Oh no you won't!' The orange beads parted and there he was in his turban, chewing a Juicy Fruit, hammer in hand; he raised his arm to deliver the final, cruel blow. Thump… thump… thump…

I lied; I am a cold sweater. I realise that now… thump… thump…

"Wilf, you tosser! Get up! We're going now, see you when we get back."

I took a few seconds to get my bearings, as the room slowed and revealed itself. I heard a final thump on the door – more of a knock, really, but I couldn't summon the energy. Honestly, I'm not lying.

After struggling for some time, I managed to raise my head a couple of inches. I rolled over onto my side, using the force of gravity rather than any force my corpse might have generated and was able to manoeuvre myself onto the floor. Never again. I am never drinking again. You can quote me on that. A few minutes later I found myself in a state of undress, standing in the hall with the front door wide open, surveying the small section of road visible through the gap in the hedge where there used to be a little wooden gate. It disappeared in the run up to bonfire night.

Was that Joe who'd just squeezed into the passenger seat of Bryan's mustard puke Hillman Imp? They weren't really going to risk taking that unroadworthy pile of junk, were they? On a public highway? In that colour? The car made a honking noise as it started to roll forwards, its vulgar *adieu* before accelerating away, the erratic drip of the oil and god knows what else leaving a trail in its wake as the pilot shifted through the gears and headed for the treacherous waters of the motorway network.

I went back to bed. Slow steps. Slow and steady never won a race. Race? My heart was racing, I'll tell you that for nothing. I'm not one of those people who can relax with a racing heart; I find it rather unsettling, if anything. Anyway, I stayed in bed for the whole day, trying to sleep and regain some inner strength.

The following morning, I was starving hungry. I hadn't eaten a scrap the previous day. I wondered: were they there yet? They must be. I wondered: was my name being dragged through the mud? It must be. And worse. It was a good job we didn't have a telephone. Equally, it was highly unlikely that they would send a telegram to say they would beat me to a pulp on their return. I was safe; at least for today.

It had the makings of a pleasant spring morning, with the merest hint of a breeze and the first signs of the natural world stirring from its winter break. I wondered where the natural world would go for a winter break. I was thinking such things all the way to the Superette. I hadn't even

# It's The Not Knowing

looked at the paper I'd bought the other day and, bearing in mind the surly disposition of the proprietor, I knew to ask him for a full refund or even part-exchange would have borne bitter fruit, if any. I let it go. Today, was not a day to be wasted. There was no time for a wasted day, not now that the clock was ticking; the procurement, *is that the word*? of alternative accommodation had to be my goal. Nothing less would do, and I was never one to spare the horses when I was in a sticky situation. Nothing must be allowed to distract me; neither snow nor rain nor heat nor gloom of night could put a stick in the spokes and keep me from the swift completion of my appointed rounds, not now. There was no sign of Miss Mistry, sadly.

I bought the regional paper, the posh broadsheet one, and sat on the wall outside to read. I thought about going up to my bench but getting there would have taken more time than I had on my hands. Things were now critical, as in life-threatening rather than disparaging, and I've been there before, so I know what I'm talking about. The front page promised A Royal Day Out; that might be worth a read later, I thought. Not yet though, I needed property. *Put your money in bricks and mortar, lad, you can't go wrong...* property... probably near the back. Hang on, what's this about a Motorway Pile-Up...?

They say you never forget where you were when you heard the news of Kennedy's assassination or when, say, your two best friends died unexpectedly. It lives with you forever. Me? I was sitting on a wall in the sunshine outside the local Superette.

# PART TWO. 2005

## Old Friends

April 30th.

"Did you read it?"

"Yes, I read it, or, at least, I tried, and I can safely say without fear of confutation that it made No. Bloody. Sense. Whatsoever. Who wrote it? You?"

"Ha! No, it's not one of mine, although I think I'm in it."

"Do you? So, who *did* write it? And which one are you?"

"William wrote it, Sue's brother, before he, y'know... I think I'm Joe."

"Really? OK, then, *Joe* – what's the ending all about?"

John chewed his lower lip and scratched the back of his neck; you know the kind of thing.

"Truth? I'm not altogether sure... maybe you're in it, too."

"I'm in it? How did that happen?"

"I think you're the Bryan character. Don't you see a bit of yourself in there?"

"It hadn't occurred to me, no. Don't you need permission for that kind of thing, and who's the other one?"

"I think Wilf is William."

"Right, so I suppose that leaves your Sue as the Suze character?"

"Correct. Or, at least, probably. She isn't actually in it."

Barney Chimes chewed his lower lip and rubbed the back of his head; you know the kind of thing.

"Why would he write about me? I know, yes I *am* an inspirational role model, but I hardly knew him; and I only *hardly* knew him for what… a year, tops?"

"Well, I suppose he needed Joe's friend to be credible and, as we've been mates for ever, if I'm Joe, then you were the obvious Bryan. Possibly."

"The fellow's taking liberties!"

"I thought the Wilf character was quite in awe of you, wouldn't you say?"

"Yes, awesome sounds about right. But then why did the bugger kill us off?"

"Dunno… maybe he was jealous of our brotherly bond. Possible*?*"

"Jealous of our brotherly bond? Get *her*! Well, he wouldn't be the first. That's sorted then. Makes perfect sense. Shall we sample another?"

John checked his watch, although time was still immaterial. "If you insist. Must be your round."

Barney picked up the empty glasses and returned them to the bar, where he ordered another two pints of Guinness, *no make that a half, please Jill: I'm watching my figure!*

# It's The Not Knowing

He and John Stilton had been friends for as long as they could remember; thirty-five years at least and counting.

This friendship, which had begun in the playground of St. Joseph's C of E Primary School, had developed steadily across the years, and was solidly built on the twin foundations of trust and mutual respect. That might make them seem like a couple of smug twats, but they weren't. Not really.

By the summer of 1986, the chums had been fully educated. There was nothing more. They emerged none the worse and a little bit wiser from the ordeal, the new owners of a couple of OK degrees. In the years since then, their chosen career paths had taken different directions, neither having much in common with the other.

John, 41 and married to Sue (41 next birthday but still looked like she was in her mid-thirties), was a stocky fellow, straight from the rugby-player mould, with a permanent five o'clock shadow discolouring a firm, resolute jaw. This mandible, which some considered his best feature, could, with practice, even be classed as 'rugged' should the occasion arise. The central dimple certainly added interest to the 'look,' although the black-framed National Health spectacles didn't. John took a different view and thought he presented as both youthful and charming.

He made a steady but unspectacular living as a wordsmith, churning out the blurb for tourist guides. If you wanted someone to describe your earthworks, castles, and monuments in words that a day-tripper could understand, John was your man. He did alright out of the secondary education market too, where his knowledge of the British Monarchy had made it to the printed page in a series of popular textbooks aimed at the State School sector. He hoped one day he might make it to the Public-School list, where the serious money was. In addition to this academic portfolio, he'd produced several short stories in the zombie horror genre and could count on a small but regular income from those. "It's crap, I suppose, but it's what the zombies like," he would say, uncharitably.

Barney, 42 and unmarried, having *never found the right one,* was a lean, long-legged specimen, ginger of unruly hair with a penchant for tailored jackets, drainpipe jeans (black), and an embryonic boozer's nose or *conk.* He had chosen to follow his dream and, after struggling in the early days, was now something of a big name in the glamorous world of television. He owned and ran an independent outlet '*Goggle Boxes,*' opposite Rumbelows on the Jay-15 Retail Park, just off the ring road. In an exciting development, he was looking to make inroads into the world of hand-held computers very soon. He was currently in discussions with Google over copyright infringement. It was something to do with his logo, apparently and his solicitors were handling the unpleasantness.

"Your very good health!"

"Yes, cheers, down the hatch and all that." Barney took a long draft. If you'd seen it, you'd have thought he'd just come out of the desert, but he hadn't. Obviously. He slurped the froth from his upper lip and furtively ejected a polite belch from the side of his mouth when no-one was looking. "Where did you find it?"

It's The Not Knowing

"The story? Thought I told you: it was in a box of his things we took from his last abode."

"Ah!"

There was a brief period of social drinking as they both paused to reflect. Barney surveyed the room with a frown.

"That's a new addition, that *tableau* in yonder frame, isn't it? Is it deliberately out of focus? Might just be me. Do you know, it pains me to say this: at this rate, I think I'm going to need spectacles soon. We'll have eight eyes between us. Oh, the shame!"

"Age shall not weary them, nor the years condemn… but in your case they'll make an exception. We're all getting old, mate. It looks like a statue of Queen Victoria in a park somewhere. Nice frame. Did you know, or did I ever tell you, he was living in an attic?"

"William? I think you did tell me that, yes – with that Irish teacher. Enya, was it?"

"That's the one, Áine, as in '*on yer bike.*' She was teaching at one time but packed it in and got into euthanasia, would you believe."

"A noble profession but, alas, a dying trade."

"I'll ignore that, shall I? We only found out he'd buggered off when she got in touch with Sue. He hadn't been home for about three weeks apparently, and she was getting concerned, worried that he might have had an accident. Áine was a proper people person. Of course, we hadn't heard from him, and she probably knew that before she asked; she obviously knew about the falling out between him and Sue but didn't know what had caused it – same as me – and he'd never told her."

"And he hadn't given this Enya *any* indication of his intentions?"

"No. Just upped and went, no note or anything, and all his stuff was still in her attic."

"Outrageous behaviour! What did Sue think?"

"Well, that was the thing: she just went funny, y'know?"

"Maybe the sudden realisation that her brother might be dead in a ditch somewhere might have had something to do with that, don't you think?"

"Of course, but it seemed to affect her much more than I would ever have imagined."

"Maybe so. Who knows how peoples' minds work! There's nowt so queer as folk!"

There was another short intermission. John sampled his pint whilst Barney made faces, trying to focus on the picture. He gradually made out the detail and concluded he didn't really need specs after all.

"Anyway, they decided they'd go to the Police and report him as a missing person."

"Makes sense; should maybe have done that sooner. And you're sure he didn't owe her rent or something, like that? Could have been something as simple as money, don't you think? Root of all evil…"

"Cynical sod!"

"Moi? How come he'd fetched up in her attic in the first place, anyway? Some sort of punishment… for her? She'd probably been up to no good, I'll be bound; Lord knows, you know what these Irish girls are like!" Barney chuckled as he said it, even though he didn't actually know what these Irish girls were like.

"Yeah, maybe. No, he knew her from Sue's college days. He used to hang around in the student bar; he was in there all the time, apparently. Do you remember, he was a bit weird, hardly ever spoke and if he did he wouldn't look at you? He'd just sit there sometimes, like he wasn't actually listening. Prat! Looked like he was from another planet, too, with that bloody pudding-bowl haircut and face. He had a really unfashionable face, do you remember?"

"That's right! A true gargoyle. I remember how he'd just get up and go without saying anything. Social niceties? Not on his watch."

They both laughed at William.

"Yes, that was him. Anyway, he was always there, like a bad smell; he obviously had a thing for Irish redheads."

"Good God, man, you can't say that! That's racist and *gingerist*!"

"Do I care? Anyway, he found her through directory enquiries, apparently; told her there was trouble at home and he needed somewhere to stay, remembered her and all that. She – Áine – was looking to make some extra cash, the timing couldn't have been better; she had an attic going spare, so he moved in the next day and stayed for ten years."

# It's The Not Knowing

"Ten years in an attic? Who did he think he was, Dorian Green?"

"Sue remembered the day he left as a 'momentous, wonderful day.' Those were her exact words."

"Momentous day... God, she really *didn't* like him much, did she!"

"It was the day the Berlin Wall came down."

"Ah!"

John returned from the bar with another couple of drinks. Historically, these get-togethers had tended to end in a stupor but, with the steady and relentless march of time, and with their bodies in terminal decline, they had simmered down dramatically in recent years. The participants were, perhaps reluctantly, just starting to accept this fact. In their prime they would have thought nothing of drinking ten or fifteen pints in a single session. Great days. Wonderful, marvellous once-in-a-lifetime-never-to-be-repeated days.

"So, anything else in this box?"

"Just personal stuff, really: paperwork and *what-not*. I've kept it just in case. I know he's not going to be coming back now but I thought she'd have regrets eventually, y'know? – if there was nothing left of him. Anyway, they went to the Police, but they weren't a lot of use, really. They said he was old enough to disappear if he wanted basically, as long as he paid his taxes and didn't make a mess if he jumped off something high."

Barney snorted through his pint. "Putting the 'care' into 'couldn't care less,' eh?"

"Yep. Of course, it was a bit unfair on Áine and we offered to help clear his stuff out in the end."

There followed another brief drinks interlude while they both took a moment. Barney discovered an itch and dealt with it.

*The Jugged Hare* had been recently refurbished and was now tastefully overloaded with charity shop and reclamation yard finds. You know the kind of thing. Blackened pots and pans hung from every beam and there were shelves filled with old hard-backed books intended to entice bookworms and avid readers to spend their lonely hours in the convivial and dog-friendly surroundings with a pint of foaming ale. Coach parties by arrangement. For those who appreciated the faded and the dead there were several taxidermy exhibits on display whilst, in the interest of inclusivity, in the vegan-friendly *Black Balls Bar* (formerly the pool room), there were assorted stuffed vegetables mounted in glass cases. Their table, interestingly, had started life in the sewing-machine game and, having been imaginatively repurposed, had recently had new life breathed into it. Along the wall, a set of paint-spattered wooden step ladders had been reimagined and mounted as lamp holders. The lamps were due any day now. It was unique, in very much the same way as many other recent refurbishments were unique. Triggered, perhaps, by the sight of some of this old tat, John eventually resumed.

## It's The Not Knowing

"You know, he had a lot of old tat and some awful clothes – it looked like he'd never thrown anything out and had kept *every* tasteless, horrible thing he'd ever worn. If you'd wanted some tangerine trousers and/or a yellow velveteen blazer, I could have fixed you up, special offer and mates' rates."

"You should have said!"

"I don't know if you were around at the time; It might have been when you went off on your mid-thirties' crisis walkabout, looking for – what was it? – *spiritual enlightenment with a good time thrown in?*"

"Ha Ha! Yes, and I certainly had a good time! Not so much enlightenment, though."

"It's overrated. Anyway, Áine didn't want anything leaving up there; even her Am-Dram group couldn't find a use for those clothes. Have you ever known Oxfam, or The Sally Army violently refuse a donation? Neither had I before this! So, the clothes and his mattress and what-have-you went to the tip. The box of diaries went straight up in the loft. And that's where they've been for the past five years or so."

"So, why bring this all up now… and why did you want me to read it?"

"No real reason. I came across it after all this time, so I read it; Sue refused to read it, so I thought I'd see what you made of it…"

"OK, well, I told you what I made of it… not a lot! Any other gems in the box, apart from this one? There's quite a niche market for old crap on eBay, these days y'know."

"Yes, there is, actually. There's another one which looks interesting, but it's going to be a challenge to decipher it; it looks like it's in Russian… of a sort."

"Of a sort? What does that mean?"

"It *looks* like Russian or Cyrillic, but it's peppered with the odd French or German word. And I have a feeling they're not actually proper Russian words, just transliterations of the English. A secret code, of sorts."

"Secret code? Sounds like something out of the Cold War! Anyway, time for a Jimmy Riddle. Same, again?"

While Barney was away pointing Percy at the porcelain (a phrase he hadn't used *once* that evening; maybe Jimmy Riddle was the new kid on the block?), John checked his phone for texts. He was struck by the thought that, if mobile phones had been around in 1977, the lives of the characters in William's story, and the incidents portrayed, would have been radically different. Joe could have called the bogus number there and then… Suze, having lost the facility for handwriting, like everyone else, would probably have sent a text message instead of a letter, and the plot would have unravelled so quickly. And if the magic of the internet had been available? Suze would never have been able to disappear, there would be so many ways of finding her… just Ask Jeeves or Google or Lycos. And yet, the internet *is* around, and it hasn't stopped William…

"Mission accomplished; one-eyed trouser snake back in the bag, and two pints as promised."

They sat and nursed their pints for a while, lost in thoughts of god knows what. Nostalgic stuff, probably.

"How many years have we been coming in here?" *Told you!*

"Good question! I dunno, 1980 maybe, so... twenty-five years probably, give or take..."

"OK. So, let's say *on average* three nights a week, for twenty of those years. Forget the five years for Uni and other unnecessary distractions. So, that's twenty years times fifty-two weeks times three nights times, let's say six, no seven pints making..."

"Go on..."

Bryan took a beer mat and peeled off the paper so he could scribble his calculation/show his working out. He looked at the result and gasped for dramatic effect.

"You ready for this? Twenty-one thousand, eight hundred and forty pints! And, let's say, at a weighted average over all that time of, perhaps, two pounds a pint? Sound right?

He picked up the beer mat and pen and resumed scribbling.

"That's... forty-three thousand, six hundred and eighty pounds! *That,* my friend, is how much we have invested in this pub... each! And not forgetting crisps and nuts and pork scratchings (except for those two weeks when you were a committed vegan) ..."

"Wow! Oh, hang on, not so fast, Einstein. You've over-cooked it, you're missing something obvious."

"I am?"

"Yes, you only had a half earlier, not a pint."

"How the *fuck* are we still alive?"

They stayed for another couple of pints, talking about rubbish mainly, as they always had. They'd already decided they wouldn't go for a curry this time; Sue was contractually expecting John back around closing time, with a grudging five-minute leeway agreed before the door was bolted for the night – *don't think I won't!* – and Barney was trying to cut down on meat and dairy in an attempt to watch his figure.

In the good old days, of course, they would have just carried on drinking in the Taj next door after the pub closed, with a vindaloo and all the trimmings, and bugger the consequences. In the good old day after the night before, of course, they would have had plenty of time to sit and consider those same consequences. It was Barney who brought the conversation back to Wilf and the events of 1977.

"You know earlier you said Suze was Sue and Wilf was William? Well, if that's the case, doesn't it strike you as a bit er... abnormal, possibly even preternatural, some of the things he said about her, his own sister? I know he said something about Suze never having the pleasure of his attentions, they were just friends and all that but then seems to contradict himself, maybe subconsciously, with the bit where he says something about '*bonking her brains out*' or that she was *'very much his type, he wished he'd known her?'* I mean, even if it's just a made-up story, you wouldn't even *think* of putting that would you? It just seems like a no-no; it isn't normal! I know if I had a sister or a brother I wouldn't have thought anything like that. D'you think it might be some kind of confession?"

John physically winced when Barney started to use big words. It wasn't a bogus wince; it was genuine. He often thought it was Barney's way of showing he was educated even though he'd never been published. It was an affectation, John decided. *'Preternatural*, and abnormal'? Bought ourselves a dictionary, have we? Confession? Maybe... I always assumed the bust-up was something to do with their dad. Did you ever meet Eric, Sue's dad? A dry old stick with rotten teeth but harmless enough; I can't say the same about her mum, though, a hard-hearted old trout... maybe I just felt sorry for him, seeing what he had to put up with."

"That's not good: you *do* know they all become their mothers, don't you?"

John shuddered at the thought of it, without actually wincing. "God, I hope not! Anyway, he never had much to say on the few occasions I saw him. We got on OK, I suppose. Then, one day, bang: heart attack and pegged it! Me and Sue were living together then, but William was still at home, sponging off the parents. That was just before we got married so... late 1989, probably..."

"Yes, I remember now; you thought you might have to postpone."

"Yeah... anyway, William buggered off shortly afterwards, didn't come to the wedding. In fact, I'm *pretty* sure we never saw him again. He was a prat and a bit weird... anyway, Sue didn't want to know and cut him dead, just like that." He snapped his fingers for emphasis.

"Well, I'm not surprised or, what's it, discombobulated by that! She *would,* do, if my suspicions are correct."

John tossed a dry-roasted peanut in the air and attempted to catch it in his mouth. He didn't; it's a hard skill to master. Instead, it bounced off his teeth and went under the table. You don't need to make a note of that.

"Yeah, it doesn't do to get discombobulated... we've been married fifteen years or whatever it is, and I still don't know what went on between them... I think she hates him. Weird. Who knows what goes on, eh? Anyway, I promised her I wouldn't be back late. C'mon, sup your beer and I'll walk you home. G'night Jill!"

## Teach Yourself Russian

The next day, John drove towards town. He parked in the B&Q car park, out of sight of the CCTV, in one of the spaces behind the *Grease Burger n Chipz* van and walked the rest of the way. By taking advantage of B&Q's 'Two-Hours Free Parking, but for customers only!' he regularly avoided the exorbitant town centre fees.

It was easy to blend in with the normal DIY crowd when he parked; a lot of them just looked like normal people. He sometimes stuck a carpenter's pencil behind his ear to really look the part and, as a result, was never challenged as he walked off site in the direction of the town. He shouldn't need more than sixty minutes, he reckoned, to find what he was looking for.

Sure enough, barely fifty minutes later he returned clutching a copy of '*Teach Yourself Russian.*' He'd just put the key in the ignition when he spotted the note which had been recently stuffed under the windscreen wipers. He pressed the switch, but the note would not be dislodged, even on the ridiculously fast and hypnotic setting – it just flapped provocatively. He felt defiled, opened the door ferociously and yanked the offending document out. It said:

*Warning! Parking re-served for Grease Burger n Chipz Customrs ONLY. £25 pounds penalty. Pay at van. OR ELSE.*

------------------------------------------

"Is that you?"

"No, just a burglar. Don't mind me…"

John was keen to get started on teaching himself Russian. He had been considering it anyway, even before the secret coded notebook turned up. There seemed to be more and more people speaking it these days, he'd noticed. Whether it was due to migration from Eastern Europe – or because Russian Oligarchs had started buying London mansions and football clubs – was open to debate. Something he might discuss with Barney, perhaps, but not Sue. She had strong opinions on such things and was very much in favour of 'kicking 'em out.' He'd bucked when she had first aired that view and had suggested that this was, perhaps, an unreasonable stance, given free movement and all that? She had reacted angrily and given him a dressing down. "They come swanning over here with their obscene plundered wealth, buying our football clubs and elegant mansions in fashionable West London… it really *pisses* me off!" Sue wasn't a swearer by nature, so he changed the subject and made a mental note never to mention it again.

Sue Stilton was now standing in the doorway, wiping her hands on a tea towel (a souvenir of something, somewhere), with her hair in a ponytail (as it always was when she was doing the housework). He often thought she could make even the mundane seem glamorous. As she approached the end of her fourth decade she had lost little of the freshness or the beauty of youth, the kind of natural beauty that turns heads and makes friends and admirers wherever it goes. The twinkling blue-grey eyes, long dark lashes and ready smile were the icing on the cake. The plain cake without icing would have been more than good enough for most men. Uncharitable types – churls and the like – would have considered John to be 'punching above his weight.' He would have been upset if he'd known they were talking about his weight.

"Where'd you go, town?"

"Yes, had to buy a book."

"Where'd you park, B&Q?"

"Course."

"Behind the burger van?"

John didn't have time for idle chit-chat, Sue could talk the hind legs off a donkey, but today was not a day for such things. He didn't want to appear disinterested and was quick to state his position. He held the book aloft.

"Er, yes… anyway, not being rude, but I need to make a start on this, so..."

"I see. I suppose if I was Barney though, then you'd stay and chat. Seems you've got time for Barney, but not for me, eh?"

"Aww, c'mon: that's not fair!" he shouted, from the foot of the stairs.

"Isn't it? Really? When do we ever spend time together? I'll tell you when – never!" She had raised her voice at this stage because he was now upstairs, on the landing.

The defendant didn't really know how to respond to the charge and quickly but unsuccessfully tried to think of something to deflect her argument or, preferably, blow it out of the water. When nothing came to mind he said, "Er…"

"But, hey! Off you go; don't worry about me, I'm just a neglected wife, no match for a stupid book!"

"It's not a stupid book. How dare you! It's '*Teach Yourself Russian*,' not that you're interested?"

"Correct!"

The spare *bedroom* was a bit of a misnomer. In the fifteen years they had lived in the house, it had never contained a bed. From Day One it had been designated 'John's study,' by John mainly, and it was in there that his '*Earthworks of The East Riding*,' '*The Cromwell Years for Young Learners*,' and '*Zombie Sex Offender*' had been conceived.

The desk, strategically positioned under the window to catch the cool northern light, featured an impressive vintage Anglepoise lamp for when the cool northern light had dwindled. The Dell laptop was John's solitary nod to the modern age, not forgetting his i-Pod: apart from this single double extravagance, purchased with the money he'd earned in royalties from his best-selling '*Confessions of a Zombie Window Cleaner,*' he was strictly a pen and paper Luddite. A bookcase to house his reference books and a few editions of his own published efforts, a faux-leather swivel chair and a small side table for the inkjet printer (another solitary nod to the modern age) completed the furnishings. John maintained that a minimalist approach was essential in establishing the kind of environment necessary for creative thinking. Sue maintained that it wasn't, and that's where she did the ironing.

Opening '*Teach Yourself Russian*' at the page entitled '*The Alphabet: Strangely Familiar!*' he surveyed the list of weird and wonderful Cyrillic characters with handy pronunciation guide. He nodded sagely. This was indeed going to be a challenge!

The mystery notebook was in the top drawer, so he fished it out, opened it at page one and surveyed the bizarre, apparently meaningless text. Gradually his frown was replaced by a newfound sense of purpose and a *can-do* attitude with a distinctly jutting jaw.

"In for a penny, in for a rouble. Here we go then, eyes down, look in!"

Taking a pencil, with the left index finger marking the first character, he scanned the list in the textbook...

"Got him! That's *A*. Good, right...

He wrote *A* on his pad.

"Now, this one looks like a backward N with a squiggle... there he is, and that's a yuh sound? Blimey!

He added *yuh* next to *A*.

"Then something that looks like an apostrophe... maybe it *is* an apostrophe? Let's give it a go.

He added an apostrophe. *A yuh.'*

"And that looks like...*d*? OK *d*. and that's the end of the first word."

He now had *A yuh'd.*

"What the hell does *that* mean? Second word. That's a B. That backward N is an I. And then the H is an N, obviously."

A yuh'd bin.

"Christ on a bike! Couldn't he have just written this in English? A yuh'd bin? I'd been? Could be! Yes! 'I'd been!' Now, we're getting somewhere!"

He picked up the notebook and thumbed through the dozens of pages with their closely packed script and the realisation suddenly dawned that this was going to take a huge effort and a feat of mental endurance that might break a lesser man. But he was no lesser man. He was a man of letters and a published writer, for God's sake; this would be his finest hour! After a cup of tea and a biscuit, obviously.

## Ice and Fire

"Cup of tea?"

"No."

"No what?"

"No."

"You're not sulking, are you? *Are* you? What have I done now? *I know what I've done: absolutely nothing, that's what!*" Obviously, he said the last bit to himself as he was reaching for the teabags.

"What do *you* care?"

"Jesus!" She'd sneaked into the kitchen and caught him unawares. She was probably the stealthiest women he'd ever known, and he'd known a few.

"I'm surprised you even bother to ask. Am I sulking? No, I'm not going to waste my breath sulking. If you can't be bothered to put more effort into this marriage, I don't see why I should!"

"Does one use one's breath to sulk? OK, you're right, I know… tell you what, let's sulk together!" He stuck out his bottom lip.

"Sod off!" she said.

He made her a cup of tea, just to show there were no hard feelings. She didn't drink it, just to show there were. She was brooding and wouldn't be deterred by a meretricious herbal infusion.

"So, what's the appeal of Russian? Found yourself a gorgeous babushka to run off with? I should be so lucky! Off you go, then; don't let me stop you!"

John scoffed.

"No, nothing so glamorous… it's just… you remember William's bits that we put up in the loft? I thought I'd have a look through them and see if, y'know, there was anything in there, that's all."

Sue let out one of her *here-we-go-again* sighs.

"And is there? No, of course there isn't! I told you he was complicated…

There was a brief silence as the words paused, unspoken.

"I really don't want to talk about him!"

"I know, I know… you've said so a million times, but *I'm* curious; you must be too, surely? Deep down? Not even the slightest bit? About where his mind might have been when, y'know…?

Again, the conversation foundered, as it often did, when the subject of *y'know* came up.

"Some of it's written in Russian script, and that's why I got the book. I'm going to attempt to translate it!"

"Why are you bothering? What *possible* purpose can it serve? If you're looking for things to do, I could find you things to do, don't *you* worry about that; there's loads of stuff that needs doing!"

"I know, I know that but... I don't know, it might tell us something?"

"Tell us why he did what he did? Is that what you think? Hardly likely, is it! And do you know what, John? I really don't need to have him shoved back into my life right now. He's gone, he's never coming back and nothing he might have written, in Russian, Chinese or sodding Sanskrit, is going to alter that fact, is it? I mean, why not just leave it alone instead of poking around, dragging up the past? Fucksake, John! Just let it go!"

There was a silence as John dunked a biscuit, considering his options, while Sue simmered and watched him with a cold and resentful eye. This was building up to something, he could sense that. He knew the signs. He knew, for instance, that she'd be watching him now; he didn't need to look round to know. It was obvious the eye doing the looking would be cold and resentful.

He always said he'd never push it; he loved her and respected her wishes, all that stuff but... as her husband, he had a right to know, surely? Maybe it would help to get it off her chest whatever it was. Why wouldn't she tell him? What was so awful that she couldn't share it with him? Could it really be the unthinkable, as Barney had suggested?

He was still dunking, although the biscuit had long since ceased to be a viable dunk, when he decided to push it, just this once, and pop the question.

"Look... don't lose the plot, right? but we talked about this last night, me and Barney. In his story, there's this bit where one of them, William's character, is talking about his sister, you… some of what he says is – how can I put this – deeply disturbing? I mean, it's really creepy stuff, the kind of thing no brother should ever say about his sister… do you know what I'm saying?

Sue clenched her fists, a face like thunder, the knuckles white, the pressure building…

"Why can't you tell me? Was there something in what Barney said? Is *that* what happened? God, I don't even want to say it but… did he ever… force you to, y'know?"

That was when she stormed out.

This was not the ideal time to be a fun-loving fly on the wall in the Stilton household; a morose silence descended. It crept into every nook and cranny, creating a funereal vibe. Vibe might be overstating it. It didn't have the energy to be a vibe. It was an atmosphere in which nothing could breathe, where the pervading mood was one of darkling, joyless sobriety. It was getting on for sombre. You've been there, I'm sure.

Sue set up camp in the conservatory, a place where she often went to sit and mope in times of stress, when a dose of good old-fashioned introspection was called for – something best tackled with both gin and tonic. Sitting there in the post-rumpus silence, with her dark mood settling, she wondered how things had come to this. How was it that the carefree, socially adept Susan Stilton (nee Skaife) had ended up drinking on her own these days in a conservatory when everyone she used to know was probably out partying with a wide circle of friends who lived fabulous lives? Not her, though; she bloody well wasn't out partying! She *eked*, she didn't *live*. Here she was, her best years behind her and not a friend in the world, no-one she could talk to about... anything! Not John. She did love John, she was sure of that, but sometimes she desperately felt the need for a confidante. The e on the end was important. She tried to pinpoint the moment in her life where her former friends, the people she'd known at school... precisely when had they ceased to be *proper* friends? When had they been divested of that particular duty? Friendships were an enormous and overwhelming responsibility. Had they even been true friends? It was all so long ago... Surely, real friends don't just disappear? Not like little brothers.

John stayed in the kitchen listening for signs of activity, ruminating and reflecting on the state of the union. It was the same every time they had words. It wasn't very often, admittedly, but each time it happened he always wondered whether this was the point of no return. Had they gone as far as they could? Was there any point in carrying on? Fifteen years must count for something though, surely? Could they last another fifteen? He hoped so; maybe more if all went well. Of course, every couple had their ups and downs but, in the main, sticky situations usually had a way of resolving themselves. They made a good team, he believed.

People often say, 'You're lovely when you're angry.' He concluded that they were talking nonsense. Those people were not his people. Sue wasn't lovely when she was angry, and he doubted anyone could be. She was really lovely when she wasn't angry, though. She was very beautiful; it came effortlessly to her. He'd recognized this from the moment he first set eyes on her. He wondered whether losers and underachievers thought he'd punched above his weight?

His reverie was brought to a halt with a sharp intake of breath and an involuntary 'ouch' when his buttocks became numb from sitting on the hard kitchen chair. He went to check in on the gin palace. She was still in there, staring past the iconic green bottle and out into deep space. The fact she hadn't moved the bamboo cane furniture to block the entrance was, he supposed, a positive sign. He fondly remembered the '*keep-out-or-else!*' sign she once had on her bedroom door, and how he'd ignored it.

She was miles away, lost in thought and swirling the liquid around the glass with carelessly expert precision. He looked in on her, hoping she would return his gaze, but to no avail. He brought out his jazz hands to try and catch her attention, grinning like a jackanapes, but there was no reaction. 'Tough crowd,' he thought.

As he stood there gaping, it appeared that her eyes were glistening – was she crying? He'd already ceased his grinning and his jazz-handing and was now unsure of his next move. When the signs of distress became so obvious they could no longer be denied, John opened the door as if he had a warrant and went in. She turned and looked at him, her face at that moment perhaps the saddest face in the Kingdom. Her lower lip began to tremble.

"Sue? What's the matter? What's this about? Hey, come here, aww c'mon now, Sue... Sue? Don't cry, please. Please don't..." He sat beside her and wrapped his arm around her shoulders. As he squeezed and pulled her close she began to sob uncontrollably.

"Shush now, it's OK. I'm sorry, I'm so sorry... hey, it's OK." He was now hugging so tightly – it might easily have been classed as swaddling – she could hardly breathe.

She settled eventually, then gasped that she was 'OK.' Could he release the clutch a bit, she was fine, she was just having a 'silly moment.'

John coughed uncomfortably and nodded in acknowledgement, knowing that the lump in his throat would play havoc with any attempt on his part to speak. He'd been overwhelmed suddenly, overpowered by his love for this woman, his best friend and his soulmate, the woman who'd shared his life for twenty years. It was unbearable to think that he of all people had been so gauche and so horribly insensitive as to ask a question like that and to push her with such a despicable lack of empathy or compassion into having to relive what were, clearly, painful and distressing memories. He closed his eyes and pondered the overwhelming responsibility of marriage, of sharing a life with another human being, of building something meaningful on just a tiny speck of dust in the vastness of the universe, struggling to comprehend the endlessness of eternity. It was a staggering thought. After a few moments he sniffed manfully and ventured,

"So he did, then?"

She didn't answer immediately. She managed both a tut and a sigh, though, as she scoffed. Speaking at first through gritted teeth, she told him straight: "No, of course he didn't!

You're totally wrong. It was nothing like that. Why would anyone even *think* that?" She still wasn't looking at him and seemed to be thinking aloud. Then she did turn and look at him. Finally, she just turned on him with the volume up.

"And, what gives you and Barney the right to go talking about me like that?"

"I don't know. It wasn't me; it was Barney's idea…"

"That's just pathetic! *'Please Miss, it wasn't me…'*" she snapped. "You've got no right to talk about things you know nothing about!"

"I've got no right to talk about things about which I know nothing!" said John, correcting her.

"*Neither* of you do!" said Sue, correcting him.

'OK, if that's how it is…' Having rattled her cage and, perhaps, having outstayed his welcome, and having definitely overstepped the mark, he left and headed upstairs, seeing little alternative. Sue refilled her glass.

William's notebook was still there, on the desk, waiting for his prompt attention. So were the Russian manual, the pad, and the pencil. His enthusiasm wasn't though. It had waned, somewhat, since he had gone off in search of tea and biscuits. A lot of enthusiasm can be waned in a couple of hours.

"Ah, fuck it!" He swept everything into the open drawer and slammed it shut.

After a pause for thought he opened it again. He got out his iPod, cursed the tangled wires, untangled said wires, lay flat on the floor, stuck a bud in each ear and pressed 'Play.'

The Jam were Down in the Tube Station at Midnight, apparently.

He lay there on the floor, unmoving until the hugely impressive guitar duet outro from *Hotel California* seeped into his brain, causing his eyelids to flip open suddenly, as if he had been prodded with a sharpened stick. He let out an involuntary gasp as he lurched into a waking state, one both unwelcome and uncalled for. He had a stiff neck. And a full *early-hours* bladder. The room was dark. He patted the floor in the immediate vicinity until he found his glasses. He peered at the dial of his watch; it was just after three o'clock. A quick visit to the loo, a cursory brush of most of his teeth and he was done.

Heading for the marriage bed, he was hoping the shoulder might be a little less cold than it had been earlier. There was a faint snore and the sound of light breathing from the figure slumbering on Sue's side of the bed, the sleek raven hair peeking from the crisp white linen. As he climbed in beside her, he whispered, "I'm sorry." There was no response. Maybe she really was asleep. He whispered: "Are you asleep?" There was no response. He whispered again: "I said, 'are you asleep?'" She whispered: "Arsehole." Sue wasn't a natural or instinctive swearer. He knew he had behaved despicably, and he'd had the wrong end of the stick; he knew he had been insensitive, and she was right to be angry. He knew all this, and he knew she would make these very same points to him in the morning, to ward off any possible misunderstanding. As he had nothing to lose, he snuggled up close and slipped his arms around her waist. He breathed in the warmth of her body, the scent of her face cream, and whispered lovingly over her shoulder, "I don't suppose there's any chance…?"

## The Last Post

Next morning, well aware that a sumptuous breakfast in bed can often prove a winning stratagem, John hopped out from under the covers as Sue slept on. He set about rustling up tea and toast generously smeared with strawberry jam. Whilst not qualifying as 'sumptuous' in the strict sense of the word, he knew Sue would be appreciative and it might help to mend a couple of medium-sized bridges.

"Here we go my sweet, a little token of my esteem."

The esteemed one eyed him suspiciously at first, but not for long, not with the offer of tea and toast on a tray! Her resistance was broken, and she sat up, smoothed the duvet, and patted her thighs.

"Put it here, then you can go."

"Go where?"

"You can go. You can sod off. Which bit don't you understand? Do you still speak English or is it just Russian now?"

She fixed him with a glare. He was perturbed. *Really, have my efforts been in vain?*

She took a bite of toast, continuing to fix him with a stare as he floundered and did a passable impression of an incredulous fish.

"Oh, you Wally – I'm winding you up!"

He thought he saw a smile. A quick half smile, admittedly.

"I might let you have some yourself if you behave. Big if, though."

He started to make his case, but his introductory splutter was quickly interrupted. "Look John... you know why I was upset and angry with you, last night, don't you? You can be a right arsehole at times, d'you know that?"

"Yes. I know. Look, I'm sorry about what I said. I didn't mean it, really. Can we just forget it and be friends again? What do you say? Friends?" He gave her a look; the kind of look he hoped would charm her like it used to do. He was out of practice though. If anything, he came over as needy and desperate. Oddly enough, though, in this instance, it worked.

It was about an hour later that they were suddenly woken by the rattle of the letter box, the snap of the flap and the sound of the post landing on the mat in the hall. And the dog next door barking. And the dog in the house opposite, set off by the dog next door, barking.

"Maybe we should get a dog?"

"You hate dogs!"

"Yes, but we could get rid after it had attacked and killed those two yapping little shits!"

"You're mean! Anyway… go and get the post, might be a huge royalty cheque!" She yawned and stretched and reluctantly started to consider getting up.

There was a pile of stuff downstairs on the mat, mainly rubbish: circulars, a pizza menu and one from *Grease Burger n Chipz* announcing the '*fantastic*' news that they were now offering *takaway* Sunday lunches, a couple of bills, reminders and a white recycled Jiffy bag held together with tape.

Sue was in her dressing gown, hunting for a slipper as he sauntered in with a lingering post-coital alpha male smile.

"Well, no big cheque today. You got a package, though."

"What sort of package?" she said, as her head and upper torso emerged from under the bed.

"A white one, want me to open it?"

"Has it got your name on it anywhere?"

John inspected it on all sides. "No, I don't think so."

"I don't want you to open it then, do I!"

She took the package and inspected the hand-written name and address, before ripping it open despite the best efforts of the tape to thwart her. Inside, there was a note and a battered notebook:

Dear Sue.

I hope you and Shaun are fine, sorry I haven't been in touch – there never seemed to be a suitable time, I suppose.

# It's The Not Knowing

I'm sending you this (enclosed). Make of it what you will. I hope you don't mind me sending it.

It was Will's. I have kept it all these years as a memento of happier times. I think it's a story about all of us: you and Shaun and me and Will and Shaun's friend. (Sorry but I can't remember his name). Apart from that, I don't really understand what it's about. I'm not keen on the ending! He showed me it when he'd finished it. I didn't get it then and I still don't. He never got around to explaining it in all the years we were together – now it's too late.

BTW I don't know if that comes as a surprise to you that we were 'together?' Maybe not, maybe you knew all along that he was more than just a lodger?

I thought you should have it. Maybe you or Shaun might make sense of it… your man's a writer so he might have a better chance, don't you think? I don't want it back. I should have said something, I know, but I'm making a clean break now, letting go of the past and moving on; I've sold the house (same day as it was listed, wooh!) and I'm packed and ready - by the time you get this I suppose I'll have gone. I'm sorry we never had the chance of a proper goodbye.

Thanks for being there; I couldn't have made it through college without your friendship, kindness, and support. Or the wine!

One last thing. I hope we always treasure the memory of our parents and the times we had with them. It's one of the most precious things in life.

Love, always. Take care, Sue – look after yourself.

It's The Not Knowing

Áine

X

Sue flicked through the pages of the notebook, instantly recognizing William's handwriting with its fierce slant to the left. A sudden, lucid flashback took her straight into a childhood *tableau*, brother and sister perched at the kitchen table with a bowl of broken wax crayons, drawing and colouring on the inside of disassembled cereal packets or on the back of wallpaper rolls. Arguing over whose was best. She could see and smell it clearly; the same hands that produced those childish pictures of square, implausible houses and a spider which looked like a helicopter, had written the story she was now holding, had thumbed through these very pages, and had, lest we forget, done something unforgivable.

She briefly felt something else mixed with the nostalgia... she wasn't sure what the last comment was about, but it wasn't anything to do with that... maybe it was simply a regret for the loss of an actual friend? No, that couldn't be it, not really. She would hardly have called her a close friend anymore, not these days. As students, yes – they were close then, but life moves on; they hadn't been in contact at all this century, had they? She couldn't even remember the last time, in fact. Did she have any kind of right to miss her? She supposed not. Maybe, more likely, it was because she was holding this little black notebook and looking at the pages, the very pages her silly, selfish brother had once looked at as he scribbled this fiction. Maybe the past was back to haunt her...

It's The Not Knowing

John was hovering at a respectful distance, chomping at the bit, hoping she wouldn't think him nosey. His curiosity rating had gone from severe to critical and might even have been touching hypercritical. His breathing was certainly shallow. Finally, she put him out of his misery, gave him the letter and the book and headed for the door. "Another one for your collection," she said as she left. When she reached the top of the stairs, she heard the plaintive squeal:

"Typical! Can't even get my name right!"

# PART THREE. 1986-89

## Communal Living

Thursday, May 1ˢᵗ, 1986.

I'd been waiting for my chauffeur for about ten minutes and there was no sign of the bastard. Why was it that when you wanted to be somewhere in a hurry, they always turned up late? Or not at all? I gave it another five minutes, exactly five minutes, during which time I rolled my eyes and tutted with the others as we waited in line. A few of us exchanged headshakes to register our common sense of grievance until eventually, with it looking increasingly likely that the 'service' had simply been cancelled altogether, I decided I'd be better off walking and saving the 30p. I sensed things might be about to kick off, if the level of customer dissatisfaction continued to grow exponentially. Don't worry, I know what I'm talking about. As I moved off, a public-spirited oaf at the back of the queue was trying to instigate a group sing-along, with an *impromptu* rendition of '*Why are we wai-ting, wh-ay are we wa-iting...*'

"Oh, shut up, man!" snapped one well-spoken, well-dressed sourpuss, drawing a few claps and a 'well said!' from the disgruntled crowd.

"Where have all the buses gone, long time pa-a-ssing...?" someone else offered, hopefully.

It was a chilly late afternoon, just before half five, and I was perhaps underdressed for hiking in the north. My holdall banged against my leg with every step as, upper body angled a few degrees to the left to offset the weight of the bag, I walked up the hill and out of town. At the exact mid-point between stops, the reliably unreliable green beast rumbled into view; it came rattling alongside and then accelerated away from me. What got me about that was that I *clearly* had my arm raised with palm suitably positioned to indicate '*Halt, Go No Further!*' It's an internationally recognised hand signal, right up there with the two-fingered salute, everyone uses it – you must have seen it. Not the grubby old loser at the wheel, though; it was a new one on him, apparently. I have committed his face to memory. It was a hideous face and they're the easiest to remember. Every action has a consequence and the consequences for this shit stain would not make pleasant reading, even if presented in the form of a clearly legible list with splendid illustrations.

I'd also remembered the bus number. I'm good with remembering things. What's the opposite of sieve?

So, I walked the two miles home. I wasn't bothered, I fancied a walk anyway. By the time I got home I was sweating like a hog; I was clearly overdressed for hiking in the north, something I'd suspected all along. I'm good at knowing stuff like that and, generally speaking, you could always rely on me to gauge the amount and, of course, the cut of the clothing required to handle most situations.

Home, in case you were wondering, was a run-of-the-mill terraced house: Edwardian, four bedrooms spread over three floors with a huge cellar where we practiced. It was nothing fancy, but I suppose it could have been done up. If pressed I'd have to say I didn't have the time or the energy for that. It wasn't my bag if you know what I mean. I'd inherited it from my parents So had my sister, Suze. She'd inherited it too, but I'll tell you about her later.

It was exactly twenty to six when I climbed the steps and let myself in. There was no post; that was the first thing I noticed. This could mean one of three things: there really had been no post or, there had been post but none for me or, thirdly, there *had* been some post for me but one of the others had taken it. This was a running joke in our place, where you'd snaffle someone's post and hide it in, say, the bathroom cabinet or, in the fridge or wherever. It had to be in the common spaces though, that was the unwritten rule. Sometimes it was a trifle annoying, I won't deny it, but it was just harmless pranking. And where's the harm in that, eh? I could hear music coming from Joe's room. Neil Young, I think. Whiney nasal voice, anyway.

Joe Boyle lives downstairs, in the front room. Mid-twenties, early seventies beard and a good mate. That's why I don't charge him much rent. I have the big bedroom at the front because it's my house. It was my parents' bedroom at one time. We hadn't been conceived in there, though, me or Suze; we moved there in 1968, just before I started school. None of that's important - you don't need to write that down.

In one of the back bedrooms, you'll find Bryan, another good mate, plays the bass in our band. Bryan Lester Grimes, to give him his full name is a modern-day philosopher; I know this because he has told me as much. He does have a peculiar slant, that's true. When he first announced this fact (him being a philosopher), he declared that he had been reading a book called '*Philosophy and Philosophers.*' There was nothing in there which he hadn't already thought long before he read the book. So that proves it, he said. He pays his way as far as the rent goes; he knows I could charge more than I do. It's true, I look after my mates but, I'm not a soft touch. Don't ever think that.

There's another smaller bedroom. It used to be Suze's room – *'keep-out-or-else'* – when she lived here and it's where I keep some of my things now. Then, up in the attic, where I lived when I was a rebellious teenager, there's a lodger. I don't know her that well. She's Northern Irish; she's called Orla and has that strange lilting accent, y'know? She seems nice, though. I was looking to make some extra cash, so I put an advert in the window at Mistry's Superette offering a room to let; she turned up at the door just as I got back from an appointment with my accountant. A redhead and skinny, that was my first impression. She liked the room, describing it as "*perfect, so it is.*" She'd always wanted to live in a garret, and she didn't mind sharing with three blokes because "*ach, no*" she had "*tree brothers*" at home, so she did; she moved in the next day. It all worked out rather well, although if I'd known it was a garret, I might have charged more. I'm only joking! I wouldn't; I'm not like that.

I'd started to make my way up the stairs when Joe's door opened. It was *indeed* Neil Young, telling us that a man needs a maid, which is something to bear in mind.

"Hey Wilf, listen to this …" Joe disappeared back into the room and Neil stopped. He returned and came halfway out, leaned against the door to stop it closing and looked up eagerly in my direction.

I couldn't hear anything, and I told him so.

"Shhh, hang on…" Then the drums and bass started up and it launched into a rocky little number.

"Think we should cover this? Nice bass riff…"

"Yeah, why not. Fancy a pint later?"

"Maybe, but I'm seeing Suze."

"Is she coming here?"

"I'm meeting her in the 'Reck so probs not…"

Joe had been seeing my sister for a few months by then so, officially, you could class them as an item. It was a strange arrangement in some respects. Legally, she owned half of this property, but she didn't live in it. Not anymore. It was our proper childhood home, the only one I could remember. Suze has had four addresses: the first place, where I was born, this one, the one when she was at college and then her current place. Although now I think about it, she did come back here after college so, maybe we should call it five, even though one was twice? It's not that important, really. You can write it down if you like. I don't know how much longer Joe is going to stay here. I suppose the logical next step would be for the pair of them to live together so, unless she is willing to sell her house and move back here into the front room, it looks like Joe will be moving out at some stage. I know she likes her own space and that's why she moved, and I know Joe likes living here because we have the cellar for band practice, but I suspect

## It's The Not Knowing

Suze might want to start a family in the next couple of years. We'll cross that bridge when we come to it.

I'm sure she had problems dealing with dad's y'know... maybe the memories were overpowering, perhaps the association with what happened, all that unexpected grief, was simply unbearable or whatever – who knows what goes on in people's minds, eh? I felt the grief, too. But she was more affected, maybe. We were suddenly alone, just us two and mother, but she had nothing to do with it. I'd never thought about it much but, in a situation like that, you do wonder about the ephemeral nature of life and how a family which has survived the eons against all the odds – which is a hell of an achievement! – can suddenly be extinguished and erased from the annals of the Human Race. Me and Suze, we were the only people I knew who had no uncles, no aunties, or cousins. Not a single one between us. That's a weird feeling; it makes you feel vulnerable. As I got older, I thought a lot about things like that. I realised in my teen angst years, the time when my voice was breaking, that there was an enormous responsibility settling on my young shoulders. I considered the heritage and the ancestry of the Mold family, the bloodline. It had survived this far, all the way back through history to an early caveman, then an even earlier caveman; before him, a monkey and, in the very beginning, a fish. Just imagine that! A fish called Mold!

Somehow, the Molds had come through; they'd survived in the face of whatever life threw at them. Plagues, two world wars, religious persecution, revolution, famine, and filth couldn't stop us because here we are, fast approaching the second millennium and still going strong. Sort of. It hit me like a bolt, actually. The fact was, that unless I could generate an heir of some sort, the family name would just fizzle out with a whimper. After all this time, it would be me who dropped the baton, me that future generations who would never be born would point the finger at. There wouldn't be any fingers in the future, thanks to me. No more pure Mold blood coursing through the veins of anyone anywhere. If there is such a thing as a sobering thought – and personally I have my doubts – then surely this was one. Life is an overwhelming responsibility. And, I didn't even have a girlfriend.

Suze said she needed to get away and find her own space so… she got away and found herself a space near where she teaches, and she moved out. I've never been there but, apparently, it's nice. She gets half of the rent monies from this place; that's our legally binding arrangement, and it probably covers her own mortgage, or near enough. If you think about it, technically, her boyfriend is paying some of the mortgage on her small house by living in our old front room. It's a neat set-up, I think, and I hope she agrees. She doesn't come around often. I wish she did, I would like to see more of her. Since our dad y'know… we've sort of drifted apart. When we were children we got on, she was a bit bossy, maybe, but I couldn't have wished for a nicer big sister. I hope she knows that. I hope she believes that. I don't see much of her anymore. On the rare occasions, less rare since things started to get serious with Joe, she doesn't have a lot to say. Not to me. She went totally weird for a while but that's probably understandable.

I opened the door to my room. There is no lock. I don't like locks, none of the rooms have them. We live together on trust and that's how I want it to be. A group of friends with a sense of community, like the old days my mum always talked about, where you could go out all day and leave your door wide open, knowing it was safe. Nobody would dream of going into someone else's house in those days. Except burglars maybe but there weren't that many about. I didn't know of any, anyway. Postmen and shop girls, yes; doctors and factory hands, even, but not burglars.

I can remember when I was an old toddler. One of my earliest memories was going somewhere with my mum. She was pointing out the houses that we were passing and telling me who lived there: "that's nosey old Mrs. Antonov's house, a dreadful woman – works in the mines and serves her right! And that's Doctor Simpson's house, look at those filthy curtains! You won't remember him, he was the idiot with the yellow fingers and stinky breath who came to see you when you had the measles, tried to make you better – for all the good *that* did!" That kind of thing. She never said, as far as I remember, "That's Mr. Manilow's house, he's a burglar." *"What's a burglar, mummy?"* Exactly.

It was a nice place to live, in those days – and it still was a nice place; I wouldn't have lived anywhere else. It felt like home and that's exactly what I was looking for. If only Suze would be my friend again, it would be perfect. I'm working on it.

You're never going to see my room, so I'll tell you what it was like. It was large, with my parents' big old double bed positioned in front of the large bay window. If I lay on it, on my back, and looked left I could see the church. If I looked right, I could see the modern tower blocks on the edge of town, poking above the treetops. If someone had asked me "hey Wilf, which way do you look when you're lying flat on your back, and you can't say 'at the ceiling,'" I suppose I'd have had to say, 'to the right.' I was more of a modernist than a traditionalist, and I still am. There's something about looking to the past that is somehow unsettling. Who said, "Show me the past and I'll give you the future but show me the future and I'll give you the past?" I don't know who said it, but they were clearly deranged and talking rubbish. Which is OK, it's a free country. Maybe it was one of Bryan's?

The dominant feature was a large wardrobe on the side wall next to the fireplace; one of those heavy old things, dark brown and impressive in its own way. It didn't impress me, though. I was never that bothered about furnishings or anything like that. It would have taken a wardrobe of unbelievable charm to impress me. It had always been there. I couldn't imagine it ever being anywhere else. It was too heavy to move, probably, and I had no plans to reposition it. I used it to keep my clothes in so, I suppose, I was something of a traditionalist in that sense. I had moved the bed, though. My parents used to have it facing the window, but I preferred it where it was, where I could keep an eye on things: comings and goings and to-ing and fro-ing and suchlike.

By half six I was in the kitchen, making myself a pre-pub snack of cheese on toast. It's a good idea to line your stomach with a layer of grease before drinking a few beers. It's a known scientific fact, actually, that a layer of grease slows the absorption of the alcohol into the blood stream.

And the bread actually soaks up the liquid so, rather than it all flooding into your system at once, it allows a more steady and stable flow. It's much more manageable and that's why all the top drinkers do it. If you don't believe me, ask anyone! Science has always appealed to me. If I'd tried harder, I could have been a boffin or a brainbox.

## Pretty in Pink

Joe popped his head in, just to say he was going out. He was taking Suze to the pictures, he said. '*Pretty in Pink*,' whatever that was. He also commented on the fine moustache I had just started to grow. In his opinion, he said, it made me look like a "Dutch porn star." He thought it was funny. It wasn't and I didn't. I hadn't heard Bryan at all since I got back, and then I remembered he'd told us that he'd be working overtime this week. He didn't mind it so much because they paid him double time or something. He could do with the money, and he was scared that if he ever said 'No,' they might not ask him again. It was what he referred to as a 'Catch-23 situation,' it being slightly worse than Catch-22.

"It's all to do with psychology. If you're mad enough to say 'No' to what they consider a generous offer, they conclude you must be sane; it's a reflection of your true desires, which you have not sought to conceal. If you say 'Yes,' they think you're lying through your teeth because the basic human instinct would have been to say 'No.' The negative always triumphs over the positive in the human experience, according to Cartland. That's why 'No' is easier to say than 'Yes.' It has fewer letters."

Apparently, they were unusually busy at the depot; he had never known anything like it.

"Wilf, man, you should see all this crap, pallet loads of it being delivered around the clock; we can't unload it fast enough!"

"What sort of crap?"

"Royal crap, Joe, wedding shit! Andrew-and-Fergie this, Andrew-and-Fergie that, mugs, tea trays, plates, tea towels, incontinence pads, the whole shebang. Who buys this shit?"

"It won't last, you mark my words, there's something not quite right about him!"

"You might be right, they're all as bad. Not the Queen, though; she's alright," countered Joe.

"Of course. Goes without saying." And we all agreed. "Absolutely!"

It was great that we all got on well together. Like a happy family, I suppose. And we did, we agreed on most things: politics, philosophy and ethics, geography, religion, the list was endless... we even liked the same music! We didn't necessarily agree on the merits of a moustache or on the ideal woman, though. Speaking personally, I liked all sorts, I wasn't fussy. Any of them would do, really. I could always find the time to make myself available. Joe said he thought Suze was his ideal woman. I suppose he'd have to say that, wouldn't he? And Bryan? I don't know about him... he always said he was too busy and having such a good time to settle down. I'd thought about having a crack at Orla; she seemed to be on her own. I did wonder whether she was expecting me to make overtures, but I didn't know how to play it: if I tried to woo her with a charm offensive, and a freshly grown moustache, would she be keen, willing, and flattered or, would she be mortified, aghast and disgusted? And if I did nothing? If I didn't make *any* kind of approach, would she think me rude or discourteous? You can imagine my dilemma, I'm sure.

So, it was just me, then. I had a choice of two pubs. The Shipwreck, where I knew Joe and Suze might turn up eventually. That was our local. Or I could go to the Angle-Grinder. That was OK; it had a decent pool room with a couple of tables, but it got full of ostlers sometimes. I don't mean hustlers, either. You would expect a pool table to attract the hustling type, wouldn't you? But no – these were genuine ostlers who worked with horses in a stable yard, just along the road. I'd had a couple of decent tips from them on a few occasions, straight from the horse's mouth, literally. I decided against The Angle-Grinder in the end. I wasn't in the mood for horse talk; they hadn't been looking after me lately, the nags. My accountant was happy though, he had done rather well at my expense in the past few days, but I'd win it all back, eventually, with interest. It was a dead cert. Fingers crossed.

I went in the 'Reck instead. I had a quick look round, but I didn't see anyone I knew. I'm not one of those people who can just strike up a conversation with anyone, never have been. I know some that can, and good luck to them. I bought myself a pint and got into conversation with the landlord, Reggie. I asked him if he was geared up for the big day, the Royal Wedding? He gave me to understand that he was, and he hoped it would prove to be as financially beneficial as the last one. He was very happy, he said, to live in a country with a Monarchy and not in a banana republic such as, he said, The Banana Republic of Ireland. He pointed out that it was a prime example of what he was talking about. I offered the view that the Queen did a great job but the rest of them could do much more to earn their corn. He was in full agreement and said as much. He had no doubt, he said, that the impending marriage would last forever, and hoped they might follow the example of Charles and Diana. He had a great deal of respect for Charles but, surprisingly and flying very much in the face of public opinion, not Diana.

"I met her once, y'know, that Diana."

"Did you?" I asked, quite impressed, "Where was that?"

"It was on the M6, bonny lad, just outside Birmingham. I'd managed to run out of petrol between the services. Maybe I had a slow leak or maybe the gauge was faulty; I never found out. Anyway, I pulled over onto the hard shoulder, and I didn't know whether I should walk to the services or stay put. Just as I was about to toss a coin, this little Mini Metro pulled over, about twenty yards in front of me. I got out and jogged up to the passenger's side, with the lorries whizzing past and honking their horns like they do. Blow me down, if it wasn't Diana herself, poking litter out of the passenger door onto the grass verge; a couple of fag packets and some sweet wrappers – Bounties, if I remember rightly. 'Your Highness!' I said, 'this is indeed a great honour! I know it's a frightful imposition, but do you think you might be able to tow me to the next services?' I sort of bowed and curtseyed at the same time; I wasn't sure of the protocol, having never met a Royal before."

"I can imagine. What did she say?"

"She called me a 'snivelling toady' and told me to fuck off! I'd never heard owt like it, not from a Royal. Then she zoomed off, straight into the outside lane without indicating!"

"Wow, didn't even indicate?"

"Well, it was a Mini Metro, so maybe the electrics were faulty."

"Ah yes, good point. Still… that was a bit rude!"

I left and went over to the fruit machines. Reggie was getting into a heated debate with Declan, one of Cork's finest, on the subject of Banana Republics and whether a landlord thought it was likely that he might get his face smashed in.

Declan is a legend and also a big surly brute, genetically incapable of smiling or not growling. Just by looking at him you can tell he's as hard as nails: anyone with a face like a welder's bench has to know how to look after themselves, or the bullies would smell fear and weakness. But he was probably a bully, anyway. Who bullies the bullies? Declan does. You will have seen his kind, wearing just a T-shirt in all weathers, not even a cardigan or a jumper; just a general all-weather psychopath.

I watched them engage in a frank exchange of views. I think Reggie would have barred anybody else for talking to him like that, but he knew that such a move would seriously damage his face and his takings so, from what I could make out from a safe distance, he apologised unreservedly. And did he just bow and curtsey? What a snivelling toady! Fuck off!

Unofficially, the big Irish lump has his own place at the bar; it's an exclusion zone for everyone else. He tends to drift between the two pubs and has the luxury of an unquestioned reservation at the Angle-Grinder bar as well: The Ostler-free Zone. There was an incident involving Declan once which, perhaps more than any other, has cemented his place in the Pantheon of Legends. I'll tell you later if there's time.

I put some money in and played for a bit on the machines, got about a quid out. I'd probably put that much in, so I just about broke even. I've seen some people blow a lot of money on those machines. Stupid people, losers. Not me, though. I always say, 'if you can't afford to lose big, don't play big.' I'm always saying it. I could see the lemon I needed for a winning line, though. I reckoned with a couple more nudges I could hit the jackpot; I didn't want to leave it for a loser to come over and snatch it, so I stuck another quid in and smacked the button hard. It was now tantalisingly close but still just out of reach. If I didn't know better, I'd say these machines were designed to just take your money. Thieving bastards.

I was about to put another quid in when Bryan came in. I might have won but there are no guarantees. You just never know.

# It's The Not Knowing

"What Ho!" I said, as he came over swinging his rucksack. It landed with a satisfying thud as it crunched into the back of the seat. Hiding behind the thud was the unmistakeable sound of something breaking.

"Ah, shit, shit, shit! I forgot that was in there."

He unzipped the bag and rifled quickly through the contents. I don't know why he was rushing; the damage had already been done, surely?

"Bollocks!" he said, biting his lower lip and closing his eyes, focussing his displeasure.

It seems he'd helped himself to a souvenir Andy and Fergie plate before leaving the depot. It was from a damaged and split pack, so it was alright; it wasn't theft, as such. With a tut and a sigh, he pulled out two evenly sized portions of the original plate, one in each hand: the grinning, sinister groom looking haughty and supercilious on the Yin, and the blushing bride-to-be looking Rubenesque and weighing heavily on the Yang.

"Oh look – they've split up before they've even walked down the aisle at the taxpayers' expense. If that's not a sign of things to come, I don't know what is!"

"It's the bag. It's cursed. What are you having, Skol?"

"Go on then. And dry roasted nuts if they've got any." I knew they did because I saw them earlier.

The jukebox was doing its thing and The Bangles were walking like an Egyptian or, to be more precise, four Egyptians or, to be more precise, four lovely Egyptians.

## It's The Not Knowing

Over at the bar, Bryan was chatting to Jill, the beanpole serving wench. He showed her the wreckage of the plate, which she was scrutinising closely. She shrugged her shoulders and looked at him for guidance. He picked up the beers and shook his head. She inclined hers and dropped Andy and Fergie in the bin. Who needs words!

The conversation, when he returned, was just as you might expect; it was formulaic: inconsequential shit disguised as persiflage, really. I asked him what he intended to do with that plate. He needed clarification: did I mean now that it was broken and in the bin or, what was he intending *before* he had broken it, when it was in a pristine, highly desirable state. This threw me, briefly. In the end I opted for the second one.

"I was going to give it to Orla. She told me she quite liked all this Royal memorabilia stuff, when I mentioned I was playing a significant role in its national and international distribution. I think she was quite impressed. I said I'd 'see what I could do.'"

"Did you *really* think a gaudy bit of mass-produced tat would impress her?"

"No, not at all, we were just chatting in the kitchen. She was looking for her post."

"Did she find it?"

"Eventually."

"Where'd you put it?"

"Down behind the cooker." We both laughed at Orla.

"Nice one. So… *would* you?"

# It's The Not Knowing

"Would I what?"

"Don't play the innocent! Would you give her one?"

"Piss off!" He started to laugh and reached for his pint.

"Why not? Not your type? She wouldn't let you near, anyway."

"Yeah, ha ha, but you know how it is… not looking to get involved, too much else going on. Anyway, Mr. Porn 'tache – would you? I bet *you* would if you could!"

"Already have," I said, as I swept up the glasses and headed for the bar. Made me feel quite superior, in a blokey way. It pays to remind one's serfs and tenants of the pecking order from time to time. But no, I hadn't.

Later on, while I was at the bar, Joe and Suze came in. As I might have mentioned, it was always awkward when I saw her; it was as if we were strangers who hadn't been formally introduced, if you know what I mean. I went over to say hello and offered to buy them a drink; Joe was quite happy to accept, but I could see Suze was reluctant. She said it was OK, they'd buy their own. She didn't even look at me. Was I upset? Yes, a little. Then Joe offered to buy the round. A nice gesture but, unless he was willing to buy the drinks for the rest of the evening, it was hardly a long-term solution.

While he was trying to get Jill the barmaid's attention, I asked Suze if she'd enjoyed the film, Pretty and Pink. She said no because they hadn't actually seen Pretty *in* Pink. She stressed the differentiation. I asked what had brought on this change of plan. She said Joe could explain it better, then she went to powder her nose. I left the bar and went back to our table. I noted that when Suze came out of the ladies she returned to the bar rather than sit with us.

A short while later, we did actually convene. All four of us were sitting together, but not for very long. Three pints of Skol and a large vodka with orange juice had just taken up positions when Suze decided she and Joe would go and invest some money in the jukebox. They were there a long time, selecting a load of songs by the looks of things. It didn't escape my notice when they went to the bar and got themselves another couple of drinks. They didn't come back straight away. I think they must have gone into the other room at some point, because I lost sight of them for a while; when I saw them again, they were chatting to the wench, Jill, and seemed to be having a good old natter.

I started to tell Bryan about the incident with Declan threatening Reggie earlier; I knew he'd be interested. He'd had a philosophical disagreement with the big lump himself, on a couple of occasions. We discussed the likely outcome, and both concluded that the Irish would have beaten the Geordie senseless if it had come to blows. Bryan wondered how you could tell the difference between a Geordie and a senseless Geordie; it amounted to the same thing, in his view. Then, something fantastic happened: the love birds came back and took their seats, smiling ominously, in tandem.

"Just talking about Declan. Thought there might have been a spot of bloodshed earlier…"

"We've got something to tell you." said Joe, interrupting and wrapping his arm around Suze. "Do you want to tell them, or shall I? OK... me and Suze we're... we're getting engaged!"

And that's all that needs to be said, really. Bryan offered congratulations. And so did I. I didn't know what to say, having never been confronted with anything like that before. And I've been around.

"Don't you have to have a ring or something?" I asked, clearly out of my depth.

"Mmm, getting it this weekend," said Suze, dreamily.

There was a spot of backslapping and a few manly handshakes. Bryan got up and went round to Suze; she turned her face and allowed him to plant a big smacker right on the cheek, smiling all the while. So, I did the same – and she didn't resist! Or rub it off! It was a fantastic moment in the History of the World.

Obviously, we bought some more drinks.

When things settled down, I picked up.

"Anyway, as I was saying to Bryan *(Would he be the best man, or would I?)* before we were *rudely* interrupted *(Wait for laughter to die down),* there was an incident earlier with Declan..."

"He's an arsehole, thinks he owns the place."

"... and I thought there was going to be blood spilled."

"What happened?" It was Suze being genuinely interested and moon-faced, I thought, like people often are after a couple of drinks have numbed the natural tendencies.

I explained what had been said, told her about Irish bananas and all that. It was the most we'd spoken in years, and it felt wonderful, on top of a peck on a cheek; it raised my spirits beyond belief.

"Is he that big lump that leans on the bar and growls at everyone?"

"Big lump – is that what you call him? Ha ha! So do I! He *is* a big lump! Yes, that's him. He's a legend!"

"Why?"

"Why what?"

"Why do you say he's a legend?"

"Well…" I said, detecting an unwelcome coolness in her tone but, at the same time, sensing this might be an opportunity to really build some bridges. And, if I could factor in one of my favourite anecdotes at the same time, it would be a real win-win, *BOGOF* situation.

Bryan and Joe sat back; I'm sure they'd heard the tale before. They might even have witnessed it themselves; I can't remember who was there at the time.

"I was in here one night a couple of years ago, maybe a bit more…"

Suze picked up her glass and took a long drink through the straw, without taking her eyes off me. We were reconnecting, I could tell – after everything that had happened, the signs were definitely encouraging.

"…it was snowing heavily on that particular night. Declan The Lump, the legend from the bog, finished his flagon and decided to go over the road for a change of scenery…"

"To *The Grinder*," said Bryan, helpfully.

"Yes, anyway. As he was crossing, having looked neither right nor left, he was knocked to the ground by a pizza delivery boy on a moped."

Suze gasped, "Oh, no!" at this point, but I carried on…

"Both parties reacted accordingly: Declan, being an immovable object, overbalanced and sat down, while the youth and moped rebounded whence they came. The brute picked himself up and brushed the snow from his fat, wet arse…"

"Was he alright, the poor boy on the bike?" she interrupted, but I didn't mind. I really didn't mind.

"He strode over towards the kid, who was flapping about on his back, the wheels of the moped still spinning and going nowhere. No bones broken, at least. Declan picked him up, lifted the visor on his helmet, probably relished the terror in his eyes and punched him through the gap! Then he dropped him back on the ground like a stone and carried on, as if nothing had happened!"

Joe and Bryan were both laughing heartily by this stage and acknowledged that it was a terrific tale.

"As I said: Legend." I smiled in conclusion.

"That's just mean!"

I remembered now, she always favoured the underdog, did Suze.

"And let's not forget the real victim in all this," I added, waving a professorial finger.

There was a gap of about two seconds, with six eyes looking at me and at least four eyebrows raised.

"The poor sod who got the stone-cold pizza delivered... late!"

We all laughed, all of us. Even Suze. Especially Suze.

The laughter settled and I went to the bar to buy another four of the same, with no refusal from anyone.

I hadn't bought Suze two drinks since she was at college, in the days when she didn't mind me going to meet her afterwards.

"So, you said you've been to the pictures. What did you see?" It was Bryan steering the conversation now, as I took time to bathe in a strange warm glow of... contentment, I suppose. I was buzzing.

"What *didn't* we see, more like!" said Joe, who seemed unable to let go the debutante fiancée's hand. Suze made a snorting noise, as she sipped at the vodka, through a straw. It seemed they had planned to see 'Pretty *in* Pink' but, when they turned up the place was swarming with young, red-haired women in their early-twenties and late teens, festooned with freckles. We both expressed astonishment at the nature of such a congregation and wondered what might have been the explanation.

"It was sold out – we couldn't get tickets." this was Suze saying this, like a friend would say it.

"Really?" I gushed, breathlessly, then hoped it didn't come over as 'needy'. I didn't need sympathy.

"Yeah, there were dozens of them!"

It was Joe who'd interrupted. Then Suze was back in the chair with the talking stick.

"They were *ev'rywhere*, ev'where you looked. It took us ages to get to the kiosk, only to find it was 'sold out.' I said to Joe, I said, 'Joe, look at them, they're *ev'rywhere!*' I said. How were we to know that we'd picked the same night to go as the regional Molly Ringwald fan-club? I mean, what are the chances?"

She picked up her glass and sucked again at the straw.

"It's true. I asked one of them…" Joe said, seeing a gap. "They'd made a block booking and were just waiting for the Harry Dean Stanton Society to turn up; they'd booked a coach, apparently! I didn't even know he *had* a society."

Neither did I. Who is he, anyway?

"So… guess what we finally decided we'd go see? C'mon Bryan, C'mon Wilf, bet you can't guess!" This was Suze, I was almost beside myself. She was getting quite tiddly, I think. On a school night!

"Erm… let's see. What would my *lovely*, not that much older, newly affianced sister want to see…?" I didn't know any films that were showing at the time. Bryan jumped in, uninvited. Well, no, he *was* invited; it just felt like he'd gate-crashed something.

"A Room with a View?" was his frankly ludicrous suggestion.

"Oooh no, but I'd love to see that. I said to Joe: 'I'd love to see that,' didn't I Joe?" she said, as she tried to find a space on the table for her empty glass.

"Yes, so would I! Well done mate, good suggestion." I meant it.

"No, we saw Police Academy. It was rubbish. I said to Joe, I said, 'That was rubbish,' didn't I Joe? but it was either that or '*The Care Bears Movie*'."

"'*Care Bears Two, A New Generation*?'"

"Who cares!" chuckled Joe, "that was nearly sold out as well; there were hundreds of little brats running around, dressed as bears. What's wrong with people, why don't they just stay at home and watch videos, like everyone else?" he wondered. I got the impression that Joe didn't like kids very much.

We chatted a lot, the four of us. The songs they had selected earlier finally came on the jukebox. *"Shhh, I put this one on."* There were one or two that I remembered she used to play at home: Spandau *Bullet* (she always corrected me when I called them that), David Bowie... '*John, I'm only dancing*', stuff like that. I always wondered if she knew anyone called John, she played it so much.

Bryan remembered that someone he worked with had had a break-in at home, while he was working overtime. We all agreed, or three of us did, that it was a horrible thing and hoped whoever did it would be caught and beaten to death.

The other, no names, agreed that it was a horrible thing and she hoped that whoever did it could live with it on their conscience. She pronounced it more like 'cushions,' for the record.

It gave me an opportunity to relate another tale; one from my childhood and one that Suze, hopefully, could relate to. I was telling the story for her, really.

"When I was at junior school – the one Suze and I *both* went to – when I was about eight years old, I suppose, some of us kids were talking about what our dads did for a job. Most of them exaggerated, I think. I didn't believe that two of them could be astronauts, not in such a small town. And I thought you had to be American to be a spaceman. So, I didn't believe them. A couple said theirs were gunslingers and that seemed OK; one was a postman. Then one kid says, 'my dad is a burglar.' A few of us gathered round when we heard that and started pushing him, daring him to repeat it. This one boy asked him, 'What, like a *cat* burglar?' When he confirmed that this was, indeed, his father's speciality, everyone jumped on him and gave him a good beating. It seems a couple of them had had cats go missing lately. I didn't feel sorry for him though. He should have kept his mouth shut. He was a loser."

This didn't produce the same degree of laughter as the Declan pizza story earlier. It got a response from Suze, though:

"Does *ev'thing* always have to end badly in your world, lil' brother?"

Me and Bryan carried on drinking until closing time; Suze and Joe sneaked off before the end, when I was in the toilet. I *was* a bit upset when I found out they'd gone without saying '*Goodnight*,' I suppose.

"Have they gone?"

"Yes, Joe said he thought it was time they made a move. He had a bit of a struggle to get her standing upright, actually; she was in a right state! And you'll like this: before he got her out the door, she shouted over at Declan and called him a *big, fat, ugly bogtrotter*! Needless to say, he wasn't happy."

"Fucking hell, what did he do?"

"He growled at her and ordered another pint of Stella snakebite."

"Legend."

"I don't suppose we'll see Joe again tonight, probably gone to hers for a bit of *''ow's-yer-father.'*"

"Hey, c'mon! That's my new sister you're talking about. And my father's dead, thanks for asking."

"It hasn't always been... y'know, you and Suze. You don't have a normal brother-sister relationship, do you? Nothing that Cartland would recognise as such. And I'm not an expert by the way, being an only child and all that, but when it's family, you have to get on, don't you, isn't that how it works? Tonight, though... I don't remember ever seeing her so... willing."

"Fuck off! What do you mean, 'willing?'"

"Just what I said: willing. Willing to talk to *you*. It's not like her; she never has much to say to you, does she? Be honest with yourself, she's taciturn at best. Tonight, though, wow; momentous stuff! And pissed; I've never seen her *that* drunk."

Yes, it had been a momentous evening; he got that right.

From that day she became noticeably less hostile towards me whenever we were all together; almost like a proper sister and, although I didn't think I'd ever get to kiss her on the cheek again, it was obvious – to me, at least – that whatever had been festering in her mind had somehow sorted itself out. Like unblocking a drain, I suppose. Who knows how a woman's mind works, eh? Bryan had even noticed it, this improvement in her demeanour; he compared it to an iceberg melting as it shifted into the warmer, tropical waters of a mangrove swamp. I remember him using those very words. Later, I'd asked if he thought that the new, improved Suze would last, or did he think she had a switch that could be flicked on and off like the weather. He enjoyed questions like this; it appealed to his inner philosopher. No, he didn't think so, he admitted. He had given it some thought, he said, and was sure it was down to the fact Joe had popped the question. He thought that the giving of the ring might prove symbolic in some way:

"Did you ever consider, Wilf, that she's not looking backwards anymore? Maybe, just maybe, she has thrown off the shackles of the Human Condition, has overthrown the innate negativity of *Mrs. Homo Sapiens?* Maybe she's no longer looking over her shoulder, seeing *you* as a reminder of an unhappy past; maybe she's happy because she can now see the light at the end of the tunnel and a future that's both fulfilling and joyous, filled with the laughter of little, tiny feet. A future where she can start a family, a new family with Joe, a future without a past. Maybe she's thinking 'show me the past and I'll give you the future?' That's my theory, for what it's worth."

Jill shouted over from the bar "Time now, please! Hey, Bryan... do little, tiny feet laugh?" She could be pedantic, at times. Best ignored.

"But, if that's the case, why is she suddenly happy to have me back in her life Maybe she wants me in her future! How does that fit in with your theory?"

"Fuck knows; who knows how a woman's mind works, eh? But I'll tell you something: Change is happening, man. And you can quote me on that."

I smoothed my new moustache and thanked him for his input. I told him it was worth a lot. I also told him that shit was twopence a pound. But maybe there was something in what he said.

Joe left and moved in with Suze shortly after the momentous *Pretty in Pink* evening. Orla who, by then, had realised it could be quite cold in a garret, moved into Joe's old room, so she did. She also become quite friendly with Suze. And with me, some nights. That just left Bryan, still busy having a good time; too busy 'playing the field' to get involved. I wasn't quite clear what he meant by that. As far as I could see the field was empty.

# It's The Not Knowing

I never thought I would be happy. Not deep down – not *really* happy. I could put on a brave face and be superficially amenable when I had to – that goes without saying. I didn't think I was ever destined to live in a land of milk and honey. I always imagined that if I did ever get there, that would be the day I found out I was lactose intolerant, the day I was attacked by bees. I didn't have a moving-in date in my diary if you know what I mean. Some people thrive on happiness. Others are less happy being happy. It's a big responsibility. Some people actually draw inspiration from adversity and struggle with plain sailing. I think I was happy sitting on the fence, occupying the middle ground.

By the Autumn of 1989 things had moved on. Joe and Suze were still living together and very much engaged but had decided to delay starting a family. They were hoping to, at some stage but didn't feel the timing was right, not at the moment. Not with '*things as they were,*' without ever specifying what these things were or what the unacceptable state of these things might have looked like.

Bryan had been promoted at work and was now spending a lot of time travelling around, dressed up like a dog's dinner. He used to try and tell me what it involved, this new junior-management role, but I didn't really know what he was banging on about. A lot of it was just words, business jargon and management-speak. I suppose I didn't want to know; I wasn't particularly interested in that world of profit margins and bottom lines. Never have been.

"I had a look at myself, and I didn't like what I saw," he told me one day, in an unguarded, drunken moment. He was happy to report that he'd sorted himself out and '*gone straight.*' By that, I assumed he meant his becoming 'Mr. Normal in a suit.' The days when he was happy to describe himself as a philosopher, a rebel poet, and a bass player (in the now-defunct blues band *Mouldy Old Dough*) seemed suddenly to be dead and buried. They were working him too hard, that much was clear. He wasn't around as much as he used to be, that's a fact; even Reggie commented on it.

"Where's *yer* mate Bryan these days, bonny lad?" he asked me, in his broad Geordie. He said he didn't seem to "come in as much these days." Had we had a falling out? I was quick to disabuse him of this by explaining that Bryan had a new job but that he hadn't really told me what it involved.

As I was telling him this he walked off and started fiddling with his pumps. Rude bastard. He said, "ah yes, I think you told me, canny lad." I hadn't and he never asked again.

I still had my on-off relationship with Orla. It wasn't going anywhere, not in a Joe and Suze way, but it was nice to have someone, sometimes. I used to spend a lot of time on my own, by then. I seemed to have all the time in the world for sitting and thinking. If life was going to pass me by I preferred it to happen whilst I was in the great outdoors, in the park, waiting for opening time. The park was a sea of tranquillity on dry land, a place where a dispirited soul could unwind and escape the humdrum.

At the time I favoured one particular location: a well-appointed bench I'd found by accident one day, when I was out and about. It had an unobstructed view of the river, and

148

I often spent an undisturbed hour or so there, watching the flow of the glacial melt waters as they headed for the North Sea or the canal, I wasn't sure which.

One early Spring day I went up there to get some fresh air and do some reading. This book I'd just borrowed from the library had caused a bit of a storm, apparently. Some people were so offended by it that they had decided they would have to kill the author. That's no way to go on, is it? Live and let live, I always say. But, as a yarn, it was fairly hard going, I'd have to say. I used to read a lot when I was younger: Dick Francis, mainly. This one was a bit highbrow for my tastes then. Not now, obviously. I could read it now and make sense of it, I'm sure. If I wanted to. On that day, it seemed altogether meaningless, and I'd had enough. It was turning quite chilly as well, so I headed off.

That was when I witnessed something which has stuck in my memory. On its own and taken out of context, even in this world of pain, misery, and horror, it might seem quite insignificant. The incident was still with me, days later and I couldn't shake it. I mentioned it to Orla; she was a good listener. I knew she was interested in dreams, their meanings and all that witchcraft *hokum* but I was quick to stress that it wasn't a dream; it was real, and I needed to share. I thought it might help to erase the memory.

"Some people had climbed up on the statue; one was *actually* sitting on her head..."

She warned me that she'd heard the park was now full of drunks and junkies.

"Yes, I know that – don't worry, I can look after myself. I avoid other people anyway, usually. Do you know—"

"Yes! Whenever you see people, your first instinct is always that they are 'just enemies you haven't met yet.'"

"That's right. Does that make sense? I always feel they represent a threat until I know otherwise. Call it a survival instinct if you like. Kill or be killed."

"Hmm… but maybe they could be friends you haven't met yet?"

"Ah! You just said they were drunks and junkies!"

She had no answer to that. I'd won.

"So you saw some people climbing on a statue…"

"Yes. There were five of them up there, larking about and then one of them climbed down and ran off."

"Well, that's one for the memoirs!"

"Maybe it is, smart arse, because a minute or so later one of them slipped and fell!"

"Oh, ouch! Were they alright?"

"I wouldn't have thought so. They landed headfirst on the concrete. I could hear the crack from where I was."

"Oh Jesus! What happened?"

"I don't know. One of them started screaming, which struck me as odd; it's not what you'd expect from a bloke. It must have sobered them up, though, because the three of them jumped down pretty quick. I didn't see what happened after that 'cos I walked off in the other direction."

"Didn't you think to go and help?"

"What could I have done? A few nosey bastards went running past, going to have a look. The ambulance chasers got there before the ambulance."

"You're unbelievable, so you are!"

"Thanks, that's very kind of you to say. I thought I heard an ambulance siren later but that might have been unrelated. It sounds like a non-event, but it's stayed with me, y'know?"

In all the excitement, I'd left my library book behind. I suppose they'll try and fine me. I didn't mention that bit to Orla though; I could see she was already quite unsettled.

## Berlin and All That

In early November of that year there was a coming together of circumstances which may, one day, be referred to by the historians as 'unprecedented.' I remember it well. I'd spent the late afternoon in the bookmakers, following the fortunes of a few of my investments. I probably just about broke even, I would say. After the last race brought bad news, I thought I'd pop into the 'Reck and see if anyone was about. I pulled open the front door and was hit by three things simultaneously: the *eternal* fug of the early evening, the *Eternal Flaming* Bangles on the jukebox and wet-fish Bryan Grimes slumped in a corner, tie askew, suit jacket in a heap and giving off negative vibes.

"What you doing in here, you tosser?" I enquired, cheerily.

"Fuck you! Why shouldn't I be? What's it got to do with you anyway?" He challenged me with a bleary and malevolent eye. I could tell he'd been drinking.

"Fair enough. D'you finish early or did you have the afternoon off?" I asked, making the two-tips-of-the-hand 'wanna pint?' signal.

"Nope. Got the rest of my life off. This day, next day, the day after… every fucking day…"

"Whaddya mean?" This didn't sound good. I aborted the signal, mid-tip.

It wasn't good. Not for him. Following a review those tossers had decided that he was 'surplus to requirements,' apparently. There was to be a company-wide restructure, they said. With immediate effect.

"What the fuck is a company-wide restructure when it's at fucking home?" I could see he was distraught, and I looked for a way of putting a positive spin on it.

"Well, on the plus side, you won't have to be a 'twat in a suit' anymore." It was poor effort; I knew as soon as I said it. I went and got a couple of pints.

There was a young professional at the bar talking about Berlin, something about a wall. My first instinct was: "So they've got a wall in Berlin, have they?" I could tell by his polished brogues he was a young professional. He'd just heard something on the news. He and *Mein Host* agreed it was hugely significant. Reggie told him his dad had been in Berlin at the end of the war, but it was 'hush-hush.' The young professional feigned amazement before he left. In fact, he said, "Wow, that's amazing." Doesn't take much to amaze a young professional, does it! After Reggie got back to pulling two pints, rather than gossiping with a young ponce, he said, "That's a shame about yer mate Bryan, eh? It's never nice when that happens, believe me – I know, bonny lad. You're too young to remember the Jarrow March, I suppose?"

"And so are you," I thought. I hoped he might say: "These are on the house, bonny lad." but he didn't. They never do.

When Bryan got his job (or his *ex-job* if you prefer), he became a different animal. It happened very suddenly; his whole world changed in twenty-four hours. One day he was one of us, a prole who liked a pint and wrote melancholic poems in his lunchbreak. A typical working class, salt-of-the-earth nobody; a loser like the rest of us. Joe was the same, a happy-go-lucky loser with a fiancée, but the right kind of loser. We were mates, all of us: two losers and me. The Three *Mousquetaires* of the Apocalypse – that's what Joe called us. But when Bryan got this job… it changed things. I suppose I probably resented him; I don't know why. Maybe he represented a seismic shift in this splendid and carefree existence, this irresponsible post-youth lived entirely for pleasure, towards a bleak new world of gravitas and responsibility, of being *accountable*. Imagine being accountable! I hated the sound of that, I would never be like that and I'm sure, looking back, I did take against him to a certain extent. He wanted to change, to become everything we had always despised. A twat in a twat's suit with matching tie and shoes. A twat's shoes. And a Filofax; yes, he had one of those, of course he did! So, yes: he was a changed man, very much so. He'd been a friend, but he'd slept with the enemy. And yet, the night is always darkest just before the dawn; the sun was up, and he was back. Good old Bryan.

Another couple of pints and he was something like his old self, waxing lyrical on what the future might hold for a man of vision and destiny like him. He could see great things coming his way, the world was his oyster. He was so drunk he even suggested we could "get the band back together, man... Joe can bring Suze, get her involved, what does she play, the harpsichord? Yes, she could play blues harpsichord in *Mouldy Old Dough*!" Then he seemed to realise something that had not occurred to either of us: he could also just go down the Jobcentre and get another job. A better one, better money than those tight bastards were paying. He wasn't going to lie down and take it like a man: no, he was going to stand up and fight like the Suffragettes did, for his right to work! There was no stopping him now. It's always alarming when they go off the rails like that.

Joe and Suze appeared later on. Over the past few months, they had firmly established themselves as a joined-at-the-hip, lovey-dovey couple; his arm was almost permanently glued to her shoulders. Maybe he didn't realise she wouldn't go anywhere or run off, not now she had that ring on her finger. It was nice to see them, of course. And they were obviously upset to hear Bryan's news. Bryan wasn't – by this stage nothing could upset him, he was desensitised.

"Hey, did you hear what's happening in Berlin?" asked Joe who, realising his arm had slipped from Suze's shoulders, was quick to put it back.

"They've built a wall or something," I said, showing I could hold my own when discussing current affairs.

"It seems they've opened the gates and people have started the chip away the concrete with hammers and drills and stuff!"

"I heard some sections had been pulled right down and people were flooding into the West side... the Commie guards just stood and watched, apparently!" This snippet came from full-time eavesdropper and part-time barmaid Jill, who was shouting from the bar. I realised that my grasp of the situation was perhaps not as rounded or as well-informed as I had supposed. I wasn't bothered. They could do what they liked in their own country, with their own wall.

"That's so beautiful, so very, very beautiful... what a truly momentous day," said Suze. Bryan and I both agreed with the summing up and praised her erudition. Joe looked on proudly. I thought he might have been about to pat her on the head when she turned and gave him a truly momentous kiss, and not just a peck on the cheek, either; it was one of those long, lingering ones that, to the casual observer, seem to go on forever. The news had clearly affected her deeply; she looked very, very emotional when she resurfaced.

Some churl shouted, "Get a room!" Joe laughed but Suze ignored it; she was about to speak.

"It gives me real hope for the future, you know. Change is happening. Not just for me and Joe but for all of us – don't you agree? It's a sign of better things to come..." Her voice tailed off and she became a little tearful, so much so that she had to fan her face, smiling self-consciously as her eyes glistened and began to leak onto her cheeks. Joe was quick off the mark and pulled her even closer, offering a shoulder to cry on, proving Neil Young's point: a maid does *indeed* need a man. She said she was OK and sniffed. If it's possible to sniff with joy, that's what she did. We were in full agreement, one of us proclaiming, "absolutely; it's a landmark event and no mistake!" I added a sincere, "Well done, Fritz!" with Joe fussing and Bryan smiling blankly.

"Hope for the future... that would be nice, for those who've got a future," moaned Bryan in hollow, self-pitying tones. He was now back at the feeling sorry for himself stage. Best ignored.

A little while later Orla made an appearance; she had been following the unfolding events over in Berlin on the radio. She had reacted in much the same way as Suze, apparently, and wanted to come out and share the joy, bathe in the warmth, and celebrate in spirit with the German people released from their chains. She was feeling, she said, a sense of hope reborn and repeated Suze's wistful "Change is happening, so it is." Joe released her briefly so the two women could hug. I wasn't sure whether Orla was my girlfriend or not this week, so I didn't know whether I should move round and sit next to her. As that would have meant dislodging Bryan, anyway, I stayed where I was but was ready to make a strategic move if and when necessary. It's so difficult to read the signals, sometimes. I've been around and I still don't know what I'm talking about.

# It's The Not Knowing

We stayed until closing time (except Bryan, who disappeared somewhere along the way; he went to the toilet and didn't return). A search party drew a blank and concluded he must have sneaked out unseen. The four of us that were left decided to go for a Thursday night curry to celebrate the great events of the day, Bryan's redundancy notwithstanding.

As we stepped out into the street, I noticed a dayglo T-shirt glowing up ahead; it was Declan looking quite paternal with his arm clamped tightly around a pizza delivery boy's neck. This was indeed a strange and wonderous day to be alive. Suze was buttoning up her denim jacket as Joe drew alongside and put his arm back around her slender shoulders. Orla was zipping up her black leather jacket, so I drew alongside and put my arm around *hers* and she didn't even flinch! We walked along chatting and laughing, taking our time, heading for the parade and Giovani's Curry House, the home of exotic fusion cuisine. I have no doubt we were happy at that moment, strolling along like couples do. My arm began to ache, so we opted for linking. Joe's obviously didn't; he'd had more practice. I wished I could have frozen time just there; it was all so perfect, so idyllic. I wasn't lactose intolerant, and the bees were fast asleep in bed. If I'd heard of Nirvana at the time, that's how I would have described it. Life, the enormous ordeal of living, was somehow suddenly bearable.

A light drizzle danced beneath the streetlights, washing clean the pavements, and releasing the earthy, fungal scent of nature. The beautiful yellow builders' lights were flashing hypnotically on the excellently fabulous, load-bearing scaffolding. It was surprising that they hadn't been stolen by irresponsible japesters or thoughtless ne'er-do-wells, or so Joe and Suze said. I couldn't resist trying to get one, though. It would make a nice present for Orla, I thought; a flashing, yellow light, a token of my growing affection, maybe even a moving-in present!

"I'll catch you up in a minute," I said, unlinking arms and going back, setting about the clamp, trying to loosen the bolts.

It was quite tricky; the bolts were securely fastened and that's why I wasn't there with them, underneath the scaffolding, when Declan fell into the road, when the truck swerved to avoid him, when the driver lost control, skidded, and smashed into the wall, when the scaffolding was toppled and when the brickwork crashed to earth with its murderous, thunderous roar.

I wasn't there when the wall came down.

# PART FOUR. 2005

## Births and Deaths

August 13<sup>th</sup>.

"There she is! There's the birthday girl! Many happy returns, lovely lady; may there be many, many more!"

Sue Stilton smiled and offered her cheek as Barney approached to give her a hug and a peck which turned into a big slobbering kiss.

"Put her down, man! What you having – the usual?" said John, laughing as he got up and slapped his old mate on the back.

"No, these are on me, I insist." Barney was beaming and hopping from left foot to right foot, like a child about to receive a big present and looking very excited at the prospect.

"OK, same again then for me and… Sue? Another one of those? And why are you looking so pleased with yourself… have your numbers come up on the lottery, or what?"

"Sort of, yes…" he hopped.

"Oooh!" said Sue, "*that* sounds mysterious!"

"When I come back, dear friends, *all* will be revealed." Barney winked and dropped the old notebook on the table.

This was a rare night out together for John and Sue; it didn't happen very often, these days. John and Barney of course had regular boys' nights out, but Sue was still more of a conservatory drinker and rarely went with them. In fact, she rarely went out. Nobody could deny her all-round allure or her charisma – with one or two tweaks she could have been the alpha female in most groups – but as she didn't have what you might call a close friend or 'bestie' her social life was limited.

Tonight, though, things were different: it was her forty-first birthday. It was *her* day, and she wanted a change of scenery.

Things in the Stilton house had taken a turn for the better since that day when John had asked the insensitive question and started to teach himself Russian. It felt like the air had been cleared, somehow. They were back on an even keel and clearly she bore no grudge against Barney.

"Here we are, then: a large glass of red for the birthday girl and two pints of freshly dispensed Skol Special Strength. Cheers Sue, here's to you!" Glasses were clinked, as dictated by tradition, then there were general enquiries about presents, had he bought her anything nice, why weren't they in a swanky restaurant, why hadn't he taken his gorgeous wife away for a long weekend and how come she'd stayed with him when Barney had been available all along?

"Aw, Barney! If only I'd known!" she flirted, flashing her beautiful eyes with a winning smile thrown in. The bonhomie was genuine and unrehearsed but it was obvious there was something else he was dying to say. He looked too excited by half.

"So, go on then, tell us about your big lottery win *pleee-eease*. We're dying to know!"

There was what you might call a 'bloody great big smile' on his face, stretching from ear to ear.

"Well…" he said, having taken a test sip and composed himself, "you know all that business with Google and the logo?"

"What, the theft of artistic and intellectual property, yes. You've told us all that… so, is *that* it?"

"No, there's more… I got a phone call this morning. It was a bit early and I thought it'd be one of those nuisance calls, the old routine, have you been involved in an accident, blah blah, but no… It was my solicitor asking me to pop into their offices… you ready for this?

Barney smiled again and leaned back in the chair. He was positively beaming. After a dramatic pause he let rip. "They've only gone and admitted they stole the design from Goggle Boxes!"

"Google? You're kidding! Really? No way!"

"Yes way! Their lawyers basically told them they didn't have a corporate leg to stand on and advised them to settle out of court!"

"Bloody hell! They must have been really scared, then!"

"Shitting themselves, more like," suggested Sue, who wasn't a swearer by nature.

"And that's not the best bit! It gets better! I thought we might be looking at a couple of grand, something like that... you ready for this?"

You could hear a pin drop as Barney consummately built the tension before the big reveal.

"*How* much? Say that again... ten million quid? Ten *million*? Ten. Million. Fucking. Quid? Jesus Christ!" said Sue, who was now definitely a swearer by nature.

John was shellshocked and couldn't say anything. He couldn't even swear.

"I know! They had to pick me up off the floor after they told me; I collapsed with the shock!"

"I bet you fucking did, no fucking wonder!" said guess who, knocking back her Merlot.

"So, now you're in the know and I'm in the money! C'mon, drink up, let's get a bottle of champers and celebrate in style! My oldest mate, one lucky bastard and my oldest mate's beautiful, gorgeous wife on her special day."

The evening, naturally, centred not so much on Sue but on Barney and what this unexpected windfall might mean for him personally and for his company. It would mean, he said, that he could afford to travel and see a bit of the world; he'd like to go back to the Far East, Thailand, and what-have-you. He was going to sell the business Goggle Boxes as a just-about-going concern and retire from the rat race. Things were certainly looking up for Barney Chimes, the self-made overnight millionaire. They weren't to worry, he insisted. He would 'see them right.'

"Do you remember, we worked out once how much money we'd spent in here over the years?"

"I do indeed!"

"And it seemed like a hell of a lot, didn't it, at the time?"

"Just a bit. It *was* – it *is* – a hell of a lot!"

"Well, y'know... now it seems like peanuts suddenly, loose change."

"Blimey, listen to moneybags!"

They had a most enjoyable evening. In fact, it was a *fabulous* evening, a celebration of a birthday and, more importantly, sudden unimaginable wealth, all funded by Barney. "Put your money away! What's the point of all this money if I can't buy my two best friends a drink?" He was most insistent. Naturally, Google Inc. was toasted as the *generous benefactor* at every turn. Sue was philosophical, and mused: "it just shows, doesn't it, these big multi-million-billion corporation tax-dodge *whatevers*, they think they can do what they like... well they can't. You showed 'em! I said to John, didn't I John, I said, 'they think they can do what they like, and they can't.' Didn't I, John?"

In all that time, amidst the excited chatter of no-expense-spared holidays, flashy cars, buying a racehorse etc, the notebook had gone unmentioned. When the conversation finally lulled Sue picked it up (at the second attempt) from the table. She flicked through the pages, smiling wistfully as she recognised once more the distinctive left-leaning script.

"I thought the ending was grim, killing them all off like that," said the man with the new money.

"Not all of them. You survived, and so did he."

"Yes, that's true. I wonder why I was spared?"

"I told you; Wilf was in awe of you."

"In the other story, maybe but this was different, surely."

"I'm not sure it was. It's like he'd taken the same characters – same names – and put them somewhere else in another time."

"Yes, but the… what's the word… the dynamic between the characters was completely different. Joe even got to kiss Suze or Sue in this one."

"Hang on, who did what, when?" said Sue, sitting up.

"Read the story!" they chorused.

"I'll concede that the dynamic seems different on the surface but he's still the same, underneath. He makes out he's a more likeable and rounded individual but there are still gaps in the fence where his true self comes out –"

" And what is his *true* self, according to you?"

"He's a miserable, paranoid bastard. He's hiding something, too."

"Yes, that sounds like my brother," said Sue, dropping the notebook back on the table.

It's The Not Knowing

The morning after the night before was notable for two reasons. The first was that Sue had a terrible hangover. The toxic '*never-again*' cocktail of red wine and champagne (punctuated with a few G&Ts), which had flowed like melt waters into a storm drain, was now wreaking havoc in the frontal lobe with skirmishes reported at the backs of both eyes. She was not at her best. If she'd had any idea what day it was she might have said: "Thank God it's Sunday." She didn't and instead emerged from the duvet and groaned, "Where am I?"

The second notable event was the phone call telling her that her mum had died suddenly in the night.

The Stiltons' kitchen was the kind of place where a large clock might be displayed prominently as a real statement piece. A big, old-fashioned, showy timepiece with Roman numerals; one which might have spent its heyday in a cold, cheerless waiting room on a branch line. Equally, it might have been a reproduction made in Hong Kong. It suited the room perfectly, though and evoked a sense of time frozen at a point in someone else's life. As did the enamelled *Lifeboy* Soap sign on show above the microwave, weathered artificially in a workshop and picked up at a car boot sale in the mid-nineties, the missing '*u*' going unnoticed. The relentless tick of the clock mechanism was the only sound to be heard in the house; everywhere was gripped by the oppressive silence of a grey Sunday on the Cheeses Estate.

Sue was slumped over the kitchen table with her head in her hands, a cup of instant cold coffee and a box of Kleenex Man-Size for company. It was sudden and painless; Sheila the neighbour had gone to borrow some full-fat milk to go with her porridge (*and* some porridge), but there was no answer. She had a key for emergencies, and that's how she was able to get in. She was lying in bed and must have died in her sleep. 'It's how we'd all like to go,' she supposed. It was Sheila who had phoned the doctor, and formally identified the body. It was the least she could do, she said.

Trying to recall, despite the throbbing headache, the last time she'd actually seen her mum, things were a little hazy. How did she look when she left, that time? She'd only ever been up there once to see her… just once! Was she smiling? It would be nice to think of her smiling! Was she happy? Was she *ever* happy! William wasn't there, of course. She'd held onto her arm, despite her protests, as they'd gone for a walk along the seafront. She could recall that she'd been her normal self that day: childish and sullen. She was by nature moody and unresponsive. That was her default setting so it wasn't totally unexpected… no, surely that couldn't be the very last sighting? That would be such a miserable, unforgiveable thing to have as a lasting memory. The mist lifted briefly and yes – she could now picture her: she was laughing, down by the public toilets in the harbour. But it wasn't a nice thing she was laughing at; it was mean, and she'd told her so. Poor little mite, slipping and skidding like that. People should clean up their dog mess! Was that *really* the last time she'd heard her laughing? It can't have been, surely… She thought it was. A cruel, vindictive belly laugh at someone else's expense. "Oh Irene, why were you like that?"

The memories came rushing in; she was powerless to resist the tide. Wave upon wave broke through, flooding the memory banks of an otherwise dehydrated brain. Random threads from the tapestry of life floated past: images of childhood, places and colours, and smells but not her voice; she couldn't hear her voice now. The face was there, but fading in and out, breaking up like an old black and white picture on the telly. Then the laugh resurfaced; that hollow, mocking cackle as the poor little girl slipped and got the dog shit in her hair and her mouth, with the hysterical young mother's frantic and futile attempts to clean up the mess.

She was cold, she had butterflies in her stomach. Now she managed to fix it in her mind: her mother's face, no longer fading in and out, wrapped in a grey silk headscarf but cold and expressionless. '*Yes, there she is*!' Then, the memories changed; they became happier and full of life, memories of good times. She was thinking about her father; she could see him now, coming home from work, smiling, bringing a present for her – not for William, just her, his little Princess, daddy's favourite.

John had gone for a walk to clear his head. Her reaction to the call, to say the least, had been restrained; he had expected there to be more in the way of tears, but she had been rather stoic. This puzzled him. He'd offered to drive and said they could be ready to go in ten minutes; they could be there by mid-afternoon. She'd shaken her head and said there was no point; it's not like they could bring her back to life, was it? What she actually said was, "Lazarus is really dead." He sensed that she might prefer to be left alone for a while. Then it struck him. She was the last one standing.

# It's The Not Knowing

She would have to go up there eventually and would have to deal with the formalities. There was no-one else who could do it. It might be tomorrow or the day after – that wasn't a problem, it was her decision. She only had to say the word and he would drop everything, take her to see the old bat and say her goodbyes whenever she wanted. He came to the end of Gorgonzola Close and, as he turned into Dairylea Way, he thought he'd go for a pint, a hair of the dog.

As he pushed open the front door of The Cracker Barrel he heard the opening chords of *Hotel California* striking up. It seemed like he'd heard this song on every jukebox in every pub he'd ever been to, a point he was still musing on when Siobhan the buxom barmaid asked him what it was to be. He ordered a pint of *Skol Lite* and a bag of vegan-friendly pork scratchings made from salted bark chippings.

He took a seat by the window and began to consider the fact that Sue now had no other extant blood family. Parents both gone, only brother probably dead, certainly missing and no other living relatives on that side of the family. She had told him once that the fact that she had never had an aunt or uncle was a personal tragedy, a connection she had craved but had been denied. He wondered about the enormity of that. Whether being the very last one in a line which must surely have stretched back to a caveman, a cavewoman and a torchlit dinner for two was an overwhelming responsibility? Did it carry some kind of stigma, a suggestion of sterility or weakness or just plain fecklessness? Would it have made a difference if they'd had kids, him and Sue? Would that have done the trick, put the ball in the next generation's court? Probably, although here he began to doubt his line of thinking. Did the woman actually contribute to the bloodline? Surely it had been diluted and dispersed from almost the very beginning by daughters who had gone a-laying and a-fornicating, who had been renamed and redeployed by marriage and who were therefore lost and untraceable. Their offspring couldn't, he reasoned, be counted as part of one single unbroken pedigree; they belonged to another ancestry, they were someone else's responsibility.

He had once briefly dipped his toes into the murky waters of Family History, using the computer in the library. He soon realised what a nightmare it could be, trying to trace earlier generations. It wasn't like in the history books he wrote, the royal stuff; that was already done and drawn up. Not for the commoners, though. Those plebs living before records began might as well have never existed as far as the genealogist was concerned and yet – oh the irony – they probably did! He was left with no choice but to conclude that it wasn't feasible or even desirable to include females when tracing the bloodline. And, what's more, if you wanted to include the cavemen's ancestors – the monkeys etc – then you were straying into treacherous and uncharted territory. He took a thoughtful swig of the tasteless beer and wondered whether a monkey had ever been married in church. At this point, having no way of knowing, he decided to call it a day.

He had a horrible, sinking feeling when he saw the Police car outside the house. His instinctive reaction was "Oh, Christ! has someone died?" before remembering that someone had. He rushed forward and opened the front door, where he received a *shock-of-his-life*: from the hallway he could hear a man laughing and Sue's voice saying "No, please don't!" What the hell was going on?

He threw open the door, not really prepared for the scene that met his incredulous gaze. The copper wedged in John's favourite chair holding his sides, convulsed with mirth; the WPC perched on the sofa next to the bereaved bent double and so beside herself she couldn't speak, and Sue pleading with them to stop. Sue, his wife, the woman with tears streaming down her cheeks as she too fought back the giggles, trying unsuccessfully to dry her eyes.

"And it went in her mouth, you say?" boomed the copper.

"Yes! And all in her hair!"

He roared again, with laughter as John's jaw gaped.

"That's a brilliant story!" said the WPC, "and such a lovely memory to have!"

They all exhaled, and there was a moment's silence before the giggles started again, sporadically.

"Hi Honey, I'm home!" said John, irked at being ignored.

The copper stood up and looked at Sue, willing her to make the introductions.

"John, this is John, my husband."

"Another John!" said John the copper. Why had she introduced *him* to him? It was his house, why didn't she introduce him to *him*? A subtle nuance but one which was not lost on him.

"We're sorry for your wife's loss, sir," said the WPC, casually putting down her G&T and rising to offer her hand. John the homeowner took the hand although he was now incensed.

"And *you* are?"

"You're not going to believe this…" she said, "I'm a Sue, too!"

The three of them exploded with delight. "What are the chances!" they said, in unholy union.

The Police officers went shortly afterwards. They said they had one more 'bereavement gig' after which they would have to go back to the station and do the paperwork.

"Bore-ring!" said WPC Sue, making a mock yawn gesture and grinning.

"Well. thanks ever so much for coming round and letting me know about y'know. We'll go up there soon and do whatever we have to do."

John couldn't wait to show them out. When he returned he looked at Sue with amazement.

"What?"

"Unbelievable!"

"What's unbelievable?"

"That woman… copper! Do you know what she said just now when we were out in the hall?"

Sue shook her head.

"Well, after she told me to take good care of you because you were fragile!—"

# It's The Not Knowing

"Fragile?"

"Yes, and that's not the best bit; wait 'til you hear this! She thrust out her hips, licked her lips and winked at me!"

"No! Really? God... that's weird. I liked her, though. She was funny."

"Funny? What's happened to you? When I left you were sad and morose – understandable in the circumstances, of course – but when I come back, you're rolling around, laughing, and joking with two members of the constabulary! I mean... what?"

"Yeah, I know... Maybe life's too short for sorrow, John. I realised something earlier. I realised that it's finished..."

"What is?"

"There's no-one left. Now that she's gone... that just leaves me. It's an overwhelming sense of failure I suppose..."

"What? No, it's not a –"

"...because it's *me* that's failed, y'know? The Skaife family blood line will be, actually, *is* no more! Do you know what I mean? All those generations struggled through and it's me that's dropped the baton..."

John was trying to dislodge a piece of bark chipping from between his molars. "Hey, you're not thinking about a monkey getting married in church, are you?"

"Every day..."

"Well, you're wrong; I was thinking about this. It's down to the male to continue the bloodline, so–"

"There's something else too: d'you know, when it boils down to it, she's gone and I'm not feeling sad like I suppose I should…"

"You're in shock. It's only natural."

"…d'you know, it sounds horrible but I'm not sure I ever loved her. I didn't even like her at the end. I came to realise she had it in her to be a truly nasty and horrible person; even when we were kids I don't think we had a real connection, me and her. With my dad I did, yes – I loved my dad, I was his Princess – but there was nothing with my mother. She was cold. I can't even remember her face now – do y'know that? It's faded away. I try and picture what she looked like, but I can't–"

Sue caught her breath. The lip started to tremble as her face crumpled. There were tears, briefly. She sniffed, took a deep breath, and resumed.

"It's the same with William; I can't get a picture of him anymore. They were so alike in lots of ways… did he think he was her favourite? I don't know if he did but I'm sure I wasn't. In fact, she always said she didn't have a favourite; she used to say she didn't like either of us!" She burst into a laugh, which sounded more like a cough.

"I didn't know she had a sense of humour."

"No, she didn't."

The house descended into silence again, shrouded by the funereal vibe of the early morning. The ticking of the clock took over and could be heard throughout. The jovial atmosphere had evaporated now that the coppers had gone (not a phrase you hear every day). They were sitting in the lounge. John had reclaimed his favourite chair, after making extravagant brushing motions to remove the indentations and imagined dandruff left by the previous and unwelcome occupant. He started thinking about his own mother; remembering what a wonderful woman she was, and *still is* – a woman who would do anything for anyone, generous to a fault, selfless and always seeing the best in people. The polar opposite of Irene, it seemed. Both his parents were still alive and very actively involved in voluntary work at a medical facility in Africa. Both were in their late sixties now but showed no inclination towards slowing down or packing it all in. He was proud of his parents.

Sue was looking out of the window, watching a couple of woodpigeons in the garden pecking relentlessly at God knows what. What do they eat? They always reminded her of one of the Thunderbird rockets; the big, fat, green one. Number 2. She surveyed the sorry show of geraniums in their pots, dashed to smithereens by the torrential downpour of a few days ago. Not enough rain to lift the hosepipe ban, though. Suddenly, something panicked the woodies and they launched themselves like a couple of airborne pigs. One flew straight into the patio door and broke its neck. It flapped for a few seconds, then no more. "Everything's dying," she thought, her senses numbed.

"John, if you don't mind I want to go up there on my own tomorrow."

"On your own? Why? Don't you want me there for support? There'll be all the stuff to arrange... do you even know how to get there? I mean, have you ever even been there?"

"Yes, just the once. I should maybe have made more effort but no, it's OK. I can do all that. I think I'd like to just… have some time, I suppose. On my own. Do you understand? You don't need to be there, honestly."

"You're mad! Are you sure?"

"Of course. I'll be OK. I'll take your car though; mine's out of petrol."

"OK, if that's what you want, but the offer stands…"

"Thanks. You didn't like her, did you."

"I did! How can you say that? Of course I did!"

"You don't have to pretend. I know you didn't. She didn't like you, either."

"What do you mean?"

"Just that; the first time you ever came to the house. She took an instant dislike to you. She said you were vapid!"

"Vapid? What did she mean by that? I'd only just met her; how could she hope to know how vapid I was after one meeting? I could have been vapid beyond her wildest dreams, for all *she* knew! I hope you stuck up for me!"

"Naturally. I said vapid was something men could often grow out of."

"Sometimes, I don't know if you're joking."

"You weren't the only one. She didn't like any of my friends. You were the first one I thought she might actually grow to despise, though!"

He mulled things over for a while. It's true, he hadn't liked her mother at all. There wasn't much to like. She was mean and petty, a spiteful woman and a miserable shrew if he was any judge of character. Ratty little eyes, cruel thin lips. But what could she have found so unlikeable about him? He was house-trained, friendly and could be charming. He loved her daughter very much, looked after her, cherished her and all that. Fucking old bitch, he was glad she was dead!

"I'd like to read William's stories. I think I should now, don't you?"

"...*glad she's dead!* What? Oh, yes. Yes! I always said you ought to read them. You're the last one left; you said so yourself, so if there's anything in there like hidden meanings, secret family stuff..."

"Secret family stuff? There's nothing secret about the Skaifes! Where's the one Bryan had, anyway? I couldn't find it. It was on the table in the pub the last time I saw it. You *did* remember to pick it up when we left, didn't you?"

"Of course... I remember picking it up. I'm sure I did... Yes, I did. Definitely."

"Well, it's not in the hall or the kitchen so, what did you do with it?"

"Tell you what, I'll phone the pub, see if it's there."

He rang 118 118 to get the number, despite his deep loathing of the Dutch porn star adverts. Then he rang the pub and asked if they'd found a little black notebook which his wife had left on the table near the quiz machine.

"Can you describe it, this little black notebook?"

"Well… it's not exactly little but it's not that big either… it's a notebook, you know the kind of thing."

"And what colour is it?"

"Black, obviously!"

"Hang on."

There was a rattle as the receiver was placed on the bar. He could hear music playing in the background: *'you can check out any time you like, but you can never leave, wah wah wah wah waaaah…'* then the voice calling "Jill! Have you found a little black notebook?" then, a few seconds later: "Black, obviously!" then, a rattle as the handset was picked up. "No, sorry. Found a black glove, if that's of any use?"

"Put it on the slate," said John, hanging up.

## Missing Believed Lost

It was late afternoon when he left the house. He was going to retrace their steps back to The Ritz to look for the book. A thorough check at home had failed to unearth it so he was now exploring the possibility that it might have been lost somewhere along the way.

# It's The Not Knowing

The irony of the situation did not escape him: the very day Sue had finally agreed she should read the stories, one of them goes missing. And who would get the blame? John Stilton, that's who!

Putting one of his best feet forward, he headed back down Primula Grove, scanning the ground, peering hopefully over garden walls, and poking around in hedges but there was no sign of it. It was the same in Rue de Boursin and Philadelphia Way, where he was set upon by a small, pointless dog called Gemma, urged on by a suspicious owner who was otherwise engaged in hosing down a second-hand Volvo, nice little runner. After jogging away at high speed for a while he reached the car park of The Ritz public house, out of breath and out of luck. He hadn't been hopeful in the first place and now it was clear Áine's bequest, the last written words (in English, at least) of the late William B. Skaife, was almost certainly lost forever.

He was about to abandon hope and was already putting together a few ideas for his defence when he spotted something small and black nestling in the hedge near the gate: a little black notebook. His spirits rocketed skywards. "Oh thankyou Lord!" he said, as he reached in among the discarded McDonald's-branded litter and retrieved the book, the property of... Doris *shitting* Hedgehopper! Fucksake! *Amateur ornithologist, if found please return to… small reward offered...*

A foul-mouthed rant towards the heavens was quickly followed by a period of incandescent rage during the course of which he repurposed the book into several pieces or tatters. These he then hatefully discarded (in the manner of a frisbee) back over the hedge into the car park.

He knew he was beaten. With his chest heaving from the exertion of spine ripping, he considered his two options. Should he go in for a pint and rehearse his apology? Should he just go straight home and face the music? He'd come out without his wallet, so the decision was made for him. Not that he should have gone in the pub, anyway. Not now that Sue was on the *Fragile* list and needed constant supervision. As he made his way home, head down and beaten, he was approached by an elderly lady called Doris Hedgehopper who enquired whether he had, by any chance, seen a little black notebook?

---

"Sorry Sue, no sign of it."

"Did you go all the way back to the Ritz?"

"Yes, I went all the way back to the Ritz."

"And you couldn't find it?"

"No, I thought we'd already covered that point. Got chased by a mutt, though."

She made a dismissive *hmm* noise.

"Sums it up, really. William vanished and now his book's vanished… mum's gone and so has Bryan's wallet," she said distractedly.

"His wallet?"

"Yes. He phoned earlier… he thought we might have picked it up. I told him we hadn't. I told him about mum."

"Was he upset?"

"Well, he offered condolences…"

"No, about his wallet?"

"Yes, of course he was. You know what this means, don't you? You'll have to translate the other one now so I can read it. There's still the first one as well, isn't there, somewhere, hidden away? Unless you've lost that one as well. And get rid of Thunderbird 2 on the patio, would you?"

# PART FIVE. 2005

## Skagness

August 15th.

It was the kind of hour often labelled 'ungodly.' The skies were threatening rain and the wind was picking up as John Stilton handed over the keys to his car. A nice little runner, the G-reg Rover 214 featured a neutral beige finish to the outside with plastic-rosewood panels and faulty electrics to the inside. It was parked directly outside number twenty-three Lymeswold Drive in the spot John had always regarded as his own and over which he had become obsessively territorial. Sue tutted as she slid the seat forward into the correct position before adjusting the mirrors so that they were fit for purpose. With a grudging promise to watch out for speed cameras (a pledge which, as a self-confessed 'extremely good driver' she considered superfluous), she revved the engine a couple of times as John hovered like an anxious parent or guardian. Finally ready, she flashed him a pained smile with a cheerless wave and set off for Lincolnshire.

She hoped to make it there and back in one day, despite John's sharp intake of breath, shake of his wise old head and discouraging *"big ask!"* She had packed a change of underwear, just in case and had also slipped William's 1977 story into her case as something to read if she *did* end up having to stay over in the wastelands of the East Coast.

It's The Not Knowing

She joined the A1 at Edgware and went straight into autopilot, leaving her free to reflect on the events of the weekend, her birthday and her mother's passing. It seemed a long time ago now, much more than twenty-four hours – the late summer day which had seen her seamlessly and effortlessly shift position from 'happy birthday girl' to 'the bereaved.'

She wondered about her reaction to it all, the hysterical laughter during the Police death squad's visit; what was *that* all about? The story of the little girl's misfortune seemed so tragic and unfunny now in the cold light of day; it was hard to imagine having ever found it amusing. And the things she'd said to John, about not loving her mum: was that true? She wasn't sure. Maybe not. What did it say about her if she didn't? Did it mean she was incapable of love? No, that's rubbish – *"Yeah, up yours too, arsehole! Why don't you try indicating next time?"* – she loved John, even after all these years, she really did. They'd never had children but, so what? – they'd never had lots of things. Deep down she knew she had never actually wanted to be a mum and she didn't have that yearning. But why? Was that natural? Had the instinctive urge been taken from her by her own unhappy experience? She had more kids than anyone could ever want… she was a qualified teacher, it came with the territory, but was that her true vocation? Could she have done something better with her life? Again, she wasn't sure. Teaching could be rewarding at times but, it could just as often be a heinous and insufferable experience. She tried to resist the suggestion, the one she knew was lurking there, that she actually hated some of the kids she taught or *had* taught. Not just merely disliked but *hated.* Strong word. Should a teacher really be capable of hatred? In one or two cases, definitely. They knew who they were! *For your homework explain how a career teacher can be capable of physical revulsion.* It made her uneasy. Little bastards, giving her physical revulsion. You would expect that in any walk of life, wouldn't you? Or is hatred not a normal human sentiment? Had we had to invent it? Had we had to have been pushed *en masse* to devise something to fill the leisure time between hunting and gathering? Maybe we came down from the trees without knowing how to hate but saw fit to nurture the seeds of resentment as we swarmed out of Africa, this small band of hominids with itchy feet, driven to search for pastures new? She wondered briefly whether a hominid had ever been married in a church, but quickly dismissed the notion somewhere near the turn-off for Letchworth Garden City.

She found the radio and turned it on. Adverts, *of course* it was adverts! She didn't know how to change channels, so she turned it off. She made good progress, heading north just as most of the traffic was heading south towards the inevitable tailbacks and expected delays.

The skies were darkening all the while and she could see the tell-tale grey smear of rain falling from the canopy in places up ahead. A few minutes later it started to splatter against the windscreen. The heavens gave up everything they had as they launched their attack, shedding their loads in wind-blown waves, the wipers frantically flapping and scraping, smearing filth in an obscuring arc across the glass. One of the blades was ineffective and in urgent need of replacement. It had been like that for the past two winters.

By the time she arrived, in what the grubby brown sign described as the *'Coastal Paradise'* of Skagness, a little under five hours after setting off, she was numb in the bum and exhausted all over. She regretted telling John she'd wanted to make the journey alone; it had been a mistake, in hindsight, and it would have been better if he'd done the driving. Hindsight is a wonderful thing, but she was here now, and the rain had started to ease, so no real harm done.

The small bungalow where her mum lived – *had* lived – was in the centre of a small, characterless estate situated at quite a distance from the charmless tourist hotspots. Cold and bracing hotspots, more often than not. Why here? Nobody had ever known why. It had seemed a random and irrational choice at the time, as it still did. Not that it mattered anymore; she would be laid to rest here, that much was probably certain.

Pulling up on the empty road right outside death's door, Sue remembered to switch off the engine before forgetting to apply the handbrake (as was her custom).

She vaguely remembered the house as it looked the other time; it was so run-down, she doubted that anything had been done in all the years to halt the decline. Number 17 Barracuda Drive, with the curtains drawn, where Irene Skaife had breathed her last, was an insubstantial dwelling, thrown together sometime in the early sixties. Built with porous, sandy brown bricks, it had a grey-green concrete-tiled roof covered in parts by lichen and mosses. It stood out like a sore thumb on a hand covered with sore thumbs,

184

one of several similarly shabby properties in a cul-de-sac, a dead-end to nowhere. The property boasted access to the beach (eventually) and was in a sought-after area with good local schools. Viewing recommended. Again the question: why? Why had she moved out here of all places? Wet and windy on a good day. Good day? A bit optimistic, or a 'big ask,' as John might have put it. Should she have made more of an effort to come up here, make sure she was OK, cranky as she was? Maybe you reap what you sow after all. And it was too late now; that ship had sailed and sunk.

The door opened in Number 19. She remembered the face, and that surprised her: Sheila Boil, the neighbour – she'd only met her once but recognised her as soon as she saw her. She made her way in a series of staccato steps towards the car, house coat flapping, unnatural maroon hair in curlers and mouth turned downwards in an appropriately supportive show of grief. A face like that really didn't take much maintenance to appear dour or downcast. Cheerless was probably its default setting. Unsettling to behold for any length of time, it was the kind of face best forgotten and yet she had held it in her memory. A strange thing, the human mind. Her physical repugnance, becoming more pronounced with the passing years, perfectly encapsulated the spirit of her mother's dismal closing chapters where charm and beauty had no business. She found herself staring aghast at the unsightly nodule on the woman's cheek from which sprouted the wispy, embryonic signs of a moustache – one quite independent of the fully formed Zapata-style growth resident on her upper lip.

"I thought it was you," she rasped when Sue wound down the window, "would you like to come in and get yourself warmed up? I'll make us a nice pot of tea. Did you bring any milk? Not to worry if you didn't, love. I'm sure I'll be able to find some, somewhere."

Sue, realising she wasn't quite ready to meet her mum, offered thanks and followed Sheila into the house. The interior brought to mind a programme she had once seen on the TV about people who hoard things compulsively, part of Channel 5's '*Pointless Losers in Action*' season. Everywhere there were stacks of boxes and plastic carrier bags filled to bursting with empty food containers. This was possibly the largest collection of ice cream and Stork margarine tubs in the Eastern counties, all stacked together in nested columns, reaching up towards the nicotine-stained polystyrene-tiles of the ceiling. The central passageway between the sitting room storage area and the kitchen storage area was crammed with newspapers and magazines piled high and bundled together with string, each stack only able to remain upright by leaning against its neighbour. She had never seen anything like it. The sense of claustrophobia and a feeling of unease was exacerbated by an overpowering stench of cats and *all they do*.

"You're a cat-lover, then?" said Sue, squeezing through and struggling to breathe.

"Oh, you mean the smell?" Sheila cackled. "No, I don't have no cats, love, can't stand 'em, shitting everywhere, 'scuse my French. I don't know why this place smells like it does do, I honestly don't; it's horrible, isn't it, when you first notice it? You *do* get used to it though, love, after a while."

# It's The Not Knowing

"Oh!"

"First few years are t'worst! Used to make me sick of a morning, worse than when I was expecting our Cliff! I don't even notice it now, not much, anyroad. Now then, nice cuppa tea was it? I'll pop t'kettle on. I'm right sorry, y'know, about Irene, your mam. She was a lovely woman, one of the best! You're a lot like her you know – you speak all clever and posh, just like what she spoke like!"

"Well, I really don't know about clever or posh but thankyou... and thank you for calling the doctor, if I didn't already say that. I'm sorry it had to be you to find her, that can't have been very pleasant."

"You're welcome, pet, though it did give me quite a turn when I saw her there. I almost shat meself! It did look like she didn't suffer, that's one good thing, isn't it? It's nice when they don't suffer. The doctor said it was old age; said something in Latin but I didn't understand that." She stroked one of the moustaches thoughtfully. "Now, set yourself down somewhere and I'll go and sort out the brew – unless you'd like something stronger, eh? After your journey, an' all? Got a can of *Carling Black Label* if you'd prefer?"

"No, just tea would be fine, Earl Grey if you have it? I'd like to have a clear head when I go next door."

When it was served up it was a challenge to drink the staggeringly vile potion made, as it undoubtedly was, with a reused teabag and sour milk. Sue grimaced at the taste before placing the cup back on the floor, the contents undrunk. *"Thank you, that was er..."*

"Oh, I'm glad you liked it. I can make you another if you like. It's nice to have company for a change, what with me being an old widow woman an' all; it's not often I have visitors, not since he died, my husband…"

"I'm sorry…"

"You needn't be pet. He went years ago, and good bloody riddance! 'scuse my French. It was that Princess Lady Diana what killed him! Now then, can I make you another cup?"

"It was what?"

"It was *her* what killed him. He was sitting there where you are now when the telly said she'd been killed in that France with them pepperonis chasing her…"

"Oh, I see!"

"And he just clutched his chest and shouted something weird, it sounded like *Irene*, actually, but obviously it wasn't. And he just died there and then! As God is my witness. August 1997 I think it was. I'll never forget that."

Having refused the threat of a second cup, Sue got the key and squeezed her way back towards the exit, keen to *get this over with* as quickly as possible.

The rain was just starting to fall again as she opened the front door of number 17. It hit her straight away: the unmistakeable smell of *old person* and boiled cabbage mixed with the stillness, the silence, and the sense of lifeless calm. Up to that point she had never in her life stepped into a vacuum in a time warp but now she had, in a bungalow in Skagness with its faux-wood panel wallpaper and tangerine-coloured nylon carpets. Unsettled by a static electric shock from the metal handle, she crossed the floor of the sitting room to open the curtains. She received another statically charged belt when she touched the window frame. Gingerly, she tested it again and then pushed it outwards, as wide as it would go, so she might breathe in the salty tang of the sea air and clear the lingering smell of dust and death from the back of her throat. She stood awhile, deliberately breathing.

In the small kitchenette positioned under the window was a Formica table and chairs on which she found some unopened envelopes. One, from Club 75-80, boasted generous discounts for early bookings: *'Be Quick! When you're gone you're gone!'* A second, from Ann Summers, was a reminder of *PAYMENT OVERDUE*. Sue winced and tutted at the thought; she re-checked the name and address. No mistake. Her mum apparently owed Ann Summers money, but for what? She couldn't begin or even want to imagine – a racy scarf or cardigan, perhaps. A third envelope contained the death certificate, signed by the Doctor at seven thirty-eight last Sunday morning. She read it twice – was that really his name? Doolittle? Cause of death: old age. Miserable old age. What did that mean... Latin? There was a business card as well; Bourke & Ayers (Undertakers & Drainage Engineers), presenting someone called Augustus Tombes, with a handwritten message: *"If you want me to arrange disposal, give us a tinkle! Gus."* The phone number had been crossed out and another one handwritten underneath. It was difficult to decipher the characters scrawled, as they were, in a child-like script. She tutted again and pocketed the card.

# It's The Not Knowing

Gingerly, she touched the fridge with her fingertip, relieved when there was no static discharge. She opened the door and checked for contents: it was empty except for one pensioner-sized jar of mayonnaise, the *use-by* date now just a distant memory. She closed the door and unplugged the unit; turned the dials on the gas cooker on and off, sniffed, looked in the bin, sniffed again and checked the cupboards which were both empty. It was strange – there was nothing in there, as if the place had been cleared. She went back to the fridge and managed to dislodge the pack of ten fish fingers (only two left) from deep within the ice in the freezer box. She was just putting off going into the bedroom for as long as possible, she knew that. She didn't know how she'd react seeing her after all this time. Maybe the sight of her, lifeless and cold, would be too painful or bring back thoughts of her dad. She still missed him…

"Would it be alright if I took them fish fingers, now you've winkled 'em out?"

"Oh Jesus, Sheila!"

"Sorry love. Didn't mean to make you jump. I let myself in with my other key. Your mam didn't mind. She had the keys for mine as well. You can never be too careful, can you? You might as well keep that one. In fact, you might as well take this one as well, while you're at it. I don't suppose I'll be coming in here again." The unexpected visitor, now minus her curlers, placed the key on the table and patted it like a dog.

"Thank you. If I find your keys I'll let you have them back."

"That's it, pet, if you could. I see you found the letters, then? I left them there for you. Now, if there's anything else you're throwing out…?"

"I don't know… there doesn't seem to be much in here, but yes, have the fish fingers; in fact, you might as well take anything else you find if you want, if it's going to go off."

"Anything. Right. What sort of limit are we talking? I mean, how much, what sort of value?"

"Sorry?"

"How much value? I mean, can I just take *anything* I want, like?"

"Well… yes, maybe, I don't know. What sort of thing were you thinking? The kitchen roll, maybe? As I said, there's not much here of any great value, really, I'm sure… it's quite empty, much emptier than I thought it would be."

"How about… let's see… this?" She held up a tea towel with a flourish, a souvenir of the gift shop at Hornsea Pottery.

"And… this?" brandishing a tall wooden pepper grinder marked "*Greetings from Girton College.*"

"Yes, go on – you can have them both."

"What about her chair?"

"One of these, you mean?" she said, pointing towards the Formica table set.

"No, the one in there, in the sitting room. The Shackletons Highchair."

191

# It's The Not Knowing

"Oh, I hadn't seen that."

"Well, it's in there, right enough, but a bit too heavy for me to shift on my own. She only got it recently, you know. First she sent for their brochure, then she went to the showroom. They had over a hundred chairs to choose from. She was delighted with it. It's lovely, she said. She thought it would be great for when she was getting on a bit or if she got arthritis. It's so easy to get in and out of. It would mean a right lot to me to have it, a nice memory of your mam. She was my best friend, you know, we were practically *inseparable* ever since she moved here. Joined at the replacement hip, you might say."

"Yes, alright, of course you can have it – I'm sure it's what she would have wanted."

"Ta very much, like, don't mind if I do. I'll ask our Cliff to help. I don't suppose there's any news on the will? Bit early, I 'spect."

"I honestly don't know, I'll need to speak to the solicitors at some stage; it's all a bit sudden, you know. I don't even know if she's made a will."

"Aye, you're probably right to speak to them. Don't you worry yourself about that. Shall we have a look in the bedroom?"

"I suppose I should, although I'm dreading seeing her, really I am…"

"Right you are, this way then, but you won't be seeing her in here, pet…"

"You're not kidding; it's so dark in here!" Sue found the light switch and flicked it on. The small boudoir was suddenly bathed in inadequate light, enabling her to take a dim view. It was different from how she remembered it. For one thing, her mother wasn't there.

"Oh! She isn't here!"

"No, pet, I thought I just told you. The Funeral Director, he came and took her back to his place."

"Back to his place? …what Funeral Director? I haven't arranged one yet!"

"Gus Tombes, he left his card. He found out about Irene, your mam, so he came over straight away on the off chance, like, hoping to land the job."

"What do you mean '*found out*'? Did the doctor call him?"

"Well, no. I might have phoned him. In fact, now I think about it, I did – yes, I phoned him, I've just remembered. No harm in it, was there?"

"Well, no I don't know but I'm not very happy about someone just turning up and taking her away without speaking to me first! And where's all her bedding gone?"

"Ah yes, you've every right to be upset, pet. He's a bugger for all that; I've known him for years; he always likes to get a souvenir or two. Cheeky beggar thinks nowt of helping himself; he's well-known for it!"

"And what… he just gets away with that, does he? Really? That can't be right!"

It's The Not Knowing

"Aye, he says it's a perk o' the job or a trick of the trade; mebbe as he's right, eh? Not for the likes of us to say, is it? If it's not nailed down, he'll take it! He's harmless, though; he's just a bit of a magpie, 'scuse my French. His mother was the same. Apple never rots far from the tree, eh?"

The room was cold and gave off a deathly vibe, and probably always had. A small white wardrobe, cheap and nasty (and destined to be unfashionable even as it was rolling off the production line), stood warped with edges peeling alongside a ... *bidet.* Bidet? The bed, a tubular steel framed, faux-Victorian reproduction, jarred with the rest of the low-budget modern flat-pack furniture which filled the space and attracted the dust. *What's that... a tripod – for what? A camera?*

"She was lying right there, in the bed, calm as you like. That's where I found her on that dreadful, terrible day." Sheila clutched the fishfingers to her chest and looked up to the heavens.

Sue, suddenly overcome by the experience, sighed, tutted, and pulled open the drawer of the bedside cabinet causing the unit to wobble and shift diagonally. She looked at her new birthday Swatch. The hands moved imperceptibly towards two o'clock as she inspected the open drawer and, more specifically, its contents.

"Oh. My. God! What the hell...?"

She was, in one fell swoop, shocked, mortified and stunned. What were *these* doing in here? Her mind raced. Surely an old lady's bedside drawer was a place where you might expect to find, I dunno... a few tablets? Medical

194

supplies, maybe a packet of Parma Violets or Werther's Originals, reading glasses and an improving book, Alan Titchmarsh, say, maybe even a copy of Readers Digest, but not this, for God's sake! You never find *this*! And yet... there they were, as plain as day: the little square sachets, each containing a flavoured condom. And an almost empty carton, too! And, to make things worse, it was a *bumper holiday pack,* promising *"More bangs for your buck!"*

Scarcely able to believe what she had just unsheathed, she reached in and cautiously retrieved one of the foil packets, holding it in the corner as if it were a dead mouse. Raising it to her eyes she read: *'Mango Chutney Flavour. Suitable for vegans.'* She turned to Sheila, her eyes approaching *max-width* and her voice faltering.

"What the hell are these?"

"They look like rubber johnnies," said the hag, leaning over and peering into the drawer with a look of concern masking a smirk.

Sue sank to the bed, lowered her head, and shook it slowly from side to side, mumbling in disbelief.

"I just don't know what to say," she whispered to begin with. "I don't know what to think any more... what's this all about? Did she have a man? In here? Who? Who is or was he, this... lifeless lothario, this decaying Don Juan? Did *you* know about this? Did you know about *him*?"

"Him? Singular? There was more than one, love! I don't recall anyone called Don, though, and that's the honest truth. I couldn't keep tabs on all of 'em. Your mam was fond of male company; she couldn't get enough of 'em!

## It's The Not Knowing

Oh, yes! She was very popular down at the bingo mixed-doubles evenings! I remember her saying she liked *nowt better than to grab hold of…*"

"That's quite enough! Thank you, Mrs Boil! Fucksake!"

"Oooh, 'scuse your French."

You know when you have a world, and it gets thrown into turmoil? That's exactly where Sue Stilton was. The situation wasn't improved by the woman with the moustaches suddenly asking: "Could I have that mirror, do you think? The big one up there on the ceiling?"

Sue began to tremble, and her voice switched to schoolteacher mode: "Leave it! Don't say any more, I don't want to hear it!"

Back in the car, bewildered and dazed, Sue leaned forward and gripped the steering wheel. She started with a few simple yet effective breathing exercises, intended to restore her equilibrium and to steady her nerves.

Breathe in… Hold… Relax… Breathe in… Hold… Relax…

Breathe in condoms?

Hold *flavoured* condoms! *Mango Chutney* condoms!?

Relax…

Breathe in a bloody mirror…?

Hold on the ceiling? How much unpleasantness had that witnessed?

Relax… How can I *possibly* relax! I've just come from a geriatric knocking shop! And what have they done with the body?

She reached over and took her phone out; she turned off the mute setting and was about to call John when it rang. It was John.

"Hey, you... Yes, I'm here – I'm sorry, I forgot. Yes, you're right: I should have let you know…"

"Yes, the A1 was fine, one arsehole cut me up, didn't indicate…"

"Yes, it *was* a BMW, funnily enough..."

"About four and a half hours."

"Yes I got caught twice: near The Hatfield Tunnel and again up near Yaxley. Sorry, that's six points on your licence…"

"They can't prove it was me."

"Yes, I'm joking."

"No, I'm going to stay over. There's still so much to do here, I can't come back today… I've got to find the body, for one thing! … Long story, never mind, I know… you were right, I was wrong… What do you want, a gold star? …I know, it *is* a pain… somewhere cheap obviously… I don't know, no more than fifty pounds, hopefully… why would they be fully booked? …I'm fine, yes. There's something else I need to tell you but… no, not over the phone… I can't, not over the phone… I said *not over the phone!* No, you'll just have to wait! I promise I'll tell you tomorrow when I get back… Hello? Hello?"

Sue stayed in the car, watching the rainclouds moving south towards the North Norfolk Coast. She had decisions to make. The first was obviously to track down the body snatcher and get her mum back and... do what with her? Put her back in the Shackletons Highchair? Easy to get her in an out of it, by all accounts. Then after that... what was the next step? Inform the local Registry Office. That seemed sensible... maybe tomorrow. She would also need to find a hotel, but there was something else she needed to do first.

She got out of the car and went back into the bungalow. Sheila Boyle had gone but the sex-drawer was still there, half open. She pulled it out and tipped the contents onto the mattress. She hadn't imagined it; there were fifteen of the little square packets. What did her mother want with all these? What was she, some sort of geriatric nympho? It was inconceivable, whatever it was. And there was more: a scrap of paper folded in half, on which was written:

cyril – get some

- tea,
- milk,
- bread,
- johnny's - don't get marmite flavour this time!

*Manita.*

She was too numbed now, too desensitised to be shocked by this. It wasn't real anymore. None of it was. It was a dream. She'd wake up soon and it would all be over. *Manita* or Maneater or Irene Skaife, Cyril the senile stud – they weren't part of this.

There was something else still in the drawer, half concealed under the lining paper – something glued in place by the sticky leakage from an old bottle of *Veno's*. She fished it out, the gelatinous linctus stringing out like treacle or chewing gum on the sole of a loser's shoe. It was a souvenir picture card, an *action* shot from the film '*Harry Potter and the Philosopher's Stone.*' She regarded the precocious little oik in his Ernest Bevin specs waving a magic wand, like Sooty or Sweep (he definitely looked like someone had their hand up his backside). Her mum loathed things like this, so why was it here? Obviously, anything was possible under this new order. On the reverse were a few words written in biro: "Don't bother, it's shit! W." The script so recognisable. So left leaning. So William. So unexpected, she froze.

## The Flotsam Hotel

"Yes, just the one night."

"OK, darling, let's have a look… and you said you *do* mind sharing, yeah?"

"Yes, of course, I do! A single room, just me. On my own! And I'm not your darling, thank you very much!"

"OK, have it *your* way, yeah?" said the youth on reception in a tone heavily laden with '*now, you're just being old and awkward, yeah?*' as he scanned the page in the register. "Wasn't *two* nights, was it?"

"No, just the one, thank you. I already told you that!"

"Ah! Yeah, here we go. The only room we got left, yeah? Your (sic) lucky! Paying by cheque, credit card or, *what'sname,* Local Authority Voucher?"

"Cash, if that's not a problem, *yeah?* How much is it for *one* night?"

"That'll be… where is it… yeah, one hundred pounds, cash."

"What? That *can't* be right! This isn't London, and it's not exactly the Dorchester, is it!"

The youth fixed her with a pimply stare. "You stay at the Dorchester much, then, yeah?"

"That's beside the point! I'm not paying a hundred pounds for a room in this… this…fleapit!" She ran a hand along the counter and brandished her dusty fingertips in the youth's face. "Look at that! It's filthy; it's disgusting!"

"Hey, cool it gran'ma, yeah? Not so much of the fleapit, right? You wanna room or not? It's the only one we got, yeah? and there'll prob'ly be a rush later, so… hey, it's totally up to you, don't matter to me. You can try somewhere else, for all I care. Yeah?"

Sue knew she was dealing with a cocky bastard of little brain. And she knew *he* knew it was getting late and everywhere else in town was going to be fully booked.

She drummed her newly dusted fingers. "I'll offer you fifty in cash."

"Fifty quid? Go on, then. Money up front."

# It's The Not Knowing

He turned and reached across for the key as Sue extracted five tenners from her purse. She placed them on the counter with a hostile slap. He counted the notes suspiciously before handing over the key. "Room 214, on the second floor, stairs on your left, yeah? Will you be dining with us tonight?"

"Oh, I don't *think* so!"

As she headed for the stairs the youth quietly slipped the money into his back pocket. Obviously. Yeah?

Room 214 was a dingy hole, gloomy and dispiriting at best. If she'd brought a cat, there wouldn't have been enough room to swing it. Sue was by no means a regular user of hotels but had seen enough in the past to know that opening the door for the first time could often bring disappointment, an experience capable of dashing even the most spirited of spirits; an occasion where a weary "*oh shit!*" might be called for.

"Oh, shit!"

She resolved to rise up in the face of adversity; she would find somewhere nice, somewhere posh to eat on the promenade, treat herself; maybe a freshly caught lobster served on a bed of samphire, a couple of glasses – sod that, a *bottle* – of crisp white wine, then an early night where maybe she would read William's story. '*You can get through this. It's only the one night,*' she said, girding her loins. It seemed reasonably quiet, though. That was one good thing, she supposed.

She hung her jacket on the back of the chair, kicked off her shoes and sank into the bed. She studied the polystyrene ceiling tiles, scarred and worn over the decades, lifting in places, and offering maximum flammability. The hum in her ears was noticeable in the early evening silence as she started to relax and gently drift. She had made it this far...

With her eyelids weighing heavy and eyes now closed, a sense of peace descended; it swept her up gently in its arms, slowly engulfing her mind, her body, and her soul. From within this near catatonic state she could hear the distant sound of the petrels calling from the sea as she breathed freely of the stillness, of the calm; the hum of the traffic she had carried in her head all day now settled into an unrelenting, pitch-perfect drone to accompany the sweet song of the gannet or the fulmar, as it swooped and soared, hoisted aloft on salt-spray thermals, its lilting, playful melody in glorious, majestic and perfect harmony with the whispered murmurings of the ocean breeze and the gentle, carefree rustle of discarded packaging as it skipped, pizzicato across the dunes. The earth, now basking in the heat of a late afternoon sun reborn knew instinctively that the time was almost upon us, that a beautiful, golden autumn was coming. Oh, God! What a glorious, magical time to be alive! Was ever one so blessed by the sheer and overwhelming paralysis of being? Of being nothing, of owing nothing, of needing nothing. Of giving up the fight, surrendering to the sweet and inevitable release from all of this horror and this pain; all of this torment? *Take me now, mother...* Her mind was shrinking, and she was powerless to stop it; her senses lost all feeling as she was carried deep, deep beneath the waves into a lifeless, deathless, painless state, where the only sound was the song of the ocean swell, the waves hurling themselves relentlessly against the shore, reducing the rocks to pebbles, turning pebbles into sand.

With the light beginning to dwindle and die, Sue thought she *had* died. She liked it; so warm, so motherly and so perfect, so perfectly peaceful, a state of grace she had longed for. Cocooned in a glorious tranquillity, she knew in that instant how it must feel in the final moments, when the business of life is, at last, done and dusted.

Ever so gradually, and against her most profound desire to remain there, unmolested, to float in peace and to fade away into a blissful oblivion, she began to regain the sense of the vulgar, the ordinary and the commonplace; the light and the sound increased, slowly at first and then all too steadily and irresistibly. It felt like she'd been ripped from the womb, flung back onto the beach amongst its piles of seaweed-tangled driftwood, take-away flotsam and sundry plastic litter spewed from the guts of the sullen North Sea.

She focused on a cobweb in her prostrate state, wondering what someone who had just paid a hundred pounds for the privilege would think at this stage of their stay. Not very much, most likely. A sense of being cheated perhaps or maybe even of having been touched inappropriately by a lothario's hand. Maybe they would now be down at reception to clarify whether, by crossing the threshold, they had entered into a legally binding agreement, invalidating any possibility of a refund and from which there was no way out. Just like Skagness, no way out. Unless you died, the last refuge of the desperate. Go Irene, you died, you showed 'em! Who has a fourteen-inch telly these days? The Flotsam Hotel and Spa, Skagness that's who. And no remote control! Really? Who the hell has time to get up and manually switch channels these days? *It's a dump Sue, but it's only for one night. Just one night.*

From somewhere outside in the corridor she heard a door being slammed and then voices, so clear it was as if they were in the room.

"So, I was like, 'no!' and she was like, 'uh?' and I was like, 'yeah? you is a slag an' a bitch!' and I may possibly have made a suggestion that her mother worked in Macdonald's. Possibly. I might have done that. I can't really recall, and she was like, 'is you disrespecting me?' and I was like, 'wot you gonna do about it, face ache?' ...I know *'faceache,'* I don't know where *that* came from, prob'ly Shakespeare innit! And she was like, 'surely, you can't expect me to reveal my intentions to a bog-beast like you,' like, coming over all posh, so I was, like, well furious, yeah?"

"Oh yes, I can well imagine, absolutely I can! As, indeed, anyone in your position would have every right to be! Do go on, this is most fascinating!"

"So anyways, I was like, 'you want some of me?' and she was like, 'you ain't worth it, sister!' and I was like, 'you is a chicken innit' and then, like..."

"Stop for a moment, Destiny. I don't know why, but I have the most extraordinary feeling that there's someone in there listening to our every word!"

"You mean, like, an eavesdropper, is that what you mean? The fucking cheek of it!"

"Let's leave it there for now, but you simply *must* promise to finish this most intriguing anecdote when we are somewhere more private. I suggest we adjourn to alternative accommodation where we might revisit this particular topic in more, shall we say, *agreeable* surroundings."

"That's a very good idea what you've had, Tiffany. Might I suggest dinner at my club? The Belgravia, it's just around the corner. They do a sensational steak and kidney pie on Mondays. My treat!"

"It sounds divine! Do they do vegan-friendly dishes, do you happen to know?"

It seems The Belgravia was very keen to attract the discerning vegan member so, yes, they most certainly did!

That being settled, there was a rumble of hooves, a cry of *"Nosey old bitch!"* another door slamming and then a beautiful silence.

She was, like, shellshocked, yeah? What she had just overheard, having had no say in the matter – the unreal and downright baffling nature of it – only served to increase her sense of alienation. A stranger in a strange land. A land where her mother was destined to spend the rest of eternity, six feet under in the muck or stuffed in a pot in a wall. *Had she ever expressed a preference?*

The events of the past forty-eight hours were, she decided, beyond her scope. She had no idea how she should react or what to do next. She wondered whether this was fitting. Was the sheer, overwhelming hideousness of this ghastly place, this awful room in this disgusting minus three-star hotel on this desolate road in this miserable, funereal seaside town the only way her mother should be remembered? It's possible, it's almost certain. A stunningly beautiful location would not have been merited, would have had no business being here; it would not have provided an appropriate setting for the dying days of a woman who had clearly failed in her duty of care, a mother who had never sought to nurture any kind of relationship with her only daughter and who had apparently chosen to spend her widowed years in depravity, doing… doing what, exactly? *Fuck knows! Irene, you're sucking the life out of me… and W too, if he's still around!*

"Why did you hang up on me earlier?

"Yes, you did.

"No, not really. It's been a shitty day, actually… and I still haven't seen her. Long story, never mind…

"… I suppose but, do you know something, John? I realise just how much I didn't know her… this woman who I thought was my mother. I really didn't know her at all…"

She rubbed her feet together to relieve an itch.

"What do I mean? I mean… wouldn't you find it just a tiny bit weird if you looked in your mother's bedside drawer and found things you shouldn't find, like… condoms, for instance…?

"*Condoms*, yes! No, I'm really not joking. Flavoured ones, too!

# It's The Not Knowing

"No, not marmite, obviously…

"Yes, it is… well, of course I'm upset! I'm more than bloody upset! Who wouldn't be! Jesus, at that age she shouldn't be doing things like that anymore, don't you agree? Honestly! where did she even get the energy, for God's sake? No, get lost! I'm not bringing them back with me! Anyway, there was something else…

"Forget that! Listen… I think William might still be alive!

"William, still alive! Why don't you listen?

"Just something I found… Do you know much about Harry Potter?" Sue reached in and pulled the sticky card from her bag. "… 'Potter and the Philosopher's Stone.' Any idea what year that was?

"Can't you look on the internet, Ask Jeeves maybe?... Or Google! If they're still in business… go on, don't be long.

"Yes, I'm still here. 2001? Yes, I thought it was around then… that's interesting…

"…because there was something else in her drawer, apart from those other things…"

John was brought up to speed on the card and the message and the W.

"I'm sure it's his writing. So, you know what this means?

"That's right. Probably written two years after he disappeared, I know…

"How do I feel? I don't really feel anything… I'm confused by it, I suppose. It's been a long day… I don't think I have the energy to feel anything else just yet… I'm

207

going to get something to eat and then, I don't know, maybe read his story, or have an early night... Tomorrow, I'm going to find out what they've done with her, registry office then home... no, I'm not staying any longer than I have to...

"Shit. Yes, totally shit... you remember the place we stayed in Cromer, downwind of the sewage farm? Luxury compared to here... minibar? Ha ha, bless you! No, there's nothing like that. Yes, I told you; it's a dump. Right... I'm going out now. I've promised myself a proper meal in a nice restaurant, locally caught lobster sounds nice, something like that. What did you have...?

"Sounds horrid... there's some Gaviscon in the bathroom cabinet... OK, yes love you too. Yes, I'll be OK. See you tomorrow... night, night. Mwaah."

After a quick shower, an experience which alternated unpredictably between scalding hot and freezing cold, she slipped William's notebook in her bag and headed down to reception. The youth was nowhere to be seen; there was now a responsible adult behind the counter.

The responsible adult, *Jacqui O* according to her badge, smiled at Sue as she approached.

"Checking in?"

Sue waved the key, by way of reply. "No, I'm just going out."

"Not dining with us tonight? We have chef's special menu on Mondays..."

Before she could continue the sales patter, Sue cut her off.

"No, thank you, I'm making my own arrangements. Should I leave the key here? Actually, seeing as you're here, can I just say, and don't take this the wrong way, that I don't know how you have the cheek to charge a hundred pounds for that room!"

Jacqui O was taken aback by this sudden verbal attack and stood, silently gaping as the disgruntled guest turned and left the foyer, in search of lobster.

## On the Waterfront

It was a cold and miserable early evening. The sun of the late afternoon was still up there probably but was now well hidden behind the steely grey clouds which loomed overhead with malicious intent. There were several restaurants that she could see; some had dining areas outside, surrounded by thick glass partitions. Many of these had been daubed by local graffiti *'artists.'* Among their number 'Daz 03' was seemingly the most prolific and least talented.

She approached the first contender, 'The Fisherman's Hut,' and scanned the menu displayed in a padlocked glass case. It looked OK... halibut, mackerel, fish fingers. Quite a dazzling array of sea food and... yes! Lobster, locally caught, served on a bed of shredded cabbage with gherkins, two slices of buttered bread and a pot of tea. £1/19/11. *Whoah! Hang on, how much? What does that mean?* As she was puzzling this and looking for a waiter, two trollops clumped past and started giggling.

"Hey, girl! You ain't finking you is eating there is you?"

"No, nobody ain't gonna be eating there, see? It's closed, innit, like."

"Yeah, innit, like. Closed. C-L-O-S-D, see?"

"Excuse me? Oh, I see. Thank you," she said and started to walk off. "Thank you Tiffany, thank you Destiny."

"That's her, innit! Nosey old cow!"

Sue hastened her step, not wishing to get into an argument with what she seriously hoped were two figments of her imagination. They couldn't be real, could they? Up ahead in the distance she saw a shimmering light outside another restaurant, which looked promising. It wasn't. The 'Hermit Crab Singles Bistro' was closed, with a sign confirming the fact that, as a seasonal restaurant aimed at the booming social recluse market, it did not open in the Summer. Not to worry. A bit further along the promenade she came to 'The Lobster,' a traditional sea-food restaurant boasting the finest selection of Suffolk wines outside of Lowestoft. She walked in and asked for a table for one, struggling to make herself heard above the noise of the diners, who were crammed into every inch of space in the very cosy and oxygen-starved dining room.

"Sorry, fully booked. Come back tomorrow if you're desperate." The Maitre D' didn't actually say this, he just pointed, with a rueful grin, to a sign which confirmed what he hadn't just said.

Not to worry. Sue headed back out onto the path. It was noticeably cooler out there than in there, and she suddenly started to feel the chill from the offshore breeze. There was one more place she could see, a bit further along. It looked like a food place, but she couldn't quite make out the name. It looked like there were people going in and out and some sitting outside so...

By the time she got there, she could read the sign: '*Cliff's Café.*' There was nobody sitting outside; the seats were occupied by black bin liners packed with who knows what.

With a growing sense of frustration and disappointment alongside the gnawing pangs of hunger and having eaten nothing since breakfast, she reluctantly pushed open the greasy door. Was that Cliff himself behind the greasy counter? Whoever it was, he had a greasy 8-track player cranked up, blaring out '*Hotel California.*' *You can check out any time you like...*

"Good evening, lovely lady. You look like someone I could trust. What can I do you for?"

Sue smiled briefly at his eager fat face and looked up at the menu mounted high on the wall: a filthy and greasy Perspex cover protecting the photographs of filthy and greasy food, making it difficult to make out what the individual photographs might once have attempted to portray.

"Do you do lobster?"

"Lobster? What's that? I don't think so; whatever we do is all up there on the board. '*If you don't see it we don't got it,*' he replied, ending with a flourish and a stupid American accent.

"Hmm." Maybe this wasn't the best time to be guessing but she was hungry, so, against her better judgment she chose at random and asked for "the top one."

"Good choice!" said Cliff (yes, it was him). "And might I suggest a crisp white wine to accompany your meal? A nice Sancerre might go very well? Or a Riesling 2005, maybe? So fresh, you'd think it had been stolen! I'm joking, of course! About the stolen, which it isn't…"

"OK, I'll have a large glass of Sancerre, then please."

"We've only got French muck, is that alright?"

"Yes, of course."

"No glasses, it'll be in a Styrofoam cup. It does the job, none of your fancy cut crystal here. Oh, and do you promise to bring the plate back afterwards?"

"Excuse me?"

"When you've finished, can you bring the plate back? We're running low, you see."

"Plate? But I'm not going anywhere with a plate… you've lost me?"

"The plate with your meal. We don't just stick it in a bag. We do things properly at this end of the parade. Always have, always will. We put it on a plate. Why do you think the Fish Hut went bust?"

"I've really no idea…"

"No plates! Stuck everything in bags or polystyrene boxes! Well people weren't going to put up with that, were they? Not when they could have it served up on a plate. Stands to reason, know what I mean?"

"No I don't; I've got no idea what you're talking about."

"I'm talking about the plate."

"I know! But I still don't see…"

"Look, love, just bring the sodding plate back, will you? Or, I'll have to charge you a deposit, and we wouldn't want that now, would we!"

"Why can't you just take it back when I've finished? You could just pick it up when you're clearing the table, problem solved!"

"Eat food *at the table*? Which table?"

"That table! There, that one there, see it? Right there! Right here, the one I'm now rapping with my knuckles. Hello?"

There was a pause as Cliff eyed the table. He moved his head from side to side, trying to expel a rick from his neck.

"What do you think this is? A diner or something?"

"Exactly that, yes, or preferably a restaurant, as we're not on Route 66, because that's what it is!"

"No! It isn't! That's where you're wrong, sweetheart. We don't have a restaurant licence anymore, so no - it's not a bleeding restaurant!"

"What the fuck is it, then?"

"It's a *take-away*, the clue's in the name! Café, it's French for take-away! You order it here, see, then we prepare it back there, see, then we put it on a plate, you give us some money and then you take it *away*. See? Now, I don't know what goes on outside Skaggy, I don't know who you are or where you've come from, but I'll tell you this for nothing sweetheart: if you think you can swan in here like Lady Diana Spinster expecting to be able to sit down in *my* café, a café which has no food licence currently, and just eat at *that* table, you've been seriously misinformed. And I'll thank you not to swear; not when there are ladies present!

Sue didn't bother checking, she knew there was nobody else there.

"Now, I'll ask you again. Will you bring the plate back?"

In a fully replete state Sue might well have continued to argue until she had bested and broken her opponent but, as she was in need of whatever sustenance or food he might be able to provide, she gave in with a shrug of the shoulders.

"Alright, I'll bring the stupid plate back but where from, I don't know."

"Washed?"

"Washed? Christ no, I'm not washing it; this is unbelievable! What do you think I am?"

"I know exactly what you are Mrs Hoity-Toity and you're going to wash that plate, even if I have to do it myself!"

"No, I'm not! And I'll tell you something else, you bloody... *grease bag*! I've changed my mind and I'm not bringing it back!"

"Oh, yes you are!"

214

"No, I'm not, get that into your greasy thick skull, you …"
Just as Cliff was about to ban her for life *(I will you know!)*,
the greasy orange bead curtain hanging behind the counter
suddenly parted.

"Hey girl, is you, like, disrespecting my father? What on
earth gives you the right to swan in here like Laydee Diana
Spinster god rest her soul, thinking you can throw insults
about like they're going out of style?"

"I told you, soon as I saw her, didn't I? I was like, 'Wooh,
she is the wrong kind of trouble!'"

"It's alright girls, I've got this. This 'lady' was just
leaving, isn't that right?" Cliff Boil folded his beefy arms
in a gesture of belligerence, a word that no one in his circle
would ever use.

Standing there, being bullied and outnumbered, in the
greasiest environment she could ever remember, Sue was
simmering with rage. She fixed the proprietor with a long
hard stare, a look which only a playground bully could
ignore. She was damned if she was going to eat anything
here now. She would rather starve than eat in this hellhole.
She was already starving anyway, so job half-done.

"Yeah, innit, though! You kick her out Dad, the nosey old
cow!"

"Yeah, do one!"

*Why do they all do those silly gestures with their hands
and prance about?* she wondered, just before being bustled
out of the door, forcibly ejected onto the pavement, and told
to never come back innit.

## It's The Not Knowing

The sun was in rapid decline as the night shift trawlers started to make their way towards the treacherous fishing grounds of the North Sea.

Alone and hungry out on the promenade, leaning against the neglected salt-washed railings and surrounded by the litter and the dog mess – the debris of modern life – a forty-one-year-old primary school teacher (recently bereaved) stared at the horizon, her spirits dashed but not broken. She didn't belong here, and she was glad; the fact in itself was a source of immense relief. It meant she didn't have to stay. She could soon be home with John, the best thing that ever happened to her. And they would never have to come back. They didn't have to bury her, did they? Certainly not here, anyway. In fact, the more she thought about it, the more she decided she would simply request her body be cremated; the ashes didn't have to be scattered or left here. She could maybe have them sent through the post, so they could be scattered somewhere nice. Somewhere else. Anywhere else. But why not just get rid straight away and have done? She could easily arrange the business at the crematorium, say her last goodbyes, wait for the ashes to be handed over and then tip them down a drain so they could be swept out to sea; make the fishes cough, it's what Irene would have wanted.

Was this a little harsh, a little unfeeling? Undeserved? Not at all. But then there was William. Was he here, somewhere? The card. The card had no stamp on it or anything, no postmark. How had it got there? By hand?

Her mind was somewhere else, lost in thought, weighing the possibilities, remembering her early life once more; the

216

image of the wax crayons and the drawing sessions at the table, Susie and little Will squabbling, the knock on the window…

There really was a knock on the window and it was coming from Cliff's Café. She turned and saw the eponymous brute banging his fist and gesturing in hostile fashion, egged on by two half-baked trollops.

"Go on! You don't belong here, your sort; move along or I'll call the Police!" And those stupid hand gestures! Sue made one of her own as she turned and walked stiffly away.

There was nothing. Nowhere was open. This was the English seaside in late August: The costume jewel in the crown of the East Coast tourist office, but the seafront shops were closed or boarded up. The wind was gusting, sending Styrofoam wine goblets swirling and skipping around corners, shifting sand into nooks and crannies, flinging salt into the wounds. This was not how things were meant to be. This should have been the busy season, one last hoorah before the golden Autumn turned into the long, cold Winter.

As she stared across the bleak terrain, her nose started to run. "Ah great, that's all I need, to come down with a cold. Thankyou mother, thank you very much!"

She rooted in her bag for a tissue but there was so much crammed inside. She took a few things out, looking for the little cellophane packet she was sure was in there. Sunglasses, reserve sunglasses, a makeup bag, a plastic poncho, William's notebook were all pulled out before the tissues were finally found, secreted in a zipped compartment. Having blown and wiped she was still sniffling as she started to put the other things back when, out of nowhere, a seagull dived and plucked something from her hand. Its shrill, mocking screech was not dissimilar to Sue's own effort. The salty maw hovered briefly before her startled eyes then spun away, wings flapping as it headed out to sea, the treasure clamped in its stinking, yellow beak. A cry of anguish and despair, one that no-one would hear, rang out before fading into the heavens. As the victim looked on aghast, hands clamped to her cheeks, a second gull, clearly not an accomplice, swooped in an effort to snatch the swag. In the skirmish that followed the item was dislodged and tumbled through the air as the two contestants engaged in an avian dogfight, a vulgar display of combat aerobatics. The pages fluttered and flapped like the wings of the dualists as they surfed the thermals briefly before plummeting spine first into the turbulent salt waters where they were engulfed and tossed cruelly by the North Sea swell until they were no more, the words scattered by the undertow, the story lost forever.

Horrified by this sudden loss, Sue leaned against the rusting, lopsided old railings on the seafront. Her eyes wedged open in shock and, feeling quite numb, she just gaped. At that moment she couldn't think what else to do; gaping came naturally and seemed altogether appropriate. She wasn't quite sure whether what had just happened had just happened before reason convinced her that it had. With a shake of the head, and a heartfelt "*Fuck!*" she turned and trudged back to the hotel, hoping the restaurant might be still serving. After a terrible evening, which she was sure could not get any more terrible, she was now prepared to slum it and desperate to eat something – even humble pie, if there was any left.

Jacqui O was still on duty when Sue walked into reception. Approaching the desk, feeling inexplicably sheepish (as if requesting a personal favour), she popped the question: "Hi, it's me again. Is the restaurant still serving? You said something about a chef's special earlier if I heard correctly?" The woman looked up from her magazine, a 1970s edition of *Cosmopolitan,* and narrowed her eyes. "Yes, I remember you. Well, no, it isn't. I'm sorry. There were no bookings tonight, so I sent chef home about two hours ago. You're far too late. If you'd only said when I asked you it might have been different…"

"Yes, I appreciate that but…"

"But you thought you'd 'try and find somewhere down by the seafront?' Not much down there, is there?" Her tone was altogether too gleeful; there was too much *I could have told you that if you'd asked!* going on.

"No, not much…"

"Did you end up at Cliff's place?"

"Erm, yes I did…"

"No luck?"

"No luck, no…"

"Did he mention the plate? Of course he did! He does that with anyone he doesn't trust."

"Doesn't trust?"

"Yes, you know, outsiders, vagrants and city types, people he doesn't know, that kind of thing."

"What? That's just mental! How does he make a living with such an idiotic approach?"

"He doesn't! He doesn't make enough to cover his bills; he's a real loser! He's harmless, though. And quite a catch!"

"Yes, I can well imagine you'd think so. So, where can I get something to eat now? Is room service still available?"

"Oh, yes; still available for the right person. You look trustworthy enough, let me get you a menu, one moment…"

Jacqui O popped out, popped back almost immediately and handed over the menu, an example of beautiful calligraphy on vellum card presented in a beautiful leather-bound case. The sheer quality of the item was unexpected, and it was perhaps the least ugly thing Sue had seen in this ugly town. Impressed by what she saw, Sue nodded appreciatively and made encouraging noises before finally ordering a platter of locally sourced fresh lobster served on a bed of samphire with parmesan shavings and a pork pie starter. "Good choice! And for the wine?" she asked, biro poised.

"A half bottle of Sancerre will do nicely, thank you; this is more *like* it!"

"I'm so glad. I'll get Warren to bring it up to your room. Oh! Incidentally – what you said earlier about the room rate…"

## It's The Not Knowing

"Yes?"

"What did you mean when you said a *hundred* pounds?"

"I meant I wouldn't have paid a hundred pounds to stay in that room!"

"Yes, I thought that might be what you meant but where did you get a *hundred pounds* from? I mean, even the *executive* rooms on the top floor are only thirty-nine pounds per night..."

"Well... that's what he told me; I didn't get his name, the young man who was on the desk earlier... he said a hundred. I have to say I was shocked. I thought the price was exorbitant, so I offered him fifty, and he took it. Are you saying he was lying?"

"No, just mistaken probably. Don't worry I'll have a word with him," she smiled. "Checkout time tomorrow is ten. Breakfast is in the dining room from seven-thirty. Ten pounds for full English. Shall I book you in?"

"Erm... yes, please."

"Right, that's all done for you. Is there anything else I can help you with? No? Enjoy your meal, yeah?"

Back in 214, Sue slumped on the bed and reflected on recent events. It had been quite an evening. She didn't mean 'quite an evening' in a good way. Not at all. It had been a total disaster. But it was nearly over, just a couple of hours and it would be done. Tomorrow would certainly be another day.

"The lying shit!" she thought angrily – trying to charge her a hundred pounds for this! And if an executive room was only thirty-nine pounds, how much was this one normally? A fiver? If she hadn't been so tired and hungry she would have been furious. They wouldn't like her when she was furious. How long before they delivered the food? She should have asked downstairs. *"C'mon, I'm starving!"* Probably time for a quick wash, though. And that's what she did; jumped in the shower for a couple of minutes, five at the most, definitely no more than ten, straight in and out, the temperature less erratic than earlier. With hair wrapped in a towel, body patted dry with another towel, if you could call it a towel – at home, it would have been called a flannel – she quickly got dressed, ready to eat.

For fifteen minutes she sat there, flicking through a *'Skagness: Where to go and what to see!'* brochure, amazed at the wealth of attractions not worth a visit and variety of things no-one could possibly want to see. Each time her stomach growled she became more impatient until eventually she picked up the phone and dialled 0 for reception. It was engaged. Of course it was! Probably off the hook. What a shithole! She slammed the receiver back down and wrenched the door open, becoming increasingly furious with this awful hotel and everything about it. What was keeping them, were they still trying to catch the fucking lobster or what?

The corridor was silent and empty. Empty except for the tray of delicious food which had been left outside her door sometime during the twenty minutes she was in the shower. On the tray, tucked under the plate was a hand-written note which said: "Enjoy ur (*sic*) meal, yeah? Sorry about the

cash thing. You'll get ur *(sic)* money back." It was signed:
*Warren.* The handwriting so distinctive, so left leaning.

## Revenge

Sue hadn't slept well – eating so late had been a mistake
– and was not in the best frame of mind the next morning
as she made her way down to reception. They were both
there behind the desk, Jacqui O, and the youth Warren,
although the latter scuttled away when he saw her coming
out of the lift.

"Good morning!

She was far too breezy, altogether too enthusiastic and the
smile was uncalled for, thought Sue.

"Oh, and by the way… what you said yesterday?"

"What did I say?"

"About the room? Well, actually, it seems Warren *did*
make a slight mistake when he quoted you the price. He's
actually new – not that that's any excuse, far from it! – but
he *did* used to work at the Dorchester, actually, so…"

"Did he really?" She wasn't actually interested in the
youth's CV and didn't actually believe her, either.
Actually.

"Yes, absolutely; the big one in Mavis Enderby. He
started there when he left school, actually."

"A couple of weeks ago, then, actually?" Sue sneered,
politely.

"No, he was there for three years before he came here. He had glowing references and we were lucky to get him, actually!"

"Of course, I forgot, they leave school at fourteen these days!"

"That's right, actually. Anyway, in view of the honest mistake and, as a gesture of goodwill, I think we can forget about charging you for breakfast, if that sounds fair? This one's on the house, as it were. So, if you'd like to go through?" said Jacqui O, actually indicating the door to the dining room.

It was a buffet affair, unlimited visits, help yourself. So, she did, overloading a plate with sausages, beans, mushrooms, black pudding, bacon, scrambled eggs, hash browns and fried bread. According to the menu, this was *'The Skaggy Special.'* Sue carried the tray over to a table in the corner, staked her claim and went back for coffee, tea, croissants, and grapefruit juice.

There was a young family sitting at another table: mum, dad and three kids, chattering with great excitement about going down to the beach to make a sandcastle. Maybe they could catch a fish? Mum thought the sea was "a bit too cold for fish." From what she could gather (as she had little option but to listen), it seems they'd never been to the seaside before, and they couldn't wait to get to the beach and "*get their cossies on.*" Dad had never had so much free black pudding in his life, and he couldn't wait to fill his plate again, encouraging everyone to do likewise. When his wife, a mousey woman in bulging purple leggings protested, trying unsuccessfully to keep her voice down,

224

*"aw, leave 'em be Spud, they've got enough puppy-fat already!"* he explained there would be no need to buy anything else if they loaded up now. If they did this every morning the cost of the holiday would work out much cheaper than they'd feared, and it would go some way towards offsetting the *'not inconsolable'* cost of their accommodation.

"Think about it, Maureen, yeah? Even with Wayne's special discount, we're still paying a hundred pounds a night for the room, right? – plus, fifty quid for *Skaggy Specials* – so, if you think about it, if we eat *two* breakfasts each it's like we're getting fifty quid back, isn't it? If we eat *three*, it's like the room's almost paid for! Trust me, I know what I'm talking about, yeah? Now, come on Josh, eat some more of them sausages, there's a good lad!"

Sue watched them as she slid the moving parts of the *Skaggy Special* around the plate. She quickly decided, even with her Liberal outlook, they had the makings of a family anyone might easily and legally describe as 'horrid.' This breed of dead-eyed loser was what she had to deal with at parent-teacher evenings in the real world – the kind who turned up early in their best tracksuits, eager to get it done and dusted so they could rush back for *'EastEnders,'* where they were keeping a keen but dead eye on the lives of other deadbeats. The brats were noisy and disruptive, unable to contain their enthusiasm; the kind of brats best kept in sedation, she thought. Little bastards.

She dipped the horn of the croissant in her coffee and chewed. They had never done this when they were young, been away to the seaside; never stayed in a hotel, not even a shit one like this. As far as she could remember Eric and Irene didn't like the idea of going on holiday. They didn't like to leave the house unoccupied, being concerned that burglars might move in. Irene would most definitely not have liked the idea. She wasn't sure what her dad thought but she preferred to imagine that he would have loved to take them to the seaside, given the opportunity. He was a good man. She could easily imagine him paddling in the sea, trousers rolled up and a knotted hanky, leaping the waves as the tide came in, wiggling his toes among the seaweed.

She couldn't face the breakfast and pushed it away. As she walked out, she heard cutlery being scraped with a gleeful cry of *"Waste not want not!"* and she smiled. She wasn't normally a spitter but, if the occasion demanded...

She went back up to the room, made the bed, cleaned her teeth, packed her case, neatly folded the wet towels, and checked out shortly afterwards. Jacqui O hoped she'd had a nice stay and hoped she'd enjoyed her free breakfast. Sue hoped to win the lottery, but you can't have everything in life.

Next stop was going to be the Registrar's Office. She didn't have an appointment but hoped it wouldn't be a problem. As she turned the key and revved the engine, something was troubling her, something at the back of her mind but she didn't know what. She had her purse and her bag; the suitcase was definitely in the boot. Suddenly, it came to her: she had been ripped off, hadn't she? A measly free breakfast did not cover the overcharge on the room, did it? No. It bloody well didn't! *Absolute bastards*! She thumped the dashboard, instantly blowing one of the bulbs in the display. Did she really want to go back in there and demand satisfaction? Could she trust herself not to hit someone or make a scene? Probably not. Maybe best not to upset the natives again: she'd seen *Deliverance.* She sighed, looked up at the storm clouds gathering overhead and thought *Fuck it!* Sue wasn't a swearer by nature, but this place would make a Saint swear, even a really good one. Through gritted teeth she decided she couldn't face Jacqui O and her flunkey again and fastened her seat belt.

As she taxied slowly and carefully towards the exit, unaware that the handbrake hadn't been fully released, she wondered for one last time whether she'd got everything. Mid-list, she spotted the two trollops. They were plodding into the car park, kicking a beer can between them. Sue slowed and fixed them with a long, thoughtful stare, pursed her lips briefly and then pressed hard on the accelerator, sending the vehicle hurtling towards them in a flurry of gravel. The beasts looked up in terror and disbelief, transfixed with slack jaws gaping as the Rover, with the power of just over a hundred horses, whinnied and gathered pace. At the last split second, they threw themselves into the bushes with a shriek as the horses swerved sharply to the side, spraying them with gravel and sending the can rattling against the kerb. Two trollops in a bush are worth less than a bird in the hand, *innit*? Sue stopped a few yards further on and watched them in the rear-view mirror as they emerged from the shrubbery, brushing themselves down. *Wait for it – yes, there they are! Silly, affected hand gestures, twisted wrists and pointy fingers, right on cue!* Sue chuckled as she blasted the horn, opened the window, offered up a single, resolute middle finger and drove off, bits of gravel and a contented smile spreading in all directions. That, she had to concede, was a job worth doing and one very well done!

## Talking of Death

The Registry Office wasn't hard to find. A brutalist concrete block situated in the Business Park, with a hand-written sign in the window: '*No appointment without an appointment.*' She pondered the thought process that must have gone into producing such a sign then pushed open the heavily rusted steel door and went inside.

An older woman in a sober grey business suit with matching hair was talking on the phone as Sue approached the main desk. She raised her hand and mouthed, "*Won't keep you long.*" Sue nodded in acknowledgement, took a seat, crossed her legs, and sat back. There were posters on the bare grey walls, sundry announcements and a variety of brochures covering births, marriages, deaths and *other*.

"No, that's right... I know, but there's nothing I can do at this end... I know... and he won't do that, is that correct? OK... I see... Have you tried Citizens Advice, they're pretty good with things like this... no, sorry I don't have the number; maybe you could try 118 118? ...Me? Oooh, I suppose either of them, I *like* a man with a porn 'tache, me... yes, it's certainly worth a punt... yes, ha ha... well, good luck and I hope you do manage to track down the body before you lose your deposit! Yes, of course. *Good luck!* Yes, goodbye." She replaced the handset, chuckled, and looked over. "Right, sorry darling. How can I help?"

# It's The Not Knowing

Sue stood up and went over to the desk to explain the purpose of her visit. Did she have an appointment? No, she didn't. The grey suit puffed out her cheeks and expelled a popping noise with a shake of the head.

"It's tight. It looks like he's fully booked today," she said, consulting the diary and making clicking noises with the tongue on the palate. It's not as impressive as it sounds, most people can do it. "Yes, unless... this might be possible. OK, we can but try. Can you run?"

"Can I *run*?"

"Yes. If you can run up the stairs now, he might be able to squeeze you in, but I can't promise anything. OK? I suggest you get your skates on; as I said, he's a very busy man! Through that door, the yellow one, just follow the signs. Go on, what're you waiting for? Chop-chop!"

She ran like a startled fawn, followed the signs and presently, quite out of breath, found herself standing and panting outside the door of *Leonard 'Len' Spiggins. Registrar.* She knocked and waited, breathing heavily.

"Come!"

She opened the heavy panelled door and was hit by the bitter smell of stale smoke and instant coffee. There was something else, too – boiled cabbage? Playing quietly in the background was a funereal piece of music, immediately calming and creating just the right kind of atmosphere for registering a death. It was impressively considerate, she thought, fostering an appropriate degree of sympathy and compassion whilst managing to avoid a sickly, cloying over-sentimentality. She recognised the music:

It's The Not Knowing

Beethoven's Ninth. Good choice. She had never heard it played by a ukulele orchestra before. The office was tastefully sombre, furnished in the brooding, classic style with subdued lighting and a rather grand walnut bookcase running the length of one wall. The ambience created by the subtle and intelligent use of light and shade could never fail to make an instant and favourable impression on all who entered, and Sue was no exception. Perhaps, if she had one small criticism, the reproduction human skeleton could have been less prominent but, otherwise, it was a triumph of sensitive interior décor, aimed squarely at the mourning-crowd.

Behind the antique walnut desk, adorned with pearl-inlay cask motifs, sat Leonard *'Len'* Spiggins, a 68-year-old career bureaucrat with a shock of white hair, greased back and held rigid with a daily dollop of Brylcreem. With his square-framed Bakelite glasses, dimpled chin, and cheeky smile, he looked a little like Ronnie Barker off the telly. He loved his job, loved everything about it; he loved being there to oversee each stage in the life of the common, mortal man or common woman: he'd been there for them all, seen it and done it. If they did a T-shirt, he would have had it. And he would have loved it even though he wouldn't have worn it. Births, Marriages, Deaths and Other. All great, life-affirming things in their own way, but he had a special preference for *Other*. That was his favourite. It was like a lucky dip. He smiled serenely and invited her to take a seat.

"You sound like you've been running."

"Yes, the lady downstairs said —"

"Ooh, the little minx! I've told her a thousand times not to do that! Anyway, talk to me lovely lady – talk to me of death," he said, leaning back sympathetically.

Sue confirmed the details of her mother's passing, replying to each of his questions in turn. The Registrar nodded compassionately as he ticked boxes and entered the details into the register. Sue began to feel a sense of relief, feeling that things were beginning to take shape and that the wheels were, at last, being set in motion. This man was a professional; he was diligent and business-like. He was just what the doctor ordered! She watched as he completed the paperwork before signing it with an extravagant flourish, the golden nib of his fountain pen gliding effortlessly across the sheet. She was very impressed by the quality of the penmanship, his beautiful handwriting a joyous celebration of the calligrapher's art.

"Ha, I can see you peeping! I suppose you're admiring my handwriting at this sad time, eh?"

"Well, yes; it is *rather* lovely."

"You're too kind!" He looked up and smiled again, maintaining the aura of serenity as he turned the opened book towards her. "If I could ask you to sign and date the entry? If you can't write your name, don't worry – an X will do."

"I think I can manage to sign my own name, thank you!"

"Ah yes, you're from out of town, of course."

Sue signed her name formally: *Mrs Susan Stilton* and sat back down before something suddenly occurred to her: the death certificate. "Oh, I'm sorry, I hope it's not too late! I should have shown you this first, shouldn't I? It totally slipped my mind, I'm really sorry!" she said, reaching for her bag.

"Ah yes, you certainly should," he said, taking the document. "I *knew* there was something missing – not that It'll make a blind bit of difference at this stage. Once you're in the book, you're in for life – or *death*!" He chuckled, but in a compassionate, caring way.

"Right. Well, there it is anyway…"

"Hmm… *old age*, yep. That'll do it, every time…

Len ran his fingers back through his hair as he scanned the document, issuing '*oohs*' and '*ahs*' occasionally.

"My Latin's a bit rusty but it looks like she was also suffering from a spot of '*mors vincit omnia.*' I expect it runs in the family, it's usually genetic."

"Oh, I wouldn't really know…"

"Nothing to worry about, I expect. Anyway, what are you planning to do with her? Going straight in the ground or having a bonfire?"

"Well, I thought cremation might be the best option."

Sue wondered whether bonfire was the normal terminology in modern registration circles? *Or was it just here, in the Fourth World?*

"Sensible choice!" Len scribbled the details on the official-looking document and passed it over. "So, pay attention: this is your Application for Cremation. You'll

232

need to fill in the blanks and hand it in at the Crematorium. There are brochures in reception but, if you want my advice, you'll avoid the cowboys…"

This didn't make any sense to Sue. "Cowboys? What do you mean?"

Len leaned back in his chair, putting opposing fingertips together and pressing inwards, hoping for a click. "Let's just say that some of these places are not quite as, er… *efficient* as they would like us to believe. It defies belief what some of them think they can get away with, it's really quite shocking. The tales I could tell! *Raging Inferno*, for instance, on the High Street… have you heard of them? No? Or *Flaming June*? Actually, she might have gone under, come to think of it. Or *Wicked Fire Starters*? Anyway, as I say, best avoided if you want a nice, respectful send-off. And who doesn't! If I might make a recommendation, you could do a lot worse than pop along to Messrs. Steadfast & Pendlebury, next to Blockbuster on The Parade. They're very good. Red hot, actually. And if you *do* choose them, if you could mention my name, I would be much obliged? It all helps."

"Helps?"

"I'm on a commission basis with them, tenner a head, so… it would be very much appreciated if you could just say '*Len sent you*?' Maybe I shouldn't tell you this, but I also get vouchers for Blockbuster as well, it's a real win/win!"

"Oh…"

Things were building up again, getting on top of her. Was it all just a dream? She hoped it was, then she could wake up and it would go away. It just could not be real, this place; how could all this – whatever it is – be allowed to go on? In broad daylight, as well. Cowboys and bonfires? It wasn't how things were meant to be, was it? It was... Len Spiggins butted in as she was searching for the word: "And, before you go, word to the wise: don't touch Bourke and Ayers with a barge pole, whatever you do!"

"But they're the ones who've got my mother's body!"

"Well, I suggest you go and get it back before it's too late. Now, if you don't mind closing the door on your way out, I'll bid you good day. And, again, sincere condolences."

When she got back to reception, she had things on her mind. Not very nice things. If the Registrar was to be believed (and she had real doubts), her mum's captors – *were they technically 'captors' if she was dead?* – needed to be sorted out. She would have to find a proper crematorium. The ones here all seemed... what? Not to be trusted, that's what! Highly unrecommended and, as for free vouchers for videos? Fucksake! Forget it Len, you've got no chance mate, not a hope in hell.

What I need, she thought, is a proper undertaker, funeral director or whatever to do all of this. I need to get mum back first, though, then find someone to take care of her. Will they be any different, though? What will they be offering by way of an inducement? Free coffee while-you-wait at Kwik-Fit? Kentucky Fried Chicken vouchers? Fucking hell, what a shit place to go and die! Maybe I should just call the police? She realised she hadn't seen a single police car or a constable on the beat in all the time she'd been here. Not one. No wonder the place was so run

234

down and lawless. She imagined it's how it must have been in the old frontier towns of the Wild West.

"Everything OK, darling?" *And her, that damned woman*! Making her run like that, laughing at her, no doubt. Well, there was something she could do about that!

"Yes, I wonder if you could help me?"

"I'll try, sweetheart."

"Is that tea or coffee you have there?"

"What – this? It's tea, Earl Grey… why?"

"May I?"

Sue picked up the mug, a souvenir of Hartlepool. It was a fine piece of hand-crafted crockery, with an exquisitely detailed landscape depicting Durham Cathedral on one side and a historic scene involving a French monkey in a noose on the reverse. She smiled. "Aww, this is so pretty; such craftsmanship… tell me: can you run?"

"Can I…? Whoah, hang on, what are you doing!" she said, shuffling back in her chair as Sue tipped the contents – hot tea, no milk, five sugars – over the woman's grey business head. Grey, as in Earl Grey.

## Plumbing New Depths

The business card gave the address as Unit 9, Avenue X on the Scotch Mist Trading Estate. In spite of the name, it was easy to find, and Sue arrived within minutes of having settled new scores at the Registry Office.

It's The Not Knowing

It was exactly as she'd imagined a Funeral Directors' premises in Skagness might look – and depressingly so. A concrete munitions bunker dating from the last war, its walls now mostly clad in corrugated iron sheeting. Like many of the buildings in Skagness, it had attracted the attentions of Daz03, who had left his mark, with little evidence of the flair for design with which the deluded sap thought he had been blessed. Obliterated in parts, there was some evidence of earlier attacks, poorly executed in white gloss and with awkward, stilted brushwork. This was apparently the work of Bert1960 who, it seemed, *"woz 'ere"* on at least one occasion in the post-war period. Possibly related to Daz03 in some way, but impossible to tell.

The skip outside, against which the wind-blown detritus of a doomed society had mustered, was seriously overloaded with soiled bedding, dead pipes, seized stopcocks and other paraphernalia associated with the plumber's craft. As for the building, every orifice was protected by a mesh panel. The painted sign at the front of the yard announced: 'Bourke & Ayers. Plumbing Engin*Daz03*eers.' A later addition, in a much whiter shade of pale yellow, expanded the business. They were now Funeral Directors, as well. She parked in the road outside and took a moment, preparing herself for a fight.

Suitably steeled she got out of the car. She rang the bell, but there was no answer. She tried again, smiting the door with her fist, but still there was no sign of life within. A tentative "Hello?" drew no response. She wanted to look through a window but there wasn't one at eye level. She skirted the building, looking for another entrance and drew a blank. There was something, though: an empty, water damaged sarcophagus leaning against the chain-link fence at the back. Someone had attempted to repair it, although it was clearly the work of an unqualified amateur. A couple of rusty nails,  hammered in in slapdash fashion, were sticking out of the side, waiting for a loser who would then need a tetanus jab. Returning to the front, she hammered one last time, expecting nothing and that's precisely what she got. There was no vehicle there anyway, which she now realised she should have spotted when she'd first arrived.

Seething at the wasted time, Sue headed back to the car. Moments later, a van came whining and rattling along Avenue X, mounted the pavement and skidded to a halt near the front entrance, expertly avoiding the skip. The door opened with a squealing grind. BBC 2 was blaring a verse from a song she recognised. It stopped on a dark desert highway as the engine died.

A figure in a long, black frock coat emerged from the driver's side, singing '*cool wind in my hair, warm smell of the heaters...*' He placed a top hat on his head, with its page-boy coiffure, and adjusted it to his satisfaction, removing any suggestion of jaunty. He arced his back, stretched his frame in a crucifix style and yawned expansively. He was a tall fellow, over six feet five, Sue estimated; if you included the topper, he was just over seven feet from tip to toe.

"Excuse me, hello? Are you the Funeral Director?" she shouted at him, expecting a denial as he extracted a length of copper pipe from the van. He hadn't noticed her down there.

"Give me one second, I'll be right with you."

A minute later – plumbers are always late, have you noticed? – he walked over and handed her his business card.

"Yes, I am indeed. Augustus Tombes, Corgi-registered and very much at your service, Madam." he said, as he bowed subserviently, clicking his heels together.

*Christ, he's even worse than I'd imagined!* Noticing that she was looking at him askance, he made haste to explain the reason for the unceremonious nature of his arrival.

"I'm afraid I had to hasten earlier to the scene of an emergency. The alarm was raised and came through when I was here *in unum proprium,* on my own, so to speak. A good friend in need, as you might say, had a little accident as she was attempting to move a Shackletons Highchair past a radiator in her home. The lady in question was most unfortunate in her endeavours, during the course of which she succeeded only in dislodging a length of feed pipe, fracturing the joint in the process. Needless to say, I was more than happy to offer assistance, even to the temporary detriment of what I like to refer to as my *Death Duties.* Now, my dear, are you in need of succour?"

Sue was momentarily fazed. A verbose body-snatching gobshite was the last thing she needed.

"Well, seeing as you ask… I believe you have the body of an older lady, so yes, I suppose I am."

Augustus Tombes looked puzzled. He retracted his chin, twisted his head, pursed his lips, and fixed her with a *look*. "Have I? Do you think so? Isn't it a bit too early to tell?"

"What?"

"Well, I mean, I've been taking the tablets *as per*, but the surgical procedures are some way off…"

"Good God! No! You have *taken* my mother's body, that's what I meant. And without permission. And I'd like her back if that's at all possible."

"Oh, my word! My poor lamb… you're Madame *Irene's* daughter. Oh, my poor girl, my most heartfelt condolences. You must be distraught. Come here, let me give you a hug, my poor darling girl!"

Sue was like a rabbit driving a car with no headlights. She froze, rooted to the spot as he strode forward, the ribbons from his topper trailing in his wake, and engulfed her. "Oh, I feel your pain, I really do." He started to wail.

"Honestly, there's no need for you to cry," she said, trying to pull away whilst thinking what she *really* should have said was: *"Fucksake man, pull yourself together and get your filthy hands off me!"*

"It's just… it's just… death, it always makes me… cr-y-yyyy!" His face collapsed and he began to sob uncontrollably. Stunned by this rapid decline she reluctantly patted him on the lower back and offered a few words of encouragement.

"Do you think you're maybe in the wrong line of work?"

## It's The Not Knowing

"No... (sniff), yes (sniff), I don't know..." and he was off again with his tears.

"Shhh, shhh... there, now, come on, stop this, eh? Maybe you should just stick to plumbing, do you think?"

He let out a fresh wave, sobbing like a fop on a downer.

"Hey now, come on, it's not that bad, shhh..."

"It is! It *is* that bad! It really is! Every time I have to fix a float valve or drain a rad or replace a cistern, it's like... it's like... an angel has died," and he was off again, lower lip flapping like a gate in a sluice valve, sobbing his eyes out.

Not knowing what else to do, Sue stood and watched, waiting for him to stop. He did eventually, wiping his eyes on a piece of absorbent blue roll, the kind that plumbers use.

"What must you think of me?"

"Don't be silly, it's alright. Are you OK now?" she said, knowing that what she *should* have said was: *'I must think you're an effete milksop.'*

"Right. OK, Gus, you can do this," he muttered, staring with renewed determination at his shoes. He took a deep breath. "Anyway, it's like this: your dear old mother is back at home. Or, rather, she's next door, at Sheila Boil's place. I know what you're thinking, it's not ideal, but I *had* to leave her there, I really had no choice. We're jam-packed in the workshop. We've just had a load of Armitage Shanks delivered, so we're falling over the blessed things – literally. You have no idea; you can't move in there for toilet ware. So, I did what any reasonable man would have done: I put her back where I found her, or near enough... funny thing is, y'know, I was going to have to maybe charge you for storage if you'd left it any longer. Oh, don't look at me like that, please... pretty please? I feel really beastly, as it is – it's not easy for any of us, you know? OK, I can see you're still upset so, what do you say we just forget it, shall we? What do you say? On the house, eh?"

Sue made a noise from the back of her throat, turned, and marched angrily back to the car. She wanted to punch him in the face, knock his stupid hat off, something like that but she couldn't reach. He was an idiot; he wasn't worth it. None of this was worth it. As she was about to slam the door, she heard his weak and plaintive *"Don't hate me! Please don't hate me!"* He was wringing his hands beside the skip, an over-sized human wreck in a top hat.

With the handbrake still partly engaged she taxied a few hundred yards to the end of Avenue X, where she executed a five-point-turn. He was still standing there, crestfallen with shoulders stooped. She pressed down hard on the accelerator and hurtled towards him, his watery eyes slowly registering what was coming. He blinked hard to clear the residual tears and, as she swerved onto the pavement, he leapt over the bonnet and landed hard on his left ankle, shattering it in the process. The whine of the engine, as it accelerated away, could not drown out the anguished howl of a broken man, a man with surplus toilets.

## Taking A Back Seat

Back in Barracuda Drive, Sheila Boil was restoring some sense of order inside Number 19 in the aftermath of Gus Tombes' visit. The columns of newspapers and magazines had been put back in their preferred location and the Shackletons Highchair was now occupying the last remaining plot in the sitting room. It was currently occupied, although Sheila hoped it would be a fleeting visit. It was now her property: the snooty daughter had said she could have it but, when Gus had asked if he might borrow it for a bit, she didn't like to say no. So, there she was, back from the dead, rigid and unmoving. With a gift shop tea towel draped over her head.

"Cup of tea, love?"

"Go on, then."

"Did you bring any milk?"

Cliff Boil looked up from the floor, where he was attempting to repair the mess made an hour earlier by that 'useless wet fish' from Bourke and Ayers. "No, I didn't. Actually, forget it. Don't bother with tea on my account. I think that's stopped it, anyway. Might need to leave a towel under it for a while in case it leaks."

Cliff wasn't a plumber and didn't have the tools to do the job properly; he'd used some kitchen implements he'd brought from the Café, but they weren't particularly suitable. It was a temporary fix, he supposed. He'd phoned the culprit, who said he was on his way to the Old Bolingbroke General and had sounded quite distressed. He thought he had a bit of a cheek bringing Irene back like that – if *he'd* been here, he wouldn't have let her in.

"Thank you, pet; I don't know where your old mum would be without you. Hang on, I'll get you one of Irene's towels. It's her chair what's caused the problem in the first place, so it seems only fair, eh?"

"Yeah, maybe. You should have told me you had something heavy to lift, I'd have come round straight away, you know that."

"I know, love, but you've got your café to run, I don't like to put you out, not when you're working …"

"Ach, it's no trouble, the café's not that busy at the moment… in fact, I sometimes wonder whether to call it a day, pack the bloody thing in and walk away—"

"And do what? Grass isn't always green y'know."

"I know. Can't help wondering sometimes how life might have been, though…

Cliff was suddenly swamped in melancholy and took a moment to feel sorry for himself.

"…ah, would you listen to me rambling on, eh!"

"You ramble all you like, pet. I like it when you ramble. Hey! Who's that?" There was someone at the door.

"Only one way to find out."

As Cliff was drying his ladle, he heard voices in the corridor, and he thought he heard them say:

"Hello again, pet."

# It's The Not Knowing

"Hello Sheila, is my mum here?"

Hearing the voice, Cliff was suddenly embarrassed and uneasy. As he got to his feet, he found himself brushing the muck from his shirt and smoothing down his hair. It was Irene's daughter, and he owed her an apology for the other night.

"She's through there, love. Mind you don't catch yourself on those crates."

"Oh – !"

Sue gasped, suddenly overcome when she saw it; she knew that was her mother there beneath the tea towel – she'd built herself up for this moment and it wasn't at all what she had been expecting. She'd hoped to see her laid out, finally at peace, resting at the end of life's long journey and preparing for the final curtain. She was definitely not expecting to see her sitting upright with a gift-shop souvenir of Cleethorpes on her head, surrounded by cardboard boxes and the smell of cats. And why was there a basket on her knee? Knitting needles and wool? What the hell?

She hadn't noticed Cliff, lurking behind the door. As she moved to remove the basket he lunged forward and grabbed the tea towel, revealing her face. The wrinkled old face of her mother was harsh, cold and beyond redress: the colourless lips with that characteristic scowl, the sightless eyes peeping through the frosted lenses of her unfashionable spectacles. Why had they put the spectacles on? *The hair, it's so white*, she thought, *she's had it permed, it looks silly. She looks like an old, clapped-out Kevin Keegan.*

Cliff cleared his throat. He apologised profusely for the tea towel and the wool and the chair. It was totally unacceptable, and he was so very sorry about it, he said, as she backed away in alarm.

"You! You're the plate man from the café!" she said, "I might have known you'd have something to do with this!"

"No, it's not like that, honestly it isn't. I was out of order last night and I want to apologise, if you'll let me explain?"

Sue picked up and removed the basket; she had no time for this, didn't want to know.

"And why is she sitting in this fucking chair? Can we have just a bit of respect, Fucksake!"

"Absolutely, you're right to be angry, definitely. It shouldn't have happened; they shouldn't have left her in this Shackletons chair."

"But it's so easy to get in and out of – what else was I supposed to do, eh?" a voice called from the kitchen.

"That's not really the point, though, is it mother. You should have shown more respect to this poor lady." he shouted back before turning to Sue, shaking his head with a rueful smile. *"What can you do with 'em, eh?"* He gazed at her with a pained, broken expression, a tormented soul clinging to a tea towel. She looked away.

"I expect you think we're all inbred peasants in Skaggy, don't you? I wouldn't blame you if you did."

# It's The Not Knowing

"Well, I—"

"It's suffocating, you see. The town, this whole area, it's... it's like a vacuum cleaner. I've never been outside; do you know that? I've never even been to Goole. I'm nearly forty-five years old and I've never been anywhere – Mavis Enderby once, that's it. Pathetic, isn't it?"

"Well, I—"

"It is, it's pathetic. I envy you; I really do. Flash car, nice clothes... you've lived, I know you have. I can see that. You've done things with your life. You must have lots of friends, successful people... I haven't done anything with mine. A miserable one-night stand and a daughter, Mavis, who calls herself Tiffany or Destiny, I'm never quite sure... I mean, what can you do, what can *I* do?

Sue was starting to feel the sense of suffocation herself, by this stage. She might have wondered where the one-night stand mother was but there was no stopping him, and he continued apace:

"Never been married, never found anyone and a disappointment for a daughter; not much to show for a life, is it...? I suppose you're wondering where her mother is, aren't you? Well, so am I!"

"Well, it's not really any of my business—"

"She dumped her on the doorstep with a note! Can you believe that? Poor little mite, wrapped in a blanket with a *polony* sandwich in a bacofoil wrapper."

"I thought it was haslet?"

"Shut up, mother!" There was no rueful smile this time, just a grimace. "I'm sorry about that... I'm nothing, am I? Not really, I've just wasted my life here in this one-horse town – and the horse is dead – stuck every day in a café, making sandwiches I'm not licensed to make and picking fights with anyone unfortunate enough to... a plate, a stupid plate! So crass, so... shit! I am so sorry I turned you away like that..."

Sue shuffled uncomfortably.

"...it could have been so different; we could have been friends, good friends! If it hadn't been for that plate you might be sitting there now, at my table, eating the finest foods, maybe even lobster like you wanted – see, I didn't forget. Lobster, that's what you wanted. You could have had it, too, second helpings if you liked. I've got glasses, proper ones, and you could have had your fill of fine wines, served in cut crystal goblets... if only—"

"Well, I'm not sure I've done that much myself. Made a wrong career choice, maybe – and I've never even been to Mavis Enderby—"

"But I bet you've been to Goole!"

"Well, yes I think I have been *there*, yes."

"Was it nice?"

"I seem to recall it was not very nice, no."

"Ah... do you know, you've been to Goole, and I don't even know your *name*?"

"It's Sue."

"That's enough now, mother! Sue, a lovely name. Is it French?"

"No, I don't think so! Anyway..." she checked her Swatch. "I think I'll—"

"You're very beautiful, Sue. You have lovely eyes, are they your own? Oh, God, listen to me babbling! What an idiot! I'm nervous, forgive me. I'm just... I find it hard to just relax and be myself with a beautiful woman – not that there are any in Skaggy, just hags but... ah, why am I telling you this? I'm sorry... that's a nice watch, did your boyfriend buy you that?"

"My husband did, yes, he did, and he used to be a judo killer, you know, so..."

"Ah, did he! Lucky man... very lucky man... such a lucky man...shall I help you move this dear lady next door?"

Sue paused and considered the options. She concluded there was really only one. One that would mean never having to come back to the dark side.

"No, thank you – that's not going to be necessary – but you might give me a hand to put her in the car?"

"The car? Oh, are you taking her somewhere? Not back to Bourke and Ayers, surely!"

"God no, that's not going to happen! No, I've decided I'm taking mum home."

With Irene fastened into the back seat, Sue took her place in the front and wound down the window. Cliff and Sheila were standing at the kerb. Cliff looking sadder than sad and his mother waving and smiling at the figure in the back.

"Well, that's us. Thanks for all your help and I'll speak to the Estate Agents about, y'know…?" Sue turned the key and started the engine, causing Sheila to raise her voice.

"Yes, we know. It's been lovely to see you, pet. Hope I get some nice new neighbours, but no-one will ever be able to replace your mum, you do know that!"

"Yes, I do… and I hope you get someone too. Well… better make a move, I suppose. Long journey ahead so… I think this is where I say goodbye!"

Sheila suddenly raised her hand to her face as her jaw snapped open. "Oh! what am I like! Hang on, don't go anywhere yet, love. There's something for you. I won't be a minute." She turned and hurried back to the house, her curlers bobbing as she tottered inelegantly along the path. Sue looked at Cliff and made a *what's going on?* gesture and received a *I have no idea what's going on* gesture in return, so she smiled insincerely and looked away, drumming her fingers on the steering wheel.

"Here it is, you'll probably need this, I think." Sheila was back, waving a large manilla envelope. "I found it down the side of the Shackletons. It's from your mam's solicitor, I think, but I haven't read it. I wouldn't read no-one else's private letters."

Sue was tempted to ask her what it said, knowing that she had definitely read it, but didn't want to hear more denials. She opened the self-seal flap and took out both the covering letter and the Last Will and Testament of Irene Skaife. As the hushed crowd looked on expectantly, she skimmed the contents, occasionally frowning, raising an eyebrow, or pursing a lip before finally smiling noncommittally and putting the papers in her bag. She thanked Sheila again and wound the window up, halfway through "Was it anything important?"

As the car moved away, the handbrake slightly on, she looked in the rear-view mirror and saw Cliff Boil sobbing like a baby.

# PART SIX. 2005

## Home Sweet Home

August 16th, 2005.

John thought he had his home-alone evening planned to perfection. Earlier in the day he'd been browsing the bargain bin in Woolies where he'd picked up a DVD for 50p – one whose name he recognised from Wilf's story; he thought that it might be worth a watch, something to pass a couple of hours. Drinks and assorted snacks to hand, he settled back in the chair and pressed *play*. It played, but after ten minutes he gave up – he couldn't concentrate and hadn't the least idea of what it was all about. If anything.

Maybe they could watch *Pretty in Pink* together another day? He wondered where he'd put the receipt.

A couple of hours later he heard the car pull up outside; the engine was revved aggressively for no obvious reason and was then turned off, the fuel gauge deep in the red. He hurried down the stairs, pulled eagerly on the door and ran outside in his slippers, arms stretched wide to welcome her home. There was a time when he would have run his eyes over the car for signs of scrapes, dents etc. but without making it too obvious. Not this time. He was delighted that she was back, that was the main thing.

He opened the driver's door as Sue was reaching for her bag. "Hey, you're back! Why didn't you phone? I was worried… good journey?" he asked. He'd missed her, more than he thought he would – less than two days, but the place seemed empty without her. The neighbours' dogs barked as they embraced. It was John doing all the embracing, really: Sue needed a drink more than a hug after a terrible journey.

"I missed you." he said, wrapping his arms around her with an intensity she could not repel.

"Yeah, me too," she murmured, as he swaddled.

"Hmm, it's great to have you back." He closed his eyes and breathed in her scent for a few moments, blissful moments rudely curtailed when he opened them again. His eyes were fixed on the back seat, but it took a few moments to register what it was he was actually seeing.

"What's that in the back?"

"John, love, can we go inside and talk about it later?" she asked, as she broke free.

"Oh, my God! Now I see." It was his car, but he didn't know if he should open the rear passenger door; it seemed like an invasion of privacy – maybe he should knock first? "Is that who I think it is in there?"

"John? Can we just go inside?"

"But we can't just leave it… is it *real*?"

"No, it's a wax dummy. Yes, of *course* it's real. Come on, let's go inside." She dangled the keys, and he followed her into the house, mouth agape.

"We can't just leave her outside, Sue! And did you lock the car?" She hadn't, so she handed him the keys and he went back out. He locked it, deliberately avoiding the cold, unfeeling look of disapproval he felt sure he was getting in person from beyond the grave. Unusually, he didn't bother to ensure all the doors were securely locked before he turned and headed back to the house at a rate pitched somewhere between a dash and a brisk walk.

He went to put the kettle on, but Sue had already been to the wine rack. Having picked one at random and, having tossed the screwcap to one side, she was now drinking straight from the bottle. She exhaled eventually and wiped her mouth. "God, I needed that!"

"So? What are you going to do now? Leave her there overnight?" John waited for a reply but there was no sign of one. "Talk to me, Sue."

"What's the rush? She's not going to run away, is she?" she giggled. "Shit, I'm sorry, that sounds horrible – just let me calm down for a bit, will you? It's all been… truly, truly horrible."

"Really? D'you mean William or the condoms?" John took the bottle and poured what was left into two glasses.

"Oh, yes, William… a false alarm, that, in the end… I'd built my hopes up y'know, thinking he might be out there after all…"

"And he isn't? So, was it finding the whatsits, then, was that it?"

"Well, y'know, I don't even think finding *them* was the worst part… it was all just… totally horrible. Every bit of it made every bit of me want to scream and kick something or someone or everyone..." Sue shivered and leaned against the worktop, clutching the glass in her palm, staring at the Merlot as it swirled around the bowl. "It was like stepping into another world. You know your zombie towns, dead zones (or whatever you call them) in your books? Well... think of that kind of place and make it worse – much worse, much worse than anything you've ever imagined, or anywhere you've ever been! Far worse..." She broke off and continued to swirl, leaving John hanging. He thought there might be more to come but it seemed not. Hoping to draw her out of herself, he eventually broke the silence and offered a tentative "worse than Goole?"

She drained the glass in one hit.

"Come on, then. Let's do this."

It wasn't as easy as he thought it would be and Sue's sudden fit of the giggles wasn't helping.

"Can you get her feet? No, not like that, you'll have to go round the other side..."

Sue did as she was told, still giggling, but couldn't open the door. "It's locked!"

"Locked? Did you put the child-lock on? Why on earth...?" This was too much for Sue, as the giggles regained control.

"It's not funny, come on, Sue; this is *serious*!"

The neighbours' dogs started barking at this point, as John became infected and started chuckling, then laughing out loud before graduating to hearty, out and out belly laughing. As bedroom lights were flicked on angrily along

## It's The Not Knowing

Lymeswold Drive, Sue gave up the fight and collapsed onto the pavement. This set John off again; he clutched his sides, gasping for air, laughing hysterically.

A bedroom window was flung open, and an upset neighbour bellowed in the darkness. "Will you keep your racket down – some of us are trying to sleep, here! It's enough to wake the bleeding dead!" This did not have the desired effect – just the opposite, in fact – and a fresh wave of hysteria broke out, echoing around the empty street, causing a spate of feverish activity in the lighting department.

"Who the hell is that, making all that racket?"

"I think it's those two at twenty-three, that teacher… she's in the road, looks like she's in a right old state! And he's on his knees by the look of it! Oh, hang on, he's gone round the other side, he's opened the door…"

"Bloody inconsiderate, that's what it is. Bloody teachers get too much holiday!"

"…now she's back on her feet."

"It's no wonder the coppers were round there, people like that. Close the window, Colin and come back to bed, I've got my Speed Bingo tomorrow."

"No, hang on… what are they up to now? Looks like they're trying to drag something out of the back…"

"That's none of our business; come on, close the window."

"It looks like an old woman, I think, some old crow… yeah, what are they…? looks like they're going to have to carry her into the house, one arm and a leg each... Jesus, Tina, you gotta see this... he's got the front door open: *mind your head, love, that's it...* gor blimey, she must be more pissed than the other one is, that teacher, she couldn't even walk! Ha ha! Go on girl, in you go, sleep it off!"

The window was closed and Colin and Tina MacHerring, returned to a fitful sleep and the dreams of addled minds: Tina was playing bingo, she needed one number. The balls were rotating in the drum, spinning, and clattering but there was no escape – they wouldn't come out. She was screaming at the caller, but her voice would make no sound. Colin was killing cats with a shovel and smiling contentedly at a job well done.

"Blimey, she's a heavy old crow!"

"Don't call her names, please John." This was the post-hysteria comedown period; nothing was funny now.

"Yeah, OK. Sorry. I didn't mean it. So, what do you want to do with her? I mean, we don't have a spare room or a bed to put her in..."

"I think we'll just put her in the front room, as it's just for one night."

They manoeuvred Irene into the lounge. It was the first time she'd ever been in there, Sue realised, with a certain poignancy. "Let's put her here."

As they sat her down, Sue instinctively stood back to see if the arrangement suited the room. John reached in his pocket and took out the unfashionable glasses, which he installed on her face, adjusting the slant of the frames. He took them off, breathed on the lenses and cleaned them on his pullover. He stood back to see if they were now straight and fit for purpose. Sue was too tired to even wonder why anyone would do that.

"D'you know, without the specs she reminds me of someone; I can't think who, though…"

"I'm going up, John. You coming?"

She looked back at the figure sitting there. She wasn't grief-stricken as such, but suddenly melancholic, hearing herself saying something she couldn't remember ever saying before – something that a loving daughter would say to a loving mother: "Goodnight, mum. God bless."

"Got it! Bloody Leo Sayer! *That's* who she looks like!"

The next morning, after a poor night's sleep, she made the call to Scrimshaw and Savile, Funeral Directors. As arranged, *the team* turned up at eleven o'clock in a proper hearse, gleaming black with polished chrome adornments. An engraved sign, discreetly positioned, offered a warning to would-be thieves that no tools or bodies were left in the vehicle overnight. The men were soberly attired in black mourning wear and were fastidious and respectful throughout the appointment. It was something of a relief to observe them as they went about their business; they were thoroughly professional in the way they carried both themselves and the body of the dear departed out to where her carriage awaited. With assurances from Mr Savile himself that there was no need to worry, that they would handle all the formalities, the hearse moved off at a funereal pace, proceeding slowly along Lymeswold Drive, back towards the High Street.

Colin MacHerring, who was dealing with an unwanted item which had appeared on his front lawn during the night and was occupied in wishing death to all cats, looked up as they passed. Seeing the coffin in the back, he bowed his head in silent prayer as the old dear departed. He reflected briefly on the ephemeral nature of the human condition, the unfathomable purpose of existence and, ultimately, the meaning of life. And cats, what was the point of them? He hated cats, no matter what.

Sue was having doubts back in the kitchen. John had adopted the position of confessor or a sounding board, as his wife tried to explain her unease. "She's in good hands, I know, but still... was that the right thing to do? I wonder if I was maybe too hasty because she never said whether she wanted this; maybe she wanted a burial, like daddy... maybe she wanted to be laid alongside him? Maybe she really wanted that, but... I just never gave it a thought... we didn't know, she never said, and we never asked... She didn't say anything in her will."

"I know, but whatever you've done you've done it with her best interests... hang on! *Will*? As in *Last Will and Testament*?" She nodded glumly.

"Have you seen it, then? When was that?"

"It turned up on Monday just as I was about to leave."

"And?"

"And nothing."

"What do you mean?"

"There's nothing. She's left everything to someone else…"

"What, the house and all? Who to?"

"Warren Beaty."


They were sitting in silence mainly, occasionally broken by a fleeting murmured thought. John watched her, aware that she was turning gloomy and introspective. He thought that it was now sinking in, and that she was at the stage of pondering all the 'never again' situations: *never again will I see this, do that, hear the other…*

"Hey, one good thing though: never again will you have to go to Skagness!" he said, hoping that might instil a sense of optimism and nudge her back towards the light.

She smiled, wanly and mumbled, "small mercies," as she leant against the worktop, picking distractedly at a split cuticle. He was about to suggest a cup of tea when she resumed but it was clearly an effort – a dispirited outpouring struggling to breathe.

"I just don't know where it went wrong or even when… maybe it didn't have anything to do with William? It seems a long lifetime ago… Is that really how mothers are supposed to be? I mean, was I such a bad daughter? 'Cos from where I'm sitting it really looks like she thought I was. Must have done, I mean… to leave the house to someone else?" John picked up on this point.

# It's The Not Knowing

"What I don't get is, who is this Warren Beaty, anyway? Not the actor, I'm guessing?"

"God only knows! Or, actually, maybe I do... I dunno, I might have met him there. I don't get why she chose that place, to live by the sea... did we ever go there when we were kids? No, never... I didn't think she *knew* anybody there, but obviously there's this Warren character... *how did she meet him*? You know when you think of the seaside you think of nice things don't you? But this wasn't, it was hell, it really was! Do you know, *nobody* I met there was normal, not in any conceivable way? Not one." She looked up, hoping her attempt at conveying the horror might have made its mark. "You don't believe me, I bet – I can't say I blame you..." John shifted uneasily by way of acknowledgement. There was no way of stopping the flow as the words seeped from somewhere deep within, the stuff of nightmares recently disturbed. After a short pause for shallow breath, she went on. "Those people who came? Proper funeral people. I know they know what they're doing, and they'll do all the right things, do them as they should be done but *there*? Ha! If we'd been *there* they would have turned up in a van, free videos thrown in. They'd be talking about bonfires... you've got no idea the stuff that goes on there... they would have offered to replace the boiler while they were here, special discount. They might have asked us to bring a plate back or overcharged us in old money... a thieving bellboy from the Dorchester, not *that* one, the *other* one, preying on old women, stupid vindictive old women..."

John was struggling to follow the gist by this stage – *was that Dorchester?* "Sue, love, you're not making much sense…" He touched her gently on the arm and this brought her back into the room and made her jump. She managed a rueful smile as she turned and looked towards him.

"D'you know what it did, John, all of that? More than anything else? It made me realise just how far away she'd gone: I don't mean how many miles she'd gone; I mean how far she'd gone from *me in spirit* – she wasn't anybody I knew. Maybe she never was. There was no bond. She was, or she had *become*, a stranger. My own cold-hearted mother, a stranger." There was another shake of the head and a sigh. The neighbour's dog barked as she said "stranger," although that might have been mere coincidence.

"Well, maybe but –"

"She didn't die on Saturday. She was dead long before that. She died in 1990 when she moved to that place, stuck a mirror on her ceiling, spread her legs and…" There was a long pause as John offered what reassurance he could. A gentle pat on the arm was like mothers' milk in a situation like this, he hoped.

"What does any of it mean? Nothing makes sense anymore, John…"

There was nothing he could offer by way of reassurance or explanation, no optimistic, motivating *bon mots* but he thought he should try. So, he began, hesitantly at first, faltering as he tried to convey his thoughts before warming to the task and getting into his stride, expressing his feelings with great care and, he hoped, great compassion.

"Do you know, I often think that there is nothing quite so indecipherable as the code, the *secret* enigmatic code of life. With it comes, perhaps, the greatest question of them all: what is the purpose of existence? What is it all about, this overwhelming responsibility, this sheer *horror* of being, of *having* to be, of having to endure the nightmares, *endure* the torments, face up to the despair, the tragedy and the agony of the eternal, insurmountable struggle towards death and decay? Why do we accept this loss of beauty and of faculty; what possible justification can there be for this feeble incapacity to resist the withering, inevitable decline, and terminal disintegration of the anguished, guilt-ridden soul – the spirit, the essence of the half-formed body ripped cruelly from the womb and thrown headlong into the abyss with nothing worthwhile in between?"

The clock ticked. Apart from that, the silence reigned supreme. Sue made no reply, did not acknowledge his contribution. A few moments later, he added: "Still, there's always someone worse off, so..."

## Too Late for Goodbyes

The service was held at the Anubis Crematorium at ten o'clock on the sixth day of September 2005. It was a Tuesday. No words had been spoken over the coffin as it rested on the catafalque, no fond farewells whispered, no wringing of hands and no wailing of the bereaved. Not one solitary tooth was gnashed. At the appointed hour, the switch was flicked without fuss or ceremony and the mortal remains of Irene Skaife took their final journey into the white heat of the unknown. There had been no witnesses.

John and Sue Stilton arrived at the Anubis Crematorium at nine forty-five on the eighth day of September 2005. It was a Thursday. There were hundreds of people there to celebrate the life and death of the clearly much-loved Mr Leigh MacDuff. A song and dance man by trade, Macduff had reached the ripe old age of 99 before succumbing to a heart attack whilst shopping in Waitrose. Another customer gone; another good man taken too soon. Another jar of piccalilli slipping from lifeless fingers.

John was particularly impressed by the size of the turnout and admitted to Sue that he was very surprised – indeed *pleasantly* surprised – that her mum had had so many *friends*. He felt it only fair to point out, however, that sometimes funerals were attended by professional freeloaders, *faux* mourners whose only interest was in what they could grab afterwards, when they hoped to stuff as much *buckshee* food and drink as they could down their miserable gullets. "They probably don't even know who they're singing about, that's often the case… well, this lot have got a nice surprise coming when we tell them there's no party afterwards!" He laughed. Sue didn't.

"This looks all *wrong*. Are you sure this is the right place, John? There are just so many people – I mean, *you* took the call – are you *sure* they said it was here? You're sure we've come on the right day? And how did they even know about it?"

There was a note of panic in her voice, but John was quick to put her mind at rest. He assured her this was definitely the place and, if anything, they were maybe a bit early:

that's all it was. As for how they knew about it, he shrugged and offered "bush telegraph, probably."

He took out the crumpled envelope from his pocket on which he'd scribbled down the details; this was his trump card. He smoothed some of the creases. "Look, see? Right there: *"Anubis Crem, Thursday 8th @ 10.00"* Relax, it'll be fine. We must be on after this lot, I'll go and ask them if they're running late, see if I can hurry them up. Honestly, you're such a worrier!" Sue snatched the envelope and peered at the hastily scribbled details, frowning and pulling faces. "God, your handwriting is *terrible*! Is that supposed to be an eight or a six? And what does *this* say? Is it… does that say *Tuesday*? It looks more like Tuesday than Thursday to me!"

"What? Hang on, let's have a look… no, it's… definitely… Thursday, isn't it?" John's heart plummeted as he checked and realised that he was now definitely in sticky situation territory. "Oh, sugary shit!" He kicked a nearby wreath which had been carefully discarded, scattering mournful roses in all directions. "OK, yes. It appears that it might say Tuesday and I'm sorry Sue but it's not my fault. I was in a rush and maybe if you'd taken the call yourself, you know you're better at these things and… well, am I right? Oh, come on, don't be like that!" He looked away and turned the envelope ninety degrees, but it made no difference. It still definitely said Tuesday. Any reasonable person would know it was an honest mistake made by an honest man who was honestly getting too scared to even consider the repercussions.

"Sue, where are you going? Sue? Sue!"

## It's The Not Knowing

John Stilton had never expected to be confronted by an angry crowd at a crematorium. Two dozen crabby strangers, assembled from the hangers-on and friends of a late song-and-dance man pushed towards him in a pincer movement. As he was being touched, shushed, and crushed he brushed them to one side as he wriggled free from their claws and made good his escape.

Sue was in the site office when he burst in, looking for sanctuary; she was being consoled by a vampire. That's what the man behind the desk looked like to John, anyway, in his long black coat, and with his glossy Ray Reardon hair shining like a healthy hound's pelt. Crematorium manager Bernie Smoker (for it was he) was eager to offer assurances that staff and management of Anubis Memorial plc had done all they possibly could – and more! – in the most trying of circumstances.

"I'm very sorry Mrs. Stiltskin, truly I am. We did try to contact you via the telephone – several times, in fact – on Tuesday, when we began to wonder whether you might have been somehow delayed but, in the end, we simply had no choice but to proceed *in absentia*, as it were. It was a question of capacity, you see; the vehicles were starting to back up and were queuing right around the block. And, whilst I never speak ill of the dead or their chauffeurs, some of those younger hearse drivers can be quite impatient, as I'm sure you can well imagine, blasting their klaxon horns and so forth... as I said, I am *truly* sorry to be the pallbearer of bad news but, rest assured, the service was conducted in a most professional manner and, if I might be allowed one small indulgence? – it was the easiest one of the day, of that there can be no question; no tears, you see? It's always

265

difficult when the tears flow but, for your mother, thankfully, there were none. If there had been anyone here, I'm sure there wouldn't have been a dry eye in the house, but as it turned out, well… we'll never know. I hope that is of *some* comfort to you, at this sad time?"

Sue, to her own surprise, felt no emotion on hearing this and realised she was, in fact, quite unfazed by what should on the face of it have been a disconcerting situation; maybe it was her realisation that there was nothing to be gained by crying over spilled milk or closing a stable door after a horse had bolted. Maybe she was becoming inured to the new reality. With a degree of self-possession that would have impressed even the coolest of customers, she asked him what had happened to her mother's ashes afterwards. Smoker replied that, in the absence of family or friends, they had been scattered in the Garden of Remembrance – *providing, of course, that one of the scatty gardeners remembered to do it.* "Sorry, just my little joke, my way of dealing with the ghastly business of death!" he explained, responding to her double take. There was a period of contemplative silence (in lieu of anything better), after which he added, "you know, it really is one of life's tragedies that you didn't make it to the actual cremation – a good and valued friend, the manager from Blockbuster, was waiting outside, handing out free video tapes – proper VHS ones, not Betamax! If I'm being honest, I found it a little too '*every man for himself*' for my taste, and it turned into a bit of a feeding frenzy. But I suppose I can have no complaints; in fact, I did rather well in the end and managed to procure a couple of really good ones. If you'd like to see them, I have them here somewhere…" He reached down into his bottom drawer and pulled out an Asda shopping bag from which he retrieved two shopsoiled, fogged plastic cases: one was "Pretty in Pink," the other "Zoltan: Hound of Dracula."

"Here they are, two *belters!*" he said, resurfacing with more excitement than was perhaps deserved, even for one who was easily excited. "Oh…"

They had already gone.

A few minutes later, they were standing in the Anubis Memorial plc Garden of Remembrance, an area towards the back of the field enclosed by a neatly clipped box hedge. The large, paved area within had been recently disinfected and was fringed by an immaculate lawn. In the centre stood a memorial tower which dated from the post-war period, adorned with hundreds of memorial plaques. The tower itself, modelled on the Ziggurat and described by Pevsner (a member of the Parks Maintenance team, known to his colleagues as Pev) as *ugly yet functional*, peaked at three metres in height. This unlovely grey brick structure was redeemed occasionally by the odd floral tribute or framed photograph. The setting was, they both agreed, *"rather lovely and so peaceful."* Obviously, they both agreed it was lovely before they came upon the small feline gift (unburied and still steaming) on the lowest level, right alongside the engraved slate commemorating the life and passing of Gordon Brigadoon MacHerring, the late lamented and much-loved brother of Colin.

"So, then. This is it. The last resting place…" The sun broke briefly from behind a cloud. The silence continued in the sudden, unexpected warmth as John considered his response, knowing it was important to find the correct tone.

"Yes."

"Where do you think they scattered her, John?"

"The ashes? Hard to say, really. Could be anywhere round here, couldn't it? And y'know, what with all the rain we had overnight..." he paused suddenly, not wanting to finish what he'd started.

"What?"

"No, nothing."

"Go on, what were you going to say?"

"Well... all that rain we've had... if they scattered her on this paved bit, well... she's probably gone down that drain over there. If my calculations are correct, and maybe they're not, she might have reached the sea by now. Maybe even Skagness. It's possible, it's always possible. Earth to sea, ashes to sludge, as it were. Sorry."

Sue covered her mouth to stifle something – possibly a chuckle? He noticed and drew encouragement from this: "Look, I'm sorry about getting the date wrong and I'm sorry it's all been so shit... which it has! Those two horrible days, you having to go and bring her back here and then... but it's not even any better *here,* is it? Am I wrong?" Sue sniffled, almost as if she was crying. His chuckle theory was perhaps ill-founded.

"Ah, Jesus, God," she sighed. "No, it isn't. You're right, it doesn't seem to get any better."

"And, I mean, did you *hear* what the vampire said back there? Free videos – what was that all about?"

"That's what I was saying… Christ almighty! Are they *all* mad, John or is it just us? Is it us? Is it? Are we the mad ones?"

"Well, you'd definitely have to wonder." he conceded. "So… where are we, then? I mean, where are *you*, in all this? How are you, y'know… how are you coping?"

"How am I *coping*? Hah! I suppose I'm fine; I think. I'm sort of… come on let's walk. It looks like rain." Sue hooked her arm through John's, and they moved off towards the gates. After a deep breath, she continued: "So… I think I'm OK. I think so. It was unexpected and the will was a bit of a shock but yeah, I'm fine. And all that other stuff, well! I don't even want to *think* about all that! But no; it's fine, it's all been done and sorted. I'm getting there. Slowly, slowly."

"That's good. I just wish there was something I could say or do..."

"It feels like it's been put to bed, I suppose. The last chapter has been written. Maybe, anyway. Life goes on – just not for my mother." John squeezed her arm, showing that he understood. "Will I miss her?" she wondered, with a shrug and a pause. "No, I really don't think I will. I mean, you can't miss what you never had, can you?"

"No, I suppose not. Anyway, I'm glad you're OK, I was worried about you, y'know. You're my mate!" She nudged him affectionately. "That's silly, you don't have to worry about me. You're my mate, too… and if I can cope with all of *this*, I can probably cope with anything – even Warren Beaty!"

As they picked their way across the field, tiptoeing or backtracking to avoid the puddles, they heard singing drifting across from the chapel. It wasn't the kind of choral work you might expect from, say, the Chapel of a Public School. If anything, it was more akin to a knees-up around the *joanna* in a downmarket boozer down by the market, full of boozers. Make no bones about it, it was a real freeform din; something in an up tempo, music hall style although the tune wasn't immediately obvious to either of them or, indeed, the singers. They were almost at the door before they realised it was '*Boiled Beef and Carrots.*' It was an infectious little tune and unprompted, they started to skip along, hand in hand, enthusiastically belting out the words. Caught up in the heady intoxication of the moment, John suddenly leapt in the air and kicked his heels together with great gusto. He landed awkwardly, turned his ankle, and skidded sideways in the mud, managing to pull Sue down with him in the process. As the shock subsided, they began to roar with laughter from the mire as a black-booted and suited crosspatch burst forth from the Chapel in a frame of mind best described as tetchy. Outraged, he fixed the pair with a steely glare and erupted: "Have some *effing* respect, will you? Some of us are trying to celebrate the *effing* life of Leigh Macduff in there and we don't need the likes of you out here making this sinful noise. It's enough to wake the dead! People like you make people like us sick!"

After a murmured apology, and without wishing to escalate the situation further, they departed the scene as the crosspatch lit an *effing* cigarette, the reason for his coming outside in the first place. He continued to glare self-righteously, grinding his yellow, nicotine-stained fangs as they went.

John was hobbling and kicking out erratically in an attempt to flick mud from his trousers; Sue did not look back. She was looking forward resolutely, wondering whether Leigh MacDuff's middle name could possibly be Don. She hoped so.

## House and Contents

September 11$^{th}$, 2005.

A dull, overcast Sunday morning on the Cheeses Estate was well under way when John Stilton groaned and rolled out of bed. It was almost ten thirty and he had a hangover, the result of an overindulgence the previous night. He'd probably overstepped the mark as far as government guidelines were concerned but he was a grown adult, and nobody was going to tell him what to do! He could vaguely account for at least two bottles of wine and a six-pack of Skol Special but there might have been more. He was aware at the time that such reckless mixing of the grape and the grain would end in tears, but he thought he could handle it. He couldn't and never had so why he thought this time might be any different could be considered a mystery, but one for another day. If there's time.

It was supposed to have been a productive tete-a-tete and something of a release: a Saturday night at home, in the same room, with the first serious discussion of *what happens next* and *where do we go from here.* John had seen it as an opportunity to contribute something, to show Sue she was not alone and could count on him for general admin at least. To that end, he had put together a flow chart and jotted down some bullet points covering what he considered to be the essential elements. He brought along a pad and a couple of pencils, but it quickly became obvious that the enthusiasm wasn't there. They decided, quite early in the proceedings, that it might be best left to another day, particularly the question of whether Sue should contest the will. She had made the point that she did not want to have to go back to Skagness or to even think about the place. Ever. She was most insistent on that matter, having no desire to return to the town which, for her, had come to symbolise everything that was wrong with the universe today, a place which she might easily have described as an *'exclusion zone'* or a *'no-go-area'* had she not already decided that *'shithole'* did the job perfectly. That was when they had uncorked a second bottle and moved on to other, less troublesome matters.

Sue looked up from the Potters Bar Times Educational Supplement as he wobbled into the kitchen and gave him a superior look.

"God, even the cat wouldn't have dragged you in in that state! Are you suffering?

He closed one eye in an attempt to focus whilst preventing the piercing light from burning a hole in his retina.

"Correct me if I'm wrong but I'm sure I told you not to mix the grape and the grain, didn't I? I seem to remember mentioning it… What will you do now? Make a cup of tea?

# It's The Not Knowing

Go on then, seeing as you're offering." He thought she was far too chirpy, almost indecently so. He might have whined if he'd had the energy; instead, he drew deep on his reserves and set about switching on the kettle. That done, he stood motionless, staring at his feet as the water came to the boil. It was ten thirty-four before he managed his first words of the day: *is that toenail fungus?*

"I've come to a decision." She waited, expecting him to ask what it was.

"It *is*! Look! I've got a bloody fungal infection in my big toe! Christ! Sorry, you've done what?"

"I said, "I've come to a decision about the will.""

"OK. You're going to fight it, yes?"

"I'm not going to fight it, no. What's the point? Let Warren Beaty have it, whoever he is. He must have done something to deserve it."

"But that's exactly the point! Who *is* he? Have we got any paracetamols anywhere?"

"I don't think I have a leg to stand on, not legally and maybe not even morally. As far as we know, she still had all her marbles when she made the will so... there's some in the cupboard."

"Yes, but don't you, y'know, feel like it's unfair? Which cupboard?"

"Course it's unfair but since when was life fair? *That* cupboard."

# It's The Not Knowing

"Well, yes but, why should this Warren tosser get what's rightfully yours? Right, *this* cupboard."

"But it *isn't* rightfully mine, that's the whole point. She made her decision; she left me nothing and it's the last bad thing she ever did. Where she actually and finally *unbecame* my mother. So, let's move on, there's nothing more to say. Did you find them?"

He had but was struggling to pop the pills from the foil-backed sheet, a fiddly operation which required a degree of co-ordination beyond his powers at that time. He muttered under his breath as Sue looked on, far from impressed. Finally, she lost patience, took over and popped them on his behalf, placing them in his shaking palm with a tut and a shake of the head. If he couldn't deal with uncooperative packaging, how would he ever deal with the fact that Irene Skaife had specifically *not* left her property to her daughter because, as witnessed by the undersigned, she detested her son-in-law 'more than one hundred percent.' The will stated that unless the daughter was prepared to legally divorce the useless waste of space forthwith (or within one calendar month) and move permanently to Skagness, the sole beneficiary in the matter of her estate was to be Mr Warren Beaty, currently residing at the Flotsam Hotel, Skagness.

Quite simply he wouldn't be able to deal with it and she would never tell him. And she would never move there or even go there. Ever.

# PART SEVEN. 2005

## The Chernobyl Diary Part 1

Wednesday, 2nd November. 07.45

"Sue? Before you go, what did you do with William's story? You haven't still got it, have you? I've looked everywhere for the bloody thing."

Sue, who was definitely not looking forward to the first day back at school, was on her way out of the door when John raised the question. She hadn't told him about the thieving seagull. It wasn't a deliberate withholding of information, more the result of his not having mentioned it and of her having a lot on her plate. She had simply forgotten, nothing more and nothing less.

"Ah, no, you won't find it because I lost it."

"What do you mean *'Lost it?'* How'd you manage that?" There was no reply. "Where did you lose it?"

She tutted and, putting down her bags, was about to explain when his dishevelled, slept-in face appeared at the top of the stairs. "I know, silly question: *'if you knew where you'd lost it, it wouldn't be lost!'*"

Wishing that she'd left five minutes earlier or that he'd woken up five minutes later, Sue looked at her watch to make him aware (if he wasn't already) that she was being avoidably delayed. "Briefly, it was grabbed from my hand by a seagull who dropped it in the sea. And that's all I've got time for, so… I'd actually forgotten about it. Anyway, look, I'm going to be late, and I have to dash. We'll talk about it tonight if you want. OK? Right, well… wish me luck!"

Horrified by this unexpected news, and not sure whether such a thing was plausible, John leaned against the banister up on the landing. His eyes wedged open in shock, he could only gape. At that moment he couldn't think what else to do; gaping came naturally and seemed somehow appropriate, so, gaping it was.

*"You know what this means, don't you?"* he mused to himself a short while later over a light breakfast of tea and toast.

"You're nuclear wintering in Chernobyl, comrade!"

For the past month John had been working on a forestry commission for The Forestry Commission: a series of pamphlets describing the various woodland tourist trails in England and Wales, provisionally entitled *'Routes to Branches.'* It wasn't the most exciting project he'd ever tackled but he made it his policy never to turn down work, increasingly so since Sue had decided not to contest the will, around the same time as he had stopped looking at expensive guitars. He had devoted himself fully to the research necessary for an undertaking of this kind, and that had accounted for most of October. The commissioners seemed happy with it, promised a cheque in due course and now his in-tray was empty. This would be the opportune moment to grasp the nettle and take on the challenge of making some sense of the coded and – following the recent receipt of certain information – only *extant* thoughts of

## It's The Not Knowing

William Butler Skaife. Now would be the right time to decipher The Chernobyl Diary.

He retreated to the study where he had to move a pile of ironing back out onto the landing before he could get cracking. The notebook was still there in the drawer, just waiting to be cracked. Next to it was his handy, barely thumbed copy of '*Teach Yourself Russian*,' where they had been since the end of April, gradually sinking beneath a build-up of desk-drawer paraphernalia; this included *The Observer's Book of Trees* which he had snapped up in a charity shop for a bargain price. Charity shops are *such a great idea* (something he'd often said, defying anyone to say otherwise). He took the diary and flicked through the pages, the majority featuring that distinctive, left leaning Cyrillic gobbledygook just waiting to be deciphered; just waiting to spill the beans on whatever was hidden within. He seemed to remember it began with a rather vague "I had –" Well, soon he would know just what *he had*.

There were no doodles, he noticed – something that hadn't occurred to him previously. Unusual for a diary, he thought. Even Pepys or Anne Frank must surely have doodled in the margins whilst waiting for inspiration? Not WBS, though. This had the appearance of a serious, academic work, something loaded with gravitas.

Well aware of the enormity of the task, he lay the notebook flat on the desktop, opened at the first page. For the reference book, he used a paperweight (a souvenir of the gift shop at Windscale, fashioned from synthetic waste plutonium) to keep the alphabet pronunciation guide in full view at all times. This done, he took a deep breath, interlocked his fingers, and applied outward pressure until the knuckles cracked, a sure sign they were ready for action. Having shifted his head from side to side a few times to expel any neck-bound cricks which might have been lurking, he was at last ready for the challenge.

"Right then, here we go *again*!" he said, leaning forward and extracting a pencil from the mass-produced yet limited-edition and beautifully hand-crafted souvenir of Hartlepool. Overhead, the skies darkened, and the rain began to fall.

# It's The Not Knowing

*I had been an unhappy child for as long as I can remember. Unhappy children rarely make happy adults.* Once the pattern has been established it's almost impossible to swim against the tide even if you've jumped ship. I know what I'm talking about. I don't know exactly what had caused or nurtured this unhappiness, but I had the feeling that I was unwanted or had ended up in the wrong place. I imagine that's how a young cuckoo might feel as he instinctively throws his new siblings headlong to their premature, featherless deaths.

The Germans probably have a ludicrously long word for this sense of not belonging, but I don't know what it is. I had a look in the library but the nearest I could find was '*Gemütlichkeit*' which actually means just the opposite, so that's not much use in this instance. Let's just forget the Germans. I blame this sense of whatever-it-is on my parents, and with some justification, I think; parents whose love I sought and felt I deserved but never had. They had their way of doing things, I suppose.

*In the beginning there was Eric Skaife*, the man I came to recognise as my father. There was no-one else, he was the lone candidate on a shortlist of one. Like any young boy, as soon as I was old enough to know how things worked, I wanted to be like my dad. Not totally like him, you understand. I didn't want to be a carbon copy or a clone. God no! Clones make me sick, so do carbon copies, and I've seen a few so I know what I'm talking about! I didn't really like his teeth if I'm honest – or the big gaps between them to be more precise – and his hair was too sparse for my liking. So, I didn't want to *look* like him, I just wanted to be able to do what *he* did; maybe in those days I wanted to make him proud of me. I wanted to have a job and drive a car, maybe have people working for me and calling me 'Sir,' because I supposed that's what they did, the people who worked for people. I didn't know at the time that he was a lone wolf, a one-man band. If you're thinking he was a back street abortionist – and God knows why you'd accuse him of something like that! – he wasn't. You must be deranged.

No matter how much I tried to please him or get on his good side, it never seemed to be enough. I didn't stoop as far as ingratiating myself. No child should have to ingratiate itself with its parents. That needs writing down unless it's an unwritten law. It always seemed to me there was nothing I could do to live up to his expectations; maybe I didn't even know what they *were;* it's possible, it's always possible. I do remember how it was when he came home after work. I can see it like it was yesterday: he'd be carrying a present – maybe no more than a trinket or a token gesture, a bauble even – but never for me, it was never for me, always for Susan, my elder sister. His 'little princess,' that's what he called her, and you'd have thought, wouldn't you, that I would have been the obvious choice for the position of Prince, me being her brother and what have you, but that's where you'd be wrong, see? If I ever said – and I did! – *"What about me, daddy, The Prince? Surely, I get a present, too?"* he would just say "Real Princes don't need presents!" and walk away whilst she, the Princess, her... why, she'd just go skipping off, clutching that day's offering, seemingly oblivious but knowing very well the injustice of it all! Is there any wonder, then, that I've turned out like I have?

# It's The Not Knowing

*'Yes, that's all very well,'* you might say, 'but what about your mother? How did she react to your father's lack of affection or his uncaring disposition?' Well, I wasn't going to mention her until later but, seeing as you ask, I'll tell you. She didn't react; she'd either chosen to ignore it or simply refused to see it. There was no support from her side. And before you speak up and table your objections, I know exactly what you're thinking so you needn't bother. Please don't underestimate me. You think that in those days the man's word was law, and the little woman or housewife did as she was told, fearful of the consequences if she dared to criticise the man of the house. Well, you may be right, but you're not. You're wrong, in her case. She wasn't scared of him at all. In fact, quite the opposite. When she had her funny moods she was inclined to be what the people of that time might have referred to as a 'nasty piece of work,' which is not a phrase anyone uses nowadays, now that we are heading for the new millennium. I think *he* was scared of *her*, in fact. That might seem unlikely but it's more common than you think. I wrote a poem about it once, a good one. It was called *'Why Do You Hurt Me So, Woman?'* I can't remember it all now but there was a bit in it, a bit I was quite proud of. It went something like:

'Oh, something something, breasts of curdled milk / Don't look for reasons to despise me / Something nurturing a purse of glow worm's silk / and then something about a sow's ear.' I wish I could remember it. I handed it in for my homework and I thought I'd get a gold star at least but all I got was a telling off and told never to say 'breast.' Ironically, the teacher Mrs. Boyle was a flat-chested harridan, and I told her as much. She gave me the slipper across the back of my head and all the kids laughed. I hated her and I hated primary school. However, let's not go down that road.

So, there we were, The Skaifes. To all intents and purposes, we were a typical dysfunctional nuclear family even though it wasn't a recognised term at the time, and you couldn't get a council grant to deal with it. I suppose, going on outward appearances, we might have passed for normal to the people who lived nearby. Some might refer to them as 'neighbours,' but you'll never hear me calling them that. I don't like to categorise people because I don't think it's fair or even helpful. I know I wouldn't like it if I thought they were talking about me like that. They didn't even know me anyway so it's hardly likely they would have much to say. Certainly, nothing worth saying, and that's probably what held them back. A life spent venting worthless thoughts to other under-achievers is no life at all, in my book. That's not to say that I'm not a people person, because I very much am but they should know their limitations and think inside the box. I hope they do for *their* sakes.

I was talking about my father and his attitude towards his children, particularly me. There's no point skirting this issue. Susan, or Suze as she liked to be called, was his favourite. No question. She knew it, he knew it and I knew it. My mother knew it, and she knew I knew it, but she would never admit she knew it; she probably didn't want to know it or to know that I knew it. I didn't mind, I didn't need presents really, it didn't bother me. What is a present when all is said and done? Nothing more than a bribe; someone's way of buying your affection and I wasn't stupid; I wasn't going to fall for such shallow gestures. When I look back now, I think if he'd offered me anything, I would probably have said, 'Keep it father and give it to an orphan.' I'm thoughtful and caring like that; I hate to think of people suffering, particularly orphans. They're my favourites.

And ultimately, what purpose did these bribes serve? What did he get out of it? And Suze: what did she get out of it except for a few knick-knacks? If you think about it, it didn't make her any happier in the long run. She couldn't wait to leave home and move in with *what's-his-name*, could she? Before they were even married too so, you could justifiably condemn her moral turpitude as I certainly did, although I kept my feelings to myself. *'Never interfere'* is one of my maxims.

I don't really know why my parents stayed together because, by that stage, things had entered what would have been talked of as *'The Great Silence,'* if anyone was talking. Which they weren't. They didn't speak to one another, and he didn't speak to me, and I didn't speak to him and hardly spoke to her, and she hardly spoke to me. Sometimes it was hard to decide who wasn't talking to whom with the greater determination. They even had the phone disconnected, just in case. These periods of silence went on for days or weeks and then there'd be a huge row when speaking returned briefly to make things worse before the suffocating silence descended again.

Apart from these deathly periods and the coming home with inducements, I don't have many other memories of the *paterfamilias*. I'm not sure I can actually remember how his face went now and it's not like there's a family album or even a single photograph anywhere, either. There is no proof and no record of family events, holidays… in fact, when I think about it, I'm sure we never even had a holiday. He once said, well before the *Great Silence* obviously, that he didn't like salt, sand or candy floss and wasn't going to spend good money staying in a guest house when he had everything he needed at home. So, we never went to the seaside if you can imagine that.

I can remember being at school, after the summer holidays, and all the kids talking about where they'd been and what they'd done. Then they asked me, and I said, "Nothing," so they laughed at me. That was another time I got into trouble.

I was trying to tell you about him, but I keep drifting. I want to commit this to paper but I'm worried I might forget something if I keep going off at a tangent. Who will ever read this? Nobody, I bet. And when they find it what will they do with it? Hard to imagine them taking the trouble to decode it, but that's OK – at least I will have purged myself and got it off my chest, whatever *it* is.

I'm finding it very therapeutic, writing in this coded way. It sharpens the mind, I think. Maybe I should have written the stories like this? It's a thought but it's too late now; they're done and dusted. Will anybody ever get to read them? Apart from Áine, that is, and I could tell she wasn't overly impressed. More of her later if there's time. I need to stop getting ahead of myself. Maybe I'll say something about the stories later. Again, it depends on whether there's time.

## It's The Not Knowing

I've mentioned my mother briefly and I suppose I should tell you more about her. She was an enigma wrapped inside a mystery which should probably have been a straitjacket. Irene Skaife *nee* Shagstaigne (pronounced *Shasteen*). I have more memories of her than I do of my father and that is probably the natural order of things. He wasn't around so much; he was always working, running his business.

Seeing as we're back on that subject, I might just say that I didn't like to tell people what he did, not the kids at school anyway. It seemed like a rubbish job when you heard what the other kids' dads did. Two were cowboys who worked on the local farms or ranches as they called them – that's what they said. I probably thought it was a lie at the time, and now I know it was. The boasting just made me despise them more than I did already. I knew their lives were worthless before that, but this just proved it, if you know what I mean. For somebody to pretend their dad was a cowboy or a ratcatcher or an astronaut (another lie, I later discovered) only goes to show what kind of low-level underachievers they are and with ideas well above their station.

I might as well get it over with and tell you what he did; there's no reason to hide it now. My father was a dealer in old, antiquarian books. Looks impressive when you write it down, but it isn't. I was ashamed because it was such a boring thing to be. I think, in my naivety, I asked him once whether that meant he was a bookie, but he didn't tell me. In fact, he ignored me. I suppose he must have made a decent living from selling dusty old crap which was not worth reading to people whose lives were not worth living. If you want to read a book, read a *new* one for God's sake!

# It's The Not Knowing

More money than sense, some people. I've seen them and I know what they're like. When I was still quite naïve I imagined a storeroom piled high with rare first editions of ancient best-sellers, probably printed on papyrus. When I got older and attained greater wisdom, I realised how ludicrous a supposition this was, and I was even more ashamed. It's not something I like to admit but I suppose if I'm getting things off my chest this is the time to do it.

Anyway, I don't know the boring fine detail about what he did and, obviously, he never said much about it. It all collapsed when he died suddenly, like that. The premises went up in smoke, quite literally; nothing remained, nothing was saved from the flames, and the Police couldn't understand it, quite literally. He never intended for me to take it on, anyway. That much was clear; he would have said otherwise, wouldn't he? I'm almost sure he would.

I know where he worked; it was somewhere off the High Street, down an alleyway next to *The Dressed Mutton*. I remember my mother taking me down there once, but I wasn't allowed inside. It was dark and gloomy in the alleyway, and it had a strange smell; like ammonia, although I didn't know that word at the time. I had to sit outside in my pushchair while she was in there, doing whatever it was she was doing. I remember it because it was the day I needed to go to the toilet and I had an accident, which was hardly my fault, but she wouldn't see it like that. When she came back, she was in a bad temper, and I got a clout but I'm sure she was upset even before she could smell what I'd done. Yes, I'm certain of that.

## It's The Not Knowing

There's something else I remember about that day, too, and not just because I got a belt for soiling myself. Before we went to his antiquarian workplace, my mother had been telling me who lived in the houses as we passed by. There was this one house, more of a cottage really, which was tucked away behind a big hedge. That was where an old lady lived, she said; I can't remember her name, it might have been Polish. It doesn't matter, none of that matters. She told me the old woman was foreign, violent, and dangerous and that she had a stick. I was warned never to go near her, and made to cross my heart and promise, or I would end up being fed to a dog. I didn't like dogs, so I promised I wouldn't. She told me I was, 'not such a disappointment after all,' and, as a reward, I could throw some stones at the windows. Now, even then I was a people person. I was born with an innate sense of fair play, so I knew such a thing was wicked and wrong. Angered by my reluctance she tipped me straight out of the pushchair and then grabbed a handful of pebbles and stones which she thrust into my hands as I started to cry. She crouched again and picked up another handful for herself and began the assault on the poor old woman's house. After the third salvo, there was a shattering of glass which produced a triumphant cry of delight and made her laugh; it wasn't a nice laugh, though – it was mean and horrible, mocking and possibly sardonic. I wasn't sure of the terminology at the time. With the ammunition spent, she picked me up, put me back into the seat and we carried on towards the town. I was still crying but I hoped the old woman wasn't hurt. I hoped she was alright, I really did. I might have prayed, I don't remember. It doesn't matter. I've always sympathised with the victims. If they're meek as well, they will inherit the Earth; that's one of the things I remember from school. I see caring for the meek as a strength and not a weakness. You must never underestimate me; don't think I'm weak and do not try to oppress me.

I want to try and understand my relationship with my sister, the sister who abandoned me twice. It might help – it might help *me*, I mean – if I can put it into words. I want to know whether it was something in me, some failing, that allowed us to drift apart. Because we did. And I dealt with that sense of loss by... well, you know how I dealt with it.

She was older than me; that's a fact and not an opinion. I told you she was his favourite, the old man's, and again that's a fact, not an opinion. How did we get on, as siblings? Strangely enough, we got on well. I wasn't jealous of her at all. This might seem strange, but I bore her no ill will, carried no grudge. It wasn't *her* fault if she was his favourite. I have to believe that otherwise how could I have carried on? Life is just too short to carry grudges.

I didn't go to her wedding, though. That's maybe the biggest regret I have. I never saw her again after the old man's funeral. I wish we'd spoken as we stood over the hole, but we didn't. We didn't even look at each other; I somehow felt I couldn't, and I really don't know why now. I behaved like someone immature, a brat possibly, and that's not something I could normally be accused of. I don't know if she ever forgave me. Maybe the fact mother was crying had shocked us into silence. I'd never seen her crying or vulnerable. It made her look ugly.

Why didn't I go to the wedding? Good question. It's haunted me ever since.

# It's The Not Knowing

My sister and I were close, I don't doubt that. And I owe her a lot. She did what she could to make my unhappy childhood happier. I would like to think I made her happy too, in my own way. She was like me; she didn't have a special friend, someone she could spend time with away from there. I often wonder whether there was something wrong with us, having no friends? We had no other family either, no aunts, uncles, or cousins. That wasn't our fault though. You can't make cousins, can you? You can make friends, though. Except that we couldn't, apparently. It's a conundrum to me because we're both people people, me and Suze. So, we had to make do with our own company.

We used to spend a lot of time in the kitchen doing school stuff and drawing. I liked her drawings, and she liked mine, I think. Mother didn't like them, any of them. There was this one occasion when Suze asked her whose was best? She'd done a pony eating grapes and I'd done a farmyard action scene with a helicopter.

"Do you like my picture or William's picture best, mummy?" she said, something like that, looking up at her hopefully with her big blue-grey eyes. When Irene entered a room in one of her funny moods, the atmosphere was instantly sucked out. If there had been a piano player at home, that's when the music would have stopped. I don't know what manner of reply Suze was expecting to hear other than a stinging put-down. She should have seen it coming and I don't know why she burst into tears when it came. It was never going to be anything positive or encouraging. That was not her style. She sneered; I remember that sneer very well.

"Hard to say. I wouldn't go as far as to say I liked *either* of them particularly. It's more a question of *which do I hate the least*, to which the only answer could be: *'Neither. I hate them both equally. I don't have favourites.'*"

As she walked away, she added (quite cruelly I thought) that the pony's grapes looked like rats' droppings and my helicopter looked more like a spider. Obviously, it was both insensitive and uncaring, but you get used to that where we came from.

I don't suppose I'd ever given much thought to how I might feel if Suze left me. Maybe I imagined she never would, but of course she did. She went to college for three years, being taught how to be a teacher, and decided to live near the college. That's where she met Áine. You might think I would be devastated by being abandoned? Well, that's another strange thing, because I wasn't. Forget what I said earlier, I was just feeling sorry for myself and that's not something anyone could normally accuse me of. And yet, you'd imagine I had good reason, wouldn't you? I was happy for her because she had escaped. I felt I could handle the situation at home better if she wasn't there because then I knew she was out of the firing line, away from the hurtful stuff and the mental abuse. She was in a safe haven, somewhere mother couldn't get to her. And the presents and bribes from the old man? They dried up and so did he. He had long since withdrawn into God-knows-where in his mind. Not a happy place, I'm sure, but better than home.

Sue finished college and came back. I was so happy, but it didn't last long; a few months and then she was gone again. She moved in with the boyfriend, a weird loser. By then I was quite independent and starting to live my own life. I was twenty-one and I had realised that I couldn't live at home forever. It was killing me, this lack of freedom. I needed to make my own decisions and steer my own ship. She was a control freak in the strictest sense; in the sense that she was very strict and controlling in a way that freaked me out. No wonder the old man went into decline like he did.

As I said, I had been an unhappy child for as long as I can remember.

In October of 1989, the situation went from intolerable to even more intolerable, if that's possible. As a dysfunctional family group, we were now definitely not talking. Previously when we weren't talking you could sense that it was building up to an explosive situation, like the accumulation of saturated fats in a sewer which needed a stick of dynamite to shift it. This would allow the faecal matter to flow again at a normal rate, ever onward to the beaches of Albion. Good old Blighty. This time there was nothing beneath the silence. In its profundity it was a *fait accompli*, at once both moribund and finished. Then one morning, as he was about to leave for another day in splendid isolation, he died. Right there in the hall. It was me who found him, lying near the door, face down.

I'd gone downstairs to see if the free papers had arrived because I was looking for alternative accommodation. I'd never seen a dead person before, and I didn't know what to do. While I was pondering whether to break the silence and call mother the letter box rattled, and a free newspaper was pushed through which landed on his head. Not the kind of impression with which a man who had spent his life in the world of printed matter and rare first editions would have chosen to be sent on his way.

## What's He Been saying?

"How's it going up there?"

The teacher was at the kitchen table, marking some homework and was bored stiff.

"Your dad just died, and I need a coffee or maybe something stronger!" John yawned, arched his back and stretched, trying to loosen the muscles. The left leaning script had given him a left leaning neck ache.

With a tut and a growl, she etched an angry red line through some precocious teenage drivel, wrote "See me!" and looked up for clarification. What did that mean: *her dad had just died? Isn't it another story?*

"No, it's more of a diary: his thoughts on the state of the universe kind of a thing… I'm about halfway through. Do you want to read what I've got, so far? See if any of it strikes a chord? It might just be some sort of mental laxative, I don't know. If nothing else, though, I'm beginning to realise how much of a tosser he was. No offence, obviously."

"He had issues, I told you. On a spectrum of his own. I suppose I get a mention?"

"There's *loads* about you. Says you were daddy's favourite. Some bits are just ramblings about nothing much, as far as I can tell. You'll have to read it and draw your own conclusions. I think there are things you might recognise – that's if *any* of it is to be believed, of course!"

"I'm still not totally in favour of this. You *do* know that, right?"

"In favour of what? Finding out the truth?"

"How do you know it's the truth?"

"Well, there *is* that…"

"It's not the finding out the truth, it's the dragging up the past again. These are painful memories for me, y'know. I think maybe I'd rather you didn't do this."

There was a silence as John sulked momentarily with the wind taking out of his sails; he wondered whether he'd been wasting his time.

"So, what you're saying is I've been wasting my time, is that it? And you're not going to read it anyway? Excellent. I don't know why I bother!"

"I didn't ask you to do it, did I? It was *always* your idea. Oh God, don't start sulking! I didn't say I *wouldn't* read it, just that I'm not sure it's a good idea. That's all. I meant… should I be afraid? How bad *is* it?"

"Well, yes, there's some libellous stuff, for sure! Can you *believe* it? He refers to me as a weird loser! Bloody arsehole! I couldn't get over that! And Irene, wow! – she hardly comes out of it smelling of roses!"

"I'm not really surprised by that!"

"Yeah, and then neither does your dad. It's like he's hitting out at everyone; *all* of us get it in the neck!"

293

"That doesn't sound particularly promising." Sue paused and wagged her red pen, weighing up the options and alternatives. "Go on then, let's get this over with. Let me have a look. I've had enough of this, anyway. Maybe a glass of wine, d'you think, or is it too early?"

"Depends on the wine but sod it! I'll go and get what I've done so far, you get the plonk."

They were now in the lounge, side by side on the sofa and sharing the pages John had just printed, hot off the inkjet. Sue had felt strangely nervous when he returned with the sheets, but she was starting to feel intrigued by what they might contain and her initial reticence was swept aside, no match for a burgeoning curiosity. Realising this might be an opportunity to put some demons in their place, she took a deep breath and began to read. John put a protective arm around her. It was just like the old days.

"Ha! an unhappy child – yeah, he got that right! Oh, that's a bit mean about his teeth, but he did, actually; he did have big gaps, ha ha! He used to whistle through them something chronic. Aww dad, you really were tone deaf!" Sue smiled and could see that this was going to be an emotional ride. She reached for the glass.

"God, what *is* he on about? Actually, I do think he was scared of her, you know, my dad? And, I remember Mrs. Boyle, the teacher; she was lovely but he's making her out to be some sort of monster... and she wasn't!"

There were gasps and moments of thoughtful reflection, there were chuckles and outright denials and a couple of instances of *"Oh no, that's just not true!"* There was the declined offer of a wine refill before she moved on to his feelings on favouritism.

"He's right, there. I *was* daddy's favourite. I didn't see it at the time but the adult me sees that it was unfair on him, you know, but when you're a kid, you don't think like that. *What's-his-name*? Does that mean *you*?"

"It's better than what he calls me in a minute!"

"Well, the sanctimonious sod! Moral bloody turpitude, ha! What does that even *mean*?"

John, in the role of translator-cum-sounding board, was ready to offer moral support if needed. He took back his arm as the neck ache was making it uncomfortable. Sue continued to read without his arm, recognising elements of the truth in some, if not all, of what he was claiming. Impossible to forget the long periods of silence at home: so unsettling and one of the main factors in her wanting to get away as soon as the chance presented itself.

She remembered the fire and how upset Irene was when the insurance refused to pay out, claiming it had been a deliberate act, a claim which the emergency services were unable to refute. Nothing ever came to court. She remembered a few times when she'd paid a visit to her dad's place down the alley. Unlike her brother, it seems, she *was* allowed in, and he'd always been happy to see her. She could picture all those neighbours, whose names and faces she hadn't thought about for decades, and the incident with the broken window; she was there when the police came to the house and had heard Irene deny any involvement, telling the constable that the Polish woman was a liar and a foreigner. She also remembered how the officer had agreed with her before departing with a cheery wave and a wink.

"Oh, here we go: *my relationship with my sister!* This should be interesting... *abandoned and drifted apart*? That was down to him! And what does he mean by *'you know how I dealt with it*?'"

John had also wondered about this and had a theory. "I wondered about that, too. I have a theory... I think he's referring to the two stories, which you never read, and you managed to lose."

Sue fixed him with a look. "It was you who lost the second one!"

"OK, we've lost them between us, fair enough, but I remember when I read them, I had the sense that he was desperate to be, what's the word... *reconnected* with you or with your character, at least. Particularly in the second one. He seemed to spend a lot of time hoping you'd be friends again. Does that make sense? Not so much in the first one. In that one he was more weird, I think. That was when Barney thought it was something... y'know?"

"Go on! Say it! Don't dance around it; *incestuous*, yes? That's what you thought!"

"OK, yes. We did. But in that story, you weren't his sister; you were someone he pretended to know just so he could take revenge on Joe, who turns out to be me. Does *that* make sense?"

"No."

"And then, there was stuff about four people sitting on a bench and getting up and walking away... it was a lot of bollocks really but maybe it was a metaphor, meant to be symbolic?"

"Symbolic of what?"

"The uneasy and unresolvable dynamic between four people, perhaps?"

"And these four people were...?"

"You, me, Barney and William. I think."

"So, what's Barney got to do with it? He hardly *knew* my brother."

"My explanation, when Barney asked that self-same question was that he's my oldest and best mate; who else would play the part of my best mate?"

"Huh! Why did you *need* to have a best mate in the story? Did I have a best mate in the stories?"

"Yes, you had me of course!"

"Then why did we need Barney?"

"Well, I er..."

"Correct. We didn't!"

John chuckled, knowing he could not win. "Just read the rest of it! Do you want a top-up?"

"Go on, a small one. How did these stories end, then – they all lived happily ever after?"

"No, they didn't end well at all. Me and Barney get killed on our way to meet you in Edgware of all places and you, me and Áine get killed in the second one. Definitely not 'happy ever after' at all!"

"That's horrible!"

"I suppose he couldn't find any other way to resolve the situation, couldn't think of a way for everyone to be happy together? I don't know, it's just my own interpretation. And I think that's what he meant by '*dealt with it.*'"

"He didn't have to kill us; there are other ways."

"I don't suppose he'd actually heard of relationship counsellors."

John laughed. Sue didn't.

"Well, that's a pity. I was hoping he might finally explain why he didn't bother coming to the wedding, but he's chickened out, there. Surprise surprise!"

"Don't suppose we'll ever know what was going on in his mind, will we?"

"This bit about the funeral is interesting, though. He's right about that, we didn't speak. If I'm being honest now, we were both at fault for that one. I suppose he'd say it was me who started it: I blanked him when I saw him there, looking sheepish. I was so sodding angry with him, angrier than I had any right to be, maybe."

"Why?"

"Oh, just because…" Sue picked up the glass and swirled the contents as her mind wandered back to that day, the three remaining Skaifes in mourning black, alone in the graveyard. The vicar, she remembered, had excused himself rather abruptly and dashed off. If she didn't know that holy men were blessed and therefore immune to earthly afflictions, she might have supposed he was heading towards the toilet in the vestry on an urgent matter. Diarrhoea, probably. Yes, Irene had been sobbing. A rare event which should have brought the family closer together, united in grief perhaps. But it hadn't.

"No come on, get it off your chest – why were you angry?"

She didn't quite know how to explain it; the way she'd felt then was hard to recreate in the here and now. Somehow, it all seemed ill-conceived and hasty, with the benefit of hindsight. She was sure that given another chance she might, no she certainly *would* have acted differently but there's never a second chance. She tapped the glass with her nails; she was still thinking and considering how to explain why she'd behaved towards him in the way she had. After a lengthy pause she took the plunge.

"I suppose… I'm not sure now if I was right in my suspicions – and there was nothing later to support it, nothing concrete – but when daddy y'know… when he died suddenly like that, I convinced myself that it had to have been something William did that caused it."

"Caused his death? What do you mean?"

"Well, this might seem daft, but for a long time I had suspected he had problems… a gambling problem in particular and you know gamblers never win! They just end up losing everything…"

"Yes, they can do, if they're not careful."

"Anyway: I knew if he *was*, it was bound to get out of hand sooner or later; he never knew when to walk away, do you know what I mean? I was worried he would take them down with him, having to bail him out. I mean, they'd worked so hard to buy that house and everything and something like that could have caused the heart attack. Do you see?"

"I do, yes. What made you think he was gambling, though?"

"Oh, he couldn't hide it. He used to come in the pub where we went after college – I thought it was so he could drool over Áine, but he always ended up on the one-armed bandit machine things, just feeding them money. I could never figure out how he could afford it, I mean he didn't have a job or anything like that and he never seemed to win; if he ever did get anything out, he'd just put it straight back in! I could see how it was drawing him in like an addict; he just kept losing and going back for more."

"And didn't you ever say anything to him?"

"Yes, I did, eventually. One day in the final term I asked him outright. I said: "Where are you getting all this money, then? Are you robbing banks?" and he lied, I know he lied! He was really shifty, told me not to say anything to anyone and then do you know what he said? He came up with some tosh about how it was daddy who was giving him a 'regular allowance!' Obviously, that wasn't true, not a chance, but he wouldn't back down and told me again not to say anything. So, I thought that he must be stealing from them. I didn't actually tell him that I knew what he was up to, but I started to hate him for it. I was certain that daddy must have found out, I don't know; maybe there was money missing from the bank account and that must have caused... y'know. He was a selfish little shit and I wanted nothing more to do with him. Horrible, isn't it?"

"Yes, but how do you know? How do you know for a fact he wasn't getting an allowance off your dad? I mean, it could have been true, don't you think?"

"No, I don't. I wasn't getting one and I was the favourite... remember?"

The rest of the pages were read in silence, Sue's mood dipped as she was forced to recall events she would have preferred to leave in the past. The cruel put downs and the references to her dad being in decline did not sit well and she was unsettled by the outright lies, particularly the one about her having no friends. She had a lot of friends in those days, and a wide social circle; attractive people always do just that – they *attract* people. Obviously as you get older they drift away, but... and what did this say about William, saying she didn't? Was he in denial, preferring to think she was somehow dependent on his company and his alone? He certainly didn't have friends. A mixture of his negative attitude towards people, allied with Irene's aura of cold, unfeeling hostility made sure there were no invites ever issued to *'come and play,'* certainly none received, and no friendships formed. William did not do friendship.

The last bit was hard to take, and she found herself rekindling the feelings of animosity towards him. This time it was simply for being there in his final moments. She resented him and was angry again, angry because, in his own words, he had just stood by, not knowing what to do. Why didn't he know? He could have saved him if he'd acted quickly and done something, surely? He could have tried; he *should* have tried to do something, anything! The selfish, thoughtless bastard could have tried!

"What are you thinking?"

"Hmm? Oh... I'm thinking about Irene..."

The sound of the clock in the kitchen seemed to increase in volume as it ticked relentlessly, seeping through the wall.

"And I'm also wondering whether anyone wouldn't think it's normal to feel how I actually *do* feel about her now that she's gone? Do you know what I mean?"

John thought he did, yes, and suggested that it was *maybe just the shock*. Sue thought there was more to it than that.

"If I'm being honest, I'm not particularly upset that my own mother is dead; I don't actually care that I'll never see her or speak to her or that there's nothing left of her, y'know? And I think this," – she waved the sheet – "*this* is all the justification I need."

There was another period of silence and introspection. John began to wonder what they were going to eat. Maybe they could order a pizza?

"What are you thinking now?"

"I suppose I'm thinking that if God exists, he made a mistake here; she was never *mother material*. William suffered; he had first-hand experience. She treated him terribly. In fact, she treated us *both* terribly. Just like she said: she didn't have favourites."

"No, well… hey, shall we order a pizza?"

"No. Do you think I would have been like that if we'd had kids? A terrible, cruel mother? It's not genetic, is it?"

"No. And no, you would have been a fabulous mother; one of the all-time greats! And there's still time, isn't there?"

"Not tonight, Josephine." Sue smiled as she doused his flames before he got any ideas. "Truth is, John my love, I just don't like kids. And I really don't fancy a pizza."

-------------------------------------------------

"Is that you?"

"No, just a burglar; don't mind me."

"Was it busy?"

John had just popped down to *Grease Burger n Chipz*. It had seemed like a good idea at the time, with neither Stilton particularly keen to rustle up something edible after the emotional strain of the Chernobyl session.

Three minutes later, in a joint effort they were attempting to rustle up something edible. Both John's burger, an incredibly inedible disappointment – *"they're never normally this bad!"* – and Sue's surprisingly greasy salad had been tossed in the bin within moments of their unveiling.

When he was queueing in the B&Q car park earlier, he'd wondered when he'd started *popping down* to places. It was an age thing, he thought. When he was younger, he didn't pop anywhere; he *went manfully,* usually. In his prime, in the Golden Age, the idea of *popping* somewhere was not something he ever considered. And yet, here he was now, heading for his fifties and *popping out* for fast food. He shuddered and moved on. He thought about Sue's reaction to the Chernobyl outpourings earlier. He thought that maybe he should abandon the idea of translating the rest. The second bit was probably going to be the same old same old anyway. What had started as a labour of love had turned out to be something of a chore before ending up a pain in the neck. If she wanted him to call it a day and leave it there, maybe it wasn't such a bad idea? He'd mention it.

"No! You can't leave it there. I need to know what else he has to say! C'mon – you can't just give up now!" This wasn't the reaction he'd expected. *But isn't it a bit upsetting?* No, apparently. It was helping; she realised that it might help her to make some sense of her family. She'd been going over it in her mind, all the stuff she'd read, when he *popped out.* He shuddered. *But hadn't she already got that sorted? Hadn't she said herself that the situation with her mother was resolved? She's gone and good riddance, wasn't that what it came down to?* Yes but…

But he didn't tackle the rest. Not straight away. For almost a month he kept putting it off by finding other things he had to do. Another commission from The Forestry Commission came in, this one for a series of pamphlets on ancient woodcrafts: carving spoons and clothes pegs, that kind of thing. Apparently, it takes one medium-sized oak to whittle enough clothes pegs to hang the washing for a town the size of Stockport for an entire year! When he read this snippet in the covering letter they'd sent, he knew this was a project to be reckoned with. Sue would just have to wait until he could find a date in his diary.

The date in John's diary turned out to be December the first.

This time, he didn't bother with the *Teach Yourself* book for the alphabet. He reckoned, with some justification, that he'd become fairly fluent in Russian, or the alphabet at least. He'd Googled a couple of swear words and had even bought himself a Russian-style Nikita fur hat, a bargain from a charity shop, for this second phase. Sue, of course, had ridiculed him when he'd proudly revealed it to her. She tittered and told him it was like something a babushka would wear. And not a gorgeous one, either.

## The Chernobyl Diary Part 2

I stuck around for a couple of months after he died. It was two months too long. There was just the two of us living there and that made things worse, somehow. She was as cold and as silent as ever but there was something else now, something hard to describe.

*The funeral was a joke;* even the vicar had the shits. Nobody was talking to anybody. I expected it from her but not Susan. I know I made an effort; I smiled at her, but she looked away like she was disgusted. Was I hurt? Yes, I was. I hardly saw her in those days, and I thought this might have provided an opportunity to reconnect. She didn't, obviously. That dickhead wasn't with her, and I wondered whether they'd split up or something. I hoped so. I hadn't wanted to be at their wedding so if it was off, that would have been a cause for celebration. She didn't even invite me to the wedding anyway. Not personally. I just got a cheap card in the second-class post. Was I hurt? Yes, I was. Again. No wonder I'm like I am sometimes. Hang on, there's someone at the door. Some loser, probably. Won't be anyone for me, it'll be one of Áine's big-mouth Irish mates. Hang on, what's your hurry! Be right back...

It's The Not Knowing


October 20<sup>th</sup>, 1996.

I'm wondering how to continue this. I've had some news which has thrown things into turmoil, tipped the world off its axis if you can imagine such an occurrence. I can. Sometimes.

Do you ever just know that things are so bad they can only get better? Or does nobody have the right to hope for something better to come along in this unjust and cruel world? For me it's probably a combination of the two. You must make your own mind up and don't look to me for guidance. You know what's coming at the end, what's waiting for you after the years of pain: a big black nothing. You live your life, despite your inner self telling you it's pointless and a waste of time and you keep going until you can't go on, and the weight of the world on your shoulders finally gets to you (sooner rather than later if you're one of the lucky ones). That's when it all comes to an end, this pain and this torment and this utter and overwhelming hopelessness which has stifled you since the day you crawled from the womb into the burning light of the fluorescent strip and got your arse slapped for your trouble. We can agree on that, I'm sure.

Sometimes you don't know what you don't know. And sometimes you're better off not knowing. Not always but usually. I know what I'm talking about; you can trust me but I'm not a doctor.

You're probably wondering who was at the door the other week. Was it someone for Áine, as I'd suspected? Well, no it wasn't! It was someone for me. A rare visitor as it turns out with an unlikely tale to tell. And that's why I'm in the

307

state of turmoil to which I alluded earlier. It's not often I'm thrown out of kilter or unexpectedly beguiled, as you probably know. This is something different though and you'd have to be a numb loser not to feel what I've been feeling since that visit. The person at the door – and I don't even know whether you'll believe me (and if you don't, it's your problem) – this cold caller has really put the cat among the pigeons, and I absolutely hate pigeons. I don't much like cats either. Or any animal, actually, if push comes to shove. And it has.

That day, when I stopped writing and opened the door, I was confronted by an old devil. He was no-one I'd ever seen before and definitely fell into the category of 'total stranger.' He must have been in his eighties at least, with a face that looked somehow familiar and somehow slept in. A rough looking loser, I thought. Overweight and shabby with a bit of grey hair sticking out at the sides. Not that I ever sit in judgement, that's not my style. There was something about him but not something I could put my finger on. Not that I would, obviously.

He didn't have a name tag or anything like that, so I realised straight away that he hadn't escaped from somewhere secure and neither had he come in an official capacity; he didn't look like one of Áine's cohorts, either – not Irish enough for that. I was looking him up and down when he asked me straight out if I was William, Irene's boy. I wasn't going to tell him one way or the other, the nosey bastard, but he smiled – at least I think it was a smile – and he muttered something like, "Yes, of course. I can see it."

# It's The Not Knowing

What did that mean and what did he want? He wanted to talk to me about something very important, that's what he said. I failed to see what this loser could possibly say that could have any importance, let alone very importance. But people do say you shouldn't judge a book by its cover until you've read it, so I gave him the benefit of the doubt.

After weighing up the pros and cons I told him he could come in if he took his shoes off.

He didn't come straight to the point, standing there in his socks, but I will.

As we were walking up to my room in the attic he came out with some boring small talk, made positive noises about the décor, which was not my department. I didn't argue, there would have been no point and if he wanted an argument, he could have one later. That might sound needlessly aggressive, but I've always been wary of having my space invaded.

I told him to sit down if he wanted, which he did. I made sure I left the door open just in case anything untoward happened, if you know what I mean. I wasn't in the mood for monkey business. The room was a bit of a mess, but I didn't apologise. I take as I find, and I expect others to do the same.

He began by introducing himself, but the name meant nothing. I may have shrugged when he said it, I can't remember now. It doesn't matter, none of that matters. He suddenly asked about mother and whether she was '*happy,*' nosey, personal stuff like that. I asked him what business that was of his, and what the hell did he want to know for?

My dander was getting up, which was only to be expected with the way things were shaping. He raised a gnarly old hand (one held together by liver spots) in apology and said he was sorry but that he'd known Irene since he was young – as if *that* had ever happened! – and had often wondered about her over the years. I wondered myself; I wondered whether he was a stalker or something sick like that. You can never be too careful with old devils who come knocking on your door.

He didn't look well, by this stage. Maybe he never had! I think the climb up to the top floor must have taken it out of him and could see he was struggling. My first thought was: "what do I do if he dies up here?" How would I get him back downstairs and out of the house?

Eventually he stopped wheezing and started to speak. I listened out of common courtesy, but I wasn't engaged. It wasn't something I felt I needed to hear, in truth. He told me he was ill and didn't have *long left*. I may have shrugged again. I certainly thought, *"here we go! Someone looking for a handout!"* and I was about to tell him he was wasting his time when he started coughing like a hag, cursing through sludge, and making an awful noise. I thought his guts were going to come up through his mouth.

I waited, patiently. He could take his time coughing and then he could go. The man was a fool and a timewaster.

But he wasn't, as it turned out.

"I've often thought about you and your sister, you know," he said when the fuss had died down. "And before you think I'm one of those stalkers, please let me explain. You might want to sit down, William or is it Will, Bill or Willy or…?"

I told him he could call me William Skaife. And I told him to leave my sister out of it.

"You might well be wondering why a total stranger has turned up at your door? I know I would if it was me. Well, it's a question of time, you see. Time is something I don't have much of, I'm afraid… actually, not afraid, no. It might be a relief… but anyway, that's nothing for you to be concerned with." *Good, because I wasn't!*

"I told you I knew your mother and I could see it got your back up and that does you proud, William Skaife, but you needn't worry, I don't mean your mother any harm; just the opposite, believe me! I first met Irene, your mum, just before either of you were born. It was an unforgettable moment in my life, one which seems like a lifetime ago now, and it is! A long lifetime and too long to be apart."

As he drifted off and gazed wistfully, I did a quick evaluation, calculating that he was probably in his mid-forties at that time. I mentioned this – I didn't want him to think I wasn't listening – and he scoffed politely. He told me that he was, in fact, in his mid-twenties when they met; it was the Spring Bank Holiday in 1960, one of the wettest on record. I did another quick calculation and, if what he was claiming was the truth, it meant this bio-wreckage was a mere sixty years old, give or take! I stifled a gasp.

He was still talking when I re-joined the narrative. He was explaining how he and his wife were on holiday and had met Irene and her boyfriend one night in what he called a 'juke joint.' It was hard to imagine Irene with a boyfriend! It might have been even harder to imagine her in a 'juke joint' but I had no idea what one was, and I didn't pursue it.

If I'm being honest, I would say I was beginning to get mildly interested – no more than mildly and certainly not to the point of being *'engrossed'* – in what this crusty intruder might have to say and he himself certainly seemed to be warming to the task. I've always thought I had a gift for drawing out the best in people, allowing them to unburden themselves of emotional suitcases and improving their mental health. I could have been a head doctor.

I told him he might put his shoes back on if he wanted.

He hoped, he said, that anything he had said (or might be about to say) would not be taken the wrong way and that he could assure me the feelings he had for "Irene, *your mum*," as he insisted on calling her, were both heartfelt and genuine. He hoped I wouldn't be shocked or in any way distressed to hear that he'd always held her, *your mum*, in the highest regard and was deeply saddened that he had not been able to spend more of his life with her, sharing special moments as they grew old together. This was what he'd wanted more than anything in the world, but circumstance was against it; he was *spoken for*, for one thing.

He could go on a bit when he got going, that was becoming very apparent, but I listened patiently. When I interact with people, I interact fully. No half measures. Definitely *private*, not NHS.

312

# It's The Not Knowing

He knew, he said, that it was perhaps 'out of order' to be talking like this. He seemed somehow obliged to point out that he did not make a habit of getting involved with women who were already *spoken for*, particularly as he himself was also *spoken* for, but in this instance, he was prepared to make an exception – indeed, he was powerless to resist! He would quite understand, he added, if I became uncomfortable at any stage that I might prefer if he absented himself, but he hoped I might *indulge* him a little longer.

Indulge him? What was this old fool talking about? Getting involved? Intrigued (but fearing this might go on for too long), I cautiously nodded my assent and he continued.

He regretted that *they* had been afforded so few opportunities to create something magical, their own Earthly paradise. The day he realised he would never again hear the sound of her laughter or see her beautiful smile was the saddest day of his life, apparently. He repeated his wish that they had been able to share more special, intimate moments and told how he had often replayed in his mind a spiritual occasion when they had laid together in the mid-summer heat of a late evening, gazing up at the stars and dreaming of what might have been. Was he talking about the same Irene? It sounded like a different kettle of cold fish to me.

He looked up from his rambling and fixed me with his rheumy eyes.

"Do you understand?"

313

I didn't know what he was talking about and that's a fact. I wondered whether he'd mistaken me for another William Skaife; there had to be someone else with that name, surely?

I didn't know how to respond.

"If you *do* understand what I'm trying to say," he continued, "you might feel it appropriate to judge me and condemn me, and to say that I behaved badly. I would understand why you might feel that way but that's not how it was, not between Irene *your mum* and me. Sometimes, you know, people are drawn together in unusual circumstances. Some people are blind, and they just don't see what's going on – how can they? That's the truth and that's exactly how and why it happened. Do you understand now?"

He had lost me ages ago and I told him so. I didn't want a babbling rambler on my hands.

He sighed when I shook my head. "You wouldn't happen to have a toilet I could use, would you? It's this infernal cold weather."

I was glad to be out of it, so I pointed him towards the facilities and went to the kitchen to make some tea and give some thought as to how I might get rid of him.

When I got back to the room he was already there, looking pale and clapped out. I suppose I took pity on him, being a people person. I offered him refreshments, which he accepted graciously. I told him no thanks were necessary and not to spill it.

## It's The Not Knowing

"This isn't quite as easy as I'd imagined but… anyway, as I was saying before nature called, it was the boyfriend. Ultimately, you see, it was *he* who was responsible for everything that happened later – you have to believe me when I say that. I mean, there's no reason for me to lie is there?" He took another biscuit and a sip of his tea. He smiled at no-one before he went rambling again.

"It was your typical, dismal bank holiday and none of us had the slightest idea of what was going to happen, all those years ago. Call it destiny if you like; it was all so life changing, really –"

By this stage I'd had enough, and I moved to expedite matters.

"Actually, I'm not following *any* of this; you're losing me here, with all this stuff about dismal bank holidays and things… what is it you're trying to say? Come on man, just spit it out, before one of us dies. What happened?"

"Shit happened son, that's what happened."

I think if there had been a fireplace with dying embers, he would have sat staring into them at this point. There was an electric fan heater but it's not really the same. I never had it switched on anyway.

He went silent for a few moments as I sat and observed him, wondering if any of this was going to make sense at any stage. I had my doubts. I wished I'd had a notebook and a fountain pen like a real doctor; I really do think I was born to play that role. I would have been good at it.

It's The Not Knowing

"Tell me about your childhood," I said, but I don't think he was listening. He was distracted by something. When he spoke again, his voice was quite unsteady and what a wordsmith or airhead would call *ethereal*.

"I'll keep sending the money as long as I'm able; you understand that I hope. I'm ill, you see... I don't think I've got long; I'll get my marching orders soon, I'm sure, but I'll do what I can for as long as I can. I wish it could have been more, much more... but I'd like to think it's been a help in some way?"

That's the turmoil, right there.

It turned deathly quiet after he said that. It was difficult to think or breathe. There was a stunned silence; so stunned, in fact, that it made no sound. The old man seemed to have ground to a halt and was staring at the floor as I struggled to untangle my thoughts. Closing one eye and arranging my mouth into an attitude of bewilderment as I angled my head, I finally raised the question uppermost in my mind: "What money are you talking about? You're making very little sense here, if you don't mind my saying!"

It was his turn to look bemused, see how he liked it!

"The money I've been sending you every year on your birthday, of course... you got it didn't you? I mean, you did, didn't you?"

I told him outright, I'd never received any money from him.

# It's The Not Knowing

"Oh, good Lord! Please tell me that isn't true! You must have! Are you saying you never received any of the letters? The thieving bastards!"

It always comes down to money with some people, have you noticed? It was time to put this matter to rest and kick this old sod into touch. He was beginning to mess with my mental equilibrium, and I feared for my sanity.

"Listen, whatever your name is: I haven't got any money, I'm never likely to have any money and I haven't received *any* money from *anyone*. Apart from my father's guilt money every year –"

"A thousand pounds in cash, on your birthday, every year!"

"Yes, that's right but that's the only money –"

"But that's exactly what I'm talking about; what do you mean you '*haven't received it?*'"

"What don't you understand? I'm talking about the money I get from my father every year, an *anonymous* donation – as if I didn't know it was him on a guilt trip!"

"Yes! That's the one. Oh son, won't you hug me?" He stood and lurched towards me.

"Back off Boogaloo!" I cried and fled the room, dodging his outstretched claws.

I couldn't leave him in the house unattended, who knows what he might have done? He was a madman, that much was clear, even to an untrained eye. I couldn't quite get things clear in my mind; did he just suggest what I think he just suggested? If so, then he'd lost his marbles, obviously.

It's The Not Knowing

I wasn't sure how to get him out, that was the problem. I remembered an incident in the papers where a huge uninvited magpie had taken up residence in the upper floor of a terraced house. The legal occupants were so traumatised by this that they decided to move downstairs until the magpie left. After a week, when it hadn't, they were re-traumatised by the thought that when it died (as it surely must, due to lack of food), they would have to pick it up and dispose of it. Being a family of crusading, tambourine-rattling vegans they did not want the death of a fancy-dress crow on their conscience so they started to feed it in the hope it would do the decent thing and leave of its own accord, eventually. It didn't. It became totally reliant upon their steady supply of tasteless vegan snacks. In the end (and in desperation), they abandoned their animal-loving principles and poisoned it. I did not want to find myself in a similar position. *And how did he know about the money? And how did he know where I lived?*

It was a good job that Áine turned up when she did.

"Would you take a look at yourself, now! You look like a frightened rabbit, so you do!"

I told her this was no time for Irish small talk and quickly explained the situation and the dilemma. She wasn't happy! "You mean you've just left a total stranger up there in my house? Well, you need to go and get him out, so you do… like now!"

I pointed out that it was easy for her to say but what if he had a magpie up there? She made a throat-based noise and left; I could hear her stomping up the stairs. Her "Hello?" was loaded with menace, if you catch my drift.

I should have gone with her, I suppose. Safety in numbers and all that but I know sometimes she likes to sort these things out in her own way and resents what she calls *'interference.'* She was gone for quite some time. I wasn't watching the clock or anything sad like that, but I was anxious on her behalf. I knew he wouldn't attack her; he was too dishevelled for that, and I know she's good at diffusing the most volatile of situations. I've never seen her diffusing volatile situations in the flesh but she's good at that *kind* of thing in general.

She's an admirable woman in many ways. I suppose she is my girlfriend; we live together so that probably makes it official in the eyes of the law. She isn't my first girlfriend, though – you shouldn't think that! I have actually had loads of women, and some damned good ones amongst them. But she's been OK for me, if you know what I mean. It's like Yin and Yan or Bill and Ben or Simon and Garfunkel or some others like that. It just works for us. It's not like Mike and Bernie Winters, though. I should have made that clear from the outset!

When I wasn't thinking those kinds of thoughts, I was going over in my mind what he'd said when he was rambling. These were not easy thoughts to think, though. If anything, they were unsettling. Why had he been sending me money? *Had* he been sending me money? He seemed to think so and what would be the point in lying about it if he hadn't? What did he stand to gain? Maybe he was looking for it back? No, that wasn't the case: didn't he say he would send more until he y'know...? If it *was* him sending it, for whatever reason, that means it wasn't my dad. And that, actually, was more in keeping with the Eric

319

we all know – or knew – giving nothing with one hand and taking everything away with the other. And what was his connection with Irene, my mother? He met her at the seaside, so what? Loads of people get met at the seaside. We didn't, me and Suze, but the point stands. I wasn't hopeful of ever getting to the truth, not with a rambling old fool holding all the cards so close to his rattly antique chest.

Obviously, as you might expect, my curiosity finally got the better of me and I made my way up the stairs. I'm not a nosey person by nature and I never have been, but if listening outside a door is ever called for, I can generally be relied upon to eavesdrop discreetly and casually, never overtly, by maintaining a low profile.

As it turned out, no low profile was possible or even necessary because, when I reached the top floor, there was nobody there. I couldn't hear anybody, anyway, so I drew the only conclusion possible in a situation like that. They'd simply vanished. I was wondering how they'd done that, managed to sneak out without me hearing them when the door opened. It was my girlfriend and she looked weird. There's no other word for it. Not one that I can think of, I mean.

"I thought I heard you eavesdropping! You'd better come in; you need to hear this," was what she said. It was actually my room, and I didn't need an invite, but I didn't say anything. He was still there and obviously reluctant to leave. Old people – seniors if you prefer – can be quite stubborn at times. He made a move, struggling to stand up.

"Do you need a hand to shift him?"

"No. Now, will you tell William what you've just told me?"

He replied that he'd been trying to tell me earlier but that I wasn't listening. *Can you believe that? Fucking cheek of the man!*

She replied that "sometimes, it might appear so, but..." *But what? Can you believe that?*

"Well, it's like I was saying..."

And then he spilled the beans from what can only be described as a can of worms.

When he'd finished, he looked up at me, and I could see the tears welling up in his sunken old eyes. It reminded me of a faithful old hound. One with tears in its eyes. Sunken ones.

"Now do you understand, son?"

Yes, I did.

Equally, I was no longer sure.

What did this mean for us, for me and Suze? Wasn't she my proper sister anymore? Was this one of those *same-mother-different-father* scenarios like you read about? I needed clarification and I asked for it.

Áine exploded and cursed me! "Oh, for the love of God! Were you not *listening*?"

"Yes, obviously!"

"Susan is the same as you, same father, same mother! What is there not to understand?"

"That's what I thought he said, so... who's Eric Skaife then? What part does he play in all of this? I thought he was my dad?"

It was the old man (literally, my brand-new old man!) who spoke.

"Eric was your mother's boyfriend, which is what I was trying to tell you."

"But... so... where do you fit into all of this? Weren't you married or something?"

"Holy Mary, mother of God! Yes, he was married – *is* married – but Eric was screwing his wife! Now do you get it?"

There was another stunned silence.

It went on for quite some time without getting any louder.

"Clem, I'm so, so sorry, so I am, I shouldn't have said that."

"No, it's the truth. That's what he did, although I wouldn't have put it like that, myself. He sneaked behind my back, and Irene, your mum's. He's what we used to call a 'blackguard.' Anyway, the dirty deed was done and nine months later my Sheila had a baby, a little boy, and I was the happiest, proudest man in the world –"

"And you're saying that was me? I'm lost."

"Oh Jesus, Mary and Joseph! No!"

"No, son. This is before your time. Late 1960, as it happens, and our Cliff comes into the world. Except...it wasn't *my* Cliff. I only discovered the truth a couple of years later; on his second birthday, actually. An anonymous birthday card came in the post. It didn't take much to realise there was a young cuckoo in the nest. Broke my heart. Thought about breaking her neck. But I didn't; breaking necks is never the answer."

"So, what *did* you do?"

"I did what any decent man would have done; I forgave her and told her I would bring him up as my own."

"That's very Christian of you!"

"Not really, I'm no saint! Far from it, in fact. No, I spent a year tracking Eric Skaife down, I had contacts in the Post Office and well, let's just say I got an address for an early Christmas present. The same way I found you, by the way... And once I had the address, I knew I had to do something. I couldn't just leave it. What sort of a man would have just left it? The question was: what? What was I going to do?"

"That's what we're all wondering."

Clem (as that seems to be what we're now calling the old goat) started to cough and splutter and even indulged in a bit of wheezing and panting. These revelations were obviously getting to him, but Áine soon sorted him out and he continued. "I got on a coach and went to see him, intending to have it out. I'm not a violent man by nature but by God I was ready to hit him! For the entire journey I played it over and over in my mind. At first, I had a speech prepared, a speech in which I called him all the names under the sun, particularly the bad ones, but the nearer we got, the more I doubted he would listen to me, listen to my grievances and if he did? What could he do about it now? The damage was done; he'd sown his seed where no seed should have been planted... and probably hasn't been planted since! No, by the time I got there I felt the only thing to do was to punch him in his bloody face."

"And did you?"

"When I got to the door, I limbered up, ready to strike the first blow. I knew as soon as he saw me, he'd probably guess what it was about and might react. I couldn't let that happen; there would be no point in going all that way only to end up on the receiving end. I was tensed and nervous as I banged on the door, my old ticker going ten to the dozen..."

"Ten? Does that mean it was slow? I'm never sure —"

"Shut up Will! Let him speak!"

"Well, maybe nineteen to the dozen. It was certainly thumping! Anyway, I was there banging on the door, in what in those days they would have called a state of high dudgeon, but there was no answer! Not at first, so I banged again and then, suddenly, there she was..."

The old man seemed to glow with a kind of inner light or aura as he relived that moment. It wasn't the kind of aura a pugilist might exude on entering the makeshift ring at a bare-knuckle fight; it was somehow gentler and more sensitive than that, the kind of aura a dreamer might exude on seeing a holy vision in a cave, that kind of thing.

"Standing there, as lovely as the day I'd last seen her. Maybe even lovelier, if that were possible!"

324

# It's The Not Knowing

"He's talking about Irene, your mam," said Áine, as if I couldn't work that out for myself! Who else could he have been talking about?

"That's right, it was Irene, your mum. Now, William Skaife, as I warned you before; what I might be about to tell you could possibly upset you so if you'd rather I skipped the detail I'd quite understand, you only have to say."

I'm no prude, God no! and I'm no stranger to the dark arts of all the sex stuff like they have in the magazines, but I told him I would prefer not to hear any of the more sordid details (if that was what all this was building up to). He looked somehow relieved and said he understood and that he wouldn't go into unnecessary detail, in that case. I sensed Áine was actually disappointed by this. She obviously denied it when I mentioned it later.

It seems, then, that what happened was this:

Having travelled inland to beat Eric to a pulp, this cuckold found that his intended victim wasn't at home. Instead, he found my mother Irene, a woman for whom he had carried a torch since she had first turned his head. It seems to me that if he'd turned his head fully, he might have seen what was happening behind his back but that's a conversation for another day – if there's time.

Irene invited him in for a cup of tea. He mentioned it several times, and I have no reason to doubt his word: the fact there was something of a spark between the two of them. I would go further and suggest they were each enamoured of the other. I don't want to mention any unpleasantness or delve between the sheets, but it seems that's where they might have ended up. Several times he tried to justify his actions, saying it was the *'Real Thing,'* and that he'd never loved anyone as much as he'd loved Irene, my mum. Loved her with all his heart from the moment he'd first set eyes on her.

Well, fancy words are all very well in their place and he could dress it up all he liked but it still amounted to just one thing in the end: a revenge pregnancy which resulted in Susan, my sister. A sweet little revenge baby. That's what she was and that's something she will have to live with if she ever finds out. She won't hear it from me.

There's one more thing. The old man as a young buck was clearly insatiable because twelve months later, he reappeared with a *bunch of flowers and a twinkle in his eye* (his phrase, and one which tumbled shamelessly from his cavalier lips). Susan was barely three months old; Eric was at work, and they *should have known better*! Except that, if they'd known better, then I wouldn't be here. And to me, that is an unpalatable prospect.

I don't think of myself as a revenge baby. Based on the events as he described them, I think I was more of a 'one-for-the-road' baby which I consider preferable; it paints me in a much better light. Some might disagree but I am indifferent to such opinions. They can think what they like for all I care. Which I don't.

W.B.S.

# It's The Not Knowing

John reached the end of the paragraph and tossed the pencil to one side, causing unseen multiple fractures to the lead inside the barrel. The next time he sharpened the pencil, about 5mm of graphite nearest the tip would fall out. In the end, the repeated effort to find a stable point would cause the shaft to reduce to such an extent that the implement would be rendered useless. This, alas, was something he would have to find out the hard way before conceding defeat and tossing the useless stub into the bin, all hope lost.

This was a mere trifle when compared to the serious stuff he'd just uncovered. How on earth, he wondered, was he going to break this to Sue? Would she be able to cope with this new state of affairs, the new world order? Would it be better all-round if she never found out about her true parentage? Yes, he thought so, definitely. She'd been nagging him to reveal his findings for the past few days, so it wasn't likely that she'd let it go now or simply forget. What he needed was a thieving seagull, but he didn't know any.

He was suddenly exhausted, worn out, wan and spent. Stifling a yawn, just as a million other early morning yawners were doing at that precise moment, he leaned back in his chair, looked up at the ceiling, closed his eyes, let out a breath of stale air through lips left slightly ajar and muttered (in what he hoped was a Russian accent): "*Drisnya!*"

The date was December 11th, 2005. It was just before six in the morning and the sleepy oil depot at Buncefield was poised to explode into the news.

# PART EIGHT. 2005

## Chernobyl Fallout

December 16th.


"Fancy a pint?"

"Good God, so you're back! Course I do!"

"How about The Cracker Barrel, half seven for eight? Bring Sue along, eh?"

"We'll see…"

So, Barney Chimes had returned to his old manor just in time for Christmas. Excellent news!

John turned up early, on his own. He didn't ask Sue; she'd made her own arrangements. He sat in what used to be called the snug, nursing his pint of guest ale, surveying the room, and struggling to breathe due to the overpowering smell of gloss paint. The whole of the downstairs had recently been opened up into one large room as part of a business rates loophole tax dodge. It had been redecorated or refurbished (he wasn't sure which) and they'd done an impressively bad job. It looked like the designer's intention had been to recreate a 1980s vibe, heavily reliant on salmon pink walls and pastel blue woodwork with plastic vines hanging from the plastic beams. As anybody who knew anything – and even those who knew very little of anything – could have told you, it was a mistake. A horrible mistake.

Even the gaudy Christmas decorations dotted around the room couldn't disguise the fact. If anything, they probably made things worse.

There was some music playing in the background; it wasn't anything he recognised. Indeed, he hoped fervently that he would never hear it again. Hang on! Is it… *Hotel California*? Actually, it was! Now jazzed up and reimagined, the opening chords of the original masterpiece were playing over and over on a loop in accompaniment to an obscenely wealthy misogynist spewing hate, venom, and bile. This hideous cacophony in the modern style did little to lift his spirits. As anybody who knew anything – and even those among them who knew very little – could have told you, it was shit. Clearly, the pub was now one to be avoided if this was a flavour of things to come. He knew Barney would feel the same. They wouldn't be staying long, that much was obvious. He was considering waiting for him in the car park when, suddenly, the wanderer returned.

"Hey! Nice paint job! Oooh! I love this version!" Barney started to *bop* as he approached, making stupid hand movements: generally, and ill-advisedly, acting younger than he was and appearing ridiculous for his pains. "Up ahead in the distance…" he snarled along, "I saw that shimmerin' light bitch, yeah?"

"Fuck off!"

He chuckled and said "*meh*," which was a new one on John, as he made the two-tips-of-the-hand 'Wanna pint?' signal. The early starter drained the last of his dregs and started to get up.

# It's The Not Knowing

"What, you want to stay *here*?"

"Why not? It's cool, man. It's funky…"

"Fuck off, funky! It's crap more like. Are you serious? Christ, really? I'll have one more guest ale and then we'll get out of this shithole!"

Barney was already at the bar by the time he heard *shithole;* a few minutes later he was back, bearing alcohol and vegan snacks. John noticed how he had been served immediately even though there was someone else (a loser admittedly) waiting at the bar. Money talks.

"No Sue tonight?"

"No, she's doing something else. She sends hugs."

"Ah, shame. Looks like it's just you and me then, buddy."

John immediately spluttered through the froth. "Buddy? When did you ever call me *buddy*?"

"Fair enough, good point. What should I call you then?"

"How about what you've always called me?"

"OK, *twat* it is then."

"Comedy fucking gold. Right, let's get these down the hatch and go."

They clinked and took one large draught each before banging the glasses down on the table in unison, like a couple of Vikings. John belched from the side of his mouth discreetly and wiped his upper lip with the back of his hand whilst Barney dabbed his lips with a monogrammed silk handkerchief. Clearly, he was in no rush to leave.

# It's The Not Knowing

"So, me old mate, me old mucker: you've been away... Good trip?"

"Oh yes, gorgeous trip. The South of France is lovely at this time of year, as I'm sure you can imagine."

"Oh yes, obviously. Top hole!" If it had been that type of sitcom, this would have been the point where John looked at the camera and pulled a face (with the obligatory canned laughter).

"And the food? Oh, my word, to die for! So much nicer than dreary old British cuisine."

"Well, yes! That goes without saying, naturally. Shitty British cuisine, eh?" John couldn't help feeling Barney was being a smug twat, suddenly. He had an uneasy feeling, one that he had never felt before in all the years he'd known his oldest friend – a feeling he was someone else. What was all this South of France babble? Pretentious? *Lui*? All that money hadn't taken long, had it? He realised he was still talking, enthusing at length about the glamour of a life on the Riviera, getting down with the other beautifully rich people. You must try and see it for yourself, he insisted; Sue would love it, absolutely love it. He could guarantee it and was happy to recommend a fantastic hotel if they were interested?

"I'll leave you with that thought. Anyway, enough about me and my great life – how are you and Sue getting along in the real world?"

"Well, I need to speak to you about Sue—"

"Oh, here he is! Colin! Over here! Colin, yoo-hoo!" He turned to John, put his hand on his arm and winked. "Hope you don't mind me inviting a friend? Let's get this party started!"

Still being a twat, thought John with a sinking feeling and the makings of a stupor.

The new arrival was a younger, healthier, and generally superior specimen: an all-over tan highlighted his perfect and unnatural teeth, which glowed like bleached pearls embedded in a salted caramel tart. Elegant and dapper in his expensive designer suit and loafers, he strode across the room as if he owned it, hand extended towards John as a broad, confident smile seeped from his glossy, rubber lips. A ludicrous gold chain, possibly weighing more than he did, hung from his slim yet macho neck for no obvious reason. And the hair! So thick and lustrous, so black and shiny, so well cut and stylish, so swept back and coiffured, so fucking what! John hated him before they'd even been formally introduced.

"John, I'd like you to meet my very good friend Colin. Colin Baskerville. Colin, John Stilton."

"Hi matey, you can call me Col and it's Baskerville as in the typeface!" The two friends laughed uproariously. John didn't. He was suddenly quite put out by recent events. He shook the fop's hand, decided he couldn't be bothered to crush his fingers and sat down with a pretend smile and a funny feeling things were about to deteriorate.

Colin made the two-tips-of-the-hand 'Wanna brandy and Babycham?' signal to ask if everyone was all right for drinky-poos. Barney fawned and said he'd love a Babycham. John, by now in shock, settled for another pint of the guest ale which, this year, was Nepshaw's *Old Weirdo*. At sixteen percent proof and brewed in the filthiest parts of the Black Country it was a manly man's man's drink and definitely not one for the Babycham crowd. One pint was usually enough to guarantee a good night out and an early collapse. Three was right up there with kamikaze and extreme parachuting with no strings attached.

"See? Told you you'd like him! He's a lovely guy, honestly."

"Yes, he sheems er... anyway, I wanted to talk to you about Shue... well, William's wotsname really and things..."

"You alright there, buddy? Slurring a bit, aren't you? You might want to slow it down a notch, fella! Don't tell me you're still beating yourself up about him and his Russian diary? He's gone, time to let it go, isn't it?"

"No, well... no..." *Buddy again??*

"Slimline would be fine! Watching my figure! Ha ha! Sorry, John. Go on?"

"It doeshn't matter."

"OK. Hey! I bet you can't guess what Colin is?"

John didn't have to guess. He knew. He was an arsehole, that's what Colin Baskerville was. "Who?" he said, making a point.

"Colin! My friend as you jolly well know!"

# It's The Not Knowing

*Jolly well fucking know?* "Oh yes, Colin Basket case. Enlighten me *buddy*, what is he, again?" The lack of enthusiasm was evident, not that Barney was deterred. He seemed altogether smitten with his new *matey*.

It transpired – that's no exaggeration – that Colin was something big in behavioural therapy. Presumably, John thought rather uncharitably, in his spare time when he wasn't gold digging amongst the nouveau-minted gay tourists on the Riviera. They say the South of France is lovely at this time of year.

John had always wondered if Barney might be homosexual. He'd never seemed interested in women and had never had a girlfriend. They'd never discussed such topics in depth, and it didn't bother him if he were. Why should it? It was none of his business and he was still his oldest friend, no questions asked. The sudden appearance of this new fop on the block, however – this strutting peacock with luminous teeth – served not only to confirm (in his own mind) his mate's sexual orientation but to fuel a degree of resentment of which John did not know he was capable. He wouldn't admit it, of course, but his nose had been what a medical professional would term 'put out of joint.'

His elbow slipped suddenly from the table. When he finally managed to right himself, he asked with bleary eyes and a mouth over which he now had little control: "So then, *mate*, how did you meet Buddy Boy?" He could already imagine the answer: in a nightclub on the seafront at Marseille, dressed as a sailor probably.

# It's The Not Knowing

"Colin? Oh, we met in a club." *Fucking knew it!* "In Marseille, of all places!" *Well, who the fuckity fuck could have guessed that!*

"Was he dresshed as a sailor? Or was it YOU?" he accused, turning and prodding Barney in the chest. The two pints of Nepshaw's were doing bad and unforgivable things to his brain at this point. John had always enjoyed a reputation as a happy drunk, fun to be around when he'd had a few; quick-witted and charming, relatively erudite, and just an all-round good egg. An egg with salt of the earth undertones. This belligerent mood that was surging through his lubricated mind would have been a cause for concern if he'd been sober enough to care. He wasn't and he didn't.

"C'mon mate, you don't have to be like that."

"Like what 'zackly?"

"Like that! Jabbing me with your finger. Ouch, fuck off! That'll leave a bruise and it bloody hurts."

"Bollocks! Anyway, you didn't question my answer, I mean answer my question: who was dressed like a jolly jack tart? Hey! I bet you *both* were. Hello Sailor! Yoo-Hoo Buddy, shut that door! Ooh, you are awful, but I like—" He didn't finish the sentence. Barney's hand was clamped firmly over his mouth. That'll be why.

The clamp certainly did the trick and stopped him in his tracks. As John struggled to extricate himself, Barney repeatedly and calmly told him to 'simmer down,' and to stop making a damned fool of himself. He refused to let go until there were signs of surrender. And not a conditional one, either.

# It's The Not Knowing

"Hey, c'mon girls! What's all this about?" Colin had returned with the drinky-poos to find the atmosphere had chilled considerably in his absence, a lengthy one admittedly. Worse things have, of course, happened in a shorter period of time – one only has to think of Sarajevo 1914 and a single gunshot which took maybe a couple of seconds – but this stand-off between two lifelong and dear friends was something altogether more disturbing.

The tendons finally relaxed, and the clamp was released. John exhaled and panted dramatically under a withering glare from his old mate. He was feeling quite sober suddenly, although in the eyes of the law he wasn't, not technically. In their eyes he would have been just another trendy, left-wing tosser who couldn't hold his ale. And then they would have beaten him up.

"Colin, do you think I'm gay?"

"You? Gay? Ha! You're the least gay man I know! Well, maybe not the least but certainly in the top three. I know this bloke – you'd get on well – Woody Wood-Pecker. The fucker is *so* hetero they had to take out a court injunction against him. Did that stop him? Did it fuck! He just went round and shagged the magistrate's wife. Twice. She was gagging for it, he said. The man was a bloody legend down the club. Anyway, you're definitely *not* gay. End of."

"Thankyou. Then perhaps, you might tell Mr. Stilton that? Perhaps you can vouch for me or provide references?"

"Why does he think you're gay?"

"Maybe you should ask *him* that?"

# It's The Not Knowing

"I suppose I might, I'll see how I'm fixed."

"I'd be much obliged, I'm sure."

"I am still here, you know!"

"OK, Johnny... Why do you think Barney is a homosexual?"

"Well, you both are, it's obvious! Look at you, with your hairdo, your suntan and your Babycham. You couldn't be anything else!"

Colin chuckled. "Babycham? You mean these bad boys?" he ejaculated, retrieving the tray from the next table, and placing three pints of Nepshaw's *Old Weirdo* on the table with a manly flourish and nary a drop spilled.

Barney sighed and shook his head as he removed the cocktail umbrella from his pint. "We were pulling your plonker, you stupid twat! I always knew you thought I might be gay, so I thought I'd play along. It was just a wind-up. I asked Colin to camp it up a bit, see how you'd react. OK, it was a bad idea: I thought you'd see through it straight away and play along too; I thought it might be a laugh. It seems to have backfired."

"Damn right, it backfired; I might have suffocated just then! That's an impressive grip though, I'll give you that. You been working out?"

"Girls, please! Get these down your neck and enough of the chick talk!"

They all three took a long draught and slammed the glasses down, like proper men do.

"You were away from the bar a long time, Col! Did you get lost? Hey! What's that grin for? You jammy bugger! You bloody pulled, didn't you?"

"What do you think? I just gave her one in the cellar to keep her interested and I'll be seeing her again tomorrow for more of the same."

"You randy old dog! So, who was the lucky girl? Not the landlady, surely?"

"God no, give me some credit, man! Fuck sake. Actually, it was Siobhan the barmaid. A most accommodating and comely wench."

"Legend!" said Barney, whose admiration knew no bounds in the face of testosterone-fuelled braggadocio.

John had always thought the lucky girl in this instance was a dyed-in-the-wool man-hater. He began to wonder if he actually knew anything about anything at all. This was just before he collapsed.

He screamed and sat bolt upright. "Whoah, Jesus!"

"What's up now?"

"Nothing… a nightmare, that's all. A horrible nightmare.

Sue reached over to check the time and groaned. "Time to get up anyway. I'll just have another ten minutes." She yawned.

"It was about Barney."

"You're dreaming about Barney? God, that's so *sweet*!"

It's The Not Knowing

"Well, funny you should say that… and it wasn't a dream it was an actual nightmare."

Sue realised her ten-minute snooze was never going to happen "Go on, you might as well tell me, let's get it over with."

John recounted the events as they faded in and out, returning to add details as they came back to him. They both wondered if it was in any way significant. John thought it might be. Sue told him it wasn't and offered a counter argument, suggesting it was more symbolic: perhaps it was his way of dealing with the loss of his best friend? John pointed out that Barney wasn't dead. Sue pointed out that he might as well be now that he'd swanned off somewhere to spend his fortune and was unlikely to ever want to swap his tropical paradise or wherever he was for an up-and-coming town on the wrong side of the M25. In short, he wasn't coming back any time soon. John thanked her for those kind words.

Sue mused awhile. There were still a few minutes to go.

"It's strange really, when you think of it, isn't it? You've lost your best friend, like I lost my brother. All of a sudden and unexpected. D'you know what I mean?"

"S'pose so."

"Talking of my brother      "

"I know what you're going to say. I've been working on it but it's really nothing to write home about. And it's getting harder to read his writing. Honestly, it's just a lot more of the same rambling. And there's no more detail about your dad or anything like that. Tell you the truth, I don't know if I can be bothered with it anymore. Anyway, I'm thinking of writing a novel, so..."

"A novel? What sort of novel? More Zombie Lit?"

"Dunno yet, a best-seller maybe."

And there he thought he had done enough to shift the focus of attention and bring the discussion to a close. Hopefully, the bud had been nipped and she would not raise the topic again. It would all blow over and soon be forgotten. It would be for the best.

## The Truth Will Out

January 6th, 2006.

*It was a cold, brooding day in the cul-de-sac as the fleet of Volvo estates made its way steadily over the bridge under steely grey skies towards the Cash 'n' Carries, looking for bargains (trade customers only). Maybe they would buy one and get one free?*

Or maybe they could all bog off! John Stilton, the author, stared at the screen with horror. The new novel wasn't going to plan. He didn't actually have a plan and didn't, in fact, know what this novel was going to be about. It was, he would be the first to admit, a novel of convenience, a diversionary tactic. A story without a plot and hardly anything to justify its existence. He was clearly ahead of his time.

Maybe he should write it in Russian? Why not? Now, *there's* a novel idea! The sketchy outline of a rough concept flowered briefly but withered as he opened the drawer and pulled out the *Teach Yourself* manual. He flipped it open, looked again at the alphabet and weighed up the pros and cons. He reached back into the drawer and was about to take out the Chernobyl diary when he realised it wasn't there.

This was most puzzling: he had definitely put both of the books back in the drawer just before Christmas. He distinctly remembered doing so. He took everything out and rooted around but to no avail. Fruitless rooting can be so unproductive. Had it fallen down the back? He took the drawer out and reached into the gap behind. Not there. Hellish strange, that. It upset him, somewhat. He wasn't the kind of man who lost things without knowing where they were.

*...maybe they could buy one and get one free? Maybe they could buy three and get the cheapest item free? Subject to availability, terms and conditions apply.* Well, they would, wouldn't they! This was no good. He couldn't concentrate, not with this latest disappearance on his mind. All the writings of William Butler Skaife had one by one been lost in unusual or suspicious circumstances. How spooky was that? It was quite spooky, he had to admit. He'd always been quite susceptible to being spooked.

He took another hopeful look in the drawer. Sometimes, things hid in plain sight. Sometimes you couldn't see the wood for the trees. He thought this scenario unlikely, particularly as he now had a decent literary canon of tree-based work, thanks to his patrons at the Forestry

Commission. It definitely wasn't there; it could not be denied.

He pounced later when Sue returned from school. Had she taken the diary? No, she hadn't. What did he think she would be doing with it? Yes, he knew that but was struggling to find an alternative explanation. Was she sure she was sure she hadn't taken it? OK, calm down, I believe you. If she hadn't taken it, and he hadn't lost it, which he most definitely hadn't, what had happened to it? Things don't just disappear. Yes, they do, she corrected him, reminding him of a tea towel that had once simply vanished from the kitchen. How could he forget that? He hadn't; he still thought about it a lot but... "OK, it's a mystery, though."

"Yes, it is, but it's been a shitty first week back and I just want to put my feet up with a glass of wine. What's for dinner?"

So, that was it. The diary had gone, and it looked like the subject was closed. If nothing else, he mused, it would mean she would never find out the dreadful secret it contained. He was happy about that. Things hadn't turned out too badly, all things considered.

It was the following Monday evening when he had cause to rethink that statement.

It was nothing he could put his finger on, she just seemed weird. She was moody, but that was nothing new just lately. He tried frantically to remember if he'd done something wrong but, as far as he knew, he hadn't. Obviously, this didn't mean he wasn't guilty but... She seemed somehow distracted with her mind somewhere else, although her hostility was still present. Taciturn probably summed it up. One-word answers where normally there would have been a full sentence, that kind of thing. If you've ever seen a volcano about to erupt, as I'm sure you must have, you might be able to picture the scene.

Eventually he could stand it no more.

They were sitting at the kitchen table. She was marking books. He was watching her marking books.

"Have I done something to upset you, Sue?"

"Yes." Having confirmed this much, she got up and walked out.

"It would help if I knew what it was I'm supposed to have done!" he shouted, unsure whether to follow her. No, he shouldn't. If she were going to be all moody and stupid, she could just stew in her own juices. He'd done absolutely nothing wrong, and he was damned if he were going to be made to carry any kind of can.

He made himself some tea and toast, hoping the smell of caramelised bread and marmite might make her hungry and force her hand. It didn't work; he ate a mouthful of the toast, but his appetite was blunted by his sense of injustice, and he pushed away the plate. His astonishment was subsiding as his anger increased. This was not good. It had all the makings of a full-blown argument or even a domestic. What was her problem? What had he done this time? She clearly thought he'd done something but what? Why were married women so irrational?

# It's The Not Knowing

He'd been brooding for a longish time when he heard her footsteps coming down the stairs. He quickly leaned back and composed himself to give the impression of indifference when she came in. '*In indifference is strength*' was a motto he would have been proud to call his own. He could play her at her own game. If she wanted taciturn, she could bloody well have taciturn, the deluxe version! He could do one-word answers as well as the next man. He was positioned and gazing with studied determination out at the garden even though the light in the kitchen made everything black outside and all he could see was an angry man in his early forties glowering back at him from the garden with studied determination. He was cool and collected, resolute and immovable in his stance.

She was wrong and he was right; he was going to give her a lecture and she would just have to listen, grin, and bear it. He knew he had done nothing wrong. What he didn't know was that she had a weapon and was about to use it.

A glancing blow to the head was the first he knew of it.

"Jesus, what the—?"

"Here! Happy now?"

"You found it! Where was it?"

"It was in my bag."

He went straight to the burning question, rubbing his head: what it was doing in her bag? It was in her bag, she explained, because that's where she'd put it when she got it back.

"Got it back? Where's it been?"

# It's The Not Knowing

"Pavel's had it."

"What's had it?"

"Pavel."

"Pavel? Who's Pavel?" John had a bad feeling about Pavel.

"He's a teacher, he's Polish, he started this term and, guess what Pavel does? He speaks fluent Russian, does Pavel!" John had another bad feeling about Pavel.

"Well, so what if he does?"

"I'll tell you *so what*; I was talking to *Pavel* about this diary, see?" She waved it menacingly, "and I told him you'd spent weeks translating it and had given up on it. I told him you were a quitter. He laughed and said he would translate it for me if I wanted. I said I wanted. I took it from your desk and gave it to him the other day and do you want to know something else?"

"He couldn't understand it?"

"He translated it in half an hour."

"Bloody show off!"

There was a momentary silence as John considered his options. He didn't have any, so he adopted a voice of resignation. "So, you've read it? All of it?"

"Yes, all of it. And I know you did too so now we both know, don't we!"

"How do you feel now that you know?"

# It's The Not Knowing

"How do I feel? I feel betrayed. I feel you lied to me and that's unforgiveable, y'know that?"

"Hang on, I didn't lie to you... I just—"

"You just what?"

"I just didn't want you to find out. I wanted to spare you that. I did it for you, Sue. Everything I do, I do it for you. You know it's true. So, what do you think now that you know about, y'know...? I mean, that's the only issue here, isn't it? It's not about whether I didn't tell you or not, is it?" He turned to look back at the man in the garden. He felt this was the best direction to face to hide his displeasure. She'd said he was a quitter and Pavel the smart arse had laughed at him. Bloody fluent Russian bastard! He wasn't normally a seether but at this moment he was seething for England. He had a good mind to go round to that school and punch his stupid face...

And then, suddenly, he wasn't seething anymore. Sue had come up behind and had clamped her arms around him and was snuggling into his back. He put his hands over hers and they connected, two spirits suddenly joined around a middle-aged spread and in harmony, the iceberg melting as nature stirred from the frost, possibly warmed by that volcano from earlier.

"Yes, I know why you didn't tell me, and that was so lovely and so thoughtful."

John turned to face her, expecting... he didn't know what he was expecting. Tears or a reproachful lower lip, perhaps, but there was neither. Just Sue's lovely face looking radiant and beautiful, her eyes sparkling and willing, her mouth luscious and begging and her hands now stroking and encouraging. If he'd had a hat, he would have spun it into the air and yipped. Instinctively their lips locked, and his tongue found hers as they kissed with a passion and a fervour he could scarcely remember. They were now breathing the same air, gasping, and panting like asthmatics in a sauna. Sue started to moan and groan – but not in a complaining, negative way – as she massaged and kneaded his buttocks and then his inner thighs, inching ever higher until she found the zip. They both fumbled to open it before she slipped her hand inside and released his bulging manhood while he struggled to kick off his shoes. Cursing whoever had invented shoelaces, he launched the second one with an extravagant flick, one which sent it spinning across the kitchen and into the hall as he made a move towards the breasts, her magnificent juicy breasts. Lifting her shirt, he reached around as she wiggled free from her skirt and, to his own amazement, unclipped her bra at the first attempt like the expert he most certainly wasn't. A lucky strike, nothing more, but there they were suddenly, unfettered and waiting for his loving attentions. He cupped the left, his personal favourite, in his hand, sucked and teased the nipple as he lifted her up onto the kitchen table. Sue's expert handiwork deftly removed her panties without fuss or hindrance; it was the same with the blouse; the bra required a little more dexterity but was it worth it! Oh God yes, c'mon… c'mon… they undid his belt in a joint fumble, before she eased down his retro Y-fronts and took him in her hand, squeezing and stroking and, as she delicately worked her way towards the best bit, he moaned, sucked, and licked voraciously before pulling away. *C'mon, do it now*! Following a desperate body realignment and search for optimum position, Sue gasped as he slid inside, welcomed into her wet and warm embrace. Happy with events so far, he started to thrust, moving in and out, slowly, and rhythmically. At the same time, she raised her legs to encircle him, moved her hips to meet him and they began to ebb and flow enthusiastically like opposing tides on a moonlit foreign shore until, after what seemed like an eternity (but was in fact twenty-eight seconds), with a shudder and a scream, they came together in majestic and fabulous unison. They froze the position, savouring the moment as their bodies tensed to hold the perfect and exquisite state of bliss for as long as any human had ever managed in the history of sex. And then it subsided, and they collapsed together, having achieved a state of grace, possibly Nirvana.

They clung on, wanting the moment to last forever. It was a few minutes before either of them spoke.

"That was beautiful. So beautiful..." John thought so too but didn't say as much. He was lost for words, actually. He managed a breathless *wow!*

"That was new; you've never screamed before!"

"I know; I just couldn't stop myself," he said, smiling at the memory. He leaned over and kissed her tenderly on the forehead and then hungrily on the lips before finally withdrawing with a resounding squelch.

"Christ, yuk... what's this sticky stuff all over my back?"

Sue had found his cold buttered toast, smeared with Marmite.

# It's The Not Knowing

Later that evening, as they were sitting together watching something on the TV about a time travelling policeman – *what rubbish will they come up with next?* – John still had a huge smile on his face.

"Hey!" he said, nudging Sue.

"Shhh, I'm watching this. Listen to Gene Hunt; what a total git!"

"Hey: what brought that on?"

"What brought what on?"

"That, y'know… earlier, the coitus?"

Sue tutted. "You make it sound so clinical!"

"OK, then, the intercourse? What brought it on?"

"Hmm, no reason. Not really."

"Ah, *not really* means there *was* a reason. Tell me, go on."

"I suppose I thought you deserved a reward. For being kind and thoughtful, for not wanting me to be upset by y'know…"

"Yes, I definitely did. Thankyou."

"Don't mention it."

"What are you thinking now? I mean, about y'know, this new situation?"

Sue took his hand and raised it to her mouth where she planted a kiss as she thought about what she was thinking now.

"I'm thinking… I suppose he's dead. He wasn't in good health, was he? And I'm wondering how many people can claim ownership of two dead fathers. Something like that."

"Did it upset you?"

"Of course it did. But I don't think of him as my father and I don't think I ever will, you can understand that, can't you?"

"Yes, absolutely. Do you want to know what's puzzled me, though?"

Sue was definitely very keen to know what had puzzled him. Could it wait until *Life on Mars* had finished?

John expressed a degree of surprise at her attitude. She'd just had her world shaken, hadn't she? Was a TV programme more important than that?

"What I don't understand," he said, regardless, "was why was your mother so horrible and cold towards the pair of you? I mean, if old Clem really was the love of her life, as he kept saying, why didn't she love you both? I mean, as the fruit of their labours, you should have been up on a pedestal eating grapes, shouldn't you?"

"You'd think so, yes. Maybe she didn't love him as much as he thought? We only have his word for that. All this talk of moonlit starry skies, lying in fields dreaming of what might have been, well, that doesn't sound like Irene does it? Maybe she thought he'd used her – twice – and then buggered off back to Skagness!"

"Yes, that could explain it. Do you think your other dad knew?"

"Yes, I think he might, at least I think he might have known about William. Maybe that's why he didn't like him very much? It's possible."

"But he didn't know about you?"

"No, I don't think he did. I was his favourite so he probably didn't."

"And he didn't have anything more to do with your mum after that, threw himself into his work and all that, died from overwork. Classic case!"

"Well, that's all the loose ends tied up, Inspector Clouseau! Except, we still don't know for sure what happened to William…"

"Yes, good point. I really don't think he can be still around, do you? This was what probably tipped him over the edge, don't you think?"

Sue gripped his hand tighter and smiled. "No, I don't think… I *know* he's out there somewhere."

# PART NINE. 2026

## The Signing

August 1<sup>st</sup>.

These days, Skagness in the holiday season is a tourist hotspot. A hot one – hotter than most hotspots, probably. When one looks back at the old days from these new days with the benefit of hindsight, it is perhaps difficult for the likes of you to imagine a time when the heat was very much off, when the icy chill of hopelessness spread both doom and gloom in equal measure across the land. In those days the boarded-up shops and run-down derelict seafront buildings provided the backdrop for the comings and goings, the ups and downs and the chiff and the chaff of the human experience. If you didn't know better – and only you would know whether that was the case – you'd be inclined to regard this activity as inconsequential mooching or aimless shambling along the promenade. These, however, were humans, just like you (or people *like* you), seeking the basic necessities of human life: fast food, warmth, and shelter.

The gentrification of traditional seaside holiday destinations is not for everyone. Some people object to the idea and claim it devalues or gives a false impression. These people are not our people. We don't need to consider those people.

Skagness had been reconstructed and improved beyond recognition since the days when Irene Skaife, Sheila Boil and others of that breed would wander down to the grey concrete precinct for sliced bread, twenty counterfeit fags and the latest copy of *TV Quick*. Cliff's Café, the Hermit Crab Singles Bistro and even the Flotsam Hotel had long since disappeared beneath the bulldozer's tracks, no match for the high-viz wrecking ball or the pneumatic drill. You know the kind of thing. You've seen them, I'm sure.

One area of this new development – the Arts Quarter – boasted a bookshop; one with real books and a coffee shop/reading area where the intelligentsia would meet regularly to discuss whatever it is the intelligentsia discuss. It's not for the likes of us to tell them what to talk about.

Situated on the fashionable Boulevard Avenue (on or about the exact spot where Blockbuster almost used to serve the needs of the popcorn-dependent VHS generation), Buck's Books had been trading at a profit for several years and was proud to promote the works of local authors. In times of famine, when no local authors were available, Buck would instead champion *outsiders*: writers who knew how to write about subjects which appealed to all local people, not just the intelligentsia. According to retail statistics, local people tend to like *local* topics, ones of local interest and with a local flavour. It was for this reason, and this reason alone, that, on this particular day, Buck's was hosting a book signing to help shift a few copies of a new work by an *outsider* called Claire de Lune.

The shop was doing a brisk trade, helped by the Saturday effect when *footfall*, a portmanteau word used by people who deal in retail statistics, is generally heavier than on a weekday. None of that matters. All you need to know is that the trade was brisk, regardless of *footfall* or even *throughput*. Try and put *footfall* and, in particular, *throughput* out of your mind.

This is not to say that the presence of Claire de Lune was in any way responsible for this healthy trading. Not by any measure of means! Sitting at a small table towards the rear of the shop, situated between the sections devoted to *Quantum Mechanics* and *Mutton*, Claire had resolved to maintain a positive outlook despite the apparent lack of interest in her book. There were several copies of the new work stacked neatly on the table, as yet unsigned and unshifted.

'*This Dying Breed*' was, in the author's own words, an attempt to reconcile life's losers with the lot of the underachiever. Based in part in Skagness, it was, in crude terms, a no-frills exposé: one that mooted the (now unfashionable) idea that, in spite of the seeming inevitability of a miserable and unhappy existence – one that can only be relieved by death – the human condition is, in fact, more onerous than that. There is unimaginable agony and despair to be borne before the light can finally die. Anyone who thinks they can improve their position, having been born a loser, has no idea of what lies in store and therein, according to Ms. De Lune, lies the rub.

A few of the locals had come over to the table for a peek. One or two had thumbed through the pages before returning them to the pile. It seemed Skagness, in commercial terms, was going to prove stony, infertile ground.

Shortly after she had laid out her wares, one particularly morose senior had sidled over and asked if it was 'raunchy.'

# It's The Not Knowing

Claire had replied that it was "not exactly raunchy but there *is* a sex scene of sorts, more a bit of a fumble on a kitchen table, you know the kind of thing." The reply to this was an indignant "I most certainly do *not!*" whereupon the inquisitive sourpuss had turned on her orthopaedic heels and exited at a relatively blistering pace.

Buck, an ex-military man seeing a lull in overall trading, thought he might offer a few words of encouragement to rally the troops. Claire, having no military training, had been keeping herself gainfully occupied doing her nails and touching up her makeup. She had thought she might sign a few copies to save time later until she realised this might invalidate the sale or return agreement. She was puckered and about to blow-dry the topcoat on her freshly lacquered nails when the proprietor marched into view.

"Yo, Claire! I'm sorry to say I haven't seen many copies going through the tills, but not to worry; it's early days yet. Things might pick up, you never know!"

"I appreciate the encouraging words, I really do, but it isn't looking promising. Trust me, I know how these things go!"

"Oh, have you had to do many of these, then?"

Claire explained that, yes, she had but not under this name. She went on to suggest, with a coy smile, that he might know her better for her best-selling works in the historical romance genre, in which field she wrote under the *nom de plume* Babba Catland and where she had enjoyed some success. Her works were particularly popular amongst short-sighted ladies of a certain age, apparently.

Buck expressed surprise and delight on hearing this and cursed himself for not having known this when she first arrived. He promptly asked if she would be willing to sign any remaining copies of Catland novels he might have on the shelves and in the storeroom? "They really are *incredibly* popular!"

She said she would be delighted. As was he, as he about turned and marched off to check his stock levels. She began to wonder why she had listened to her agent when he'd suggested this; there were surely better things to do on a Saturday, particularly in modern-day Skagness!

"Excuse me, I know you're probably busy, but as this is a book-signing – I read the sign in the window – would you mind signing one of those books for me?

A man in his mid-sixties had approached the table and was now standing in front of her, nervously wringing his hands. Clearly unsure of himself, he grinned sheepishly as Claire smiled pleasantly and took a copy from the top of the pile.

"Of course, yes, I'd be delighted to sign one of my books... just for you!" she beamed, encouraged by his request. He immediately expressed surprise, having not realised she was the author of the work. That made it even better, he said. She was briefly deflated by this, but a sale was a sale, so...

"Is Claire your name, then? Claire de Lune? It's a lovely name: is it French? You're very beautiful, Claire. You have lovely eyes... are they your own? Oh, God, listen to me babbling! What an idiot! I'm nervous, forgive me. I'm just... I find it hard to just be myself with a beautiful

woman – oh dear, why am I telling you this? I'm so sorry…
would you have dinner with me tonight? Please? I'm just
passing through, and I don't know anybody… I live in
Goole, now; I used to live here, but I moved on and made
something of myself when mother died. Oh, there I go
again, babbling on, would you listen to me! So, what do
you say? Will you have dinner with me tonight? I'll bring
a plate for you too; you won't have to – "

"I'm sorry, but I have made other arrangements. Maybe
some other time? Possibly. I'm not in Skagness often… so,
I'll just sign my name, shall I?" With pen poised, Claire
watched him as he shuffled uneasily, realising he'd be
spending another evening alone with an empty plate for
company.

After a moment he said: "could you put 'to Jay-Zed?'
That's my grandson; I'm sure he'd treasure a book if he had
one. Even this one. Are there any pictures in it?"

Claire confirmed that unfortunately there were no
pictures. He took the signed copy anyway, smiled ruefully
and shuffled away, head bowed. She watched him approach
the till where he glanced round, placed the book on the
counter and walked out of the shop.

She frowned, picked up another copy of the book and
flicked through the pages before returning to the inside
cover, where there was a brief biography and a photo. Lost
deep in her own thoughts – *I mean, what was Cliff's
problem?* – and distracted by the details of her early life
laid bare, she was quite unaware that she was being
watched.

357

It's The Not Knowing

A young woman of about twenty had been flicking through some Haynes Manuals while that rude old man who had pushed in had been talking to Claire. She'd watched them both, Claire in particular, from behind the pages of *Ford Capri MkII All Models 1974-87*. Now, as she approached the table, the sound of *Hotel California* booming out in the street from a passing Ford Capri dragged Claire's mind suddenly back into the room.

"Sorry – Sorry! – I was in my own little world there for a moment! Hi! So...?" She sat up straight, smiled and was going to ask *How may I help you?* but felt it sounded a little too *call centric*. She left the question hanging, unsaid, waiting for the young woman to make the move. It was a good tactic, and one which paid dividends immediately.

"So, hi... so, *you* wrote this book?"

"*This Dying Breed*? I did, yes. There are no pictures I'm afraid, and it's my first in this genre. You might know me better as—"

"So, I don't think it makes sense."

"Oh! Do you mean you've read it?"

"Yes."

"*Actually* read it?"

"So, yes, *actually* read it. Twice. Actually."

"OK, I see. So, what bit doesn't make sense, would you say?"

"So, why would he just disappear like that? He wouldn't. Nobody can really just disappear like that. He would have been seen by someone eventually. But what gets me is *why*? Why did he have to disappear? That's the first thing…"

"Well… oh, there's more?"

"So, secondly, why did the mother, Irene, why did she hate her children? That makes no sense. Thirdly, why did Irene stay with Eric if they were so miserable? Why didn't Irene and Clem just get off their arses and run away to start a new life together? And why did Wilf pretend to know that girl Suze when he didn't? That was just silly. If you don't mind me saying so!"

"No, I don't mind constructive criticism… Well, y'know… maybe William changed his appearance so much and so drastically that nobody could possibly recognise him? Maybe he had surgery on his face? People can have face transplants these days. People can change themselves in so many ways, who knows? That's possible, isn't it? And as for why he went and took himself off, well… maybe he just felt as if he no longer had a purpose living the life he was living. It's so important to have a purpose, don't you think?"

The girl agreed that it was absolutely important to have a purpose. Claire tipped her head so she could peer over her glasses. She removed them and thoughtfully chewed the temple tips for a few seconds before continuing. "I believe it was, in fact, an accumulation of several factors: finding out his father wasn't really his father, coming to terms with the devastating realisation that his mother had never wanted him, struggling to accept that the sister he idolised didn't need him in her life. Didn't some of that seem plausible? I thought I'd hinted at some – if not all – of those possibilities, no?

There was a pause for a spot of umming and ahing before Claire continued,

"And perhaps Áine, the woman he was living with, that whole relationship might have seemed somehow empty or devoid of meaning… maybe that was why he needed a total change, needed to make a clean break. Wouldn't that make sense? When you consider the sheer weight of the burden he had to bear, there's no wonder he disappeared."

"So, yes, I suppose that might make sense. But, what about the other bits?"

"What was the second thing… hating her children? Well, she hated her children because they were the living embodiment of the betrayal of Clem, their genetic father. You see, Clem might have whispered sweet nothings and filled her head with fancy ideas, he might have promised her the moon and stars, but he wasn't a nice man. He used Irene. To him, she was probably just one of many. And Irene? Well, she wasn't nice either. and she was naturally bitter about the way things had turned out, how she had been *used*, as she saw it."

"Yes, I can see that…"

"So, I think the instinctive thing for this woman – a woman who wasn't *naturally* maternal – the instinctive reaction for her would be to reject and discard. Don't you agree? And that's why they didn't run away together: she knew he'd already used her and would discard her eventually, when he found something better."

# It's The Not Knowing

"But he said he loved her!"

"Oh, my dear – you should never trust a man when he says that!"

"Oh wow! Really? I mean, that's a very cynical attitude!"

They both laughed. A serious bookworm looked over and raised her index finger in front of her moue and made a 'shh!' sound. The young woman lowered her voice slightly and continued: "but if she hated him in the end, why did she end up in Skagness? Surely, she'd want to avoid him like the plague rather than go looking for him."

"Well, it doesn't always work like that does it? You're too young to know, but sometimes it's the *poisonous* fruit that's the most appealing."

"Really? Hey, maybe she wanted to make him jealous by sleeping around? Although, *afternoon napping* around was probably more appropriate at her age. Is that what you were thinking?"

Claire laughed, causing another moue over in Penguin Classics. "Yes, I suppose that might have been a possibility although I'm not sure that occurred to me at the time. It's an interesting view. I do sometimes wonder why I based it here in Skagness; maybe I just thought there probably weren't many books set here. Not that I knew of anyway."

The girl pondered briefly. "No, I can't think of any, either. So, *I'd* like to think she was trying to make him jealous in some way though, y'know? Men deserve all they get – some of them do, anyway!"

"Yes, I suppose they do!"

# It's The Not Knowing

"So, why did he *pretend* to know her?"

"Ah yes, why did he pretend to know her…? I think he *did* know her. Not physically, but in his mind. She possibly *reminded* him of someone…"

"So, is that a good enough reason for pretending to know her? And, if you think about it, that stupid lie ended up killing Joe and Bryan, didn't it?"

"Yes, but only in the story within the story. I mean, it's not real, remember? None of it's real, it's just a story within a story within a story… actually, someone disappearing, maybe that happened."

"So, do you mean Suze Moon or William?"

"Well, both of them, I suppose. Yes—"

"OK, so did you ever consider, Claire, that when Wilf or William wrote that Suze had disappeared, the writer was presaging his own eventual disappearance?"

"Presaging? Hmm, that's a particularly good word – I'll remember that one! – and a good point. A *very* good point. I suppose that *might* have been in my mind."

"*Might*? But you wrote it! Surely, as the author, you *know* these things before you write them?"

"No, it's not always the case. Sometimes you have no idea what you're writing—"

"Gosh! That's what they said in the Potters Bar Times Literary Supplement!"

# It's The Not Knowing

"About me? Really?" Claire chuckled. "Blooming cheek! God! Potters Bar Times? When was this *so-called* review in the *Potters Bar Times Literary Supplement*?"

"So, it was weeks ago. That's our rubbish local paper back home – that's where I live, or near there, anyway. Someone's got to, I suppose! It's a dump."

"I'm sure it can't be all bad?'

"So, it is, trust me. Even the zombies have moved out. But if you're ever in the area…"

"Thank you, that's very kind. So, are you here on holiday?"

"Yes, with my parents. It's on their bucket list, apparently. Something to do with an exorcism, I think."

"That's nice. So, you've managed to escape your folks and you thought you'd come along and buy my book?"

"So, something like that, yes. They've gone off for the day with my uncle and his partner Sam. Barney's not really my uncle, just my dad's oldest friend, and coming here was his idea. He saw the poster in the window and told me about it, said it might be useful – I'm studying English Lit at Uni, you see – so, here I am. I honestly never expected I'd get to discuss a book one-to-one with the author!"

"Oh, excellent I'm so glad you came along and I'm very pleased to meet you… er?" The positioning of the head indicated that this was a question.

"So, Chloe."

"So Chloe! That's a lovely name, So Chloe. Is it French?"

## It's The Not Knowing

"Maybe, yes, and thank you – so, it's been *really* interesting – and certainly educational – to meet you too, Claire. Anyway, I'm sure I've taken up enough of your time, there's no stopping me when I get going! My mum says I could talk for England. I've already got my own copy, of course – I *wish* I'd brought it with me – but I want to buy a signed one; this will be for my mum."

"Oh, my word, that's so sweet; what a lucky mum. I hope she enjoys reading it."

"I hope so too. I might even ask my dad to read it too, but he probably won't."

"Oh, well never mind. But at least your mum will – she sounds like a nice lady."

"Oh, she is! She's lovely. She used to be a teacher – since she retired she reads a lot."

"A teacher, really? And your dad – was he a teacher too?"

"My dad actually used to be a writer, he wrote school textbooks – history, stuff like that. He also wrote some Zombie books, can you believe! Not my kind of thing but, as he always said, it's what the zombies like."

"I see – zombies and history… sounds like a fascinating mix…"

Something troubled Claire about this young woman. A sense of something she couldn't quite put her finger on. It was possibly no more than a coincidence. Silly really…

"Honestly, you should hear the way he goes on about modern life and pop culture… the modern novel, that's what he'd put in Room 101. He has a special name for all modern stuff, but erm… it's not very nice – perhaps I shouldn't say…"

"Oh well—"

"*Shiterature.* Sorry, but that's what he calls it."

There was a lull in the conversation. Claire wondered why moderns tend to start their responses to questions with 'so…' and whether the younger generation were more forthright than they had any right to be.

She was pondering something else, too, as she peered over the top of her glasses and gave the younger woman a thoughtful look. She wondered how many times she'd driven past Potters Bar, unaware…

Chloe wondered whether she'd overstepped the mark, now wishing she hadn't mentioned *shiterature*. She looked down and shifted uneasily. She really hadn't intended to upset anyone.

"So, I shouldn't have told you that, I'm sorry…"

"Don't be silly, I'm old enough and I'm quite thick-skinned! What is it they say? 'You can't please all—'"

"'Please *all* of the people…' Yes, that's true, but my dad is *notoriously* difficult to please – *all* of the time! Anyway, I'm going to buy this one," Chloe said, reaching for the pile. "So, would you mind writing a personalised message inside? To my mum? I want it to be a nice surprise for her birthday!"

"Of course, I'd be more than happy," Claire said as she uncapped her Waterman. She wrote '*Happy birthday,'* then paused while a pensive Chloe stood, reflecting on the conversation.

"Do you know, So Chloe, I don't think you told me your mum's name."

"Didn't I? So, it's actually Sue, same as the woman in your story! I know, isn't that totally weird? *And* my dad's called John! I mean, what are the chances! *And* strangely enough – and this might sound a bit bizarre, but when I first saw you, it was... you *do* look a little bit like my mum, you know – you could be sisters!"

Claire chuckled. "I think I might like to meet your mum, in that case. That would be quite strange, wouldn't it. So, another Sue and another John? That *is* quite a coincidence, though! My word..."

"I know, it's *uber* spooky isn't it!"

"Tell me, do you have grandparents still alive?"

"Grandparents? Why?"

"Just an idea..."

"Well, no, they all died before I was born – I never knew any of them. Grandma Irene, that's mum's mum, she was actually living here in Skagness when she died – I only found that out in the car on the way here... small world, or what."

That was all the confirmation Claire needed. "I see. That's sad. I'm sorry you never got to meet any of them. Family is so important... I never knew mine, either."

"Aw, that's a shame. Irene wasn't a very nice person, though, by all accounts…"

"No? Oh dear… anyway…"

"Yes, anyway… so, can you put: 'To Sue (mum), with love – no, *much* love – from your husband John and daughter Chloe, and…' She paused and looked over at the Doris Hedgehopper promotional poster, which towered over the Ornithology section. As she was considering the wording for the inscription, she was unaware that she was being closely monitored and appraised.

The monitor's hand hovered above the page, waiting for instruction. She shrugged, willing her to continue. As Chloe deliberated, Claire made a clicking noise with her tongue – it's not as impressive as it sounds, anyone can do it. She tipped her head and looked over the frame of her glasses again. There was a pause as everything went eerily quiet. Even the thieving, salty seagulls held their beaks.

"Well, this is taking quite some thinking about!" Claire smiled.

"I was just wondering if you should put something about you being her sister, just for a laugh… but no, it's a lame idea. OK, let's say… 'To legendary teacher, wife and mother, Mrs Stilton (Sue) with much – all our? – much? *much* love, from Chloe and John.' That would be great, thank you so much."

It's The Not Knowing

If she were to describe it in words that even a day-tripper could understand, Claire would come to think of it as a sign that the time was right, that it might finally be time to go back and reconnect. The sun came out as the sense of an ending and of a new beginning filled the room.

Once done, she turned the book so Chloe could approve the wording.

It was perfect. The ink not yet dry, the sentiment so sweet, the handwriting so distinctive.

And so left leaning.

*To legendary teacher, wife and mother, Mrs Stilton (Sue) with much love, from Chloe and John... and William xxx'*

Printed in Great Britain
by Amazon